Kate & Ozzie

Enjoy!
Bev Hopwood
Dec. 2013.

A Historical Novel

Beverley Hopwood

KATE AND OZZIE
BMD Series #2

ISBN: 978-1-77069-950-2

Printed in Canada

Word Alive Press
131 Cordite Road, Winnipeg, MB R3W 1S1
www.wordalivepress.ca

Cataloguing in Publication may be obtained through Library and Archives Canada

table of contents

preface

Beginning the search for ancestors in Jamaica has proven equally frustrating and exciting. I knew my great-grandfather was born in Jamaica and was likely a person of colour. My grandmother and her brother, John, had some features of blacks, even though some family members disputed this fact. Then Great-Aunt Clemmie married a black man, according to a cousin's note to my mother. The records for Jamaica were few and far between on the Internet. Other factors indicated that the possibility of slaves in the family went generations back. My great-grandfather Philip Summers was a ship's purser, and his father, John Pink Summers, was a master mariner, so some were white and some were black, and as Jamaican records indicate quite distinctly, some were of varying degrees of colour.

Trolling through the records on Jamaicasearch.org gave me a start half a dozen years ago, and gradually a general picture of the lives of slaves and whites was created as I became familiar with the Jamaican parishes and the development of the country in the eighteenth and nineteenth centuries.

I wasn't expecting to find much on Jamaica at the National Archives in Kew, London, England, but much to my surprise there were all kinds of colonial records. There were maps, hand drawn, coloured, and detailed, and there were West Indian records from the mid-1500s when England first took Jamaica from the Spaniards, and for nearly three centuries following.

Books this old seem from another world and are handled with extreme care. White gloves, sponge props, and weighted beanbags all help maintain the heavy leather-bound record books. The reverent page-turning process I felt compelled to use brought surprising and stunning information to light. Although much of my introduction here is of a general history, I can't help feeling a tie with the past generations that inhabited this island. Sometimes the arrogance, or the shame, and certainly the frustration of the people came to light in the official records of military, government, and church.

The following "vignettes" are quick glimpses into moments in history that shaped the island. Some are directly based on records, and some are what I personally pictured might have happened.

The family story, as far back as I can document it, starts in part I. The amazing coincidence that the London branch of the LDS was housed at Kew while I was visiting in 2012 was indeed a bonus. Thank you to these volunteers. My only regret is that I have not made a trip to Jamaica before publication, but I plan to do so someday.

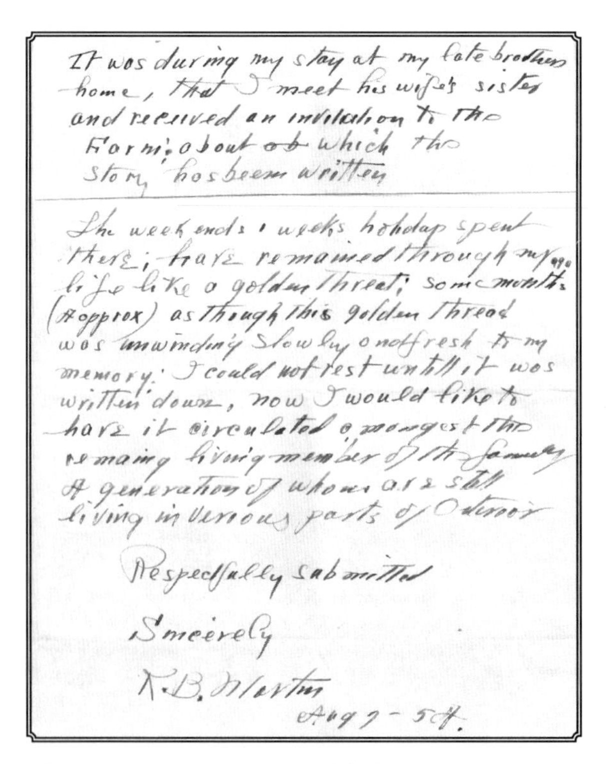

It was during my stay at my late brothers home, that I meet his wife's sister and received an invitation to the Farm; about of which the story has been written

The week ends & weeks holiday spent there; have remained through my life like a golden thread; some months (approx) as though this golden thread was unwinding slowly and fresh to my memory; I could not rest until it was written down, now I would like to have it circulated amongest the remaining living member of the family A generation of whom are still living in various parts of Ontario

Respectfully submitted

Sincerely

K.B. Martin

Aug 7 - 54.

Grandma Martin, I hope I have filled your wishes. With many thanks and great love, Your granddaughter, Bev

acknowledgements

I FIRST NEED TO THANK MY FAMILY FOR THEIR SUPPORT AND FOR ALLOWING ME the time to research independently, travel, and write. A thank you to all my friends who have allowed me to disappear for weeks at a time, only to reappear for another dose of your support. To my mother, who saved everything—I wish I had completed this before her passing, but I think she would have been pleased that I was able to use so much of the material she so conscientiously saved and valued.

I wish to acknowledge the cousins I was able to contact on Ancestry.ca: Beryl Martin, Lois Howison, John Leonard, Dianne Youden, and John Linton; also Geri Moon, Vickie McKinnon, and Kerrie Findlay. Thank you for your own research, which helped me to add to or verify mine, and for your additional stories and photos.

The detailed maps included in the 2001 Road Atlas: Great Britain and Ireland published by the Automobile Association in Britain were invaluable in finding locations of ancestral hometowns. A special thanks to the helpful hands at the Napanee Archives, Napanee, Ontario; the Calgary Library and Glenbow Archives, Calgary, Alberta; the National Archives, Kew Gardens, London, England; and the Barnardo After Care facility—especially Karen Fletcher, whose tour of the historical grounds on Tanner's Lane was so enlightening.

editorial acknowledgements

A SPECIAL THANKS TO PAULA D. CLARKE, WHOSE HOURS SPENT EDITING AND tightening up language in this book were immensely helpful and enriched our nearly five-decade friendship.

Thank you to Larry Hincks, whose edit ensured me that this novel came together as a story with as much historical accuracy as possible.

A huge amount of gratitude to my cousin Paul Miller, graphic artist, etc., who worked on the family tree segments to make them workable in publishing format.

And last, but not least, to my fellow Word Writers, Brian Austin, Ruth Coghill, Sara Davison, Donna Mann, Heidi VanDerSlikke, and Kay Watson, for your continued support, encouragement, and prayers. Your tuned-in listening gave me the hints needed to put ideas clearly into words. To Helena Smrcek and Sara Davison, who make great writing retreat roommates, may we continue the time-stealing treats of writing in companionable silence, sharing meals, and watching late-night movies.

introduction to jamaica

Summers Family

Southern Jamaica, 1515—1660

Padre Gomez bent to shake the dust off the hem of his long black robe. Workmen hollered instructions to each other. Birds chattered in nearby mango groves. As he looked up to check the next rafter being raised, he shouted, "Juan! Juan! Quidarse! Watch out! La viga!" as a large timber slipped from its precarious position off the crossbeams of the new cathedral. God, not another death!

Juan Decampo flung himself out of the path of the falling timber just in time to avoid being crushed. Succumbing to gravity, one end of the beam slid from the braided reed rope and dug into the hardened earth. The other end bounced with a thunderous whomp right where Juan had been standing.

"Gracias Dio," whispered the padre. They crossed themselves and looked skyward in gratitude. Sun-scorched workmen hurried towards the scene, fearful eyes wide.

"Gracias, Padre, gracias!"

"¿Esta bien?" asked the padre. "Are you well?"

"Si, Padre, si. Muchos gracias. Mio Dio, gracias!"

II

After Sevilla was deemed unhealthy because of bad air, the Spanish colony on Jamaica was re-established inland away from the low-lying swampy flats of the coast. The priests had decided a cathedral should be the first priority in St. Jago de la Vega, so Spain gave permission to construct what would become the oldest cathedral in the West Indian colonies.

Years later, in 1655, the English began to take over the islands. The Spanish fled St. Jago de la Vega, Jamaica, freeing their African slaves as they scrambled to outrun the British troops. Some of the Portuguese and Spanish Jews who had come to find refuge in Jamaica were also left, gradually integrating with the British colony. Many remained in St. Jago de la Vega, which became Spanish Town, Clarendon Parish. By 1660 there were 4,500 white residents and an estimated 1,500 black, many of whom were in the hills fighting off possible recapture by the British.

Central Jamaica, Trelawney Parish, 1700

The midday jungle was quiet except for the macaws crying high in tree branches and the rustling of palms. Where the sun pierced through the heavy canopy, light played with the hundred shades of green foliage.

Filiptor was searching for his sister. Faint sounds of a struggle were ahead. His friend followed closely, also scantily clad in a ragged loincloth. They clambered from the undergrowth just above a drop into a small ravine.

"Maria!" Filiptor yelled, but he was too late. Her hands bound behind her back and her clothes torn, she had thrust her body's weight against the point of the sword one soldier had been tormenting her with. The other had been foolishly dropping his weapons and pants.

Rage surged through Filiptor and Byou. Filiptor sprang ahead angrily and threw his primitive but lethal bayonet straight into the man's heart, darkening the wool uniform around the wound. Byou threw his bayonet at the retreating redcoat, who was twisted in his own tangle of breeches and gear. Then Filiptor stood still, intensely listening.

Quiet had again settled in the midday heat of the mountainous jungle. They lifted Maria's lifeless, bloody body off the sword. Byou moved ahead, checking the nearby area for any other British soldiers lost on patrol. He planned to retrieve the weapons as soon as time allowed.

"They are gone now. You are good, Filiptor?" his friend asked in Spanish when he returned.

"She was a strong, brave woman. No one was going to get her as slave." Filiptor wiped away an unwanted tear and faced Byou. "Thank you, my friend. You go to bring back the weapons and look for the firing arms on the dead. It will better prepare us for the next attack, for surely there will be many more men in the red coats."

Byou nodded and scrambled through the jungle to the gully they had left. Filiptor carried Maria's body to a safer site near their camp, fighting his anger and heartbreak.

As Filiptor moved, far away drums throbbed in his inner ear. Their pulse beat along the bloodlines coursing through his body. The air seemed to thicken. Darker, heavier jungle closed around him; memories, generations old, fed his heightened anger until he felt he was one with his grandfather, his great-grandfather, and shadows of generations gone before.

A cool breeze gently drew Filiptor out of his mesmerized state and made him aware he had reached the summit of a brightly lit and thinly vegetated area where he could bury Maria's body under the stones. After placing a traditional arrangement of branches and leaves over the mound, he moved slowly back to camp, still plagued by ancient memories and sounds.

II

Filiptor returned to his fellow Maroons, the escaped slaves, who were gathered in the hidden encampment. They had been captured from different tribes in Africa and brought to the West Indies by the Spanish, whose language they now spoke fluently.

"We must try to contact the leader and make peace," advised the young, slim thinker Claudos as Filiptor joined the group.

"Never," growled the oldest, Gull. "My back reminds me too often about cruel masters. These whites could be even worse. I will die before giving up to be a slave again!"

"There are more large ships in the bay over the mountains. We cannot fight all of them with their swords and firing arms. We must negotiate," Claudos tried a second time.

Filiptor still had a hard stone in the pit of his stomach, but Maria's bravery had ensured his loyalty to the independent tribes of Maroons. He would never become a slave on this island as his ancestors had. They had been brought here from a great distance, with no way to escape. A few of them had come from other islands in this turquoise sea and reported the conditions of the people from the dark continent across the water. They were worse off, their masters not having fled from the British troops and navy as their former Spanish masters had done.

"We have no choice but to fight. These men are made weak by the heat and air. They foolishly wear heavy clothes and carry too much with them. They will do little after the rains begin in two months' time, and we know the mountains and gullies. I believe we can keep the redcoats from our people for many years. We must lead them into fighting, but away from our shelters and children. We must stay united, or we are lost," Filiptor concluded, searching the group's tired, determined faces. Many nodded in agreement and began to hunt for edible berries and fruit. Gradually they all relaxed, and the small sweet-wood grove lay quiet.

"What have you there, my friend Byou?" Filiptor asked as the jungle leaves opened. Byou grunted his answer while he dragged a body along in short jerks.

"He is alive, but not for long when he runs out of blood. Can we use him? He knows the language our Spanish masters taught us, and he knows the language of the redcoats too. We can keep him alive to teach us, and then we get rid of him."

Claudos came up beside them, hopeful in the situation. "We have someone then to tell us what the redcoats plan. We do not let him know of our location, but we keep him fed and try to revive him so we can use him when the time comes. It is a guarantee to our freedom."

Filiptor nodded in agreement but warned Claudos, "It will be some time yet before we are in that position. You must be patient, Claudos." He studied the bewildered black face of their prisoner and wondered at his being in a red coat. Why was a dark brother helping the men in red?

Months of heavy rains and high winds followed, thrashing the treetops on the mountains and laying flat the growth by the seashore fields. The groups of Maroons hidden in thick jungle camps, faces blending with shadows, peered out to sea and studied the few scattered British camps. The day would come when they would not have to hide, but now their fierceness, strengthened by hatred and anger, helped them to keep the British military at bay. Their prisoner had become one of them, not anxious to return to the redcoats, who had promised him freedom if he fought with them. The English language lessons passed on to others quickly. The Maroons would be prepared for war by 1732.

St. James Parish, Northern Jamaica, 1710

Ann was just beginning to relax in the warm freshness of a Jamaican morning. Unfamiliar fragrances stirred her senses. She studied the smooth-barked cotton tree overhanging the ford and gently massaged the now uncomfortable expansion of her stomach. After weeks at sea, the calm turquoise blue of the still ocean before her felt like a dream. The horrible smells of human waste and sickness on board were nearly wiped from her memory. She turned then to report back to her husband, Thomas, but jumped in alarm at a figure whose white-toothed grin captured her focus. Her feet turned to lumps of lead, immobilizing her. The heavy perfumes of the air suddenly nauseated her.

"Ah, no worry, ma'am, no worry. I be your helper in da house, if you be da new missus," reassured the heavyset woman of Negro blood. To Ann, brought up in the city life of central London in England, the black depth of the Negress's skin was a startling new sight. Except for their white wrists above ratty sleeves, only the chimney sweeps of Whitechapel resembled the same colour.

"Da boss man tell me find you an show you da house. Please, you to come?" The question was more pleading than demanding. Ann could have turned to escape to the men on the wharf but instead took a deep breath and followed this person, a slave. She had had a young girl for domestic help at home, trained in every way to meet their family's needs there, but she had been warned that slaves were not to be trusted here on the island and could not be given the slightest privilege; otherwise troubles would begin.

"What is your name?" Ann asked, forcing her voice to be firmer than she felt.

"Mary, and I been done baptized with my chil' William."

Ann thought she should feel some relief at that, but new anxiety crept in as they approached a wooden building with its door open. A cooking pot was hung over an outside open fire pit. Care had been taken to line the pit with sand, and a large area around the pit had been cleared of plants and roots to ensure no fire would creep into the nearby savannah and plantation.

"Where do the field workers stay?" Ann asked, peering through surrounding stands of cottonwood.

"Through dose trees dere. Dere is a long path to our houses, but they is nothin' like 'dis one," Mary stressed as she waved her arm in welcome. Cane chairs on the comforting veranda invited Ann to sit and rest, as the heat seeped through her pores in beads of perspiration.

"I think I shall wait here for my husband and children to join me."

Minutes later Thomas Summers, bright with enthusiasm, joined his wife. Three children plodded along behind him, and he carried the youngest on his hip.

"Well, my dear. Don't you think this will be a splendid new start? Tomorrow, Prince and the overseer will show me the plantation and how things work here. I hope you will be comfortable with ordering the slaves in an appropriately firm manner. There have been cases, I understand, where the Negroes have taken advantage of white women. They have no rights here, you know, and can be severely punished."

Ann continued to fan herself with a palm but was still troubled about how she would cope with slaves. "How am I to know what is expected of them and when they are shirking their duties?"

"You'll learn. If you need something, tell them. If you are in doubt, ask the overseer's wife." Thomas began to feel somewhat drained himself. "My, it is warm, is it not? I say, dear, would you like to go in and rest? You must learn to pace yourself, in your condition. I hope it will be cooler after the fall rains."

Ann grasped her husband's hand and said, "I shall be fine once we settle. My only wish is that you will not be away for long on your expeditions."

"We shall see how well the present overseer has been doing. I hope that there will be produce to sell soon. I learned that there is a church of England called St. James in the town. It has been surprisingly well-established since the Spaniards left, which I suppose is to be expected, as the government pays the diocese to build churches and keep the parishes."

Thomas recalled how the military had relinquished political control in 1661, and a restricted representation system had been established. The primary seats were held by the largest and wealthiest plantation owners who lived on the island. Despite the fact that 30 percent of the landowners were absent, sufficient numbers of well-educated and well-bred white men who saw fit to protect the interests of the plantation owners had been hired. Men like Thomas Summers moved from London, the port cities of Bristol and Plymouth, or small manor-dominated towns to increase the white population, run the plantations, and, hopefully, to improve their lot in life.

II

On May 15th, 1710, four-day-old John Summers, son of Thomas and Ann, was baptized at St. James. The rector gladly welcomed the newborn as the first white child within his congregation to be baptized.

The rector and plantation owners were always happy to help new settlers who might increase the minority white population. Numbers of people with varying degrees of blackness and brownness were increasing more rapidly than those who controlled the slaves; at times, it was frightening for white men.

Many coloured freemen were allowed to work at fishing, be indentured to captains on the navy boats, or run businesses, but they could not own land or property. Some coloured had earned their freedom after doing outstandingly brave deeds against the French during the wars of the last five years of the seventeenth century. Perhaps, as preached by some, they really were human.

Of course, gentry from the British Isles felt they should still be treated the way their ancestors had been. The plain folk and tenant farmers on the small holdings and in the damp cottages in Britain had always regarded the landlords as superior. Here in the West Indies, the expectations were even higher when it came to people of colour.

Portland Parish, Eastern Jamaica, 1723

The two clerics showed little Christian love between themselves as they fought for control of the amalgamated parishes. St. George and St. Thomas in the east were joined to become Portland Parish, and Hanover had been separated from Westmoreland in the same year.

"These Negroes will not be tamed by whipping and beating. There needs to be teaching so they can learn some rules of Christianity," the Reverend Wright firmly stated.

"They need stronger penalties for disobedience. They are next to animals that need to be trained with whipping, not cajoling. Punishment is what they need, not rewards for disobeying their plantation owners. Their masters have purchased them, remember? They need to get work out of them for their investment," argued James Rowe.

The plantation owners were determined to own slaves and gradually pushed anyone with thoughts of abolition out of the parish. They were strong-minded men, focused on getting as much from the land for as little cost as possible. Sugarcane had become their life, and they hired white overseers to control the dispirited slaves, who worked with little reward for their masters.

II

"Move back, woman!" shouted the overseer, John Stone, as he shoved Sarah to the ground on the sharply cut cane stumps, some of which dug deeply into her flesh, leaving abrasions and bruises.

"No! Caffee! Caffee!" Sarah cried out.

"Stay down, woman, or I will beat you too!" shouted Stone as he drew up the dripping whip to continue beating the bleeding man on his knees. The intensity of the noon sun beat down on the three. Perspiration dripped from Stone's brow, off the end of his nose, and down his chin. The adrenaline was flowing.

His repeated attacks on the broad black back continued until Caffee fell on his face. Stone dropped the whip.

"Get down, woman! Don't fight me," directed Stone as he unbuttoned his trousers. "Get your dress up and your hands away," he growled, slapping her fearful, wet face while forcing himself upon her. Sarah cried out. There was no protection for her during this savage attack. The white overseer was ripping her new bloomers down from her waist to below her knees, and she screamed as the sugarcane stumps shred her backside into strips. She tried backing away on her elbows, but sharp stubbles of stalk dug into her. She turned to see the bleeding welts on her husband's back—crying and moaning in agonized pain, praying and beseeching an unknown god.

Sarah and Caffee had never formally married. They had two children, now seven and eleven. Once they realized it simply meant new stock for the slave owner, they found ways to prevent any further births. Most children would stay with their mother until sixteen but could then be sold off to another plantation owner. No doubt, a word of complaint to the landowner from the overseer and Caffee would be sold, an attempt to weaken any family bonds and threaten Sarah's security from any more forced attacks.

Kingston, Jamaica, 1755

"And furthermore, honoured gentlemen of the council," continued the riled plantation owner, also the king's representative in the assembly, "if the Consolidated Slave Act should pass and a committee is allowed to report on the letters and allegations of these reputed distresses of slaves in transportation, we will suffer the consequences, which could be severe. As colonials, we know the importance of having a secure labour force, and should a committee be swayed by emotional views, rather than clear-headed business reports, they may be tempted to reduce or stop all slave trade."

Papers, which moments before had crackled throughout the assembly room in a futile effort to move the deadly still air, were waved wildly by the representatives like flags above their heads. Many more thumped the tables or clapped in agitation.

"Here! Here! We must not let them interfere with the trade, transportation, or treatment of our labourers," expounded another.

"A letter should be sent. Ask for the sake of justice that there need not be any further security for the slaves, but for us!"

The meeting carried on, and immediately thereafter, the corresponding secretary sent the request to hold off the Consolidated Slave Act proposed by the House of Commons in the British Parliament.

Two gentlemen met outside of the chambers after the meeting.

"I have already written to Stephen Fuller, the agent for Jamaica, to request military help. After the insurrection in St. John's Parish, I am sure that this Negro business will cause trouble. There is already unrest in Vere Parish."

"I am surprised that they are having trouble, in light of the strict fierceness with which they control their slaves. St. Thomas in the east has the highest percentages of slaves per white person. Even Clarendon and here in the city of Kingston there is a much greater percentage of Negroes to whites. The problem with taking the white militia from the plantations is they can't leave without increasing the danger of rebellion from their own slaves, on their own land. There is also no point in commissioned officers coming here and forcing the militia to march unreasonable distances in this climate. The dark- skinned people can take the heat, but the white men cannot."

"I did suggest that some man-of-war ships be sent rather than just troops. A few anchored in harbours for a fortnight might send the message more clearly."

"Well, let's hope the resolution is not passed, once they see our side."

The two men parted.

II

Weeks later, another meeting resulted in the reading of two acts not favoured by the representation of the people at Parliament.

"Sir! This is outrageous. With the passing of the Consolidated Slave Act we are allowing a committee to report not only on the slave trade and the transportation of the slaves, but also on their treatment in the whole West Indies. What qualifications do those reporting have to judge the colonial treatment of Negroes?"

"Point taken, Mr. Rhodes. There is the danger that these homeland lawmakers do not have a clear understanding of the unruly, heathen behaviour with which we plantation owners and overseers have to deal. It is ludicrous to even consider these supposed avaricious and unfeeling taskmasters as anything but out of the ordinary. We don't hear of slaves in distress. They are clothed, fed, and trained in Christian ways. Britain does not understand that the Negro is unwilling to put forth any effort in daily labour; they bring forth any excuse not to do a task, and even worse, their unclean habits cause deadly disease among them."

"The question, honourable sir, is what will happen if these temporary regulations to stop the slave trade in British ships become law?"

III

The honourable member's question was soon to be answered by a letter from Lord Sydney to Colonel Sloane and Lord Hawksbury in England. He had been observing the shipping status in the Dutch ports of Le Havre and Honfleur. A great number of freighted ships preparing to leave for Africa had alerted him to the fact that the French were tired of being inconvenienced. They resented having to get their slaves transported by the British and were certain to take advantage of the stoppage of British slave ships. "Not only that," he wrote, "but the French are tempting our ships to get French licenses."1

Up Park and Port Royal, Jamaica, 1760—1788

Time passed. John Leard and his assistants had been drawing up maps for Philip Afflect Esquire, rear admiral of the white and commander in chief for the past four years. His fees were substantial. Only John's assistants-in-training would be considered for his enviable position upon his retirement.

"Sir, I am here to present the maps you have required." Leard spoke in a cultured, moderate voice and bowed respectfully in greeting.

"Very good, Leard. What have we here?" Afflect leaned over his desk as Leard unrolled a number of very neat, detailed maps of the coastlines and harbours of Jamaica.

"You see here the north coastline, sir, with St. Ann's Bay, Martha Brae, Montego Bay, and Savanna La Mer."

"Yes, very good. Mmm. Are these sketches necessary?" Afflect asked, looking at the detailed landscape sketches.

"Oh, just something we sometimes do when waiting for ships to arrive. It helps to give some perspective to the coastline. Now here are the ones for Old Harbour and Port Royal, which you were wanting immediately."

"Yes. Good. I see that the fathoms are marked. This shows that Hunt's Bay is nearly blocked off. Why is the depth not recorded here?"

"Well, from our investigations, the depth is mainly about three feet—hardly navigable. And the passage between Fort Augusta and the shoals is about a cable and a half, which is still manageable, except perhaps in storms. The whole harbour is particularly difficult in high winds."

"Well, I see we have our dredging marked out for us. The plan is to get another harbour master for Old Harbour, Salt River, and Clarendon Bay and keep these buccaneers from finding refuge. If there is ever a stop to the slave trade, it will necessitate more patrolling of our coasts."

Afflect continued poring over the maps and dismissed Leard with a cursory wave. He felt a great deal of responsibility on his shoulders and was troubled by the heat. He needed to finish up here so he could join all the town and many other white inhabitants from the surrounding areas to make their way together to Kingston's Harbour, where the son of Britain's king was disembarking.

Prince William Henry gave a very favourable impression to the public. Though young, and the dream of many a hopeful young woman of privilege, he was proving to be professional and appropriately subordinate to his superior officers.

"Oh, sir, you must write to the king and tell him how his illustrious son has given the navy an exciting honour by his presence here in our station!" suggested an impressed magistrate. And the thought sparked an excellent, complimentary, and exhaustive letter to His Majesty in the year of 1788.

Afflect concluded his writing on behalf of Lieutenant Clark: "We cannot doubt that the Royal Navy of Great Britain continues to be, as it hitherto has been, the Terror of the World, and that under its protection, the National Commerce will flourish, until it encircles the whole inhabitable Earth."2

Kingston Harbour, Jamaica: 1787 -1788

Lieutenant Governor Alvord Clarke loosened the collar on his uniform. The April humidity of a Jamaican spring sucked the life right out of him.

"Dunlop! Are those papers ready for signing at present?"

"Sir, I have three more lines to complete. The pen is as slippery as a wet herring. I'll have them done momentarily." He had already completed a letter dictated to him earlier this morning in its formal presentation for the king's council. "The total number of Negroes on this island is two hundred and fifty-six thousand," he had written. That was, at least as far as they could tell. The landowners were not particular in recording details of their slaves. Most only had a first name.

"When I finish signing these, I need to get the current cash prices of commodities. I wonder if there will be any difference from last month."

"Likely there will be very little, sir." Dunlop finished the document with a flourish and moved it over to the lieutenant governor's desk for signing.

"Even this heavy linen paper feels moist. How do things ever dry here? Why is there never a breath of fresh air to be had in this godforsaken country?"

The lieutenant governor shuffled to the door, fastening all the buttons of his tunic but the top one. He headed down to the naval office to collect the reports of British and foreign ships that had entered Kingston Harbour that week. Along the winding path towards the wooden naval base near the docks, he saw men lazing around in groups as they deftly hid rum bottles behind bunches of grass. Clarke was suspicious that they were the lookouts for buccaneers and pirates, observing his every move, and those of his men. They would report to their captains, who were often responsible for terrorizing legal trading ships and stealing their goods. There could be no planning of surprise attacks by the military. Parliament did not appear willing to send funds or troops to squash the pirates, and there was nothing he could arrest them for doing.

PART ONE

Summers F A M I L Y

one

Kingston, Jamaica, 1813

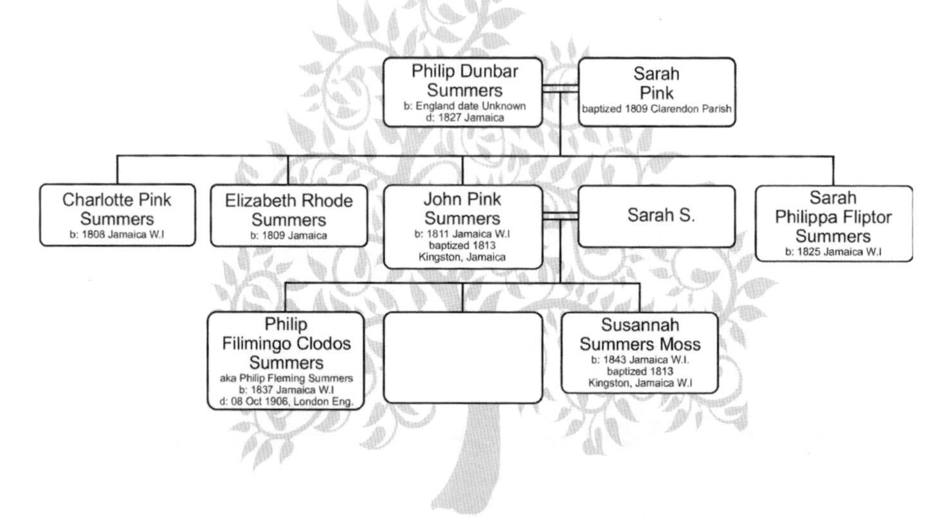

Jamaica – 1700's, unknown artist (see endnote #2)

Philip Dunbar Summers shuffled the papers in front of him. He glanced through the most recent edition of the Supplement to the Royal Gazette, covering the week of June 26 to July 3. He skimmed the article on Napoleon Bonaparte, who had ordered four men hanged because, reportedly, they had borne arms against France. No trial had taken place, just a special military commission. The writer asked, "Is Napoleon alone to be blamed for this dreadful outrage?" Well, he didn't know.

Ah. Page sixteen had descriptions under Runaways: "Lewis, a Mendinga, 5'1"; William, a Congo, 5'7"; Charles, a Creole, 5'2"." The list filled two columns. He wondered if his friend William DaSilva had found his own two slaves who had disappeared.

Then he perused the column under Strays from the pounds, first in St. Andrew, then St. Catherine, a closer, more likely place to find his missing companion. "Old brown Spanish he mule; mouse-coloured horse with Spanish markings; Bay horse, marked B in one ear; Bay Spanish mare, marked F near buttock." Well, none of those descriptions fit his black beauty.[3]

This was not what he had intended to do when he sat down at the fine wooden desk by the window. He was thinking of his son's future. Since he himself was a white and Sarah, mother of his children, was a free mulatto, what did that make his son, John Pink Summers? Ha, here it was in a simply printed act, handed out to voting citizens along with the Gazette.

"Any child of a white and a mustee is considered white," read Philip, "meaning one-sixteenth or having one great great-grandparent who was black." That might not fit, as Sarah was a mulatto. If their son married a white woman, then his children would be considered white. Philip had given Sarah permission to have John baptized the next day at the Church of England in Kingston.

"Sarah," Philip called to his wife, "do you know what your mother was?"

"My mother was a very fine woman, so don't you be saying anything against her. She did the best with us as she could at Drax Hall."

Philip smiled and took her hand gently. "She was a fine woman, and I am sorry she is among us no longer, but I was trying to establish what degree of colour our John will be considered."

"Oh my." Sarah sighed, rolling her eyes upward. "I have no firm knowledge, but my mother was more Negro than not. My father was definitely white."

"Did he, you know, force her?"

"I don't know, and she never said, but he looked after us. I had some free schooling before taking care of my mother and the house. It was preferable to living on some piece of swamp the government gave out. There was nothing but tiny brush and cane huts with inside fires. My half-brother—now he's a wonderful businessman. He's done well for himself. Perhaps he would help us if needed. He is fully white, Father always claimed."

He smiled at Sarah's apparent pride in her heritage. Although she spoke of the Negro side of her family, she always made sure people understood that they had been free Maroons, those former Spanish slaves who had fought off the British for sixty years until given their own lands. Sarah highly praised the Pinks of Drax Hall near St. Ann's Bay, Parish of St. Mary's Parish. Through them she had been educated, probably more than many wealthy white women, who were considered too delicate to need education. The sons of the wealthy were sent to Britain or Scotland for university education and polishing. The daughters were sent there to find suitable husbands.

"Well, it will not be necessary to take anything from him," Philip said. "I don't suppose we need worry too much about owning land after I sell the house. Now I must be on my way to the harbour. A foreign bark has arrived. and the fees must be collected. Is Rose working with the children in a satisfactory manner? Are you sure you need to keep her so well dressed? She has another new outfit on this week. It looks like a Sunday dress, too long for real work."

Sarah, not unsympathetic to the slaves, nodded. "She's a house servant, and I like her to be well-dressed. She enjoys seeing that the children are entertained. They love her jolly ways."

"She doesn't move very much, does she? Even with our three children? Sometimes I think she enjoys eating excessively."

"Perhaps she does, but no one moves quickly in this heat. You go now and do your business. We'll eat fresh fish tonight if you bring some home from the wharf." And with that request, she handed Philip his hat and pressed against him for a kiss.

two

PHILIP HAD THOUGHT OF MARRYING AGAIN AT ONE TIME. HE WAS A WHITE and still under forty years of age. His first wife, Charlotte, and his daughter, Sarah Summers, had both succumbed to the fever in 1803 and were buried in the Church of England graveyard outside of town. When he had returned to Kingston, Jamaica, from an extended voyage, it was a shock to him to learn of their deaths from his solicitor.

"Eh, William," lamented Philip, "and I wasn't here to say goodbye. It was always a joy to come home to Charlotte and Sarah. Well, I'm glad you have been helping them these years. It was a comfort for me to know that." Philip swung his arm over William's shoulders.

"I'll show you their resting places now, if you like," William offered, somewhat embarrassed. He respected and admired this man, but long separations had not allowed them to get to know each other well.

Philip asked about some of the merchants and inhabitants of Kingston as they strolled slowly down the hard earthen road towards the cemetery. Some had added to their family, and a few had left.

As they passed the new barrel and vat-making shed, he reflected, "It will be four years now since William Summers died. He tried leaving to improve his health, but by then it was too late. Either we stick out this sickly hot weather, or we succumb to it. I did not think this last epidemic was as widespread as the 93–94 fever reported being. Of course, we were not yet in Jamaica. It is much healthier on the ships above deck, and I'm never sorry to feel a breeze on the sea. I don't think Sarah and Charlotte had a chance to grow acclimatized to this weather and the diseases."

"I took the step to inform your daughters in England of their mother's death, but perhaps you wish to write to them yourself," suggested William.

"Yes, of course. I will write to Rhode and Elizabeth myself. I haven't heard about their weddings. Had there been correspondence with Charlotte?"

"I kept all of Charlotte's personal papers and letters, of course, so that you might go through them. I'm sorry, Philip, that you had to learn of their deaths this way, but there was no method to get letters to you before your return."

"I'm beginning to dislike being on the open sea. Perhaps it's time I turn to piloting boats in the harbour and then apply to be a harbour master. These last trips have been too exciting for me. There are so many buccaneers and privateers that life can get downright dangerous, especially with so many firearms stolen from the government." Philip stopped talking and tried to take in the fact that his wife and daughter were gone. Life would be lonely here.

"There's been a tremendous increase in sugar exports in the last ten years, so the ports have become increasingly busy. Things are improving in town and plans being made to enlarge the Up Park Camp for the military. It's been left to weather and is in quite a ruinous state," William continued.

"They only built those barracks fifteen years ago. I guess the hurricanes have done their share of the damage. Are the house help and slaves behaving adequately? Do we need to trade or sell any, or should I be thinking of sending some on board as apprentices? The ship Charlotte needs some refitting. I could use some of them for that."

"I've been putting them to use in the gardens for the time being. Only Samuel and John are freemen and suitable for sea. Are you going to be staying for a while this time? John and Philip Dunbar have some pimento, ginger, and sugar for export. They asked me to speak to you about it."

"That is a possibility. I think if I take a short trip this season, I will not have the hurricanes to deal with in November. Can you continue looking after the house and help until then?"

"Yes. I was hoping to get someone to rent the house, if that is your wish."

"If you find short-term renters, it will be fine. When I return, I hope to get some experience at Salt River Bay and maybe Clarendon Bay."

Philip and William turned in at the cemetery gates. William pointed Philip in the right direction and then discretely left the graveyard.

three

Philip Summers returned to Kingston Harbour just before the hurricane season began. Last year's storms had been mild, and so far this fall there'd been no indication of any brewing. It was a relief not to spend time repairing after nature's tempests.

Philip worked away for a few years, preparing for the position of harbour master. Then, in 1806, Parliament in Britain prepared to pass an act forbidding bringing any new slaves to British colonies. As feared, they had abolished the slave trade. Plantation owners were distraught with the whole idea, because their profits would start to dwindle. Sugarcane had remained at the top of the list of exports for decades. Although a variety of products such as indigo, salt, pimento, Jamaican peppers, fustic, brasiletto, and ebony woods had been important exports for over a century, now the main cash crop was sugarcane only.

How could they run plantations effectively when new slaves were not available to replace the weaker workers? Slaves did not last long, especially on plantations where inhumane plantation overseers whipped and pushed them cruelly on hot days, past any human's endurance. These overseers wanted a steady amount of work done, and done willingly. Some had begun to import Chinese coolies, but they expected wages and refused to be enslaved for the good of their masters.

Better off were the slaves on the few plantations where treatment was reasonable. An early start to the day was followed by a two-hour rest period at the peak of the day's heat, and then they could continue working until late in the day. None of the work was easy, and no allowance was made for the heat's effects.

For a century, the wealthy plantation owners had been petitioning the British government through letters, asking for an act of Parliament to allow their claimed mulatto children the right to ownership of property. Either there were no white heirs or their children were not interested in coming to Jamaica.

II

Kingston, Jamaica, 1806

Philip stepped out of the customhouse onto the wharf on a humid, sticky fall day and stood with a few friends. Smell, Pike, Parr, and Strangeways liked to gather in the shade and eye the brown beauties that would pass them in this particular part of the wharf to purchase fresh fish. Most were already housekeepers, women who had children with white men, married or not, and were kept by them in small houses or shacks. Philip had taken note at times of a beautiful caramel-skinned young woman with that natural sway of coloured Jamaicans when carrying baskets or babies on their hips. She stood her full four-foot-six height, adding a dignity that many like her had had beaten out of them. Bright scarves circled around her shoulders and hat, protecting her from the sun, and a long skirt swished around her bare ankles. For several days his eyes had followed her retreating figure along the wharf and down the dirt road to the middle of town. Today, he had to pull his attention back to the men once again.

"Well there, fellows, I believe we have a storm brewing. I feel it in my bones," John Pike said.

"Ah, never mind your bones; look at the sky and the colour of the sea, ya daft one. That will tell you we're in for a steady gale any time now," retorted Parr.

Far past the sand spit of Port Royal, small white caps threatened, and greater swells beyond that promised trouble. Both sea and sky were darkening rapidly.

"Well, better head home before the rains start," suggested Pike, but it was already too late. Gusts of wind were fiercely blowing the tops of trees, and pellets of rainwater dampened the dust. Dry leaves and debris swirled over the pathways and roads.

"Better hurry!" yelled Philip as he scurried in the direction of the figure he had been admiring. Philip briefly thought of captains and crews out on the open water of the Caribbean, but he knew that a sensible sailor would have moved to the lee side of an island or had his rigging reduced and everything tied down on deck before the first serious gales began.

Walking into the wind, Philip pressed on but made headway slowly. Heavily bent treetops pointed in his direction. Cool rain pelted his bare skin until it smarted. He couldn't see the figure he had intended to follow, but there were dozens of others scrambling in all directions, parcels, hats, and skirts held close as they headed towards home.

He reached his own bulletwood door, forced its brass knocker to turn, and opened the door wide enough to squeeze into the hall. It closed with a slam, the heavy weight of the aptly named wood a godsend in hurricane season.

"There ye be, Mr. Summers! I bin waitin' for you come in. I get 'dose wet tings off and hung to dry. I got William and Henry up de stairs pulling de window slats and shutters closed. We's in for a real storm!" exclaimed Juliana, head housemaid.

Philip tried to read the Gazette, but the fierce winds distracted his attempts. After several hours, he was ready to call for his dinner, relaxing somewhat as the rains settled to a steady beating and the winds gradually quieted.

"I am headed out for a while, Juliana. Be sure to remind William and Henry to get things cleaned up and repaired, but only when the rain stops. I don't want them complaining of a fever if they go out while it's wet." With that he placed his hat on his head, straightened his jacket, and started his search for the street where that young woman had disappeared. He passed Orange Street and wondered if it was that one, but no, it didn't seem right. When he came to Princess, he turned right and followed it to the block where he had last seen her. Unbelievably, there she was, hurrying down the three steps of a solid-looking house.

"May I help you, Miss?" Philip asked, tipping the brim of his hat slightly.

The young woman looked startled, somewhat afraid of him and his offer. Perhaps the whiteness of his skin or the politeness of his greeting set off her nerves.

"I'm helping my men to locate our runaway horse, which was tied to a fence by the house here. But he reared up and ripped away from his anchorage during the storm. I don't blame him, but he is rather skittish and I am the only one who can calm him. It really isn't necessary for you to help." All this she said while walking smartly down the street without even a sideways glance towards Philip.

"I will help, and please let me introduce myself. I'm Philip Summers, from Bristol, England. I believe you are a Pink, are you not? I have seen your face before." He followed alongside Miss Pink. She nodded at his identification. Under the guise of searching for her horse, the young woman began stealing glances in his direction.

They both might have unwittingly passed the runaway had it not let out a familiar whinny. They turned down the narrow lane between two buildings, where the horse had dragged the rig as far as it would go. It was well and truly stuck, so they walked around to the other end, Miss Pink calling its name. After releasing its tangled harness, Philip assisted in leading it out to the road.

"I would very much like to make your acquaintance, Miss Pink, so I wonder if you would allow me to call some evening for a walk."

The young woman hesitated, but then nodded her head, wishing he were not so attractive to her. They parted, leaving it at that.

five

Sarah Pink had been strictly warned by her half-brother after her mother died. She must be careful of making acquaintance with young men, particularly white ones, for they often took advantage of women of colour, even if they were free. He wanted her to be sure of having at least some support, if not a husband.

"Keep your distance. Don't pay them any attention when they speak or stare at you. You're a beautiful young woman, even though you are mulatto, and I think you can choose a gentleman who will treat you well," volunteered John.

Sarah had been on edge since the death of her mother, who had drilled into her that she must behave like a lady: "Ignore those young rascals that eye you up and down. You don't want to get caught without support. I was fortunate, and Mr. Pink Senior treated me good." Sarah had suddenly felt the seriousness of the situation after her mother was gone. She never discussed what her life had been like before she was allowed to live in her own dwelling with her children, supported by John Pink Senior. Sarah knew that he already had a wife and son, his heir, who had been introduced to his half-sisters years before.

At the time of these warnings, Sarah would lightheartedly brush them off and swing her cane basket on her way to market or to a sick neighbour needing food. No coloured person had rights, she had learned, especially women. There was no pretense at treating Negroes, sambos, mulattos, quadroons, octoroons, or mustees with respect. They were not even considered persons. A 1677 Act of Parliament dictated that Africans, slaves, and blacks were less than human and had no rights to own any land, vote, hold office, or stand witness in court. The same went for "free" coloureds, although they were allowed to move and to ask for a wage.

Fortunately, Sarah's father, John Pink, a landowner in two or three parishes, had favoured her mother, who had been descended from the feisty Maroons. As a free black, she was hired as his housekeeper, and later she was set up in her own home to raise Sarah, a "free mulatto," and her sister. Sarah had not seen him since her mother's death but received word by letter of financial matters, guaranteeing her a place to live as long as she remained in the house. Her half-brother was kind to her, but he was busy buying up property for himself as it became available, the most recent being Tunburym in Clarendon Parish.

Sarah had begun attending the Church of England at a young age and continued to do so. She had felt uncomfortable when groups of slaves were brought in by their masters for baptism. They did not attend regularly, but perhaps their masters thought baptism would stamp some of the rebelliousness out of them and make them into hard-working, courteous Christians. Perhaps some slaves figured that if they were baptized, they would somehow become free, or at least protected. The church didn't explain where the rules for the white people were written.

Sarah gritted her teeth when she saw slaves being whipped and abused by their hot and angry owners. She had hated hearing the preachers use the word free. They didn't help slaves become free. They just told them that, as God-fearing Christians, it was their duty to listen to their betters. The white men knew nothing about how it was to be a slave. Would they ever?

Within the week, Sarah had a caller.

"Is Miss Pink at home?" Philip asked the black servant at the door. He wondered if the slave was owned by Miss Pink or if was she a paid "free" servant.

"One moment, please. You wait here," and she shut the door.

Seconds later Sarah appeared. "Good evening, Mr. Summers. How are you this evening?"

"Please, it's Philip. I'm fine and wondered if you would care to walk this evening?"

"Yes, that will be fine. I shall return in one hour, Rose," she said, a signal that if she didn't, her faithful maid was to raise the alarm.

six

Philip and Sarah took their time getting to know each other. Sarah began to feel comfortable with their relationship, and Philip remained respectful. He had never taken to the habit of drinking rum down at the tavern; nor had he taken liberties with any young women at the local crimp houses, as some of his acquaintances had.

"Do you attend a church, Philip?" Sarah asked innocently four months into their courtship.

"No. It just has never seemed important. My parents did not deem it a priority enough to take me, but they trained me in reading by using a Bible. I found the stories somewhat frightening as a child and irrelevant as a youth. Do you attend yourself, Sarah?"

"Yes, although I must say not weekly. I have yet to be baptized. Do you believe we are damned if we are not? My Catholic friend believes we must be baptized before death, or we will suffer in hell forever."

"I believe that we should respect all people, and I don't think that God will condemn us if we are not baptized because we don't have the opportunity. These preachers who admonish their congregations to love one another, then turn around and beat their slaves within inches of their lives are to me hypocrites. I do not really care to attend church, other than funerals or weddings of relatives and friends."

"Do you know many people who are married under the church law?" inquired Sarah.

"Very few, in fact. It is a great cost, for one thing. I cannot understand why Parliament must charge church rectors who wish to marry people. They of course have to pass on the price to those couples. Their licenses used to cost as much as a license to draw drink. Surely the situation is not equal. When a couple wishes to marry in Jamaica, it's usually for appearances and status with the law."

"I understand that in the British Isles, everyone tries to marry before any children are born, and the rich women are highly supervised."

"That is as it may be. Our life is very different here. Many are more concerned with the colour of their flesh or the colour of their family, don't you think?"

"Are you saying that you do not care for my colour, Mr. Summers?" Sarah stretched her shoulders back and rose proudly to her full height.

"My dear Sarah, I adore the glow of your beautiful skin, and it charms me to see what little I can of it. I adore all of you and wish you to be the mother of my children."

Sarah had felt charmed as well. She was somewhat alarmed at the joy she felt with his arm about her and his open desire of her, but it felt natural to bring him into her home that late afternoon.

Sarah leaned her back against the door after Philip's lingering kiss goodbye. She smiled. She would see him again soon.

II

Months later, their first child was on its way, and Sarah broached the topic of a house together.

"Well, as I am away much of the time, I have not improved my house since Charlotte's death. But what of this house? Will you lose it if you leave? It is preferable in structure to mine, but who owns it?" asked Philip.

"It will revert to my father's possession until his son can purchase it or inherit it."

"And would you mind staying here, then, until after the baby is born? It will be some time before I can afford to purchase our own house, although I'm certain to be harbour master soon."

Sarah nodded, somewhat saddened but determined to accept Philip's wishes.

On April 5, 1807, their first daughter, Charlotte Pink, was born. Within a year, before the birth of their second child, Sarah decided she should be baptized herself. She almost changed her mind after speaking to the condescending rector of Clarendon Parish, but she thought of her children and the need to record their parents and their colour.

"Now, Mizz Pink. You need get that chil' baptized so her name be on the records. They's lookin' for new slaves. If we ever get the 'mancipation, no telling what some white folk might think they can do with our babies!"

"I don't think that will happen, Rose. I don't hear of it happening too often now, but I suppose you're right. Slaves are difficult to purchase now; fewer are brought legally to the Caribbean and fewer have come to Jamaica than are needed." She wanted no chance of her child being taken from her later and claimed as a runaway slave by some powerful plantation owner. The turnover was so fast because they pushed slaves hard while young, and they often died before having a chance to grow old.

seven

THE TEN READY TO BE BAPTIZED WERE LINED UP AT THE FRONT. ONE AT A TIME, they bent before the priest, who read their names from a list and quickly made the sign of the cross while pouring copious amounts of water down their faces. Sarah wasn't sure if she felt any different, but no harm had been done, and only slight humiliation had occurred while she struggled to lift herself up and became slightly over-balanced by her bulging stomach. Each one would have their full name, age, standing, and colour entered in the volume of baptisms for Clarendon under the date of January 8, 1808.

"Bring the baby back when she's born, now, do you hear, Miss Pink?" instructed the elderly Church of England rector in his quavering voice.

"Yes, sir. I plan on it," smiled a flustered Sarah, and she moved on as quickly as her ample size and the January heat would allow.

She began thinking about her firstborn daughter, Charlotte, who was at home with the house servants. Sarah had not had her baptized. Perhaps Sarah should get her baptized before the birth of the child she was carrying.

On February 25, 1808, she did take Charlotte up to the front for baptism. Although the Summers' name would appear on the records, Philip's as the father would not, as he was not in attendance. Sarah was surprised that Philip noticed her disappointment at home later.

"So you had her baptized? Should I have come along?" he naively asked.

"Of course I would have liked you there!" Did he have any idea what it was like to walk up to the front of the nave and back alone? Back alone, facing the stiff necks of those proud white women with their frills, their own primly dressed white children, their pale-faced husbands uncomfortably attired in formal church wear at the order of their wives—the very same men who provided a second home for their second families of colour in much meaner accommodations. It just wasn't right.

The big news of 1808 was the nearly complete destruction of the Port of Falmouth, Trelawny, by fire. The wooden buildings were flattened and the wharves rendered unusable. The port authorities moved everything to Montego Bay to conduct shipping business from there.

Sarah and Philip welcomed their second daughter into the world, and life was agreeable and calm. Philip enjoyed being at home when not working.

He began to see the four of them as his little family, and his previous losses diminished in time.

II

Sarah approached Philip in October of 1809 with a request. "I would like to have you with me for the record, if you don't mind. I know their baptism means nothing to you, but I feel that it may be a help to them someday."

Eliza Rhode Summers was baptized on October 23, 1809. Philip was quite somber while his smallest child was registered in the books. His own name this time, Philip Dunbar Summers, was used as father.

The little family walked back to Sarah's house, where Philip was determined to be a more responsible parent than he had been in the past.

III

Two years later, Philip's son, John Pink Summers, was born. He was delighted to have a son after so many daughters but held off having him baptized until June 24, 1813. Sarah was proud of her half-brother's achievements and was more than happy to name her son after him. John had gone from playing the cornet in 1797 to being a second lieutenant in the Clarendon Troop in 1802, an assistant attorney in possession of Brownberry Estate, St. Elizabeth, and finally an assistant judge and magistrate in St. Mary's and St. Ann's Parishes. Sarah's father, having died, left a large estate for his son John and daughter-in-law Rebecca Hiatt to add to their own properties.

"I thought you would be happy to have our own place. Little Goat Island can be seen from the wharf. It is only a matter of minutes to get there by boat," encouraged Philip, taking Sarah by the arm and sitting her on his knee. "You look like an unhappy schoolgirl," he laughed.

"Well, I feel like one. I know I should be grateful, but I enjoy the town and shops. There is nothing on Little Goat Island."

"You will enjoy the countryside. It will have lots of space for the children to play, and you will have plenty of help. There will be twenty-two slaves on the plantation there, and I can work with the pilot boats handily."

II

It became apparent during the years of 1816 and 1817 that the move had not been very successful. The breezes from the sea were very slow and warming even at the coolest time of the year. Perhaps the heat and humidity made everyone a little bad-tempered, or perhaps Sarah was unhappy having so many slaves under their care. She had a streak in her that resisted the white way of thinking slaves could be owned. She did her best to care for those who were ill, but medical knowledge was limited and threats to good health were everywhere. Her children loved to play with the younger slave children; however, schooling was limited to what Sarah could teach all of them. Philip, too, found getting back and forth to town was not as easy as he had predicted. Then a new situation arose.

"My dear, my dream has finally emerged into reality. Please greet Philip Summers, harbour master of Old Harbour, Clarendon Bay, and Salt River. All these waters before you," and he swept his hand around the three bays in front of them as they stood on the end of the wharf, "are under my jurisdiction." His arm around her waist tightened in excitement.

Sarah smiled at her husband, pleased about his promotion. Slyly she looked sideways at him to catch his reaction to her next hopeful remark.

"I suppose this means that we must find a place on shore and move again, does it?"

III

Milford Lodge sat between Clarendon and Bowers Gullies. The verandas on two sides provided shade for Sarah and the children while they read and studied in the afternoons.

"Mother, do you think I can grow up to be a ship's captain like Father?"

"Oh, John, I see no reason why not. It's unfortunate that your father has retired from captaining a ship. If you don't feel ill, then it would be grand to have a master mariner in the family again." Sarah was sad for a moment, thinking of her only son being away and facing so many dangers on the sea. Thankfully, pirates and buccaneers were no longer as much a threat and French and Spanish ships even less so now.

When his father came home, John sat on a stool beside him while he rested and took refreshment. He liked listening to his father's stories of catching illegal fishing boats or foreign ships that had not paid customs duties. Sometimes the port authority called Philip away in the night to help man a pilot boat. He made many trips searching the morass that dominated the low-lying shorelines from Salt River Bay right around to Cabaritta Point near Long Bay. Their torches often caught a lonely night fisherman, but their search was for larger vessels, unlicensed or foreign. Regulations did not allow ships' crews onshore except by special permission. At times, they found an empty boat drawn ashore where some sailors were looking to hire draymen or carriages to take them to Spanish Town, and even as far as Kingston. There they would be found in grog shops, punch or tippling houses or at some liquor retailer willing to supply them with alcohol illegally. Old Harbour had the best wharves and the only decent beaching facilities for landing small boats.

"You know that a seaman must be very good with numbers and able to calculate fathoms and feet. He must be an excellent map reader and a man who knows and understands the weather. Would you like to do all that, John?" asked his father.

"Oh, yes, Father. Do you think you can show me your maps so I can begin learning? I'm tired of reading stories with the girls."

"What do you say you attend school in Kingston for a year or two and get proper training before we start?"

John frowned and asked, "Would I be caned if I didn't know my lessons?"

"Well, only if you did not try to learn your lessons. I think you would enjoy the classes with other boys who wish to be sailors and captains."

John smiled at the thought of being with other boys and quickly agreed to his father making the arrangements.

nine

According to Philip, there were few free or parochial schools that gave a broad enough education. He felt the rectors in every church parish spent far too much time on catechetical instruction. What was the point in having slaves and coloureds able to say the catechism?

He smiled at his son beside him sitting up smartly in the trap. "Are you satisfied with our choice of Wolmer's Free School in Kingston? It is a very good school and has turned out many scholars since opening in 1729. Your time there will pass quickly, and before you know it, you will be apprenticing aboard Mr. Johnston's ships."

John smiled eagerly, and then hesitated. "Do you think Mother will miss me very much, Father? Will you be sure she doesn't worry too much about me?"

"You have no need to worry about your mother. She has a great devotion to you children, however, and she will miss you." Philip leaned over his son conspiratorially. "Women need to express their emotions in an exaggerated way, just to be sure that we notice and can interpret them." John nodded confidently. Philip felt a pride in his son, sure that John would make a fine seaman, even captain someday if he put his mind to it.

John was excited to see the busy streets of Kingston, Jamaica's largest city. Men were lighting the gaslights as he and his father arrived at the home of a friend of Philip's. There were new ordinance buildings in town, a hospital that had been built in 1819, and bridle paths that had become carriage roads. There were plenty of free coloureds looking for work at the docks. Philip realized that John would face challenges here and on the ships that he, as a white Brit, never had to face.

II

Sarah Philippa Fliptor Summers was born on June 14 in 1825. Little Sarah cried upon entering the world, and Philip was again amazed at the wonders of new life. He had thought perhaps he could rest easier these days, but now here was a tiny new baby. Fortunately, her fifteen- and sixteen-year-old sisters delighted in helping their mother since there were fewer slaves around Milford Lodge these days. John had already begun his apprenticeship at sea so hardly would get to know his youngest sister.

Two years later, a frail Philip succumbed to old age and disease, leaving the Milford estate in limbo while the courts sorted out who could own it and who would benefit from its sale. John carried on as an apprentice, rising to mate and a master mariner himself, carrying on the tradition of the seafaring Summers.

Sarah did her best to raise the three girls, but life was not the same without Philip. She was happy enough when her son John married Sarah Fleming and blessed her with a grandson and granddaughter, even though it meant he was not allowed to inherit any of Philip's land or wealth after she died. John Summers and his family attended the newly organized Methodist Church in Kingston, and the pastor baptized Philip Fleming Summers there in 1837.

ten

London, England, 1861

Philip Fleming Summers was happy on the sea. Although his father, John Pink Summers, had captained a ship, his own interests were with the transport of goods and provisions. He wanted to travel and see seaports all over the world. His ambition was to move to Great Britain, where the largest shipping nation in the world controlled vast areas of the oceans and commanded many ships in the western hemisphere.

After the ship and crew cleared the port authority, Philip was now in the large, crowded, and busy city of London.

"Have ye lodgings, young man?" asked the bent and bearded man leaning on the wall of the port authority's office.

Philip instinctively drew back from the man, wary in his new surroundings and determined not to be taken advantage of in his first day in London. "I do, thank ye, and am on my way now."

He moved on, heading toward a busy street, which he hoped was Commercial and would lead him to a room at 18 Gray Street. Philip walked as steadily forward as his sea legs allowed, studying the dark streets with awe. The buildings were tall and massive, of heavy solid stone or dull-coloured brick. There were crowds of people and carriages struggling to share the cobblestone streets. Young people, often shoeless, wore clothing that had been handed down from older siblings, or perhaps pulled from refuse piles. The ragged and dirty hems caught the dust of the street, the coal, and the ashes. Their faces appeared as dark as the Negroes he had left behind in Kingston.

"Watch out there, mister," shouted a ruffian with bare ankles. Behind him, an irate fruit peddler raised his fist.

"Ye'll pay for this, young master David. Wait until I see the bobby next round!" and he swung back to protect his cart from any other bold thieves who might try to trick him into distraction while swiping an apple.

Philip felt he had to be constantly on his guard. He had heard how quick the practiced young children were at pickpocketing. Of all the world ports, London was not the worst, but today it felt the darkest and dirtiest to Philip. The fact that he had been at sea at Christmastime made Philip fondly remember the bright, warm West Indian holiday time of his youth. Warmth, fresh green foliage everywhere, and colourful clothing even on the poor were a stark contrast to this crowded, cold, industrialized city.

(E-1) CERTIFICATE OF DISCHARGE.

For Seamen discharged before a Shipping Master.

MARINE DEPARTMENT

SANCTIONED BY THE BOARD OF TRADE MAY 1855. IN PURSUANCE OF 17 & 18 VICT. C. 104.

28

Name of Ship.	Official Number.	Port of Registry.
Trossachs	15089	Dundee

Registered Tonnage.	Description of Voyage or Employment.
340	Foreign

		Capacity.
Name of Seaman	Philip C Summers	Steward
Place of Birth	Jamaica	
Date of Birth	1840	

Date of Entry.	Date of Discharge.	Place of Discharge.
March 20/62	Dec 6/63	London

I Certify that the above particulars are correct and that the above Seaman was discharged accordingly.

Dated this 9 day of Dec 1863

For Signature of Seaman see back.

Signed John Imlach Master of the Ship.

[illegible] Shipping Master.

NOTE.—One of these Certificates must be filled up and delivered to every Seaman who is discharged whenever the discharge takes place before a Shipping Master.

Printed by Authority of the Board of Trade.

(E-1) CERTIFICATE OF CHARACTER.

MARINE DEPARTMENT

SANCTIONED BY THE BOARD OF TRADE MAY 1855. IN PURSUANCE OF 17 & 18 VICT. C. 104.

Character for ability in whatever capacity: VG

Character for Conduct: VG

28

I Certify the above to be a true Copy of so much of the Report of Character, made by the said Master on the termination of the said Voyage, as concerns the said Seaman.

Dated at London this 9 day of Dec 1863

Signed John Imlach Master of the Ship.

[illegible] Shipping Master.

For Signature of Seaman see back.

NOTE. Any Person who fraudulently forges or alters a Certificate of Character or makes use of one which does not belong to him may either be prosecuted for a Misdemeanour or may be summarily punished by a Penalty not exceeding £100 or imprisonment with hard labour not exceeding six months.

Printed by Authority of the Board of Trade.

Earliest Known Discharge Paper Of Philip Summers

PART TWO

Pepper FAMILY

eleven

London, England, 1850s

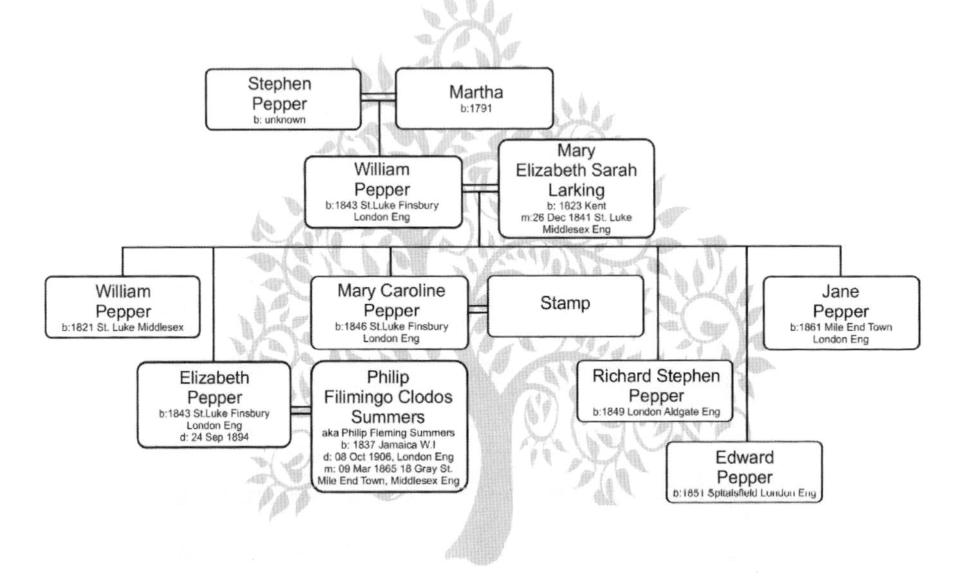

Barnardo Trunk sent with children being Emigrated

"Mother, where are you taking us?" asked William, now a young man and head of the household. After the death of his father, Stephen Pepper, just weeks before, William felt he should be consulted as to what the family was doing.

"William, don't let Thomas drag behind. Your uncle has put us in touch with a house on Rahere Street just to the west in Finsbury. There will room for us there, and we will carry on. Here, Thomas, hold my hand. William, will you please take both handles of the trunk? It's not much farther." Martha Pepper handed the rope handle of the trunk to her son and grasped her four-year-old grandson's hand.

"Mother, what about me and Mary? We were planning on getting married. Do you expect us to move in with you and Thomas?"

"Mary's home is three doors away, and if you speak to Mary's father, James Larking, I'm sure they will have room for you to live with them."

Since Stephen Pepper, her husband of forty-nine years, died, Martha continued caring for family members and her grandchildren every day of the week. She was looking after young Thomas until his mother was on her feet after having a difficult birth. Martha's oldest five offspring had all married and were busy with their own children. They had all been baptized at St. Luke's, Finsbury, and many carried on their Christian duties within that same parish, for which Martha was thankful. She was very hopeful that Mary Larking would make a good wife for her youngest son, William.

II

Banns had been published for three weeks prior to the marriage of William James Pepper and Mary Larking the day after Christmas. After the ceremony at the parish church in St. Luke's, James Larking brought his daughter and new son-in-law home, and they joined in the evening meal as though nothing had changed. William carried on with his position as warehouseman. With a busy port such as London, there was always work out on the docks, but it was preferable to be out of the wet, dreary weather in a warehouse.

William enjoyed the smells of foreign goods that arrived daily. He was responsible for finding broken or damaged items, which meant prying open the wooden crates and unpacking the straw. Invoices were carefully checked against contents, and the goods were loaded onto wagons for transport to the shops throughout the city or out to the towns by special order. Most of it was headed away from the docks in the west end to the more influential and lucrative districts.

After the birth of their first four children, the Pepper family moved to 13 Palmer Street, Christchurch Parish, in the borough of Tower Hamlets. This allowed the children to attend day schools for a small fee. Three-year-old Richard was still at home. It was a challenge for the other three to get to school safely.

"William, please wait for us," begged six-year-old Elizabeth, who was pulling the reluctant Mary Ann behind her. William had to walk a little farther to the school for charity scholars, and he didn't want to be a minute late. He was fortunate to still be in school at eight years of age.

III

At the time of the 1861 census, William was an earthenware dealer, Elizabeth a tailoress, Mary Ann a lace collar maker, and fourteen-year-old Stephen Richard was a butcher's apprentice. Edward, at ten, was still in school, and Caroline Jane was only seven months old.

There was a richness to the decor of the house, with numerous articles that had been purchased for little more than the cost of transportation from the country of origin. William acquired exotic wooden furniture, a desk, a vanity, stools, and earthenware items with only small irregularities or repaired cracks. Majestic stuffed peacocks, a few feathers short of a full panoramic display of colours, graced the entryway.

twelve

London, England, December 1863

Philip Summers was busy discharging his goods from the deck of the Trossachs when a familiar face and voice greeted him.

"Good afternoon there, Philip. How was this last voyage?"

"Afternoon, Mr. Pepper! Glad to see you again. I have your parcels here." Philip pointed to a few bundles at his feet. "Your crate is ready for loading from the dock. Did the company order a cart to haul it to the warehouse?"

"Well, indeed they did, young man, but for safety purposes I am to collect these smaller parcels myself." He frowned at the total size and weight of them, figuring that he would not be able to take them on his own after all. Philip was also sizing up the situation.

"Sir, if you would wait a few minutes while I clear the rest of the merchandise with the office, I can help you carry them to the warehouse."

"Splendid, Philip. Splendid. I shall wait right here beside them until you can join me." And with that Philip headed to the port authority to finish his voyage business and pick up his discharge papers.

Philip was still awed by the large banks and commercial buildings that lined the streets. They were old, he thought, perhaps fifty or one hundred years old or more. None like this would have survived in Jamaica through the seasonal hurricanes and earthquakes, and that was why they didn't build them so grandly there. Repairing and restoring buildings was not a priority, because of a population struggling with poverty. The former slaves had no jobs and were given only small pieces of land if any, and the formerly wealthy plantation owners couldn't afford to pay wages to those who had worked their land for nothing as slaves. The sugarcane markets had also shrunk. Things were different here.

Philip followed the large strides of William Pepper, who forged ahead through crowds without seeming to notice. After arriving at the doors of the warehouse, Philip slowed his breathing and followed William into the office.

"How long are you in London, lad?"

"The Trossachs leaves Dundee, Scotland, on the 11th of January, Mr. Pepper."

"Well, it sounds like you might be in need for a bit of company around the Advent season. How would you like to join my family for a great goose dinner and a bit of celebration afterwards? And it's William, by the way, Philip." William smiled at the gratitude with which Philip accepted, and they made plans for his first visit the following week during tea so that William might introduce Philip to the family.

II

William's oldest daughter, Elizabeth, sat quietly pouring the tea and passing the bread, meat, and relish, only occasionally, glancing up to listen attentively to her father and his guest's conversation about the trading business, oriental textiles, and shipping costs. It was after she retrieved the guest's muffler that William knew Philip Summers would be back before Christmas dinner.

"Thank you for the tea, ma'am. I appreciate the invitation and company." Philip accepted his muffler and wool jacket from Elizabeth and shook William's hand. Elizabeth's sister and mother stood at the kitchen door, smiling their approving goodbyes.

Elizabeth resumed her tailoring of Lady Sarah's extensive wedding trousseau, once or twice pausing to stare thoughtfully into the fire pit of the working parlour's fireplace.

III

By Christmas dinner, the following week, Elizabeth was much more relaxed and responsive to Philip's attention.

"Yes, please write to me while you are at sea. Would you like me to write in return?"

"Please. I can let you know where to send letters. It won't be often, but I would be delighted to receive anything you write." Philip took her hand and brought it to his lips, searching her dark eyes. He could sense her controlled interest, and a joy welled up into his heart to know that his own interest was reciprocated.

thirteen

London, England, 1865

Elizabeth's father granted Philip permission to marry her, and Philip was not willing to wait for his next leave.

"Elizabeth, say yes. Please be agreeable and let us marry soon."

"Oh, Philip. You know I want to marry you, but how can I stand to have you away at sea so long at a time? I'll be so lonely."

"You may have company once you're a mother. I'd like to have many children. I had only one sister, Susanna. The families in Jamaica were much smaller than here in England. You do want children, do you not?"

"Yes, of course." Elizabeth blushed demurely.

"We'll set the date then?"

She nodded her assent, studying his smooth olive-toned skin and his very wavy dark hair: very handsome, very exotic, and very interesting.

II

At their Thomas Street dwelling, Elizabeth's mother and father heartily greeted the newly married couple on their return from the registrar for the district of Mile End, Old Town. Mary had prepared a lovely light tea for the celebration, but the excited young couple hardly touched it. The Pepper family was happy for Philip and Elizabeth and clustered around them, asking questions and making comments.

"It's not too far to Gray Street, Mother. We will visit often."

"Yes, dear. I'm sure you will," answered Mary, as she wiped her nose with the hem of her apron. "Give us a hug, and be off with you."

The cold winds of March 9, 1865, whipped around their ankles, but happy anticipation hurried their walk to Philip's well-kept room. Elizabeth gratefully removed her grey satin-lined bonnet and her cape overcoat before she smoothed her hair in the rippled glass of the tiny mirror.

III

"You have experience, young man?" asked the shipping master, Dunlop.

"Yes, sir," answered Philip. "My father, Captain John Summers, began to apprentice me aboard his ship nearly ten years ago, and I have served as a steward on Caribbean ships for the past five. My last ship was the Blornee from London, and discharge was July 10th of this year. The captain offered no discharge papers at the time because of some interference with the port authorities."

"All right. The Nautitus leaves for St. Kitts at the end of September. As steward, you need to board the 26th. Captain Henry Laws is the master of the ship, and you will report to him on the aft deck by five in the morning." Dunlop shuffled a few papers on his desk to bring the logbook into view.

"Full name?"

"Philipo Clodos Filimingo Summers." Philip stood erect. He had learned from experience that it was more effective to bring out the "Spanish" side of his family, rather than the black African.

Dunlop raised his head, briefly studying the dark, curly-haired man, and wrote "Philip C. Summers."

"Date and place of birth?" he asked.

"1837, Jamaica," Philip answered.

"Good. Report on the 26th, then," and he smiled approvingly at his new recruit.

The Nautilus was felt-sheathed with marine metal, an older barque of 346 tons registered in the Port of London for voyages destined to the West Indies. It was a young crew, but since the mate and two nephews of the captain had already served on the Nautilus, Philip deemed it a desirable ship to join.

The weather being agreeable, the ship's voyage was uneventful, and it returned to the Port of Cowden, Poplar, in London on January 31, 1866. Thomas Williams of Bermuda had been discharged as a cook at St. Kitts, by mutual agreement. His conduct had been good, but his meal-making skills were rated as "middling," leaving something to be desired by the crew. The return to London was uneventful.

Philip decided not to reengage with the Nautilus, as it would be leaving within the week, and he wanted more time with his new bride. He had no trouble signing up a few weeks later on the Trossachs.

fourteen

London, England, 1866

Elizabeth desperately missed her husband while he was away. She worried about storms, pirating buccaneers, and disease. The cholera epidemic in London during the year following her marriage had alarmed her. Hundreds were sick and dying. Her parents and siblings remained healthy; however, the disease had affected her neighbours, and she was almost glad that she had not yet conceived. She continued work as a tailoress, keeping busy with the handwork by candlelight in evenings. She wanted a gas lamp sometime, but there were other things she needed to furnish their simply decorated rooms.

Philip sometimes arrived home from sea sooner than expected, surprising and pleasing her.

"Well, dear wife! How are you, Elizabeth? Any news for me?" asked Philip, as he affectionately wrapped his arms around her waist, drawing her towards him for a long and welcomed display of affection. "I've been worried about the cholera in the city here, but I see you are well and healthy," he said with relief and a smile.

"All are well. Mother, Father, and the boys are fine, but we were worried about Caroline near the new year. Please say you'll have weeks to stay and visit, not just days."

"It seems I must earn a good wage to keep my wife in style," Philip gently joked, but his demeanour remained serious. "The Knighton leaves Leith on June 28th, and it's a yearlong foreign voyage. You shall be all right, my dear?"

"Well, I suppose I shall be perfectly fine, but I miss you on these long journeys."

II

After Philip's return in July of 1867, Elizabeth and Philip had two months of wedded bliss before he was bound for a short term as cook on the Hamburg line. Elizabeth went only as far as the street door to see him off, and her sadness was heavy indeed. No child had been forthcoming as of yet. Although her mother, brothers, and sister were not far away, they were all as busy as she was, trying to earn a daily living. She recalled some of the times her father had returned after travelling, bringing surprise gifts and delightful packages. She looked with fondness at the brilliant stuffed peacocks at the foot of the stairs that led to their present rooms on Devonshire Street. They were a gift from her parents that she held close to her heart.

Within a few weeks, a smile replaced the downturn on the corners of Elizabeth's mouth and grew as her abdomen grew. Philip would be so pleased when he returned.

They named her Sarah Arabella, after Philip's mother and grandmother. Within months of her birth on May 12, 1868, her dark curly hair had grown to frame her delicate face. She had only just met her father, who was again preparing for another voyage.

"I leave for Liverpool to pick up the Miami on the 26th of July," Philip informed Elizabeth. He looked down on his daughter, and his happiness was complete.

"Am I to have her baptized?" Elizabeth asked hopefully.

Philip, who was unsure of infant baptism because of his unconventional Methodist upbringing in Jamaica, shook his head. "No," he sadly replied, "it's too costly, and I say wait for them to attend and grow into the church as they get older. Take them to St. Luke's or St. Peter's, which are both close."

Elizabeth nodded and rocked the baby girl in her arms.

fifteen

London, England, 1870

"Mary Ann Kitchener, our neighbour, was with William when he died. Oh, I wish I could have been with him. I've been trying to make enough in my meagre wages to add to Edward's wage to pay for food and the rent, so I was away getting more laundry from Mrs. Smith. Times are getting so tough, and it won't be easy with your father gone."

"Oh, Mother. Has this been a terrible shock to you? I thought Father seemed more comfortable on Sunday when we last visited. Would you like me to stay with you for a while?"

"It would be a comfort dear, and Caroline would be a help with Sarah and the new baby."

Elizabeth looked at her mother with eyebrows raised. "What new baby? How did you know my special news?" she asked.

Her mother just nodded and replied, "A woman just knows these things," and Elizabeth understood that women with experience such as her mother would recognize her condition almost sooner than she could herself. She released her mother's red, raw hands, which had been chaffed recently by her work doing laundry. She recognized that it would become more difficult in the near future if Edward finished his training and went on to marry. She wasn't sure, but she suspected they might have to do with less than they had been accustomed to.

London, England, 1871

Captain James Hindsen gave orders to leave the Port of London shortly after the tugboats were tied on to the hull of the Olga, January 12, 1871. He was proud to captain this newly built 863-ton iron steamship. At this period in time, four-fifths of oceangoing vessels were still sailing ships. Philip Summers was belowdecks, overseeing the provisions for the crew. Besides a daily issue of lime and lemon juice with sugar, bread, beef, pork, flour, rice, tea, and coffee, the steward issued three quarts of water per day. The cook and helper would do the rations, prepare the meals, and clean up following each meal.

Philip checked the orders for the cargo he would deliver along the route. Ports in the Suez Canal and the India, China, Japanese, and Arabian Seas were on the list, as were the Pacific and Atlantic Oceans, Cape Australia, New Zealand, the western coast of the colonies of the United States of America, the West Indies, the Mediterranean, and ports in the continent of Europe. The termination date was to be the June 26 this same year, although a voyage that had many stops or delays could take as long as two years.

II

"Philipo. Donde esta l'agua?" asked Juan. He was the only one who spoke any Spanish fluently, and Philip made a point to practice with him whenever they came in contact. It kept life while at sea from becoming dreary and reminded him of his home in Jamaica, where some Spanish was still spoken in Old Harbour and Spanish Town.

"Esta aqui, Juan. Quanto quieres?" answered Philip while pulling out a barrel of water. Juan would need to take it to the galley for the noon meal.

Philip enjoyed the planning and organization of his position. Getting goods ready for delivery at the correct port and receiving others for transport was fascinating when it meant stopping in at foreign places around the world.

sixteen

EDWARD MURRAY, JOHN JENKINS, AND DAVID GARDINER CLAMBERED ABOARD the Olga at Port Said, Sunday, May 20. They were laughing loudly, speaking boldly, and shoving each other in the process. They smelled strongly of spirits, and their appearance was dishevelled. The clerk for William Methovitch approached Captain Hudson at 2:00 p.m.

"Sir, one of the watchmen from the ship alongside us came on board for a little water to drink, and three sailors started shoving him about. They've injured his leg."

"I shall come up top immediately. Keep a watch!"

"Ha, there, Cap'n. Did ya see this blighter trying to steal our good water!" shouted Murray.

"Men, stop this behaviour and get below deck. Your wages will be deducted accordingly," replied the captain.

"Ya miserable sod, ya can't take what we earned," retorted Jenkins.

"An' who do ya think ya are, bringin' the cap'n atop?" growled Murray, his face inches from the clerk's face.

"I'm the clerk of William Methovitch," answered the man civilly.

Without warning, Edward Murray struck him a severe blow to the eye, causing it to swell and bleed profusely. The captain separated the two men with great difficulty, almost gagging on the fumes emanating from the intoxicated Murray. At the same time, a man from Methovitch's crew drew a knife.

"I'll stab any of ya that come near me!" he threatened. The crew swelled from the surrounding decks and below, and all was in a huge uproar. The captain shouted to the first mate to remove the intoxicated men with the assistance of four other sailors. They were being incarcerated below deck just as Philip Summers finished working at his desk in the storage room. He stepped out to investigate the ruckus but had to retreat quickly to allow the sailors to wrestle the men into a holding cell.

At four in the afternoon Her Majesty's consul and a file of soldiers boarded the ship.

"Where might these men be?" asked the consul crisply. He had no tolerance for sailors who disobeyed the rules. Quickly the mate led them down to the brig. Edward Murray and John Jenkins marched ashore under guard, where they would be charged and tried.

"Sir, you might take me as well," slurred in a third sailor as he staggered towards the soldiers, obviously in a state of intoxication as well. A fourth had already been picked up on shore by the police, charged for drunken behaviour and being ashore without leave.

The consul charged Edward Murray and John Jenkins with the two pounds sterling penalty, covering a medical certificate, medical treatment for Methovitch's clerk, and police and prison expenses. The court charged James Smith with taking leave without permission. An escort returned the men after the short delay to the Olga, and the ship carried on without further incident to London. The Olga docked expertly on June 26, 1871, and Philip returned home with relief.[4]

(SUBSTITUTE FOR E1, C11, AND CC5)

Dis. 1.

CERTIFICATE OF DISCHARGE

FOR SEAMEN DISCHARGED BEFORE THE SUPERINTENDENT OF A MERCANTILE MARINE OFFICE IN THE UNITED KINGDOM, A BRITISH CONSUL, OR A SHIPPING OFFICER IN BRITISH POSSESSION ABROAD.

SANCTIONED BY THE BOARD OF TRADE JANUARY, 1869.

No 175

Name of Ship	Offic! Number	Port of Registry	Regist! Tonnage
Olga	61222	Hull	863

Horse Power of Engines (if any)	Description of Voyage or Employment
130	Calcutta

Name of Seaman	Age	Place of Birth	No of R.N.R. Commission or Certif.	Capacity. If Mate or Engineer No of Certif. (if any)
P. Summers	30	Jamaica		Steward

Date of Engagement	Place of Engagement	Date of Discharge	Place of Discharge
12 Jany 1871	London	26 June 71	London

I certify that the above particulars are correct, and that the above named Seaman was discharged accordingly; and that the character described on the other side hereof is a true copy of the Report concerning the said Seaman.

Dated this day of June 1871

James Hudson MASTER

AUTHENTICATED BY SIGNATURE OF SUPERT CONSUL, OR SHIPPING OFFICER

Signature of Seaman: P. Summers

Discharge Paper of Philip Summers from the Olga

seventeen

When Philip arrived at 65 Devonshire, he had to ask the neighbour where his wife and children had gone.

"She's gone to her mother's on Thomas Street. I don't think they had the rent, and there was trouble at her mum's."

Foreboding gripped Philip. Was Elizabeth's mother so in need of her daughter and granddaughters after her husband's death? He picked up his gear to haul over to Thomas Street, questions on his mind. The traffic along Mile End Road did not alarm him as it had at one time, but he increased his pace when he turned southeast onto Stepney Green. The shade of the mature growth of trees along the green was refreshing and reminded him just a little of the lush Jamaican vegetation he missed.

A preacher pounded the makeshift podium on the edge of the green. "Parents, you must be aware of what your drinking of spirits will do to your family. Too many are under the control of this evil substance. Children as young as two years of age are left to wander the streets while mothers and fathers are lounging around in mindless stupor. These waifs must fend for themselves, getting to the desperate point of stealing food to relieve the hunger they feel in their stomachs. Never mind the hunger they have in their hearts! Pledge now that you will abstain from taking any intoxicating drinks!" Young and old were gathered around, many of substantial means. These folk, mainly men, were horrified at the apparent immorality within their society.

Down the street, poorly played bugles sounded; shouts and songs, barking dogs, and flag-waving children formed a cacophony of lively activity. Dr. Barnardo's boys were holding a colourful banner in support of Thomas Barnardo and representatives, who had begun evangelizing in Stepney three years ago, taking homeless children to shelters and schools. Then Charring of the brewery family began competitive evangelizing in Mile End Old Town with parades of their own supporters. This caused conflict when the opposing groups collided in the streets.

Philip stepped aside to let the parade pass, still listening to the preacher. He knew only too well what alcohol did to people. In Jamaica, it was rum. Here, it was gin. Youngsters were often seen carrying brown paper bags from the pub—paid by their parents to bring them home.

Philip walked along Ben Jonson Road, past the Commercial Gas Works and its fumes, across the bridge over the Regent's Canal, and along Rhodeswell, which intersected with Thomas Street. At number 6, his young sister-in-law, heading out to purchase a few groceries, met him.

"Oh, Philip! Elizabeth will be so glad to see you!" exclaimed Caroline.

"And how is everyone? Are my girls fine?" Philip asked, but Caroline continued on her way, waving him inside the door. "Hello! Elizabeth! What! What is the matter?" he asked as she hugged him with baby Florence bundled between them.

"Oh, Philip. It's been horrible. First Papa died, and then Sarah. She had meningitis and a high fever for days, and finally her little body couldn't fight it any more. She died in my arms on May 6th." Elizabeth laid her quivering chin on his chest, allowing tears to drop as he held her closer.

"I am so sorry, Elizabeth. Our poor beautiful child…Did you move in with your mother then?"

"No—before then. It was getting difficult to pay the rent and feed the three of us. Mother wanted the company after Father died, so Richard and Edward helped us bring everything here. Now that Richard is married, there's another room, but I think we must move soon again."

Philip was somewhat alarmed that the money he had been sending was not covering their costs. Nor was Elizabeth saving any of it as he had hoped.

Philip signed up with the Alpha for just four-month voyages to the Black Sea and the Mediterranean. It would allow him more frequent visits with Elizabeth, and he hoped it would allow them to get on more solid footing with a little bit of savings.

eighteen

When Philip was due back after his second voyage, he was very late arriving at South Grove, St. Paul's Terrace, a tiny set of two rooms tucked in a bleak courtyard on the third floor. Elizabeth was anxiously waiting, stepping out to the landing that served as laundry and coal bin. She cried when she saw him—back bent and foot dragging. He had been injured!

"Oh Philip!" she greeted him. "What has happened to you?"

He didn't stop to hug her but tried to smile through his pain to greet her while he struggled to the bottom of the steps, where he could at last release his bag and collapse to rest on the stairs.

"My dear, I've had an accident, and it's a poor relic of your husband you have to greet you so badly as this." He grasped her hand and tried to draw Elizabeth toward him; Elizabeth threw her arms around his shoulders and tearfully hugged him as best she could.

"Never mind, my dear. A few weeks rest and I shall be good as new, or so says the ship's surgeon. It was a crate coming down the chute. I had turned to place a large package on the floor of the receiving room aboard the Alpha, and the next crate came quickly and unannounced. It should not have happened. James up on deck didn't ring the bell but just let the thing slide down. Next moment I lay on the floor, face down, with that blasted crate on my back. It took two men to manoeuvre it out of the way. I feared at first I was crippled, as I had no feeling in my legs for hours. I am not usually afraid, my sweet, but this time I was, even as I was praying to the good Lord to send help quickly."

Florence played shy with her father, hiding behind her mother's shoulder, but soon warmed to the dark-haired man on the bed. She became a great relief to him as he lay flat on his back for most of the next month. He would get her to find things he wanted. He read to her, and they played together with a ball of paper tied to a bit of string. However, he felt discouraged that their income was very much reduced now with him unable to work.

II

At the beginning of October, he sent a note to the dock master at Bristol, saying he would be ready to sail with the Alpha on the 13th of the month. It was a smart-looking iron screw steamer built in the 1860s in Glasgow for the Cunard Line's Halifax to West Indies route.

On the return voyage, he had the chance to be around when his next child was to be born. At the end of his leave, Philip asked hopefully, "Any sign yet, Elizabeth?" It was the evening of March 24, and he needed to be in Hull the next day for the Alpha's departure.

"No, Philip. I can't help but think this baby is just waiting until you leave. I would really like to have you here. Ellen will come, so I'll have help, but I miss you so much. It just can't be helped though," and she got up to make the tea. At least Philip had filled the larder with enough food staples for the next few days.

In the early dawn, he tenderly kissed his wife goodbye and left South Grove for Hull.

II

"Oh, Ellen. Am I glad to see you! Can you get the midwife? This baby will arrive soon, and to think that Philip just left!"

Elizabeth continued to pace, placating Florence with a rag doll and a scrap of fabric for bedding. Her pains had seemed to ease off, but she felt cramping in her back. The minutes passed agonizingly slowly.

Ellen finally returned with the midwife, who calmly settled, drinking tea and tonic while waiting. It appeared Elizabeth was ready, but, obviously, the baby was not.

Night hours passed into the early dawn light. Elizabeth's labour pains began in earnest. Her cries frightened young Florence, who clung to Ellen, but she finally fell back to sleep. The bedroom had no door, so there was no privacy. At this point Elizabeth was past caring.

Finally, a baby boy appeared, welcomed by his mother with a weak and tired smile. He murmured a while before nursing but settled quickly, content with his new little world. Ellen brought Florence in to view Philip Juan de Delgloria on the morning of March 26, 1874.

nineteen

London, England, 1875

James Hay, master, signed the Chiswick crew agreement on February 15, 1875. Philip was on board as ship's steward. The return trip was expected to be on July 4; Philip felt that was a good amount of time but not overly lengthy. The iron ship had the same gross tonnage as the Alpha, and along with twenty-five crew, it had been making shorter voyages to the Mediterranean and Black Sea ports. Philip felt his back had healed as well as it was going to, and this longer trip to Rangoon, Burma, would prove him fit or not.

On July 17, the Chiswick left the port at Poplar, London, captained by twenty-five-year-old Newry Baer. They sailed despite being unable to engage a carpenter. The apprentice, John William Calman, deserted in Cardiff early into the voyage. The British consulate at Constantinople, on August 16, 1875, certified that P. Kelly was discharged on the grounds of sickness. Without a carpenter, Calman, or Kelly, they were short-staffed, but the mates and captain filled in to cover the missing crew, and no major calamities occurred.

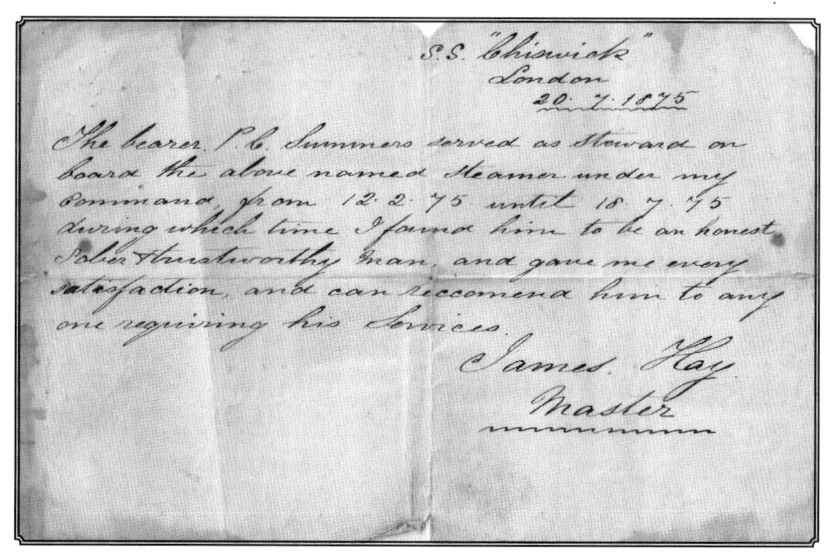

S.S. "Chiswick"
London
20.7.1875

The bearer P.C. Summers served as Steward on board the above named Steamer under my Command, from 12.2.75 until 18.7.75 during which time I found him to be an honest Sober & trustworthy man, and gave me every satisfaction, and can reccomend him to any one requiring his Services.

James Hay
Master

Character Reference of Philip Summers

The agreement with the British consulate at Galatz, signed by the consul, allowed the ship to enter the sea on August 23, stop at various ports of call, and return by September 15, when they continued on their way to England. The days spent at sea were busy, but between many ports Philip found time to write his wife letters of greeting and encouragement. He was still polishing up his Spanish and had been working on some Swedish and German, depending on the origin of the crew. He spent time learning seafaring phrases in other languages so at times he could act as translator among the men, who were mostly able to speak only a few necessary phrases in English.

Philip left the ship on November 4 at the port of London carrying his discharge papers, with his character rating as "Very Good," signed by James Hay, master.

II

Philip anxiously hurried to Bridge Street and had to inquire about where he might find Schrier's Terrace. He wove his way down narrow side streets and through a courtyard, then hurried to the door of number four. There he hesitated, listening to sounds of an infant crying. Had the newest baby arrived already?

"Elizabeth! Are you there?" Philip called upon entering the dismal room, dropping his kit bag. Five-year-old Florence was carrying a pan of water, which was not slopping too much until she saw her father.

"Father!" she declared with glee, and quickly Philip reached for the pan before Florence could spill the rest down her pinafore.

"Well, Florrie, my dear girl," Philip exclaimed as he gathered her in his arms. "Do you have a little brother or sister who is making all this noise?"

"We has a sister, and her name is Clemmie, or something like that," Florence said, by now dragging her father in to see the newcomer. Elizabeth smiled tiredly, putting her arm out to draw Philip close.

"She was just born yesterday, but she's a hungry little pet. Do you like her? She's beautiful, is she not?" asked Elizabeth.

"I see she takes after my grandmother. Her skin has the same tone," Philip said cautiously. Elizabeth knew he was not willing to concede the Negro strain in the family, but of all so far, Charlotte Clementina was the darkest and, to Elizabeth, the prettiest.

III

London, England, February 1878

Florence walked slightly ahead of her father as he accompanied her to register at grammar school. He wanted to be sure that she would be signed up, paid for, and attending before he left on his next voyage.

"Slow down, Florrie! We'll be there in plenty of time to see the headmaster. Do you remember what the name of this road is?"

"Of course, Papa. It's St. Paul's Road, just like the name of the school, St. Paul's Road School. And I know that it's a new school, only five years old, and that it's in the borough of Tower Hamlets. Do we live in Tower Hamlets, Papa?"

"Our house is in Mile End Town, but we are very close to Tower Hamlets. There shouldn't be any difficulty. Florence, I need you to promise to go to school, and even when your mother asks you to stay home, be sure to remind her that I have paid for the term and that you need to attend every day. Education is very important, even to young ladies, who need to know how to read and write properly as well as speak correctly. You will find that education can open many doors for you that would otherwise be shut in your face. And never be anything but proud of your British heritage."

Florence Anne nodded as she took her father's outstretched hand to climb the school entrance steps. She had heard the speech before and would remember it in later years.

IV

Philip signed on as crew for the SS Bengal, then the Bombay, and lastly the Gamma, three iron ships that sailed to India and the Baltic. He was at home, their new residence at #13 Goodliff Street, when his son John Pink Summers was born on April 25, 1879.

Conditions in the London district of Poplar and the west end were not good. There were many of those young ruffians that the good Dr. Barnardo was so concerned about. Now, at least, there were some training schools for them. Philip and others, who could not afford to send their children to school, recognized that free schooling was their only answer. As soon as an opening was available, it was filled, and still there were so many destitute children. Sending them out to play in the streets was just asking for trouble. The authorities knew that children died in the streets, from either starvation or exposure to inclement weather.

Goodliff Street was as close to the newly built West India docks as Philip wanted to be. It made his coming and going easier, but he continued to warn Elizabeth about the evils of gin and drunken sailors and the dangers of young thieves and gangs in the streets. The girls were not exempt from these dangers. He was beginning to suspect that during his long trips away, his wife was using spirits to fill the loneliness. He sent money home regularly, hoping that Elizabeth might be able to put some away, but there were more mouths to feed each time he returned home.

twenty

London, England, 1881

Philip Summers bid the crew of the Georgian a hurried farewell.

"Mind ye, Philip, we leave in the dawn of October the sixth for Antwerp," called the master of the ship, Baines, after handing Philip his certificate of discharge.

"I will be here, never fear." The captain knew Philip's word was good. Despite Philip's daily pain from his back injury while aboard the ship several years earlier, the captain had always found his character and deportment to be very good and indicated such in the records.

Philip hurried through the dockyards towards the nearest tram stop. He was most anxious to meet his new daughter, Barcelonita Catalonita. He and Elizabeth had agreed upon the name, as unusual as it was, because of its supposed Spanish connection, which Philip preferred. Besides, during this trip he had been very close to Barcelona, Catalina, Spain. The baby would be almost four months old already, having been born on January 23.

The walk from the docks to the tram was far enough to force Philip to pause, dropping his heavy sea kit bag on the cobblestone pavement. He took a long rest while studying the dry docks, which had been completed about three years before.

"Long voyage, mate?" called another seaman, whose weaving stagger could not be contributed only to sea legs.

"Nine months, mostly the Mediterranean," answered Philip in a friendly way. There were lots of the navies who couldn't wait to dock at a British port so they could indulge in the intoxicating beverages that were not allowed on board.

He approached the dusty station and had enough change to buy his ticket to Burdett Tramway—a stop within a few short blocks of Edinboro Road in Mile End Old Town. It was a pleasure to ride, but he didn't remember there having been so many people, nor so much noise. There seemed to be vehicles of every description with loud sounds to match. Some people walked slowly with parcels and prams. Some hurried more determinedly, either home from work or on to church services. Some looked vacantly about them as they trudged along in oversized, worn-out clothing with grubby sacks or items wrapped in bedding. Everyone was headed in different directions as Philip stepped off the tram, hauling his bag behind. Never mind. He would soon be home in the arms of his loving wife and children.

Philip passed the tiny door of Edward Griffiths, the nearest fishmonger. He never minded the smell of fresh fish, but the odours that wafted out of this small shop were of day-old seafood, offensive to Philip. At #7 Edinboro Road, Philip rapped on the dusty glass of the green grocer.

"Joseph! How are you?" Philip asked his neighbour as he waved. Joseph Sealey waved back, a surprised look on his face.

"You're back from the sea, then, Philip. You've been missed, yah know. Come in tomorrow and we can settle up your bill. You've got a hungry lot to feed, and I know it may not be the time to say, but that wife of yours don't know much about stretching the pennies."

Philip's shoulders drooped a little further as he nodded farewell and wondered how the money he had sent disappeared so quickly.

II

"My, Florrie! How you have grown. Such a tall young lady." Philip smiled admiringly at his oldest daughter, nearly eleven now, and he put a strong arm around her shoulders. "Is that you, young Philip?" he asked, ruffling the seven-year-old's curly top. "And who's that hiding behind you? Is that my Clemmy? Already five!" He bent over, gasping quietly as the muscles in his back pulled. Clementina gave him a puzzled look and stepped up to him, unafraid.

"Hello, Father. We've been waiting all day for you to arrive."

He smiled and got a much needed hug from his middle daughter. He looked over at John, who, after glancing up briefly to look at the strange man the others called Father, had busied himself with two wooden blocks painted like ships. Philip knew that during his four days' leave his two-year-old son would not get to know him, and he would see little of his wife if he let the children take up all his time. But he loved each one.

"Elizabeth! Are you here?" called Philip into the back room, which served as a kitchen, temporary nursery, and laundry room. Elizabeth had always insisted there be one room that could be furnished decently, where visitors could be met, and where she could keep her hand-tailoring jobs in a basket without the kitchen steam deforming them. Now both living and working quarters were in the same two rooms, and there was no basket of hand-sewing present.

"Oh, Philip, come in, love, and meet your newest daughter," Elizabeth said quietly so as not to disturb the sleeping infant in her arms. She stood up to return Philip's warm and comforting embrace before handing over the four-month-old to him.

"I've called her Katherine. I did register her as Barceloneta Catalonita as we agreed, but I just can't call her by that name. Remind me, what were you thinking at the time?"

Philip gave his wife a long hard-pressing kiss on the lips and smiled. "We will call her Katherine. She looks like a Kathy. You, Mrs. Summers, have delivered a very beautiful baby, and I think she will look just like you. Look at that dark curly hair already!"

Elizabeth would have blushed, had she not been so exhausted. Her consumption of gin might have contributed to that, but with just having had her sixth child and without enough help, she hoped Philip would be home to stay for a while.

"Do you have any news of your family, dear?"

"Yes. Mother surprised us and moved in with my brother Edward and his wife, Maud. I didn't think Mother liked Maud too much, but apparently they are making it do for now. Edward is working as a labourer as he no longer wants to be a plasterer. He's working small jobs until he's trained for steam fitting."

"Well, that sounds like a good plan. Any sign of children yet?"

"No. It seems as though God has ordained them to remain childless, and here we have six and hardly the means to feed them."

Philip was saddened by his wife's talk but thought that he might encourage her to take the children to church and Sunday school more regularly. It was the right way to start the younger ones with a good, solid moral foundation. As well, he could always hope that Elizabeth's consumption of alcoholic spirits might be tamed by the temperance of other churchgoers.

A few new charity schools were being opened for the children of those without means to send them to paying schools, and they were fed a little just to keep them alert. Perhaps some of his children could attend one of these.

twenty-one

London, England, 1883

Philip continued as a steward on the Georgian while they completed shorter voyages of three and four months to Europe and the Mediterranean ports. Then, after a week's leave in November of 1882, Philip had an eleven-month voyage.

Upon his return home for a few days leave, this time at 57 Carr Street, he was surprised to meet his new two-month-old son.

"This is Jose Modesto. Meet your father," introduced Elizabeth. Philip was concerned about his coughing and his tiny size, but he was pleased that Elizabeth appeared well after this seventh birth.

Philip felt refreshed enough after a light tea to plan taking the older children out for a walk. They all began chattering at once, as this was an unusual event.

"Well, get your jackets and we'll be off to the park. I believe we might find a surprise there to entertain you." He felt in his pockets for a few loose coins and smiled as Florence, Clemmie, Philip, and John scurried around and out the door to the street. As they approached the park, young Philip began hopping about, pointing and hollering. "Punch and Judy! A Punch and Judy show!"

Philip Senior delighted in their smiles and excitement as they joined the group of other youngsters. They all stood transfixed in front of the brightly painted orange and red theatre where Punch clumsily dropped the baby and Judy began pounding and smacking him. They gave their pennies to the collection lad as they first arrived, settling into positions within two yards of the stage. The lower half of the theatre hid the performer behind curtains. The narrow stage was bordered by brightly painted wooden sides and an ornate curved top. By craning their necks upwards, onlookers could watch the colourfully dressed large-nosed puppets travel to the beach.

The small crowd of children laughed at the antics. They were completely immersed in the performance, an exciting, bright spot in their lives. Philip stood a distance away, still able to hear what the puppeteers were saying. He waited for the political and social comments on the times, as the policeman, the dog, the hangman, and the crocodile characters made their appearances. The situation of the underdog being bullied by the law and a wife and his own ineptitude was delivered in such a way that all ages were amused. Only when the puppets made their last bow and the curtain flap was pulled up, signalling the end of the performance, did the children reluctantly leave.

II

Philip also took the opportunity during this shore leave to register John Pink at the Halley Street School in the infants' class. He was only three years and nine months, but Philip wanted him to begin as soon as possible. Philip Juan had refused to regularly attend any school, having run about the streets at an early age, and it had spoiled him for sitting on hard benches in a classroom for very long.

III

A subdued group of five children met Philip at the door on the 29th of December 29 in 1883. There had been little celebration at Christmas this year: no father at home, no surprise gifts, and no sweets from Grandmother Pepper. There were only recent raw memories of a baby brother coughing and gasping for air and a doctor's visit too late to help the little fellow. On December 12, Jose Modesto had died of bronchitis. Philip collapsed on the nearest chair, forcing himself to greet his children affectionately, despite his aching back. The loss of yet another child left him heavyhearted.

"Elizabeth, my dear, I'm so sorry you had to bear this alone. I believe the innocent young lad will be with his heavenly Father until we join him and his sister." He drew her close as she silently shed tears, mopping them with his topcoat. The relief of arriving home dissipated in the sorrow and the chill. "Do you have an extra comforter close by?"

"Your back is troubling you, is it not, Philip? Oh, what are we to do? There is nothing left of your last wages, and the tailoring business has been slow. I cannot work with six children around as I could when there were none. Mother is living with Edward and his wife, Caroline is newly married, and Richard has no room." Elizabeth could no longer count on help from her family members, and Philip's were either dead or living in Jamaica, where Elizabeth was sure their poverty was equally distressing.

Philip knew there would be hard times if he was unable to work at all. "You must not fret, Elizabeth. The good Lord will provide. I shall see about working as a custodian for the terraces nearby or ask for the superintendent's position in this building. I know how to fix many things, and it will provide a little wage and give us a place to live."

Elizabeth was glad to have Philip on shore for now. The children needed attention, and when he was feeling able, he liked to entertain them as well as teach and discipline like a schoolmaster.

twenty-two

London, England, 1884

Philip registered Charlotte at the Dalglish Street School in Tower Hamlets. She was pleased to be admitted to a new school, and like Florence in her first experience, she was seven years old and was most anxious to be in school. She was a very enthusiastic pupil and kept up home studies at 94 Maroon Street, where she taught John and Kathy what she had learned that day. Charlotte wished her mother had more enthusiasm for looking after them, but she seemed very tired these days.

About this time, young Philip began to stay out later at night, and his father was troubled by his behaviour. It hurt him to have the young lad arrive home with a brown paper bag from the local public house.

"What is this, Philip? Where did you get the money?"

Young Philip didn't like to tattle on his own mother, but it would save a stropping. "Mother. Mother gave me money and asked me to get it."

Philip Senior was angry because this was unlikely the first time, but he hoped with his plan, it would be the last. He examined the top, and it had been tampered with.

"She never asked you to test it!" exclaimed Philip in exasperation. "Philip, I have made enquiries, and you will have the opportunity to go to school and work in a workshop for two years. I have been greatly concerned about your activities, the dangers on the streets, and your lack of training. I cannot take you along as an apprentice because of my injuries, so tomorrow we will go down to the office of Dr. Barnardo's training home for boys."

Young Philip threw his father a look of defiance and was beginning to protest when Philip Senior commanded him, "Philip, there can be no argument. You will be trained, and then you can find good work. If you do well, they may send you to Canada, and that is a land where, I hear, you can work your way to a much better life than you would have here roaming the streets."

The next morning, after an exhausting trip, they arrived together at Barnardo's office. It looked somewhat dull and intimidating, but Philip was determined that there was no better solution for his son. Not yet twelve years old, he had been close to getting into trouble with the law, and Barnardo's workshop offered training, discipline, and structure. Philip made it clear that the family was destitute, but should their position improve, young Philip would be welcomed home. Philip Senior filled in numerous papers but left before they had finished photographing Philip Juan de Delgloria Summers. He felt sick at heart, but back pain reminded him there was no other solution.

"Papa, where is Philip?" asked young John as his father walked in the door at home.

"He's going to a training workshop where he will learn things like carpentry and tin work," answered Philip.

"Is he coming home? Is it like school? Philip doesn't like school," John continued.

"Well, when he has learned a few skills, he will be…he might not be coming home for quite some time, John." Philip decided not to add any further details that might upset the children.

Within a short time, Florence was talking about getting training as a domestic. She had no desire to be trained in tailoring and really not much talent for holding a needle, despite repeated demonstrations by her mother.

"Mother, can't I go and see if there is an opening at the Sturge House for Girls? It's only up on Bow Road. I could be a day student."

"I need you here, Florence. We can talk about it in a few months."

twenty-three

London, England, 1885

Philip and Elizabeth waited until they thought the children were asleep. For a year, Elizabeth had resisted sending any of the other children to training centres, but now...she was in the family way again. There was often only stale bread and thin broth for a meal and porridge for breakfast if they were lucky. She wanted to hold their family together, and she felt she needed the older ones to help, but the one room to share for sleeping, eating, and living was too crowded and unhealthy. Her secret consumption of gin was an expensive burden, but Elizabeth couldn't seem to change her ways. She knew of no other comfort for the long, lonely nights while Philip was at sea. Some women might take another to bed, but she wanted none of that. Elizabeth loved Philip and knew that his work required many absences, though fewer since his injury.

Florence was a great help, but with a few months of training she could be working as a domestic in a good situation and perhaps send along a little money to them. The others might have to follow suit if there was not enough to feed them all. Now the discussion was about who and when, not if, they would go into care. Philip had signed up for a trip to Hong Kong on the Odessa. They only had until March 6 to make arrangements. These were desperate times.

In the morning Florence was dressed in her only "good" dress. It was a dark green plaid with a small velvet collar that Elizabeth had taken off an old dress of a kindly client. She had stitched a row of pearl buttons down the front and added crisp white cuffs. Florence was of short stature and had a gaunt slimness to her. With her black straw hat and bow she still appeared much younger than her fifteen years. She herself was ready to start on this new adventure but gave a concerned last look at her mother as she and her father headed out to Sturge House. At least she might get enough to eat there.

"You can't go, Florrie," and John, and Katie grabbed her tightly about the waist, pulling her away from the door.

Florence looked down on them kindly, eyes teary. "I must go, and then you can have my share to eat."

Elizabeth started to sniffle. "Ah, my dear girl. I'm sorry you have to make this sacrifice, but your training will be over before we know it, and you can go into service somewhere and make a good living for yourself. You might even find you have a little left to help with these young ones." Six-month-old William began to howl, both from hunger and neglect. He didn't understand why all his family was paying attention to this leaving and not him.

"Kate and John, leave Florrie to go. She will be back. Clemmi, here. You hold William while I give Florrie a hug. Godspeed, my girl," and Elizabeth turned in a hurry, taking up William in her arms again so that she might not burst into tears.

"Write to us, Florrie," begged Clemmi. "Tell us where you are so we can visit you," she said, wishing it might be true.

Hong Kong, October 1886

My Darling Elizabeth,
It pains to have to send so little this voyage. I must keep enough for a month of recuperation here in Hong Kong while waiting for the Chollerton next month. That will seem like a short voyage, but it has been too long since I felt your arms around me and heard the sound of our children playing and laughing. Though I struggle each and every day, I am sure it is not the struggle that you endure with our young brood, trying to feed them and watch their behaviour. I had hoped to be a better provider, but since the accident, work has been challenging and painful. Be sure to keep extra care with letting the young ones play outside with neighbourhood children. I believe there is a great deal of danger on the streets these days, despite all the evangelizing. The city has reduced the number of gin palaces with their fancy writing on the big plate glass windows, but the drinking of spirits is a terrible temptation, as you might know, and segregating the public houses has done little to reduce serving malts and hops to all who find the money for it. I pray that none of ours will fall under such influence. I hope that Florrie and Philip will be grateful for their chance to get some training. Give a special hug to our son William, who will already be a year old now. If you are not well enough yourself to take the children to church or Sunday school, perhaps Clemmie and John would do so. I think

of you every day and pray for strength to deal with life as He would have us bear it.

Your loving husband,

Philip

twenty-four

London, England, 1887

Philip had returned at the end of the year in 1886, unable to straighten or lift any weight. He had greeted the children from a chair and even pulled his wife down towards him to hug her with a desperate grip. After a few days of rest on his back and gentle play with Kathy and William, he was determined to go to Sturge House and find out how his daughter and son were doing.

"Philip, you must rest. Don't think about going just now." Elizabeth looked at him sadly.

"I must see what the school is like, and if they are unhappy, perhaps they can return home and find some work that will help us support the family."

"I'm sure that you won't get Florence back home. She'd like to migrate to Canada if possible. I've never even heard from Philip." Elizabeth finished up her next pair of trousers, ready for return to the shop.

Philip found his way to Sturge House, an impressive four-storey building with gateposts and a five-foot iron fence surrounding the yard. He saw numbers of girls dressed in black uniforms with white starched caps and aprons as they went about their daily chores. Younger girls in plain dress carried mops, dusters, and dirty bedding. The smell of starches, lye, and soap from the laundry permeated the premises. They certainly were clean. He remembered the Jamaican maids of his childhood who had looked after all the domestic duties in the wealthy homes of his birthland. Their whites had been spotless and almost shining compared to whites hung in the coal-dusty air of London.

The matron showed him into the office. "Well, Mr. Pepper. Your daughter Florence has progressed very well. She is clean, well-groomed, and standing with some pride in her accomplishments. Florence has also expressed an interest in going to North America, and I feel her independent nature would be most suitable to a situation in Canada.

"You have asked about your son, Philip Juan de Delgloria. I see by my copy of the records that he was migrated on March 24, 1886, aboard the SS Parisian, arriving in Halifax on April 4, 1886. He was sent to Halton, Trafalgar, Ontario, where he is satisfactorily working for a farmer, Mr. Mitchel."

Philip simply nodded, realizing that he had seen his son for the very last time two years ago.

"May I see Florence Anne for a moment?"

"That is not usually encouraged; however, in this situation, I feel that a few minutes with your daughter will not go amiss. Please wait here while I see if she can be found." The matron did not say what she really meant to do, and that was to see if indeed Florence even wanted to see her father.

Florence gave Philip a wary hug, unnecessarily concerned that he might ask her to come home. Her concern was short-lived. Philip was happier knowing that his daughter was healthy and appeared happy with her situation.

By September 1, 1887, Florence was aboard the SS Sardinian, and she arriving in Quebec only ten days later. She was taken with a group of young ladies to Montreal to be placed in domestic service positions with mainly English-speaking families. Florence caught the eye of a red-haired Irish woman pushing a perambulator toward her. Unaware that she should be following the woman escorting them, Florence smiled and agreed to engage as a domestic for this woman's family on University Street.

II

Charlotte, to her delight, was readmitted to school at age twelve on December 19, 1887. The same day, John Pink was admitted to Doctor Barnardo's school on Copperfield Road, where he remained until "being migrated" to Canada.

Just after Christmas in 1887 Walter De Compo was born at 13 Maroon Street. This meant there were Clemmie, Katherine, William, and baby Walter, only four of the nine siblings, at home. Both Philip and Elizabeth liked this street because at the west end were a public garden, St. Dunstan's Church, and its rectory, all in one large common green. They were directly north of the Regent's Canal Dock, the London and Blackwell Railway, Ratcliffe, and St. Anne Limehouse. They were south of Mile End Town, which placed them in the Stepney Division, Tower Hamlet. Green grocers were not far away, and Katherine could help her father bring food home every other day or so. There was no good in buying very much as it would spoil quickly in the tiny flat.

twenty-five

London, England, 1888

Katherine was now Kathleen or Kathy. At age six, she was still fascinated by the young babies. She ran to them when they cried, held them as soon as they were big enough, and helped her mother wash their nappies and bedding. She had not been very old when Jose died, but for days after his burial she had wandered over to the dresser drawer where he had been placed and had pulled at the corner of the bedding.

"Where Jose? Where Jose go, Mama?" Kathy would ask, causing Elizabeth to pull her onto her lap and give her a big hug.

"Let's have a cup of hot drink, shall we?" And Kathy would smile, easily distracted.

When three-year-old William took sick and died in November of 1888, Kathy was devastated by his passing. She looked at the wooden ship and blocks they had all played with and turned away, unable to express her sadness. She was genuinely concerned for her mother, who spent more time in a chair, rocking back and forth. Kathy spent much of that winter entertaining and caring for baby Walter, but when spring came, she dearly loved to get out and play with the neighbourhood children.

Clemmie was at school some of the time and withdrawn when the school fees could not be found. Her mother coughed a great deal and was bringing in less and less tailoring work. Philip and Elizabeth discussed the dangers of the street when the children were asleep. Rumours of a serial killer they were beginning to call Jack the Ripper had been active in White Chapel, very near their home, and though he didn't disclose any details, Philip tried to protect the children.

"Now you children know," and their father would face them with a severe look, "that there is a nefarious murderer out in the streets. We hear he has been committing evil deeds in Whitechapel, but he could come to our district, which is right next!" He was always careful to know with whom his children played and what they were doing. They knew this, but Kathy loved the idea of playing school so much she was easily swayed to disobey her father's warning. Just let Annie Blundle call up the stairs, "We are going to play school, Kath..." and Kathy could not think up an excuse quickly enough to get to her house. Her father, who had been an invalid for years by now, always wanted to know where they were. There were only a few neighbours whose homes they were allowed to visit, and they were not allowed to play on the streets.

Annie having called up the stairs, Kathy, knowing the rules, decided to make her excuse by telling her mother that Mrs. Bird would like her to go to the store. Elizabeth answered at once, "Yes."

She went, but not to Mrs. Bird's rooms. As fast as her legs would carry her, she went straight to Annie Blundle's, where school was in progress. Once there, everything else was forgotten, including the thought that her father would soon be home from his walk.

A little girl who had seen Kathleen knew where she had been heading. She asked Philip, "Are you looking for Kath?"

"Where is she? Have you seen her?"

"Yes. Kathy went to Annie Blundle's."

Going upstairs Philip asked his wife, who, not knowing the real excuse, said, "Kathy has gone to shop for Mrs. Bird." Philip frowned, dissatisfied with the two different statements, and went to Mrs. Bird's house.

"No, Mr. Summers. I have not seen her."

Seeing the girl again, he asked her to go to Annie's house and tell Kathy he wanted her.

Father was waiting for Kathleen at the door, razor strap in hand. What a strapping she received, the memory of which remained in her, making it hard for her to ever tell a lie or listen to one.

Mrs. Bird, knowing Philip strapped his daughter, said to Kathleen later, "You should have come to me first. I would have sent you to shop."

Kathleen's father never had to worry much about her afterwards because it was mostly adults in whose company she could be found. A man putting in a pane of glass, another laying bricks or mixing cement, someone attaching pipes: young Kathleen would do her best to be on hand to observe. Unfortunately, she was born in the days when children were to be seen and not heard.

One day looking out of the window, she saw a dreadful accident. When the police came on the scene, they at once glanced up at the window and saw faces. It was not long before the Pepper family heard a knock at the door.

"Did any of you see the accident?"

"No," said Philip. Kathy turned at once, but not quickly enough. "Kathleen," was all her father said, and her mouth was closed. The "be seen and not heard" stage was a great detriment to her. She never got to explain to anyone what she had seen during the accident.

twenty-six

LONDON, ENGLAND, 1890

ELIZABETH CLOSED THE DOOR ON THE MAIN FLOOR. HER SISTER, CAROLINE, HAD just paid a visit. She turned to go up the stairs at 113 Maroon Street, eyes glancing at the empty corner where the stuffed peacocks had stood. They had been sold to put a few meals on the table for the family. No pictures hung in the hallway, which was not their hallway any longer. As she came into the room the family shared, the lines between her eyes furrowed deeply.

"Philip, Caroline has told me that mother has remarried my father's cousin John Pepper, and they are living on Beaufoy Road in Plainstow."

"Well, Elizabeth, the woman is fortunate indeed if she has a future with some happiness. I would wish that you do so well when I pass out of this world," and he gave her a somewhat playful hug around the waist before she broke into a coughing fit.

"Did you hear that the new electrically operated underground system has opened between King William Street to Stockwell?" Philip asked, trying to change the subject.

"What good is there in knowing that? We'll never use it, although I doubt that I would have the nerves to try it anyway," Elizabeth responded edgily. She trudged back downstairs to where the washtubs concealed her tonic.

II

"Oh, Father, please do not let them send John away. I'll miss him so much."

"Kathleen, please! You know the circumstances cannot be avoided. I do not want to send him away, but he will have a brother and sister in Canada. You still have Clemmi and Walter, who adores you. We cannot have everything we wish for in this world; we must learn to deal with the circumstances God has given us in the best way we know how."

Kathleen had heard the same concept many times at Sunday school and church, but she would miss her brother John terribly.

After a few weeks, John was prepared for a second photo—the "after" shot. The bandana tied around his neck was gone. New pants, white shirt, clean fitted collared waistcoat, and renewed topcoat allowed John to stand with a sense of pride and confidence that stood him in good stead. His previously roughly hacked hair was neatly cut much shorter but still wound itself into tight curls.

Dr. Barnardo's dream of having individual cottages with house mothers, clean cots with the specially made white and blue woven covers, a children's church with rows of child-size pews, gardens, dining areas, and classrooms had been fulfilled by wealthy patrons who could name the cottage for which they paid. The semicircles of buildings with treed greens, a fountain, and walkways became wonderful reality.

Young children sometimes accompanied their wealthy mothers, who used a variety of tin boxes to collect funds for orphans. The women's groups enthusiastically recruited anyone willing to help this good cause in hopes of clearing the streets of wandering, starving, and destitute children, who cluttered the crowded warren of alleys, terraces, and narrow lanes.

Dr. Barnardo's efforts appeared to have come to fruition, but soon crowding increased the numbers going overseas, and all the philanthropic institutions were overflowing. The English orphanages and training schools were filling to overcapacity because the movement to clear up the streets was in full force.

John Pink Summers was soon migrated on the Norwegian, and he arrived in Boston with a large group of boys. They were transported to a new Barnardo Home on Farley Avenue, Toronto, Ontario.

Early in 1892 Charlotte Clemintina entered Sturge House for an accelerated course in domestic services. Cleaning, mending, and limited kitchen classes gave her the basics to be migrated on October 13 aboard the SS Sardinian, which arrived in Quebec City, Canada. She attempted to make contact with Florence when passing through Montreal but did not have the means.

Charlotte was placed in Toronto to work, and she was sorely disappointed when she noticed the difference with which she was treated. Charlotte had more features and colouring of her mulatto grandmother than anyone else in the family, except perhaps Walter. There was a mix of nationalities in Toronto—a variety of cultures, clothing, languages and stores—but the wealthy still treated people of colour with some disdain. She felt relatively comfortable in the large, busy city. Despite the muddy streets, Toronto felt more open; it was cleaner and fresher than the tenements of Mile End. She sent a letter of inquiry to Barnardo's and found out that Philip was working for a Mr. Mitchell, in Halton County, Ontario. He finally responded to her letter months later, and she was thankful that he seemed happy enough to be working with a large crew of hands on a farm. She received notice from her parents that John Pink had been migrated and was also in Toronto. She had no time to look him up before he was placed in a home.

On February 6, young Walter was admitted to Halley Street School. His father, at home now since 1886, made sure of his attendance. Financially it was a struggle. Food was scarce in the home but was served on lovely china, which Elizabeth refused to give up. Philip Sr. was able to secure the rent of their room by doing the cleaning and management of the building. He often lay on his back, eyes closed, praying for God's help in managing his pain, in improving Elizabeth's health, and in the protection of his children.

twenty-seven

London, England, 1894

Kathleen's schooling was very intermittent, owing to what was known as nephritis or kidney trouble. It was a sore trial for her and caused many bitter tears. When allowed to attend, she joyfully smiled after putting on her clean pinafore, and she would trot off to school with Walter. This time Elizabeth slowed her down. "Here, Kathy, put on this scarf. You can put it over your head if you're cold. Walter, don't let go of Kathy's hand."

The two headed out the door, Kathy so happy she nearly dragged Walter along, faster than his short legs could take him.

"Kathy, slow down. I ain't excited like you 'bout getten there."

"Walter, it's 'I'm not.' We don't want to be late."

"We'll be too early, we's going so fast."

Because it was November, the children were dismissed at 3:00 p.m. The fog was so thick Kathy felt she could slice it with a knife. She went to the infants' door, where she hoped Walter would be waiting. Sometimes he was impatient and went on ahead of her.

"Walter. There you are! I'm glad you didn't go on ahead."

"I couldn't now, could I? You got the 'night lights,' and it's getting dark already." Kathy handed Walter a light. They had made these at home by rolling up pieces of newspaper that were three by eight inches and dipping them in boiling wax. Walter was shivering in the dampness.

"Hold still, Walter, while I light this," said Kathy, expertly striking a match. There was no sense wasting matches. There was little enough to spare for what was really needed without squandering things.

"Do you think there will be anything to eat at home?" asked Walter as he patted his growling tummy.

"I don't know, but maybe we can put some sugar in some boiling water and have something to drink to get us warm." She was more worried about getting home in time to use the privy out back.

II

At Kathleen's school, girls were chosen each month according to conduct and academic standing to wait on the governess and the teacher. These girls' duties included buying lunches and carrying messages to and from classrooms. The boys' and girls' buildings were separated by a brick wall that divided the two stairways. In the wall was a door used only by the head master and the governess should they wish to confer with each other.

In the classroom, the teacher's monitor would be sent down each aisle and would ask, "Are you co-operating? Sit erect," and so on.

One day the monitor approached Kathleen and said, "Teacher wishes to speak to you."

Kathleen rose in surprise and went to the teacher's desk.

"You are wanted in the governess's room."

Kathleen went, with fear and trembling, to find the door ajar and her mother saying, "I need Kathleen home."

Then she heard the governess's voice. "It grieves me to let her go as she is getting on so well. Could you possibly do without her?"

Knocking on the door, Kathleen walked into the room.

"Come in," said the governess. "Kathleen, your mother wishes to take you home."

Kathleen's heart was heavy, and tears filled her eyes. Instead of remaining in her office, the governess followed Kathleen and her mother to the stairs, still trying to convince Elizabeth that Kathleen should be left in school. Elizabeth carried on resolutely, as though she did not hear the pleas of the governess.

The school, which stood in a residential district, was surrounded by a brick wall and iron gates. Hansom cabs were not allowed to wait in residential districts, so Elizabeth had been forced to let go the one she had taken. This meant they had to walk a block or more to a cab stand.

They had not gone half a block when Elizabeth stammered, "Kathy, I must sit down—"

Opening the gate leading to a large house, Kathleen sat her mother on the steps. She ran up to the door for help, but just as Kathleen was about to knock, the door opened and a gentleman asked, "Little girl, is your mother ill?"

Before she could give him an answer, he took her by the hand, sat her on the hall seat, and disappeared. From the time she sat on that seat, she did not remember a thing until waking up to see her father sitting at her mother's casket. What happened between the time her mother sat on the step and the three days until her death was a complete blank in Kathy's life. Shock had set in. She later realized that the red cheeks of her mother were not those of health but of a heart condition.

III

At that time in London, relatives and friends who attended a funeral did not remain long. It meant that Kathleen would have the dishes to wash, which was something she knew little about. Should she wash pots and pans first or cut-glass tumblers? So busy crying and wondering was she that she didn't hear a step until feeling a hand on her shoulder. She turned to see her Sunday school teacher.

"Kathleen, please don't cry. Is there anything I can do?"

"Miss Aulstin, I don't know how to wash these dishes."

"Would you like to know the right way?"

"Yes, I would."

"Well, do the best you can now, and I will come back this evening." That afternoon Miss Aulstin went to the schoolteacher's house and told her of Kathleen's problem. Bringing Kathleen's day schoolteacher, Miss Muggerton, with her, Miss Aulstin said, "I will take you to see my sister, who's in charge of a domestic science school, and perhaps we can make some arrangements to have Kathleen take part of the course."

Arrangements were made for Kathleen to take nine months of training at Sturge House. During that time, every opportunity would be given to her to learn all the practical work and as much theory as possible.

The two returned to the Summers' residence in the evening, and they told Kathleen what they had done. She sat listening to them with a straight face while her heart was pounding with joy at such an opportunity. The two teachers would even pay the fees.

"Well, Kathleen? What do you think about it?"

Kathleen replied, "I don't know how to thank you. There's only one thing I would like, which is that I pay you back with the first money I earn." She later did this, saving all her salary, with the exception of a few shillings for pocket money.

twenty-eight

London, England, School, 1894

Kathleen wrote to her father,

> *Dearest Father:*
> *I have been putting every ounce of mental and physical energy into my work. At the end of nine months I should have absorbed a great deal of knowledge. The course covers everything from scrubbing floors to receiving nobility! We have sewing, knitting, darning, mending, opening and closing doors, walking, waiting on table, playing with children, and learning to conduct games correctly.*
>
> *When my turn to study cooking came, Miss Scott did everything in her power to have me make good French pastry, but I could not reach her requirements. Miss Scott said, however, having high marks in all other cooking, I would probably pass my exams. I shall return to you very soon when I have finished my nine months of training. Then I will have received my certificate, with, I hope, some praise, which will make me contented and happy. Soon the question will be: What would I like to work at? I have been thinking about it for some time and have decided I want to be a babies' nurse. Goodbye for now, Father. I will see you soon, and hope you are pleased with my efforts.*
> *Your loving daughter,*
> *Kate B. Summers*

Although she still retained the hope that someday she would become a qualified nurse, Kate completed her nine months of the domestic science course. She bubbled upon greeting her father. Kate threw her arms around her father's shoulders. After releasing him she drew a hankie-wrapped article out of her pocket.

"What's this, then? Have you been given a prize?"

"All the students received them, Father. See, here. It has my name on it, 'Kate Summers' and 'For Good Conduct and Length of Service.'"

"Come in now, dear girl, and tell me all about your school. I just saw you a week past, and yet you are so happy to see me! I thought you liked going to school?" responded Philip as he led the way to the kitchen, where he would make them a cup of tea.

"Oh, Father, you know I do. Ever since I was young my chief aim in life has been to learn and find out how things are made, done, and studied. You remember, the only children's game in which I was interested was playing at school."

"Oh, yes! The infamous Annie Blundle's 'school,'" recalled Philip, smiling at his daughter, who at fourteen had developed into such a strong and honest young lady and as loving a daughter as a man could want. "Now, tell me about your school." He quickly pushed aside thoughts of having had to deliver his children to the orphanages and training schools, where they were sent so far away to Canada.

"Well," began Kathie, "the school was a beautiful house, more like a mansion. Our dormitory for intermediate girls is a large room with a ceiling ten feet high and three large windows reaching from the ceiling to within five inches of the floor, and about four feet in width. Our wash basins were stationary, built along the centre of the room. There were eight of these, with pipes extending up from the floor, all very compact. There were eight single beds. The rising bell always rings at seven, breakfast at eight, prayers at nine sharp. It was at prayers that I first saw a blind lady read Braille. She conducted all the Bible studies, lectures, and morning and evening worship, and it was wonderful."

Kathleen placed her elbows on her knees, forgetting for a moment her usual good posture. She sat reminiscing. For quite some time afterwards, she could envision the massive stairway. The banisters were about eight inches wide and were a great temptation to slide down. This was strictly forbidden, as a student, some years previous to Kathleen being there, had fallen through, struck her head on the hall floor, and died.

The girls' dayroom, like every other room in the former mansion, was very large and beautiful. It contained two long tables in the centre, with all kinds of cupboards along the sides. In this room they did their lessons and learned to sew, darn, and do all kinds of fancy work. When mending table linen—and it was real linen in those days—they had to draw threads from old table linen and fit them into the pattern. All indoor games were played in this room.

Kathleen's teacher secured a position for her in a lovely home, where she remained four years, spending all of her spare time studying elocution, vocal, and dramatic art, and so her life of independence began. It took about eleven months to pay the money back after she had completed her schooling, and she was free to accept another position in London, much to her father's relief. With her meagre wages, she might be able to help keep him out of the poorhouse in his later years.

twenty-nine

London, England, 1895, Work

In the neighbourhood there was a private nursing home. The matron had a little girl with whom Kathleen spent some very pleasant afternoons.

One day her mother asked Kathleen, "Would you like to work in my nursing home?" This was just the opportunity she had been waiting for. She was what would now be called a nurse's aide. Her duties were posting letters, changing flowers, shaking up pillows, in fact anything that would make the patients more comfortable. She knew now that nursing must be her life's work.

"Madam, I have been offered a position in a private nursing home," stated Kathleen to her employer.

"I quite understand. I know your heart is in nursing," responded the woman.

"I hope you won't think less of me, because I have enjoyed staying in your home and helping with the children. I will miss them." Kathleen hurried off to the matron to accept the new position.

There were three patients, all of whom were financially well off. One patient in particular was a Mr. Jacobs, over eighty years of age. This gentleman took a great interest in Kathleen, so much so that each time he sent her to the store he would give her a sovereign, telling her to bring back the change in a half crown and two shilling pieces. These were silver coins equal to fifty or sixty cents in Canada. The first day as she was counting out the change to him, he told her that she had taken great pains with his flowers and keeping his bed comfortable. He knew she didn't get very much money, while he had quite a good amount and knew he would never live to spend it, so he was going to give her some. Every day from then on when Kathleen went to the store, he would give her two shillings or a half crown.

This went on for a long time until one day the matron came in just as he was giving her the money. Calling Kathleen into the hall she asked, "What did Mr. Jacobs give you?"

"Half a crown," Kathleen said.

"Well, you're not to take money from any of the patients," and she nodded in the direction of Mr. Jacobs' bed.

Kathleen went over to Mr. Jacobs' bed, telling him he must not give her any more money.

"Very well," he complained, "this pillow is not straight." Kate was obliged to lean over him to pull the pillow loose.

While doing so, he slipped a half crown into the pocket of her apron, and then he said, "I'm not giving you any money."

This went on for some time until he decided to leave Kathleen something in his will. He gave her a letter, telling her not to let any person see it, and she ran at once to the post box and mailed it.

In a few days a tall gentleman came to see him. Noticing the gentleman looking at her when leaving, Kathleen wondered who he could be.

"Now, little girl," said Mr. Jacobs, "you will be well looked after." He had, however, not reckoned on his niece and nephew, who, when they heard from the lawyer what he had added to his will, immediately took steps to have things changed. Coming to see him the next day, they told him it was too late for his will to be changed.

Calling Kathleen into the hall, they told her what they had done. Not being satisfied with this, they asked the matron to let her go, which of course she did. She was getting a good fee and was obliged to cater to them.

Kathleen had only been gone two weeks when the matron came to see her, telling her Mr. Jacobs had died. "Would you come back? Mr. Jacobs continually asked for you."

As young as Kathleen was, she told her just what she thought of her, adding that she would not go back with her any more. "I will not return. Mr. Jacobs wanted to provide me with something, and his niece and nephew, who never came to visit, were greedy to begin with, and mean. They knew how much Mr. Jacob's enjoyed my care, and they wouldn't allow it. It was very disheartening for me to know that you agreed with them."

thirty

One of the great ladies whom Kate knew was Miss Burke, another of her Sunday school teachers. She lived in a large, beautiful home and had once been dressmaker to Queen Victoria.

The first time Kate met her was one Sunday afternoon after she had accepted a new position as nurse to a new baby. Having moved to a new neighbourhood with her father and Walter, Kate had to find a new Sunday school, so putting her Bible under her arm, away she went to the Anglican church at the corner, asking a passerby which door led to the Sunday school. She went around to the side and very quietly opened the door. Confronting her was a white-haired lady and a group of grown women.

Just as she was about to close the door, the lady said, "Come in, little girl. What would you like?"

In a very quiet voice Kathleen said, "I was looking for a girls' class."

"Would you like to stay here for today? Yes?"

"Thank you."

When Miss Burke's class was over for the day, all the other young women asked for Kate to stay with the class. Kate did stay for four happy years, becoming almost a mascot for the older girls.

Once a month, Miss Burke would invite her class to high tea. The girls would call it a banquet with the gold and silver salt cellars with their gold and silver spoons, the finest of English china, and cut glass. On Kate's first visit, Miss Burke explained her reasons for such a display.

"I wish you girls to see how the luncheon was set at Buckingham Palace and also to have you use the same table service that Queen Victoria used. Gold and silver may be very common, silver very cheap, and most big houses use hallmarked silver all the time, so it's not the silver and gold but the fact that it had been used by Her Majesty that is so important. On their retirement, any persons in personal service with Their Majesties were given presents that had been used by them, and that is how I obtained it." The girls were suitably impressed and took great care to use their very best manners.

PART THREE

Johnston, Leonard and Howard FAMILIES

thirty-one

Napanee, Ontario, 1875

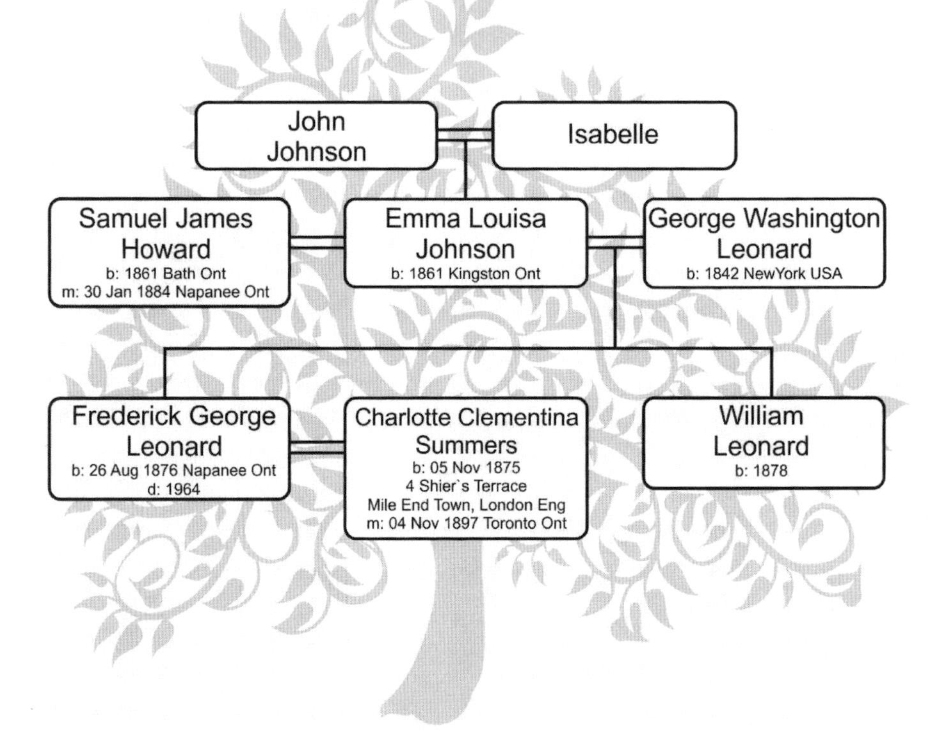

John Johnston brought his family from Kingston, Ontario, to Napanee in the late 1860s. Their daughter Emma Louise had been born in Kingston, but no record was left of it. There were no records of John's birth or his wife Isabella's or the births or deaths of their parents or grandparents. This was not unusual for the former slaves of Loyalists.

"You childs behave for your mam, ya hear?" commanded John. He was off to do barbering, a respectable profession for a person of colour.

II

"Can you tell me where da post office might be?" asked the handsome Negro of the young, attractive fourteen-year-old.

Emma Johnson fluttered her eyelashes, trying to cover her embarrassment but only succeeding in looking more coy. "It's right next door to the general store, down that side street and to the back."

George Washington Leonard tipped his hat with a smile. "Thank ye, ma'am," and went on his way. He had emigrated from New York State in 1871, still concerned about the way Negroes were treated in the United States after the Civil War. He worked as a barber but also cut wood in good weather for other people.

Emma Louisa was breathless after the encounter, and every day after that, when she had opportunity, she would gather her hat and mother's shopping basket and head out to the main street of Napanee, keeping an unobtrusive look out for the handsome black man she had met.

George Washington Leonard had seen her on the street several times but hid himself between buildings and watched her from the shadows. He was struck by her beauty and mature looks, though he knew her to be young. Finally, he could no longer stand it.

"Good day, to you, ma'am. May I carry your basket?" He had his large well-manicured hand on the handle of the basket before she could close her mouth. She nodded while releasing the basket to his grip and touched his extended elbow with her hand. She was so thrilled at seeing him again, and having him pay her attention, that she didn't notice the neighbour lady stepping out of the general store across the street. The woman made a mental note to herself to tell Emma Louisa's mother, Isabella, what she had seen. There was going to be trouble; she could just tell by the way that the two across the road were looking at each other.

By the time Emma Louisa got home, flushed and with her basket empty, her mother was prepared. "What you think you're doing with a man old as your father? Look at that! An empty basket. You're not making any more trips down to the main street to shop. Your younger sister can do it. You are heading for nothing but trouble, young woman. I'm warning you. You keep yerself to yerself, or your father is going to cut a new switch to use on you!"

Emma was completely exasperated but knew better than to argue with her mother right then. She would wait until she calmed down.

Isabelle did not calm down quickly, and her father, John, kept eyeing Emma whenever she got near the gate. She felt trapped, and anger began to flow. She really had to see George again. He was so solid, so handsome, and oh, she found herself as attracted to him as he was to her.

Emma began to contemplate ways to sneak out of the house, and Mrs. Gilbert down the way gave her an excuse. "Mama, it's time I went over to see Mrs. Gilbert. She'll be lonely without a visitor now and then. You know I'm the only one who goes to see her."

"All right, you go. But don't you go anywheres else, and come straight back here."

Emma nodded her head, with fingers crossed behind her back. She had to at least see George and let him know about the situation. Maybe he could meet her in the night somewhere close.

Napanee Cemetery – People of African descent did not have headstones but were buried along the fence row

thirty-two

Winter began to close in. Emma and George met more often than weekly if possible. Emma tried to get George to attend their small Baptist church so they might "officially" meet, but he was against that, mainly because he didn't abide by formal religion. It hadn't been that long since his family had escaped from slavery in the South of the United States, and as far as he was concerned, organized religion hadn't helped the slaves any.

It was a bitter and windy December, but Emma Louisa didn't see too much wrong with sneaking out of her house late at night to spend time with George. One thing led to another, and when Emma discovered she was in the family way early that spring, she didn't tell anyone except George.

"Emma, Mama wants you to go out to the garden to help her," her sister told her.

"What can she want? The ground is too wet to dig just yet," answered Emma.

"I don't know, but she told me to tell you, and you better git out there, or you're gonna cause trouble."

Emma went out slowly, thinking of all the things her mother might want to tell her or ask her, and she couldn't think of anything important enough, unless her mother had discovered her secret.

"Emma, I'm not gonna mince words with you. I'm certain you're in the family way, and I want to know the truth. Have you been having relations with that George fellow?" Isabelle Johnson handed Emma a long-handled hoe and kept her other hand on her hip.

Emma slowly took the handle as she made up her mind to tell her mother the truth. There was little point in denying it, since there was nothing to be done now.

"Ya, Mama, I been seeing George, and we is in the family way. I was hoping that we could get married, but George ain't said nothing yet about that. He did say he would look after me, so I'm not afraid to leave here and just go to him," Emma said nervously.

"Well, I don't know how he's gonna feel about you showing up on his doorstep, but his greeting will be a lot better than anything your papa is gonna say or do to you. We tried to warn you and watch you, but you just wouldn't listen, would you?" asked her mother.

II

Emma Louisa turned up on George's doorstep a few days after her fifteenth birthday, and George calmly waved her into his house with her sugar bag of personal items. He studied her and then gently drew her to him as she tried to tell him her situation between sniffles.

"It gonna be just all right. I'm gonna look after you and the baby, and we will be a lovin' little family," George reassured her.

III

His grandmother, Isabelle, delivered a healthy Frederick George Leonard on August 26. Emma was so relieved to have her mother there, she cried through the entire process.

Within two years Frederick had a brother named William, and the four managed to survive in a poorly insulated house, with a woodstove and a large pile of dry firewood that George kept topped up. At least it was away from the river, where others had damp conditions to deal with.

George always felt the Canadian weather was brutally wet and cold. He got a fair wage as a barber, but the rent to the property owner of the shop took a big percentage of his profits.

When George saw the posters and heard they were looking for strong workers to help dig the Welland Canal, he argued with Emma to let him go so he could earn a good wage. He promised to send whatever he could back home to her and return when he could. Jobs were that difficult to get that Emma didn't argue too much. She believed he would send them what he could, and he did—a few times.

After nothing came from him for a year and she had spent what little savings she had, she decided he must have returned to his family in New York. She heard tell that many working on the Erie and Welland Canals were infected with malaria. He could have been one of those that died.

Emma never became despondent. She looked after her two boys, dressing them and feeding them well for having so little. She was frugal with her money and took whatever jobs she could get in order not to appear destitute, especially in front of her father. Soon, Frederick was able to handle an axe and brought in the firewood every day. William pumped water from the well, and on occasion a bundle of baking would mysteriously appear on the step.

One day Samuel James Howard approached Emma. "That man of yours isn't going to return to you…is he?" asked Samuel.

"No, I don't reckon he is, as it's been six years now."

"Miss Emma, I know this might be hurtful to you, but I have to ask. Did you get married?"

Emma's lips tightened. She had always hoped to be married. In a way, she still loved George, and she harboured no hard feelings towards him but was terribly lonely. She shook her head.

"Then, that solves the problem. I can ask you to marry me, if you agree to let me court you," replied Samuel. He had been very attracted to her dark beauty for some time, and she was quite happy for him to court her.

They were married January 30, 1884, with both Emma's parents in attendance. Samuel, although hoping for his own sons, took care of Frederick and William, as well as Emma. He and his family were well thought of in the community, and Emma's shoulders straightened noticeably.

PART FOUR

Summers-Leonard
F A M I L Y

thirty-three

Toronto, Ontario, 1897–1898

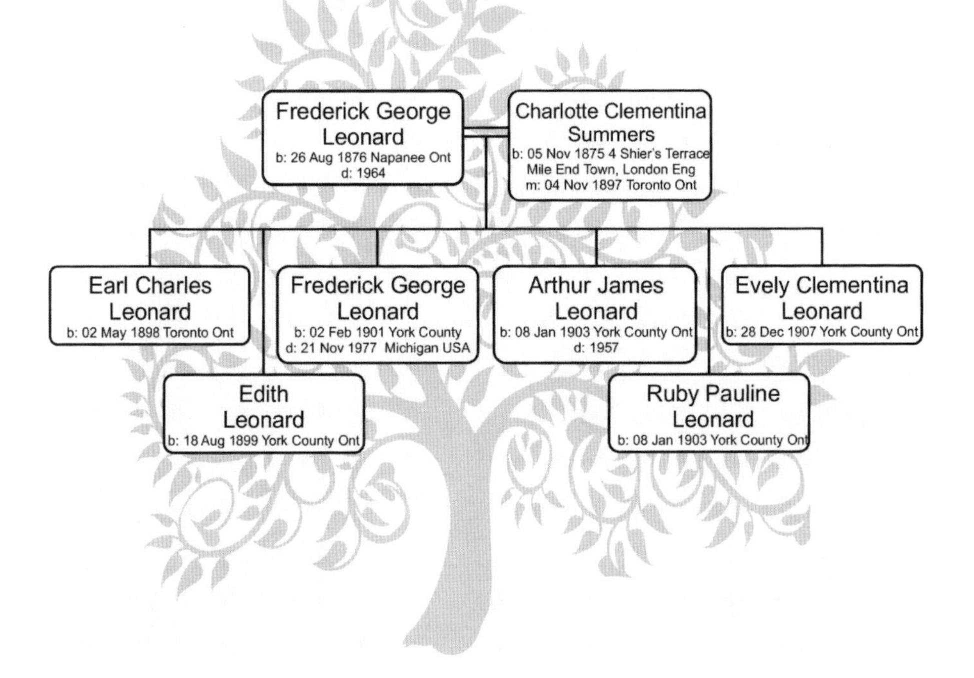

"Ticket, ma'am?" asked the young porter on the coach headed to the city centre.

Charlotte fumbled with her small purse in search of the ticket. She ended up having to remove her gloves to bring it forth at last for stamping by the porter. She triumphantly thrust it towards him as she apologized for the delay, but he appeared to be in no hurry.

"Do you often take the train, ma'am?" he casually asked.

Charlotte forced herself to breathe deeply before answering him. "Just on my half-day off."

"You're not from around here, are you?" he asked as he returned her ticket.

"No, that's true. I was born and raised in London, England." She didn't feel there was any harm in telling him that much. It wasn't as if he asked her where she lived or worked.

"Do you like it in Canada?" he continued, although he was moving backwards toward the next seat, where curious patrons held out their tickets.

Charlotte lowered her eyes away from the intense look of the handsome porter's dark face and shyly nodded. She wondered if she would by chance see him again. She had been working for five years as a domestic servant and wondered if she would ever have her own home and family to care for. Already she was twenty-one and had so few chances to make friends or meet eligible young men. Well, as her mother had always said, "Leave it in God's hands"; she tried changing her attention to the sights of new buildings and the city streets. She had only a few hours if she was to return to her dwelling before dark.

The following week, Charlotte was surprised to find the same young porter assisting the ladies up into the coach at her stop. He tipped his head in a slight bow as he firmly held her gloved hand while helping her up into the coach.

"Mind your step, now," he warned, with a smile.

This week Charlotte was ready with her ticket, but still, she startled when the young porter called "Tickets, please." He didn't pause long but gave her a very broad smile, then carried on with his work. She was disappointed not to see him again before leaving the coach.

The shops didn't really hold too much interest for Charlotte this trip because she had no intention of buying anything. She looked at fabric for new dresses of the season but knew she might not have the opportunity to make one if her mistress would not let her use her new Singer treadle sewing machine. Charlotte knew all about hand sewing and pattern design but had never actually used a sewing machine before. Her mother had taught her what she could before Charlotte went to Sturge House, and then she became expert at repairing clothing and linens.

Charlotte made a big effort to keep in contact with her family. She would send Barnardo's office in London any updates she received. John Pink was in Peel County, and he had written to tell her he had signed up for the South African war against the Boers. She didn't understand why he would go so far away, but it was obvious in his letter that he wanted to travel, and the pay was better than the labouring work he had been doing. She supposed the call of the British army was stronger in men than in women, who were left behind to wait and mourn their losses.

II

Frederick was just becoming resigned to the fact that the British lady was not going to show up this week when Charlotte came scurrying out through the engine's steam, hurrying to catch the train before it left the station. He beamed at her as he assisted her into the coach, swung the step up to its place, and grabbed the handrails to swing himself up just as the final whistle was warning all that the train was about to move. This time Frederick followed the young woman until she chose her seat. Not wanting to miss another opportunity, he leaned over her conspiratorially.

"The name is Frederick, miss, Frederick Leonard. I hope it is Miss..."

"Yes, Mr. Leonard. It's Miss Summers." And so began their courting.

Frederick would arrange to meet her on her return to the east end of Toronto. If Frederick was finished his shift, he would accompany her to her stop and carry on his trip to Napanee to visit his mother and stepfather.

On November 4th of 1897 Charlotte Clemintina Summers married Frederick George Leonard. Their first son was born on May 2, 1898, and he was named Earl Charles Leonard. After their second child, a daughter, was born in August of 1899, they moved into 11 William Street, Toronto. Charlotte was delighted they had a home to themselves. There were four rooms on the main floor and two more up the stairs.

"To think that six of us lived in one room and the privy was shared by another ten from the same house! There were no spaces between the houses. It kept things a little warmer in winter, but there were no gardens to plant or sit in. Even the parks had gates and fences, and of course there were private ones, and very few that the public could enjoy," Clemmie was fond of telling her young children.

Frederick was saddened by the news that his grandmother Isabella Johnston died in October of 1900. Although eighty years old, she had always seemed much younger and was the kindest woman he had known as a lad.

Edith Leonard at nine months old –
Photo found among her cousin's papers

PART FIVE

Summers FAMILY

thirty-four

London, England, 1900

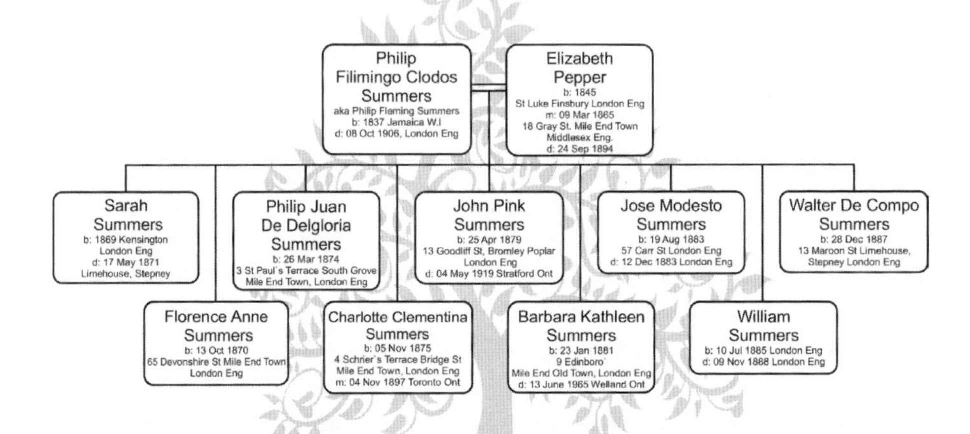

Philip Summers – first to leave Britain

Florence Summers – immigrated to Montreal through Barnardo's

While Kathleen had been earning a small wage and receiving gifts from Mr. Jacobs, Philip had been able to keep the one room on Maroon Street for doing custodial work inside the building and out. Walter, still a young lad, attended the Ragged School for boys down near the almshouse. Other times he would be helping Philip do some of the bending, which otherwise caused Philip so much pain. There were so many people without a steady position or with a disability such as what Philip had that soon Martin Henry Cain, Samuel Snell, and Robert Rushmore shared the room with Philip at 113 Maroon St. There was very little to eat, and Walter would often go to bed hungry. He was small for his age, not having had good nutrition, and finally Philip was forced to take Walter to be admitted to Barnardo's in April of 1900.

Kathleen, who preferred to be called Kate now, was working as a general servant at 24 Tivoli Road, in Crouch End, London. Kate enjoyed the family of Edgar Brown, but it was very different from Mile End, Old Town. New underground systems were being built, and in 1900 the central line was completed, allowing her much faster transportation, but she had little free time to check on her young brother Walter and her father.

In August she visited her father and was dismayed to learn that Walter had been migrated July 29 and was working for Mr. James Brown at Lumsden, Saskatchewan. She would look up a map of Canada at the library to find the location of this province and town and also check how far it was from Toronto and Peel County in Ontario. Although all living in Canada, her brothers and sisters were so far apart from each other, they might as well have been in different countries.

London, England, 1901

The population of London had reached 6.6 million by 1901. It was a busy, crowded city with the businesses centring around Westminster and the poor crammed into the west end, where ports and industry alternated with tenements. Martin Cain had left 113 Maroon Street, but J. Cannon had joined Philip, Robert, and Samuel. Reports from Charlotte let everyone in the family know she had found Florence working as a domestic with Henry Rouselle in Montreal, and Walter was a chore boy for Ariel and Martha Bedek in Assiniboia, where they farmed their parents' property and spent evenings teaching Walter to improve his reading and writing, as well as mathematics. Charlotte let them know her third child was to be born in February, and Frederick would take their son Earl to live with his mother and stepfather in Napanee. Although they had never had children together, Emma and Samuel were delighted to have young Earl live with them and Frederick's brother William.

II

John Pink Summers had been discharged from the British army's South African troops and was returning to Canada. On his way there, he was in a position to visit his family. He wasn't sure who was left at home, it having been some years since he was there. He hiked his kit bag over his shoulder and took a long detour to Maroon Street.

He paused in front of a small, dark bookshop where new and used books were sold. He saw Kim, Rudyard Kipling's newest novel, and The First Men on the Moon, by H. G. Wells, which sounded exciting. And there also was Joseph Conrad's book Lord Jim. Conrad had been writing about Africa, and John thought briefly of purchasing some gifts, but not knowing what kind of reception to expect at his father's last known address, he decided against it. He might have to buy food for some meals and find his own lodging. Whatever the situation, he hoped to see Kate, his closest sister.

Neighbours were able to direct him down a few houses to where his father still lived. He rang a buzzer and waited. Finally he could hear someone shuffling about, coming to the door.

His father had aged tremendously. "Papa. I stopped for a visit." John's eyes were tearing up as he gazed at his father's own tear-filled eyes. It was the gift of a special surprise, because Philip had never expected to see any of his children from Canada once he had taken them to Barnardo's.

"Oh! John, you're back from the war, and you're all right?" Philip's voice quivered with excitement and shock. "Come in. You must come in. I can't believe it's you. Oh, wait until I tell Kate."

"Is she here, Papa?"

Philip shook his head, but before he could explain John began questions.

"Walter? Is Walter here?"

Philip shook his head. "Walter was migrated in 1900, but Kate is working up on Tivoli Road for a family. You must stop by and see her. But now, come in and meet my roommates."

Philip ushered John into the hall and up the steps. The large room had been divided into four with drapes, dressers, and a divider from China, now rather stained and torn. Philip introduced him to Robert, the only one present at the moment, and then offered him a chair by his desk.

"You take the chair, Papa. I can sit with my feet up here on your bed. Will you have room for me tonight?" asked John.

"Oh, yes. Of course! Oh, I can't believe it's you. I never thought I would see you again, and here you are a man, grown up from the little boy I last saw."

John didn't ask his father how he was. The heavily stooped shoulders and back, the gaunt cheeks, and the shaking hands all told John of his father's condition. The fact that he managed to stay in the house was by grit and grin. His father had not complained of being an invalid much after the accident, except to express regret at not being able to look after his family. It must have been so difficult for him to release the care of his children to the home, John realized now, although it had done him no harm. Others had not been so fortunate in their placements.

"Papa, I would like Kate to come to Canada, and I'm giving you money for her passage if you will allow her to visit me in the future. I have been corresponding with a young lady whom I hope to marry some day."

"Well, lad, you have done very well for yourself. Now, tell us something of this war in South Africa you've been to."

John Pink pulled a somewhat dusty brown booklet from his bag and handed it to his father. "You can read some of this while I'm here. I tried to write every day, so there are quite a few details. May not be the best writing, but things were so different there, and I wanted to remember all that was going on."

Kate was thrilled her brother came to visit and wanted her to come to Canada, and he had given her father enough money for her to do that. When was another question, but the money was in safe keeping, so she would keep working until there was a set date.

III

This same year, Charlotte and Frederick celebrated the birth of healthy twins on January 8. Ruby Pauline and Arthur James were born in York. Charlotte was thrilled, but exhausted. Fortunately, neighbours were helpful, but it wasn't the same as having a mother nearby. Keeping five under the age of five fed and clothed was difficult, although Fred had worked as a porter at the Hotel Calmo for two years, and the extra tip money assisted with housekeeping expenses.

Because education was legally mandated for everyone up to the age of fourteen, Charlotte and Frederick knew their children would have more education than they had had the opportunity to take, and they would make sure the children took full advantage of it.

As soon as Emma found out she was a grandmother twice over, she placed a notice, which appeared in the February 6, 1903, edition of the Napanee Express: "BIRTHS HOWARD–At Toronto, on January 18th, the wife of Mr. Fred Howard, formerly of Napanee, of twins, a boy and a girl."

Emma used the Howard name because her friends and neighbours would know better who it was. Fred had gone back to using Leonard, but living in Toronto, it didn't matter. It was such a large, dusty city compared to their quaint town of Napanee. He missed the large architecturally interesting buildings like the courthouse and post office and the grand homes along Dundas, Bridge, and Adelaide Streets, but of course Fred had to live where his livelihood could be made.

Barnardo's Children's Church – all windows reflected scenes with children and Christ

Barnardo's Children's Church – pews made to fit children

Cottages in Tanner Lane – now seniors' residences

PART SIX

Puckering and Summers FAMILIES

thirty-five

Great Driffield, York, England, 1773, to Caledon, Ontario, Canada, 1897

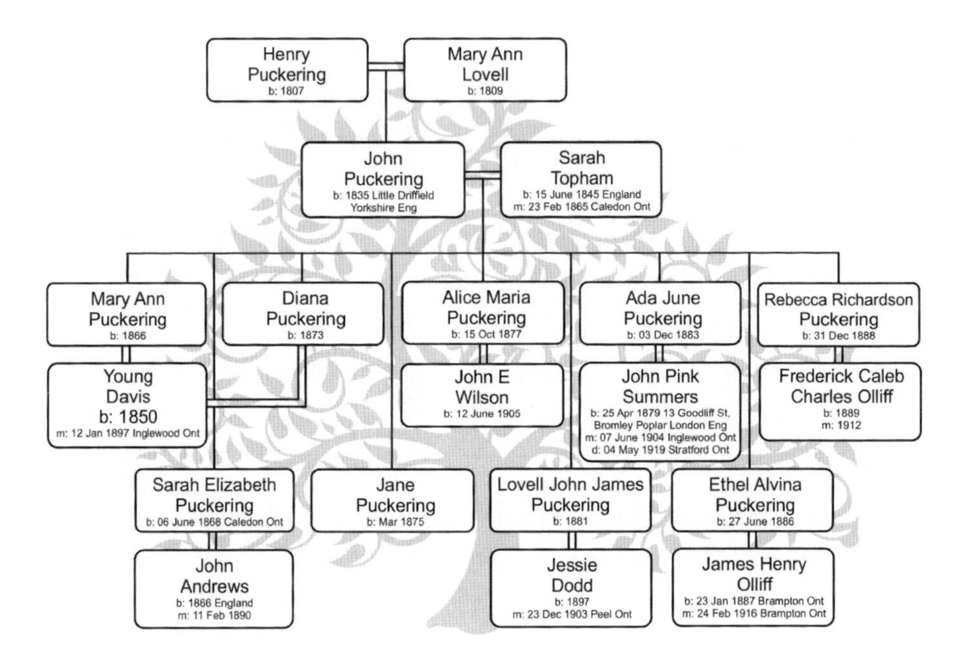

Thomas Puckering named his son, born in 1773, Thomas. Thomas married Catharine and farmed in Great Driffield, as had his father and his father's father. Their son Henry Puckering was an agricultural labourer in Great Driffield, York, England, and his wife was Mary Ann Lovell. John, second of Henry and Mary Ann's eight children, was also a farm labourer. Fewer labourers were needed because more farm machinery was used. At fifteen, John became a servant at the big house. He married Sarah Topham in February of 1865, and after a year, they set off for Ontario, Canada.

II

When their second daughter, Sarah Elizabeth, was born in 1868, John and Sarah established a farm in Caledon, Peel Township. Mary Ann was two. Little Jane, born in 1875, only lived three months. After five daughters, a son was finally born in 1888. Three more sisters followed Lovell John James Puckering. The large family needed accommodation, so the storey-and-a-half log cabin was increased in size. The family added an extra bedroom and a big kitchen on the main floor. The older girls were helping both Father and Mother with indoor and outdoor work.

John built a large barn with the help of neighbours, and livestock was gradually increased. The girls had no time to spoil their only brother, Lovell, and their father had him working alongside as soon as possible.

Whatever Sarah did, she taught her daughters well. Handwork on bedding and table settings was done by candlelight, and like almost every other farm family at the time, winter evenings were spent knitting and mending after chores in the barn were done.

At some point, Sarah noticed her husband's behaviour change. He spent more time at the barn, he became somewhat surly, and he complained of ailments. She realized he had started consuming more than the average amount of spirits, and that was not making him easy to live with. Sarah kept her family organized and working to make life the best they could on a pioneer farm.

The first to marry was Sarah in 1890 to John Andrews. The surrounding countryside was growing in population, and the city seemed to be expanding their way from the lake. Rail lines and improved road conditions soon made Peel much less isolated than it had been twenty-five years before.

III

After John died in 1891, Sarah Topham Puckering took on the farm work with her daughters and young son. She did this with determination, but not without humour. Diana, the Puckerings' third daughter, helped nurse the first wife of Young Davis, and then she married him in 1897.

Life on the farm was hard work. Diana continued on the Davis farm doing the same hard work her mother did. Her coughing during the winter months increased in frequency, until the telltale sign of tuberculosis—blood in the sputum—showed up in the spring of 1900.

"Diana, it's Mary Ann. I'm here to help you." Mary Ann entered the room, which had been made into a bedroom so that Diana could use the privy whenever possible. She needed assistance and was weakening daily. Mary Ann looked at her sister and thought, She must have watched his first wife go through this, just the way I'm watching her now, but Mary Ann tried to greet Diana with a cheerful smile and carry on with nursing, cleaning, and housekeeping.

By this time, their older sister, Sarah, had three boys and a girl. They joked about how John would have loved having a brother or two, rather than eight sisters.

Mrs. Puckering and children

thirty-six

London, England, 1902

Kate accepted a position as nursery governess to two boys and a little girl. While with the Porters, she had the opportunity of putting her knowledge to work. The children were ages five to nine. This meant each one went to bed at a different time. Dana, who was the oldest, remained up another two hours. Kate was startled to see this little black-haired boy kneeling on the nursery floor, drawing maps and more maps. Night after night he would do this, until Kate would say, "Bedtime!" Then he would jump up, come to her chair, sit on the arm, and ask, "Please read?"

Always ready to comply with his wishes, Kate would finish another chapter of their story.

London, England, to Ontario, Canada, 1904

Kate's friends, when they knew for sure she was going to Canada, made plans for going-away parties. Even though she was born in London, Kate had never been to the city.

"We must arrange a day to the city centre for Kate," one exclaimed.

"How will we do that in such a short time?" another asked.

One of the boys said, "I'll take Katie to every place of importance in one day." How the group did laugh, because it was almost impossible to go through just the art gallery in one day. However, Harry made his plans, and then asked Kate to give him one day and he would take her out.

After asking for the day off, Kate caught a nearby bus to Findsbury Park, transferred to a city bus, and got off at Buckingham Palace. Harry took Kate's hand, and it was a rush from then until 11 p.m. at night. They scarcely stopped to eat.

They went through the British Museum, the art gallery, the Tower of London, on to the outside of Westminster Abbey, Buckingham Palace, all around the Marble Arch, into St. Paul's Cathedral, and so many other places. They ended up at Madame Tussaud's Exhibition. Here, just before reaching the steps of stone with an iron railing to hold, Harry quietly spoke to Katie.

"See those two policemen standing there? Yes, well, the one standing inside the door watches every person going in and out. He expects you to speak, so say, 'Good evening' so that he will know you are English." Harry led Kate up by the hand and gave her a little push, which sent her right in front of the policeman.

"Good evening," Kate said, giving him her sweetest smile. He never moved or spoke, and all Kate could hear was the peal of laughter from the crowd behind her. The policeman was wax!

They rushed from room to room until coming to a beautiful hall. On the walls hung large paintings. Down the centre were two rows of seats back to back. On the left were two long desks, one at each end, where a woman sat selling programs. Harry and Kate were so engrossed in looking at the paintings that Kate never noticed the crowds. After a while, Harry said to her, "Katie, will you go and buy a program from that girl?"

"Certainly," answered Kate, and taking the sixpence from Harry, she held out her hand towards the girl.

"A program, please," she said, but the girl never moved or spoke. All Kate heard was an uproar of laughter from behind her. Kate sighed, but she smiled at Harry as she turned around. Let him have his fun, too, she thought.

Harry had left the worst until the last, which was the room of horrors. "Will you be afraid, Katie?" asked Harry.

Kate read the sign: "The Room of Horrors. Admittance 6 pence." "No," she answered.

"Do you want to take this little girl in there?" asked the guard.

Kate was surprised at that, because she was twenty-three years old, even though quite short.

"Will she be nervous?"

"No, I have asked her," Harry replied and paid for their way in.

The first thing Kate noticed was a family who had been murdered by their father. The next was titled Ten Nights in a Bar Room.

This story took up the whole side of the length of the room and showed how a young man had been led astray. He had been a trusted bank clerk. The first night he met a man who enticed him to a drink. The first drink led from bad to worse, until the young man, coming to his senses, realized he was deep in debt to the bank. He killed the man and was consequently hanged for it.

This was one day Kate would never forget.

thirty-seven

London, England, to Ontario, Canada, June 1904

"You must go, my dear Kate," her father said as Kate stood waffling at the door. "Your brother wishes you to join him, and I know that you have wanted very much to go to Canada. There's the blood of mariners in you, and I know you will enjoy the sea voyage."

"Oh, Father! Thank you. I'm very excited to go and have a bag prepared for a voyage already. Will you be all right while I'm gone?"

"Yes, yes. You see I have friends who have joined me in this residence, and we all get along well. What one cannot do, another is often able to do. Wish your dear brother a hearty greeting from me. Now be off with you. I have arranged that you will travel first class under the care of the captain. The ship leaves Liverpool on June 9th, so you will have to make arrangements to take the train there yourself. God bless you, Kate."

II

Kate settled herself in her compartment and learned she was in first-second class and that there was still another first class, the only difference being that that first class had a bugle call for meals, whereas she was to listen for a bell. The dining room was carpeted and separated by a glass wall built partway up from the floor.

Kate was delighted to find that next door was a woman with her three daughters, ages six, nine, and twelve years of age. She spent a great deal of time in their company, playing and skipping about on the deck. Though much older, she fit in with the young girls and delighted in the sights of the sea and the intricacies of the ship. Kate, being of a lively character, was enjoying freedom for the first time in her life, but she felt guilty about leaving her father alone in England.

On two occasions, the sea began to roll in huge swells. Waves splashed against the bow, sending streams of spray everywhere. Some people began to feel ill. Kate was one. The steward carried her over to the rail, where, as she later told her brother, "Did I ever feed the fishes!" Her upset stomach made even her head hurt.

"I felt so bad," she wrote to her father, "I didn't care whether I reached Canada or went overboard." However, once over the sickness, she felt so much better that the steward was able to carry her on deck, where he brought her ice cream. She remained on deck until the evening, when the same steward would carry her back downstairs. She had the sympathy of many of the passengers who knew she travelled alone and was usually such a happy, lively young girl. They were amazed when she was up and around skipping and playing the next day, glad to be well and enjoying the sea once more.

In the dining room at breakfast, she and another lad her age were the only ones at the table. She had toast and almost finished her porridge, then made a dash for the railing, where she again fed the fishes. By dinner, she was able to keep food down, and life carried on in a delightful way for her.

III

Kate wrote to her father later.

> *We had a dreadful storm, also saw some icebergs, which delayed the ship for some days; the sky after a storm at sea is magnificent. When we docked at Montreal, I was very sorry to land. The second and third class passengers were landed at Quebec City, which gave the remaining passengers an hour or more to go ashore and see a few shops. The narrow cobblestone streets were lovely, and dear old French ladies with their quaint bonnets carried their baskets of shopping with them.*

The next night the ship reached Montreal, where Kate was placed under the care of the stationmaster. There was a Mr. Donnel going west as a home missionary. He attended to Kate's customs and luggage, which made things less frightening. Her boxes of books, hand Singer sewing machine, and two tin trunks were looked at but not opened.

Kate sat stiffly on the bench where the stationmaster had directed her. All at once, she heard a scream. Looking up she saw a four-year-old boy with blood streaming down his face. Forgetting she had been told to stay on the bench, she jumped up to run to his assistance. A woman came running.

"Oh, dear! I'm this boy's aunt. What have you done, Tommy?' she asked, but he continued screaming with the blood running down his face. Kate and his aunt managed to get him to a water fountain, where they tried washing the blood off. Others came to help, and just as Kate was about to return to her seat, someone took her by the elbow.

"You gave me quite a fright. Didn't I tell you to stay on that bench?"

"Oh, I was just returning, sir, but thank you for your concern. The little boy has been badly cut. He must have run into something, and he was very alarmed. It must have been two inches long, and I don't know how deep," replied Kate.

"Now, don't move until I come for you," he said, but Kate had no intention of moving, with the noises and crowds hurrying all around her. Steamers' engines billowed smoke, the porters hollered in French and English, and seagulls cried. She was thrilled watching, despite the strong odours of smoke and fish.

The stationmaster asked a porter to show her through to the pullman and sleeper of what Katie thought was the largest train she had ever seen. She was so nervous of its great height she thought of nothing but the train tipping over and crashing. Then when the plush curtains came down over the seats, she remained bolt upright in her seat and stayed awake until the train reached Toronto at about 2:30 in the morning. Since she was already two days late for her brother's wedding because of the storms at sea, Katie found it no hardship having to wait for her brother to meet her, now that she had landed. There was so much activity and so many people coming and going, the time passed quickly.

Kate glanced at the day's Beacon newspaper. She couldn't see it all but got the idea from bits and pieces. Seventy-five apprentices lost their jobs with the Grand Trunk Railway because they went to the circus. How terrible! She wasn't sure if it was terrible that the apprentices had dared leave their responsibilities to go to a circus or if it was terrible that the railway had fired the seventy-five apprentices. That was a very large number, and she wondered why there would be so many.

thirty-eight

Caledon, Peel County, Ontario, 1904

John was stretching his neck, scanning the train platform, when he spied her. Kate jumped up and ran to greet him, as excited as a young teen.

"Kate! How good to see you. You look so well. I'm so sorry you missed the wedding. Ada and I were both so disappointed with the ship's delay. Was the storm so terrible?" he asked, picking up her valise and keeping his arm encircled around her waist.

"I'm just glad it wasn't worse. There were just two very bad days, but it was a wonderful trip. I thank you, dear brother, for giving me this opportunity. Father sends his love. You know, you're the only one of the family who calls him Papa. He was so delighted to see you. He misses all his children but thankfully has faith the Lord will keep us all safe. We must write immediately to let him know I have arrived."

"I think I will send a cable. That will relieve him much sooner." It had never occurred to Kate to spend money on sending a cable or that the untamed country of Canada would have such a device, but of course it was not too much money to relieve her father's anxiety.

The hustle and bustle of the city of Toronto dwindled as they approached Caledon, and they passed quiet country roads and villages. The hills and farms were the brightest green Kate had ever seen. She struggled to keep her eyes focused.

They pulled into a laneway, where John helped Kate down with her bag and took her to the front veranda before he took horse and carriage to the backyard stable.

II

Her first breakfast was a T-bone steak, after which she went to bed and slept until six p.m. Kate was so tired, she could hardly talk, but she took everything in. It didn't stop her from asking questions after she awakened fully.

"Where do you cook?" All Kate could see was a massive thing standing in the kitchen area, shining black and polished nickel.

"This is the stove," answered Ada, John's wife. She opened it wide so Kate could see and wonder at the space it took. Later, after enjoying sumptuous meals at John and Ada's Brampton home, she understood the need.

"I've been used to having bread cut as thin as wafers with butter. Here I can't believe all the food: buns, cookies, thick sliced bread, meat, and pickles." Kate thought it was very delicious and enjoyed every bite.

In England, corn on the cob was dried and hung in the windows of homes and feed shops. Those shops sold only feed for cattle and chickens, so all English people first arriving in Canada wondered at humans eating it.

John passed his sister a plate piled high of steaming golden corn. "Kate, would you like to try some?"

Seeing everyone else eating it, she took the fork and placed a cob on her plate. The others were surprised and amused because they expected a turned up nose to the Canadian corn on the cob. Instead, Kate ate one, then another, until she had finished six cobs.

"Kate, why don't you come and stay with us at the farm?" asked Ada's sister, Ethel. "We would love to have you come and visit," chimed in the others, including their mother. Kate immediately wrote to her father to ask permission to stay a few weeks longer so that she might visit the farm in Peel.

"John, why do you suppose there were so many apprentices working for the Grand Trunk Railway in Stratford?"

"Oh, you heard about that, did you? Well, there's a great deal of construction going on. Stratford is the county seat, important government buildings are going up, and the railways are coming in. Back when the Grand Trunk came into Stratford, there was the Buffalo, Brantford and Goderich line blocking the route they had wanted to expand to St. Mary's. I don't know why there were so many apprentices there, but most of the railway trainees are there for some period. They might be doing more expansion; I don't know. I wouldn't mind working there someday."

thirty-nine

Peel, Ontario, 1904

The Puckering farm was located in the quickly developing Peel Township. When John Puckering and Sarah Topham immigrated to Canada, they could not believe the space. They built the traditional log cabin but added a complete sleeping loft. There were nine children born to them, the last being Rebecca Richardson Puckering in 1888. After John died in 1891, Sarah worked hard to pay off the remainder of the mortgage and raise the children.

By 1904, when Kate visited, the oldest daughter, Mary Ann, had married her sister's widower, Young Davis. Sarah and John Andrews had six children. Lovell, the only son, had married Jessie Dodd and had two children, and Ada had just married Kate's brother, John Summers. Alice, Ethel, and Rebecca remained at home.

Now that things were a little easier, it seemed to the others that Rebecca had much more than many of them at the same age. They all called her Reva, not being able to pronounce Rebecca when they were young.

Kate wrote on scraps of paper whenever she could find time after those wonderful months of what she considered a holiday with the Puckerings. She didn't want to forget a thing of her experiences on the farm.

"Downstairs consisted of one large dining and living room, which ran the full length of the house," she wrote.

Off the living room on the south side was a bedroom where Sarah slept, a pantry, and a washroom. On the north side, a lean-to kitchen and men's washroom had been built. All these windows were not long, but wide. On the east side was the front door, leading to a gravel path, which extended to the road. A low wire fence protected the flowerbeds on each side of the gravel walk. The beds were a mixture of all kinds of lovely flowers, which, in the early morning, to smell their fragrance and see their beauty, and listen to the birds overhead, certainly made one happy to be alive.

Upstairs consisted of one large room, heavy beams separating it into four parts. Here is where all the pillow fights took place. The beds were very comfortable feather beds and most of the bed covers were handmade.

Lovely they were; I used to lie and look at them wondering how these dear people found time to do such lovely work. There was one wide window, which had, like the rest of the windows, pretty curtains worked with some pretty design to relieve their plainness because they were made from cheesecloth. The side curtains, made from sugar bags, were bleached.

The barnyard proper was fenced in with a high wooden fence which gave the farm a very neat appearance.

The Call

At 5 a.m. dear mother Sarah would call up the stairs, "Time to get up girls."

The first thing I would be aware of would be a pillow at my head, and then one thrown from behind me; by this time we would all be awake, and although we had fun, there was still no waste of time.

Milking

One day Ethel asked, "Katie, would you like to learn to milk?"

"Yes," I answered. So that night after supper, we, Ethel, her younger sister and I, went to the barn. Ethel gave me a pail and called the dog.

"Go fetch the cows, Teddy." Away went Teddy, and by the time we reached the cowshed, there they all stood waiting for the door to be opened. Ethel, turning to her sister, said, "We'll let Katie practice on Dorothy." Every animal on that farm had a name, and they all knew Ethel and loved her. Having settled the cows in their stalls, Ethel took me to one, saying, "Katie, this cow's name is Dorothy. She is quiet and patient so you will be safe to practice on her." Putting her arm around the cow's neck, Ethel said, "No, Dorothy, do not switch your tail, and stand still," which the cow seemed to understand and stood perfectly still while Ethel showed me how to handle things.

First, I must learn to sit on the stool properly!

"Now, Katie," said Ethel, "take this stool and place it here," which was at the right side of the cow's body. "Sit down with your feet apart, under the cow's body. Now place the pail on the ground between your two legs." Therefore, I carried out these instructions. Stooping down beside me, Ethel said, "Now take this teat in your right hand and this one in your left and gently squeeze upward and a little firmer downward," which I did, but could not get any milk. This practice went on for some days until one day, much to my delight, some milk came. I became more efficient at manipulating the teats and the cow relaxed, which made milking easier.

One day Ethel asked, "Katie, would you mind if I leave you alone? We will go and milk the other eight cows. Now see how much milk you can get." Ethel was, as usual, laughing, and away they went. Coming back, in what seemed to me a very short time, they asked, "How much milk, Katie?"

"A half a pail," said I, turning to let them see, when to my great disappointment, my heel caught the handle, and away went the pail of milk spilling on the ground.

As usual, Ethel, with her beaming smile said, "Never mind. You have learned how to milk, and the spilled milk will not be wasted. Here come the cats."

forty

The Chicken Bee

One day Ethel asked, "Katie! Would you like to go to a chicken bee?"

"A chicken bee," I said. What would that be? I had been on a farm in England only for two weeks' holidays, when we never saw the farm proper, only the brick house with its lovely green lawn and tennis court in the front, and, being a Londoner, I did not come in contact with chickens until after they were cooked.

"A chicken bee," said Ethel, "is where a group of women and girls meet on one farm and pick a large number of chickens." Then she laughed, brought me an old coat, overalls, and cap, and said, "Carry these, Katie."

"What for?" I asked.

"You will see, and feel too," said Ethel.

On reaching the farm, we found a group of women waiting for us, all wearing old coats, overalls, and caps. I knew by the expressions and concealed chuckles that mischief was in the air, about which I knew nothing so decided to ask no questions, feeling the laugh was on me.

"Now," said Ethel, "Katie! You put on this coat, overalls, and cap," which I did.

"Now, here is a chicken for you pick." Taking the chicken, which although dead was still warm, I promptly dropped it, much to the amusement of all. When I questioned her, Ethel explained that chickens had to be plucked as soon as their necks were wrung, so that the feathers would come off easily, without breaking the skin. Also, they must be hung up so they will remain white for market.

So busy was I watching what was going on that I did not notice my coat, until they began to laugh and look at me. Wondering what the women could see about me to cause so much fun, I glanced at myself, to find I was smothered in—what?… Pinfeathers! I jumped up to shake myself, but they didn't come off. Ethel came to my rescue and told me not to mind, these feathers would not remove themselves, and that was why we wore old clothes and cap, so as not to get them in our hair and everywhere else. Now I could see why they had such fun, and I laughed too. We had many more chicken bees, all of which I enjoyed, becoming an expert at picking chickens.

The Colts

At another time, Ethel exhibited her courage. There were two colts to be broken in. The men were able to break in one, but the other could not be tamed. Try as they would, we would always be thrown. I spoke of this each day at mealtime, for some days, but Ethel, sitting next to me at the table, was silent. I had noticed whenever Ethel was quiet, one could be sure there was something on her mind.

After dinner one day, while washing dishes, Ethel said, "I will break in that colt."

Her mother replied, "Don't try that. She might kill you, and what would we do without you?" However, each night at a given time Ethel would disappear, not saying where or what, until one evening we heard a horse's hooves clattering on the gravel path. Looking up we saw that Ethel was riding the colt. That is where she had gone and what she had been doing when we missed her each evening. What courage that girl had! From this night on, Ethel and the colt were fast friends, and the colt came to the kitchen door each day to put her nose into Ethel's pocket and get an apple or carrot or sugar. What pals those two became.

Near Drowning And The Cow

One evening Ethel asked, "Katie, would you like to come to the barnyard?"

"Yes, I would," I answered. The barnyard had a small door through which we went, back and forth, unless the large things—cattle, buggy and horse—were going in or out. The girls, running ahead of me, thinking I was following, which I was until, noticing some long boards lying, as I thought, on the ground, I stopped to investigate. Finding they would move up and down, I decided to play seesaw.

All of a sudden, I heard a dreadful shriek and Ethel's voice calling,

"Katie, Katie!" I looked up and there was Ethel, her face like death, running towards me. With one bound, I ran to meet her, which I think saved my life, for those boards were covering a very deep well half filled with water.

This was a Thursday evening, and the following Sunday we were all ready for church, waiting for Ethel to bring the buggy and horse. Thinking her a long time, two of us went to find what was detaining her, as she was always so quick. Then Ethel came, looking so pale. We helped her to the house, and when she could get her breath, we asked, "What is wrong?"

"Thompsons' heifer has fallen in the well, and that might have been your fate, Katie, had I left you much longer to see why you were so long in following us up."

There was no church that Sunday. Like a flash, we all ran to the well. Here, a group of farmers were standing, not knowing what to do. The cow had jumped over the fence right onto the boards, and being heavier than I was, it plunged in, in such a manner that its body was doubled in two. Ethel, as usual, being quick, spoke up, and we all made plans, for all this time the men were trying to bring the cow up but could not move her. The only thing to be done now was some man must go down the well, try and loop a rope around the cow's body, and pull her up.

John, the farm's hired man, said he would go. It was at this moment we saw that John and the daughter Alice were in love. The paleness and look on Alice's face was enough to assure John that his love was returned.

Finally, it was decided that we four girls should stand behind each other pulling one end of the stout rope through the fence. The other end would be fastened around John's waist. Taking another rope in his hand, we let him down the well. He just managed to loop the rope around the cow's body when he fainted. Now for presence of mind and courage, Ethel at all times was best. She gave the order. "Hoist! Hoist!" Therefore, we pulled like a tug-o-war, finally bringing John up, and laying him on the ground. The men, all this time, were trying to rescue the cow, but she had fallen in such a doubled-up manner that she did not live long.

The men came and carried John to the house, then went back to the well, while we girls secured hot bottles and blankets. Finally, he came to. Then we gave him a hot drink of water and milk. Knowing how Alice felt about John, we three girls went back to the well, to find the young heifer lying on the ground surrounded by men, and, of course, the owner.

"What a loss this is for me. The cow jumped over the fence onto other property, so I can't claim any damages. Well, I wouldn't claim any from a dear pioneering mother and neighbour like Mrs. Puckering." Ethel, as in other difficulties, was the heroine.

forty-one

To Town and Shopping

Usually on Thursdays, the mother, Sarah Puckering, would go to town, five miles away, in the buggy drawn by the horse, taking her chickens, eggs, butter, and cream that were kept on a block of ice. Ethel, who was the second youngest daughter, would bring the buggy and horse from the barn, place everything in it, and see that her mother was comfortable. Then away Sarah would go to town to the grocery store, where she would exchange butter, eggs, chickens, and cream for groceries and staples. Then she would go to the dry goods store, where an exchange would be made for notions, cottons, and yarns. There was not much money paid out at this time.

Gum

"There was always great fun on this farm. We went to bed laughing and got up laughing. Of all the girls, Ethel was my favourite. She had a delightful disposition and was ready for fun at any time. The only time I saw her mad was one day when we were going for a walk along a country road. Looking sideways at her, I noticed her mouth moving. Watching this movement for some time, my curiosity finally reached its peak.

"What are you chewing?" I asked Ethel.

"Gum," she replied. "Would you like a chew?"

"What does it taste like?" I asked.

"Like sticky toffee—only it does not last as long, that is, the sweetness doesn't last," then she laughed. Ready to try anything, I took a piece, gave one chew, and threw it into the road. Mad! Was she mad!

Her face, which was always like a rosy apple, went redder, and she just said, "Katie! How could you? That piece was all I had." At the time, I did not know how difficult it was for those girls to get candy or gum.

Thrashing

Never will I forget that experience! We three girls would sit in the summer kitchen and peel pail after pail of potatoes. There were no potato peelers in those days, at least not on this farm, but the knives were so sharp and the potatoes so fresh that the work was light. We would laugh and joke until the tears would run down our cheeks. The potatoes washed and on to cook, I would have time to watch the pies being made—pumpkin, lemon, cream, and raisin pies. And what pastry! All were made with butter.

Now to set the table we put in an extension board and covered this with a silence cloth, which was an old gift, and then the white tablecloth, which would usually be used only on Sundays. Ethel had the work so arranged that each person knew her part. In this way, there would be no confusion when the men came in to dinner, and what a dinner! My work was to put on salt and pepper shakers, which I made sure were full, sugar, mustard, vinegar, pickles, and what delicious pickles. There were mustard bean, pickled onions, sweet mixed, and tomato mixed. Next, water and cream, cold iced tea with lemon, delicious homemade bread, and butter were put on the table. Of course everything was "home made." I could feel my eyes getting wider with amazement seeing all this delicious food placed on the table at 11:00 a.m. sharp, dinnertime.

Ethel said, "All ready?"

"Yes," answered her mother, Sarah. Alice took the cowbell to the front door and rang it loud enough to be heard all over the farm.

Now, to watch Ethel's face. She had told me to stand in a certain place that was just behind the kitchen door through which men would come from the washroom. Surmising she was up to some trick, I quietly obeyed.

Finally, the men came in from the fields. They all knew Ethel, and from the beaming face sensed she was up to some mischief. To make sure, one young man put his head around the kitchen door, to behold—me! A stranger and a girl at that! Darting back into the washroom he said something to the others, and then to hear the calls, "Give me that comb. Give me that comb!" while Ethel was convulsing with laughter. The joke was that at noon, the men never combed their hair, just washed their faces and hands. Ethel, knowing this, as usual, must play some joke on them.

They would all come in to dinner at once; by the time they were settled at the table we were laughing and the men's faces were as red as beets. So it was in this happy frame of mind and heart that we commenced to serve dinner.

Dinner! Did I say dinner? It was more like a banquet. I had never seen such quantities of delicious food served at one meal. There were dishes of mashed potatoes, beets, corn on the cob, creamed carrots, cabbage, chicken, ham, beef, and gravy, brown and luscious.

There were five of us girls waiting on tables, each one knowing her work. We just served, laughed, and joked. The men, having satisfied their tummies with the first course, now waited while we cleared away the plates in readiness for dessert. Having never been to a thrashing before, my eyes just kept getting larger, thinking these men would be sick after eating such large pieces of pie. My curiosity was such that, after they had gone in the yard to rest a while, I had to sneak out, expecting at least some with a pain, instead of which, they were all convulsed with laughter. Was my face red!

The girls had a chance to clear the table and get their own dinner after the men went back to work. After enjoying the meal, we cleared and scraped dishes for washing. There were piles and piles of them, but this did not bother us, as we had so much fun, no matter how hard the work was. There was never a straight cross face, and even dear Mother Sarah would have to laugh. The pots, pans, and mixing bowls had been washed and put away while waiting for the men to come in to dinner. There was never a wasted moment in that house. That was how they found time to do all the fancy work. You should have seen their beautiful quilt that took first prize years in succession at Toronto Exhibition.

Having finished the dishes, swept, and tidied everything, Ethel took me to see the men thrashing. What a sight to see that golden grain running through the funnel to the ground. A little later, it was shoveled up into bags ready for the bins.

At 6:00 p.m., another meal was made with leftovers from dinner, following which the men took the thrashing machine to another farm, ready for the next day. This would mean the men would not finish their day's work until about 7:30 or 8:00 p.m. In spite of the late hour, the young men would wash and change, hitch up Dobby in the buggy, and go off to visit their girlfriends.

Meals

Having been used to small helpings and my cup only filled to within three-quarters of the brim, I found it quite difficult to accustom myself to the bountiful meals served in Canada, but I did not say anything, my brother having previously advised me that Canada was not England and for me not to expect English conservative ways. Always sitting next to each other at the table, Ethel and I were able to play tricks on each other, to the delight of her dear mother. And so, the weeks flew, and then I had to return to my brother's house and back to England.

forty-two

London, England, 1905

Kate went to visit her father, still living on Maroon Street. She walked past the park area and breathed deeply. She did enjoy walking, and the green was a welcome contrast against the dull grey of buildings and sky. There had been typhus this year in the city, and many had died from drinking the contaminated water.

Kate rang the bell but knew she would need to walk in and up the stairs to her father's room. Since her trip to Canada, Kate had noticed more of a hunch in her father's back. His clothes seemed ill fitting, and she wondered where his jacket might have come from, being an older style than she had seen. She hoped the news of another grandchild would cheer him up.

"Her name is Sarah Elizabeth, and she was born July 27th. John and Ada are very excited by the sounds of their letter to me. Did you receive a letter from them?" asked Kate.

"Not yet. Imagine! A granddaughter named Sarah. Your mother and I were so sad to lose our oldest child. My mother and grandmother were named Sarah, and, come to think of it, I had a great-aunt Sarah too. I expect that I will hear from Clemmie before long. She does her best to keep the family up to date. I often wish we had had the means to keep all you children at home, but it was too much for your mother and I. I hope you and the others can forgive us, Kate…"

"Oh, Father, we know you had no choice, and the family is doing much better in Canada than if they had stayed here. Moreover, everyone got some training. You made sure of that."

"My dear Kate. I wondered if you would be coming back to your old life here in London after the joy you found on the farm in Peel. I thought you might forget about your old father after a while."

"Oh, Father. I never stopped thinking of you, and I wouldn't have left you alone here; you had no fear of that," and she gently patted his hand. "Let me read you the letter I had from John.

"Dearest Kate,
We have God to thank for the safe arrival of a beautiful baby girl. Her aunts are all doting on her, and Ada has had some time to rest. We are very happy and remember the days of your visit with fondness. Do you hear of Philip or Walter? Clemmie has written to tell us of some of her difficulties with five children so close together in age, but the twins are quite fun, and Frederick enjoys playing with them when he is off shift. The city of Toronto is growing rapidly, she tells us, and streetcars and electricity are common now. Frederick's parents in Napanee like to keep Earl or one or two of the others for a period, especially when it's so hot in the city during the summer. Here, there is always so much work to do on the farm in summer; we sometimes go over to help. You might know already that Alice and John married, at last.
Affectionately,
Your brother John."

II

Kate returned to her duties as a household maid at the home of Mr. and Mrs. Brown. Her employers were expecting to host a dinner party that Saturday evening, and Kate was expected to help with the table setting. Mrs. Brown had polished the larger pieces of silver herself, and the kitchen girl was finishing the silverware in the dining room.

"Now Kate, you have had the training, you say, so let's see how you would place the setting for this menu." Mrs. Brown watched carefully as Kate looked over the menu. She would set for the salad, the soup, and the bread and butter plate.

"Are the dessert silver to be placed after the silver from the main course has been cleared, or do you wish to have the dessert silver across the top of the place setting?"

"You may place the dessert silver across the top of the dinner plate. The fewer times Nancy has to interrupt, the better. She will have to do the serving and the clearing. We can't afford a butler, but I want a wonderfully attractive table with these dishes filled with flowers, the napkins fan-folded, and those ornaments from the sideboard arranged in a formal but attractive placement. There will be eleven, so let's see if you are as capable of placing these in a symmetrical fashion as you are at setting a formal table. I will return in an hour to check your final work."

Kate set right to work with placing the eleven dinner plates evenly around the table. She would remove these so the smaller plates and soup bowls could be placed in their stead, but she needed the dinner plate to space everything correctly from the three forks on the left and the spoons and knife on the right to the bread and butter plate on the left, butter knife turned outward, to the three drinking glasses at the top right, largest at the back. She carefully measured the distance between each setting with seams in her apron, redistributing them to even out the space for eleven. She was confident in the placement of all the silver and dishes because this was something she had been trained for at school.

Kate checked the menu again to ensure all the appropriate utensils were in their place. The matching china was all in position and she was finishing the centrepieces after folding the napkins when Mrs. Brown returned with fresh cut flowers from the market stall down the street. The colour added a delightful mix to the china's pattern and the white tablecloth and napkins.

"Don't forget the dessert fork and spoon, Kate. And would you please get the serving dishes out on the sideboard for Cook before you go upstairs to put the children to bed. They are in the kitchen having their tea and are quite excited about the activities around the house. They seem to know Cook and Nancy are busy, and they might likely use this opportunity to cause mischief. Please remain in the nursery on the cot tonight, so I can rest assured that they will remain upstairs." With those instructions, she was off to the kitchen to continue instructions and check on the front hall entrance to ensure that things were tidy and unnecessary items removed.

Kate supervised the children's bath, lined up their Sunday church clothes, read them two stories because she knew they were listening to the company arrive, and then said their prayers with them as they all knelt beside the bed. She enjoyed tucking them in and placing a kiss on their foreheads before reposing her aching body on the cot. She had to stay alert but was having trouble keeping her eyes open. Her short visit with her father seemed ages away.

Suddenly, a loud thump sounded on the bare floorboards of the nursery, and Kate jumped up from the cot. Her night candle had gone out, and there was no moon to put light in the room. She trod carefully towards the children's bed and almost tumbled over Eric, who had fallen asleep and tumbled to the floor. This action had not wakened him, but his older brother was sitting up, his high-necked linen nightgown gently illuminating his face enough that Kate could ensure that everything was, indeed, all right.

"Go back to sleep, Kenneth. Eric is fine. He's still asleep even though we were awakened."

After lifting the dead weight of Eric's sleeping body onto the bed, Kate tucked him in more tightly so he would not fall out again. She hoped that bump had not heard on the main floor. She didn't think it would be, but she would spend the rest of the evening in the rocking chair until the last of the guests left. She adjusted the open window a little wider so she would be sure to hear the cabs on the street, and fresh air kept away childhood diseases better than anything else did.

forty-three

London, England, 1906

Kate had been worried about her father's health all summer, and she had to ask for time off when she received a note from William Tagg that her father was very ill.

William greeted her at the door. "Ach, Kate, I'm sorry. You are too late. There was nothing you could have done. He just fell asleep early this morning, and then I couldn't wake him. There, there, Kate. You were a lovely daughter to him, and he was so proud of all his family."

William put his arm around Kate's shaking shoulders as she wept tears of frustration and sorrow. Her father had had such a hard life, and she would miss his gentle ways and kind wisdom.

"Well, nothing to do but clean up his things, which I will do right now," Kate determined. She lifted the cover off the tin trunk that he sometimes had used for his long voyages. Kate carefully sorted through his papers and found the bundle of discharge papers in a worn black leather pouch. After wiping away any sign of tears, she gathered up a few of her mother's good china cups, which had been kept just for company, and these she wrapped in a few ragged linens that her father had on his bed. She hadn't expected to find too many treasures, but there, under some old blankets, was a silk baby quilt, as soft and fluffy as the last time she had seen it. A few corners of the green and pink paisley-patterned silk quilt were frayed, but she didn't care.

By the time she was finished packing the trunk, it was too heavy for her to move. She went down to the street and found two men willing to load it on to a hansom cab. Then she returned to pay for the rest of Philip's rent and the doctor, who would be returning for his fee the next day. After getting the address of the morgue where Philip's body was resting, Kate bid her father's old roommate goodbye and left 113 Maroon Street for the last time.

She saw her father buried at Ilford Cemetery and had some cards printed up with his death notice. These she sent to friends and relatives in her spare time. Kate wondered if her Grandmother Pepper would acknowledge the notice or not. Kate knew that her mother's brothers' and sisters' families would keep her grandmother busy, but Kate just hoped that she could stop taking in laundry now that she had remarried. Then her rough, red hands might heal.

II

London, England, 1907

Kate was delighted to hear John and Ada had a second daughter, Harriet Florence, born on August 24. Then Charlotte and Frederick had their sixth child, Evelyn Clementina, after the Christmas holiday. With each birth, Kate became more and more determined to get back to Canada and find training as a nurse.

She found it harder to be with friends on her half-day off. She hardly had time to attend worship on Sundays, and this troubled her. Her friends had begun to marry and have their own children, but she was waiting to save enough money to cross the ocean to join all her living brothers and sisters. Since her father had died and her mother's family was all settled, she frequently thought about her siblings and the Puckering farm and girls, as well as the plentiful food.

Kate dutifully and carefully saved some money from her positions as domestic servant and governess. She made plans and then sailed for a second time to Canada. She was delighted to see her brother and Ada's four girls, born about two years apart. Annie Willard was only a few months' old when Kate first saw her.

Reva, Ada, Ethel Puckering

PART SEVEN

Kate Summers
Leonard, Puckering
F A M I L I E S

forty-four

Beverley Street Nursing Mission, Toronto, Canada, 1910

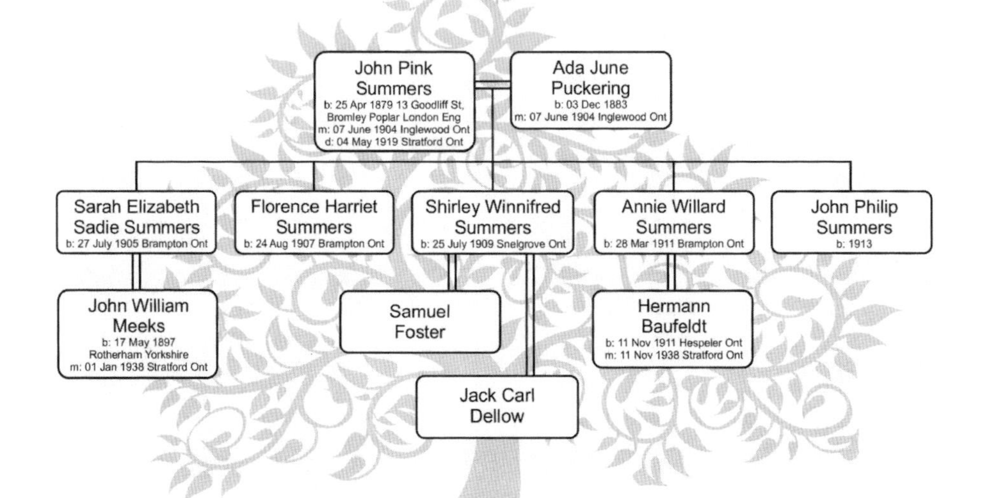

John Pink Summers

Kate realized that the general public heard a great deal about the public lives of men like Goldwin Smith, but perhaps few knew about their private lives. The mission was at 55 Beverley Street, opposite the church, and Goldwin Smith's was on the northeast side. Kate was among the district nurses who benefited from the support of Goldwin Smith. He was at all times doing something for or entertaining the mission nurses.

Goldwin Smith was a retired tutor to King Edward VII, and on his return to Canada, he married a widow living at the Grange on Grange Avenue. He felt at home there because it was much like the English style. Walls surrounded all the grounds, and his staff had their lodges on the grounds.

Each month, Kate and the other nurses would receive an invitation to tea at his home, and it was always understood that they would wear their uniforms. How he enjoyed seeing the uniforms! So two by two the nurses would go to be admitted by his servery housekeeper. At the time, Smith's health was such that he could not receive the young women himself but would shake their hands and then leave them. He became too weak to see them at all, but they were still invited to be served tea from royal cups, royal silver spoons, and plates, all from Buckingham Palace. Kate recalled the times she had been served with a royal tea service in England at the home of her Sunday school teacher.

Goldwin's health was rapidly failing. He had to have two nurses, and of course, one of these had to be a mission nurse.

II

"Did you hear, Kate?" asked a fellow nurse. "Mr. Smith's will has been read, and he left $5,000 to the mission and the request that, before his body is viewed by the public, we, the mission nurses, are to go first for viewing. What do you think?"

Excitement crept into their voices, dissipating some of their grief at having lost such a kind patron. "That is quite the honour. Goldwin Smith must have thought very highly of the mission to do that."

"Yes, and not only that, but we are to have time to view the Grange's rooms first; then after the viewing we are to have afternoon tea."

"That was so kind of him, but it will be sad that it will be the last afternoon tea at the Grange, now that he's passed on," reflected Kate.

Later, the nurses from the mission went over to the Grange at the appointed time, two by two as always and in their spotless uniforms. The housekeeper invited them in, and the butler led them from room to room.

"Oh, my!" exclaimed Susan. "Look at the silver and china setting used by King Edward."

"Look," one of the others said, "there's the golden chair that was used by King Edward."

"Each one of you is invited to sit in that chair for five minutes, if you wish," smiled the butler, pleased with their awe and respect for these items that had been roped off from the general public. Each girl took her turn in the chair, wishing that a photographer might capture her image in this unusual and special situation.

After a somber viewing of Goldwin Smith, the girls were led to a sitting room for their tea. Once they finished, public viewing was to begin. The nurses returned to their residence, quietly discussing the honour bestowed on them.

III

In February of 1911, Kate found a small package delivered to her residence. It was a book of poetry. She opened the cover and read, "To my little nurse as a token of gratitude from Mrs. George Scott / To Miss Summers." Kate carefully thumbed through the pages and then held it to her chest, thinking of the dear woman, who had fought illness with such determination that she recuperated against the odds.

IV

The eight young nursing women were in residence, where they received their board as well as eight dollars a month. The area around University Avenue and Elizabeth Street in Toronto, as well as the surrounding districts, was dirty and poverty stricken with struggling immigrant families. The nurses went to homes where, after cleaning up, they assisted at confinements, circumcisions, tonsillectomies, and many operations, especially for women. In spite of the poor conditions, Kate could not recall the superintendent ever having to sign a death certificate. Kate attended eighty confinements, the mothers receiving as much care as the newborn.

"Well, so this is the eightieth confinement you have attended, did you say?" asked Doctor Baker.

"Yes, it is, sir," replied Kate, somewhat proudly.

"Well, I have attended one hundred and ninety confinements…and only been paid for ninety."

Kate eyed him with respect and continued cleaning up the birth remains. She was anxious to be done in time to clean herself up before going to dinner with Dr. Clutterbuck and his wife, who was also a nurse.

She and Susan arrived at the door of the doctor's house and turned the brass bell ringer. Mrs. Clutterbuck answered the door and welcomed them.

The dinner was a pleasant change for the girls, and the conversation got around to Kate's situation.

"How long have you been in Canada?" asked the doctor.

"Just over a year," answered Kate. "I have always wanted to be a nurse and was given the opportunity to work at the mission last year."

"You enjoy the work, then?"

"Oh, yes. I have had so many experiences and truly wish to become a qualified nurse."

"Well, young lady, my advice to you would be to go to a hospital and train where you can get your certificate."

"That would be a splendid idea," agreed his wife. "You can always come back to the mission if it is in your heart."

forty-five

Toronto, Ontario, 1912

Kate entered the Toronto Hospital at Weston, which was a training school for nurses. Here she spent two years. Then she went for one year to the Bellevue and Allied Hospitals in New York, New York. There were all types of training, such as obstetrics, surgery, and tuberculosis training. Weston was a T. B. hospital, but many of the women who became pregnant after they left the hospital would come back for special care in the delivery of their babies. They would stay in the Davis cottage, where there was a wonderful nursery. This was a three-month stay to ensure that the baby had a good start in life.

Kate never mentioned her "secret" training at the mission or the knowledge she had gained there, because she had been advised not to mention that she knew anything.

Dr. Dobbie was quick to notice a student's interest and took great pride in this work at Weston. The student nurses received eight dollars per month as well as uniforms, room, and board.

Kate would often be found off in a corner studying. She was so thrilled to have the chance to become a nurse that whenever she could she studied and read. When it came to physical studies of the heart, liver, lungs, and other organs, just reading about them was not enough for Kate.

"Mr. Reid's Butcher Shop," the cheerful neighbourhood butcher would say. "How may I help you?"

"Mr. Reid, this is Kate Summers. Do you think you could save me a lung sometime today?"

"Oh, you didn't want to get to the heart of the matter, eh?" he would joke. He knew Kate well and always managed to save a good specimen for her to purchase and study.

Kate studied at the Fordham General Hospital in the Bronx, New York, from October 1913 through August 1914. Even in her maternity medical course with M. J. Maloney, she was considered above average. It had been the most difficult one to complete because of her own throat illness. Miss Tibbits still considered her ability, tact, deportment, neatness, and practical work above average, though, and her observance of regulations to be far above average. She did very well in the practical nursing and childhood diseases, but her real thrill and capability shone in obstetrics.

"Well, Kate Summers, can't we persuade you to stay here and work in the New York hospitals?"

"Oh, Miss Jones, I appreciate the offer, but my family is in Ontario, and I would like to be closer to them." She shook the hands of the superintendent of nurses and the general superintendent of the hospital firmly goodbye.

II

In April of 1912, Frederick Leonard received news of his stepfather's death.

Dear Fred, Charlotte, and children:
I am writing to inform you that Samuel has passed away. I knew you would not be able to attend the funeral because it had to be Wednesday last week. He was more of a father to you and William than your own birth father, and I am so saddened by his passing, I can hardly function. He had been out fishing with friends; you know how the men liked to visit down by the river, and he was cleaning the mudcats that they caught. One of the barbs must have caught in his hand, and it started swelling so badly that after a couple of days he had to be taken to Kingston General Hospital, but they could do nothing for him, and after six days of a very painful delirium, he died. I have enclosed the obituary from page 8 of the April 5 Napanee Express. I hope you understand my not informing you sooner, but everyone has kept us so busy with bringing food and well-wishes, I could not find time to write. I hope to see you and the children sometime this summer for a holiday away from the hot city.
Your loving mother,
Emma

Bellevue And Allied Hospitals, The Bronx, New York, August 1914

"Miss Summers, congratulations on your strong work. Here is your mark sheet to take to the registrar at the Toronto Free Hospital. You will see that your record of standing is far above average, and we will be sorry to lose you. I'm not sure why your rating for medical terminology was only seventy-five, but perhaps you didn't have the opportunity to study Latin?"

"No, Miss Tibbits, I did not have the opportunity, as I was taken out of school at that time to look after my mother. We didn't study languages after that."

"Well, I can see you will make a fine nurse. All the best to you back in Canada."

Kate was left to ponder her mark sheet for a few moments while the other girls received their reports. Their bags were packed ready to return to Toronto via the T, H and B—the Toronto, Hamilton, and Buffalo line. There was yet another year to complete before she would be finished her training, but she felt gratified that she had used some of her savings to take the course.

II

"Dear Kate," wrote her brother Walter at the end of the year.

> *I have gone to Melville, Saskatchewan, and enlisted for the war. I think it will be a bigger war than any the modern world has seen. I enjoy the farming and fresh air out here and have my own small piece of land but will rent it while I go to help the boys in the homeland. Keep yourself well. I don't expect there will be any of the fighting come over this far, or even as far as the east coast of Canada.*
> *All the best, Walter*

forty-six

Brampton, Peel County, and Brantford, Brant, Ontario, February 1915

Kate Summers – Registered Nurse

This was the first time in her life that she'd had a photo taken at a studio. Kate was so proud of her achievements. It had taken thirty-four years of her life to reach this goal, and she felt she could afford the extravagance of a portrait. She pulled her dark hair up behind her head in a tidy bun, but small curls and tendrils were jumping out all over with each bit of breeze. Her dress was a soft off-white crepe, high collared with a frill around her neck.

"Oh, Kate. You just need these choker pearls to enhance your lovely long neck!" Ethel exclaimed. "Your dress is beautiful."

"You do look beautiful," agreed Ada as she fluffed the gathers of lace that edged the shawl-like upper bodice around her shoulders.

"It's such a delicate little flower in the print. It almost looks like a wedding dress," teased Ethel.

"Well, with all the hard work to get this diploma, I am not about to waste it getting married," replied Kate sadly, but laughing as well. She could hardly believe how her dream had come true.

"You must be very proud of your accomplishments. Papa would have been so pleased. You know you were his favourite?" teased John, joking to keep the tears back.

"The girls will be delighted with a copy, if you will give them one too," beamed Ada. They were all thrilled with the moment.

II

After graduation in 1915, Kate accepted the position of head nurse of the Brantford Sanatorium, successor to Miss A. Cringle. Mr. E. L. Cockshutt had donated a tract of land called Strawberry Hill, where the new two-storey brick building with wide verandas was built. The beds could be rolled outside easily. The best cure at the time for T. B. was fresh air—summer, fall, winter, and spring. Patients were bundled according to the weather and encouraged to breathe deeply.

"All right, everyone! Get ready to say a big cheese! Please! Here we go. One. Two. Three!" The camera shutter clicked, although it and the photographer were so far away from the building that everyone wondered how they would be seen. Three weeks later, very clear large copies were distributed to the staff. A copy had already been printed in the local newspaper.

Kate enjoyed the small number of patients at her hospital, as she liked to refer to it. Everything was so new that things were easy to keep clean and organized. None of the patients was particularly difficult, and all hoped for a full recovery.

III

Kate kept busy, and once every three months she had a quick visit with her brother John and sister-in-law Ada and their five children, who now lived in Stratford.

"How do you like the railway work, John?" Kate asked.

"It really is fine. They have a pension, you know, and the work is steady. This is a booming town. How do you like our new house here at 28 Crooks Street?"

"I think it's just beautiful. The entrance on the corner the way it is makes it quite remarkable along the street. Stratford seems to be a very busy town."

"They did a grand job on the city hall, didn't they?" piped in Ada as they walked past the impressive red sandstone building that dominated the town square.

"Stratford is quite a central location for all the trains and transport for this southern part of Ontario. There are enough large homes in the area to prove that business is booming. What say we take the children for a walk this evening, and we can show you the river and station and stores?"

It was a lovely evening, and the streets had quieted. John Philip was asleep in the perambulator, and Willard was nearly asleep on her feet, but the entire family enjoyed what they knew to be a special time that they would remember. Their Aunt Kate was always cheerful and gave each one special attention.

IV

Brant Sanatorium, Brantford, Ontario, July 3, 1916

Late this night was one of those hectic times when night duty becomes a nightmare. The storm began at 12:30 a.m., reaching its peak at 2:30 a.m. After going room to room, closing approximately thirty windows, Kate then moved downstairs to close more windows and comfort the women. They were terrified when a clap of thunder sounded so close that the windows shook. Then the lights went out.

Kate found her way to where the lanterns were kept. She filled one with oil, lit it, and then filled some others, which she carried to stairwells and down hallways. She took time to check the very sick patients in private rooms.

By 4:00 a.m. the rain had subsided enough to reopen most of the windows. Kate noticed that her uniform was soaking wet, but she went into the office hoping to make a cup of tea. The phone rang, and after dealing with the caller, she turned to find a man behind her moving his lips but not making a sound. Kate recognized the man as the one from the boiler room. She brought him into the office.

"What's your trouble?" she asked.

"Nurse, will you please call these three numbers?" he asked.

Kate had dialed the third number before she got an answer. It was the engineer. "A man wishes to speak to you," Kate said and handed over the phone to the man from the boiler room. The power had gone off, paralyzing the lifts, food conveyor, and other important things in a hospital.

Kate sat down thirty minutes later, hoping to be able to get to work. She had many duties besides the patients. One thing she needed to do was get rid of the tiny green flies that came in everywhere.

forty-seven

Ontario to London, England, 1916

London was being bombed by the Germans. Kate decided to go to Britain to help with the war effort since it hadn't finished in the short time everyone had previously thought. She had no idea that her brother Walter was seriously wounded; word from her brother John only reached her afterwards. Letters were not easy to send during this time. She had no specific location in mind but knew they were looking for nurses. If she had to go to the front line, she would. She found passage aboard a navy steamer that was taking volunteer medical staff.

She was directed to a military hospital in the south area of London and was fortunate in finding transportation in an ambulance headed to the hospital. The hospital was really a makeshift ward in a large mansion, and she was directed to the recruiting desk in the estate's magnificent hallway, which could not easily be disguised.

"What qualifications do you have, ma'am?" she was asked.

"I had fifteen months of training at a nursing mission in Toronto, and then I received my certificate after three years at Toronto Weston and Bellevue hospitals in New York City. Here's a copy. For the past eighteen months, I have been head nurse at the Brant Sanatorium, Brantford, Ontario. I just couldn't stop thinking about how many would need nursing care."

"We're happy to have you. Matron on the second floor will direct you to where the nursing sisters are to begin." The desk sergeant indicated a wide set of stairs leading to the crowded ward on the second floor.

Her time at the T. B. hospital had not prepared Kate for the open infections, amputations, and burn wounds among the young men. Her heart went out to them, but she kept a smiling, confident outlook as she sterilized wounds and stitches, rebandaged short appendages, and took temperatures and pulses. Kate recognized fear and despair in many of their eyes.

"You remind me of my younger brother," she said, too many times. They were too young for the depths of their physical and spiritual pain. She did her best to cheer them up. She would make up little rhymes like "The Thermometer":

I am a little thermometer
So thin and frail they say;
They make my bed of absorbent cotton
And carry me on a tray.
The house I live in
Is made of glass
With black markings
That do not last.
I am supposed to be someone of renown
But when I am down they run me up,
And when I am up they shake me down;
So more often, I'm like a clown.
For long hours each night
My pals and I are soaked
In that nasty stuff they call "greensoap."
Then we are rinsed in sterile water, wiped for sure,
Because this is the perfect way to take the "cure."
Should the water be a little warm,
It is then I create a storm.
The nurse calls, "This thermometer registers 105!
Are you sure the patient is still alive?"
Then I laugh and say, "Hee, hee,
'Twas the warm water did that to me."
Should I strike a table or a chair
My mercury starts rolling everywhere;
Then I laugh again and say, "Tee Hee,"
Because the nurse pays ten pence for me!

III

In January 1917, Kate could not stop coughing. Her chest hurt, particularly on the left side, and her temperature was causing beads of perspiration to collect on her forehead and along her collar. As she finished making Mr. Simon's bed, Kate thought she would report to Matron. Suddenly she collapsed, crumpling on the floor.

"Miss Summers! Summers! Are you all right?" asked Matron, forcing Kate to sit up where she was on the floor. Two nursing sisters gathered her under her arms and half carried, half dragged her into the sitting room, where a doctor could examine her.

"You are not going to like this, Miss Summers, but there's nothing I can do about it. You have pleurisy, mainly on the left lung, but it's reaching to the right as well. Do you have relatives anywhere in England?" the doctor asked.

"No, no one here; they're in Canada," Kate whispered as loudly as she could. It hurt her to breathe, and her fever was making her head cloudy.

"Well, we'll take care of you here until the worst of the fever is gone, but I think you will need to go to a dryer climate to fully recuperate," the doctor informed her.

Kate's head drooped. She had hoped to be of more use in this war, and now here she had to be looked after, but she knew as well as the doctor that England's dampness in winter would not be conducive to regaining her health. The war was not even over, and she would be sent back to Canada as soon as she was able to travel.

forty-eight

London, England, to Canada, February 1917

"Please take this onboard as well," Kate asked the porter. She hoped he would find her room. The ship was large, but because of the war there were only twenty passengers travelling on the RMS Ausonia. She carried her handbag up the gangplank, keeping the shawl blanket around her shoulders and neck to keep the raw wind from chilling her. Despite the pain in her left lung, Kate felt a thrill to be boarding a ship. The busy London port was filled with ships of all sizes. Some were merchant ships, but the majority was naval and carried troops or weapons. It seemed such a short time ago that she had landed, fully intending to stay, nursing the wounded until the end of the war. She now turned briefly to the shore, wondering how many times her father had left this dock, headed out to sea for six months or a year.

London looked sleepy. Few lights were on, although there was activity on the streets and on the docks. The dawn was just beginning to lighten the cold fog, which had been creeping in from the River Thames. Perhaps this was safer than a clear day, thought Kate as she turned to locate her room. Downstairs and through a corridor she wandered, looking for the room number matching the one stamped on her ticket. Finding it, she turned the key in the lock, opened the narrow door, and there was her luggage.

On the desk beside the lamp was a little booklet. "Europe…America" was printed across the top in blue and "Cunard Line" across the bottom. A fancy gold frame surrounded the coloured sketch of a tall sailing ship. Inside the first page, seventeen services from and to various ports of call were listed. She turned to find on the next page, "Information for Passengers," which she read thoroughly. Meals were to be served in the "saloon." Breakfast was at 8:00 a.m., luncheon at 1 p.m., and dinner at 6:30 p.m. She would have no need to go to the bar and smoke room, which stayed open until 11:00 p.m. She had reserved a seat at the dining table ahead, as suggested, but she had not insured her baggage, as there was little of value in it. Her fellow diners might get tired of the two suitable outfits she had with her, but she had had no need of them in the hospitals.

On the next page the cabin passengers were listed. Under Captain D. S. Miller were the chief engineer, surgeon, chief steward, chief officer, the purser, and the assistant purser. The next line indicated the ship would be travelling from London to New York, via Halifax. The passengers at her table were Mrs. J. Craig, Mr. Harry A. Ives, Mr. Frank P. Larson, and herself, Miss K. B. Summers. She hoped the ship would have a smooth sailing, recalling her first voyage to Canada in 1904.

Kate turned the page and found the additional names of Mr. Miroljab Todorvich, Mrs. L. C. Wilson, and Miss L. C. Wilson. Six other passengers' names had been added in ink, bringing the cabin passengers up to thirteen. Third class had seven unnamed passengers and a crew of 126.

Kate wondered what third class was like. She had a narrow bunk and a desk where she could stand to see out the porthole. Perhaps third class had no windows, and they didn't eat in the dining room. Today's luncheon and dinner menus were printed up neatly on embossed cards. Oh, Kate thought, I hope I can enjoy eating some of the meals. Of course, if I were not ill, I would not be going home or be on this ship at all. When she surveyed the menus, she realized the ship must stock up in America, because some of the things would not be available in England.

Later that afternoon, Kate sat at her desk polishing a poem:

To Lonely Soldiers
God bless you, soldier lad
Whoever you may be
I wonder where you are to-day,
As I write these lines to thee.
Perhaps you're on the battlefield
Perhaps you're in a trench
Perhaps behind the lines, in camp
Taking rest with a brother French.
Today I've been quite busy
Around the kitchen fire
Making cakes and candy
Trusting this is what you desire.
And if there is something else you'd like
Just write a line and say.
And I will sew, knit, buy, or cook

For you…some other day.
When you eat the middle of the cake
Do not bite too hard
For there you'll find a quarter please
For bacca or cigar.
I trust the box will reach you
And give a tiny bit of cheer
So goodnight, brave soldier lad,
Fighting for "freedom" out there.

Kate stopped again to think of her brother who had been injured, but she didn't know where he was or if he still lived. He had been wounded on June 27, 1916. She thought of the little lad she had led back and forth to school. Of all the children living, he was the one with bluest eyes, but he still had dark curly hair and skin that tanned so quickly in the sun. She wished she knew where he was. She would pack a box as soon as she arrived, and she began thinking of things the boys would enjoy. She fortunately had an old sweater from which to unwind the yarn, and then she could begin knitting a pair of socks.

forty-nine

On the first Sunday, after the divine service at 10:30, Kate thought she would rest in her room until lunch. She had some reading material with her, a few past issues of English nursing papers and, of course, her Bible, but she was so tired she slept until the bell rang for lunch. Most of the table was seated when she arrived.

"Good afternoon, Mrs. Craig, Miss Wilson." Kate smiled and nodded to the gentlemen at the table, who stood while Kate seated herself at the chair the steward pushed in for her. The men had just reseated themselves when the ship shook quite violently. The warning horns sounded but stopped almost immediately.

"My goodemus! Vat vas dat?" exclaimed Mr. Todorvich.

"That, my good man, was a very close call with a torpedo, if I am not mistaken," answered Mr. Hicks. Mr. Kelly nodded in agreement.

"It's all right, dear. It didn't hit. It came close, but it didn't hit," said Mrs. Wilson, putting an arm around her tearful daughter.

"Wow!" exclaimed young Master Wellwood. "That sure was something!" His eyes remained wide open for another few minutes.

"Do you think there is any damage?" asked Kate. "Do you think we were hit, or was that a near miss?"

The chief steward came towards the table with a tray. "There is nothing to worry about, ladies and gentlemen. That was a torpedo fired by a German submarine, but we are far beyond its range now. I'll serve the beverages immediately, if that's all right with you."

Kate bowed her head in prayer, thanking God for their safe delivery. Her thoughts were interrupted as Mrs. Wilson asked, "Could you please say a blessing for all of us, Mr. Larson?"

The others, some of whom were not in the habit of praying, looked side to side and then bowed their heads while Mr. Larson spoke the words of an extended grace and praise of thanksgiving.

The remainder of the trip was uneventful, other than rough seas. There were sightings of a few icebergs, which slowed the voyage, but that was to be expected. Kate found the sea air somewhat refreshing but thought there was still some infection as her lungs pained her when breathing deeply.

She took the train from New York to Buffalo, then to Hamilton and to Stratford. The mission had indicated that she would be travelling to Canada West to open some new nursing mission stations, and Kate saw this as an adventure. She had a few weeks to rest and to prepare herself for nursing in the west.

II

Stratford, Ontario, 1917

Kate was so pleased to be able to get to Stratford, Ontario, by train herself. Her brother, now working for Canadian National Railway as a switchman at the main crossing in town, was able to meet her at the station. She would have a quick visit with John, Ada, and their five children. There really would not be too much space at 28 Crooks Street, but Kate was glad to share a room with the children. She was feeling so much better that it was no longer a concern that she would be spreading the illness.

"Oh, John. You look a little thin. Are you all right?" Kate asked her brother.

"Yes, just fine. Oh, Ada and the Puckering girls are looking forward to seeing you. They all want to share so you can have a room to yourself. And Ethel is coming to town tomorrow to see you, and she's bringing Jessie and her three. Ethel's new husband is the brother of Rebecca's wife, James Olliff. His name is Fred. So all the girls are married now or gone. Poor Young Davis. He has been wandering the streets in Caledonia nearly out of his mind with regret. He found out that he is a T. B. carrier; never showed any symptoms himself, but he figures he is responsible for the death of his three wives, Ada's sisters Diana and Mary Ann included. His son Bill doesn't know what to do for him. You know that Lovell died recently, right?"

"No. I am so sorry for Jessie and her children. She's such a lovely person. Are they staying over or just for the day?"

"Just for the day."

"What is she doing for a living?

"She's taking in boarders and lodgers. Just to warn you, Jessie is expecting a third child in the next two weeks. She just carries on, but it can't be easy. We were all shocked when Lovell died so suddenly."

"I hope she is taking care of herself. She must be exhausted." Kate quietly contemplated the loss of so many of John's in-laws. It must be hard on all of them, but she wondered if John weren't keeping something back from her about his own health.

John carried on, "By the way, I've had a letter from the armed forces to say they have sent Walter back to Canada on the hospital ship Essequito on the 22nd of March. He has had months of recuperation and surgery. He should be in Regina, Saskatchewan, by the time you arrive out there. Are you anywhere near there?"

"I don't know. I'll be in an outpost where there are very few people, never mind hospitals. There are few doctors too. Did they say what the extent of his injuries was?"

"Well, I don't understand the terms, but the wound was caused by shrapnel on the left side of the sacrum, and there's a wound in the sacral region that's still not healed," reported John.

Kate was immediately concerned. She knew he would not be able to sit for a long time. It would be a horribly humiliating type of injury, and he would have to have a special sack that would collect solid wastes. Constipation might be a problem too. "Did they say he had any type of sack? How was he injured there anyway?"

"Apparently, from the letter I got from him, he was diving into a foxhole when he was hit. Two of his buddies were killed during the same firing. He felt fortunate to be alive, but I think he has suffered a great deal since. He had a colostomy, and that wound has healed."

"I must write to him, if you can let me have his address. Perhaps I may be able to visit him when I have time off, if it's not too far. I don't know how far north the trains go. But now, tell me about the family. I can't wait to see how much the children have grown and to see Ada again."

fifty

Saskatchewan, Canada, 1917

Leaving Union Station, Kate prepared to travel the long journey to Winnipeg on her own.

"Oh, excuse me, please. I am sorry to bump you," apologized a young woman.

"That's perfectly all right. The train certainly is jostling at the moment."

The young woman appeared to hesitate and looked uncomfortable as well as a little nervous.

"They say the muskeg is worst in the spring and makes the ride interesting. The freezing temperatures and thaw of this boggy ground must be a challenge for the railway men. Are you going to eat alone?" Kate asked.

"I would be, unless you would allow me to join you..." answered the young woman.

After introductions, during which Kate discovered that the other young woman was a graduate of the Hayter Street Mission, they planned to share a room when they arrived in Winnipeg. Kate would be going on in a day or so to Fairlight on the Regina train, while the other young woman was going to take up mission work in Winnipeg.

The trip to Fairlight was interesting at first, then monotonous, but gradually, as time passed, the realization of how isolated they were began to settle on Kate. There was only one man on the coach. He was loaded up with a whole variety of things, making Kate think that he was going to homestead. Kate's friends in Toronto had packed her a club bag with sandwiches and a bottle of grape juice. She now thought she would like to eat one of the sandwiches.

"Oh, no!" exclaimed Kate. As she took the first bite of the sandwich, the grape juice bubbled up and all over her sandwiches, which she was obliged to throw away. She had spent all her time looking out the window but now glanced at the man, who was watching her. She turned away with embarrassment when she saw the fellow had tears in his eyes. He must have felt sorry for her, knowing how she probably had been looking forward to the lunch. He might have guessed, too, how lonely she was, as he, being a single homesteader, was also lonely.

Kate, in her new navy blue suit, navy hat, black Oxfords, and kid gloves, got off the train looking like twenty years old. She carried her bag and a mandolin, which she had been learning to play. The moss green cloth cover of the case was held together with leather straps, and inside, the bowl mandolin with mother-of-pearl inlay nestled in the red felt lining. It was one of the few items she purchased wholly for herself that wasn't useful.

On the station platform, a small group of women was standing, waiting to greet the new district nurse. Observing this well-dressed petite youngster, they tried to contain their surprise, but one or two stepped aside to whisper something to the others.

Their surprise at Kate's appearance did not equal Kate's surprise at what was supposed to be her bedroom. Kate dropped her bag on the floor.

"Thank you very much," Kate forced herself to say to the woman who had shown her the way to her room. She surveyed the tiny room in a glance—an old iron bedstead, one rickety table, one chair with a broken ring, a black and rusty stove pipe coming up from the kitchen for heat, and last, but not least, a bed chamber with no handle. The only thing that kept Kate from turning back to return the way she had come was that they had purchased a new mattress. This was to be her boarding house.

The wife made supper, but Kate couldn't make herself eat it. She then went up to bed, but not to sleep. She just lay there and sobbed her heart out, not realizing that there was only a thin wallboard between the rooms. Of the three bedrooms, Kate's was the only one with a door. The others had curtains.

II

It was no wonder that the rest were staring at her when she went down for breakfast the next morning. Having heard her crying during the night, they were surprised to see Kate in a blue uniform with white collar and cuffs, looking calm and smart and ready for duty.

Kate had her first case within the hour after eating.

"Mason, could you see about getting a doctor here? I'm not sure that I can stitch up this wound. He's losing a great deal of blood."

Kate was annoyed to see the man stand there without making any effort to move. "Come on, man. Get a move on."

"Well, there be no doctor within two days travel by wagon. Nearest is Doc Neeley, who's twenty-five miles away. Jason here could bleed to death."

Kate stood still for thirty seconds, in shock. Of course, she would have to clean up the wound and stitch it up. That was why there were all those supplies in the kit she was given. "Go and get some water boiling, please, then. I have to sterilize some things. Oh, and bring some clean flannelette pieces." Jason moaned from within the room, and Kate added, "Bring a tumbler of some spirits for him to drink while I work."

The young man's cut was a wide and deep gash, ragged on the sides from the blade of the saw. Kate prepared to do the stitching because there was no choice. Delivering babies did not intimidate Kate like abscesses or broken limbs where bone had broken the skin, but she learned to deal with most emergencies. Her work in the ward of the soldiers' hospital in England had prepared her for many of the gruesome injuries she faced in the isolated West. The smells could be the worst. She often had to clean up some part of the house to be able to function in the soddy or log cabin of the homesteaders where injuries, births, and deaths took place.

fifty-one

Kate Summers in northern Saskatchewan

A NUMBER OF MONTHS LATER, KATE RECEIVED A LETTER FROM THE MISSION.

Dear Miss Summers,
We understand from the town representative that you have done an admirable job in setting up a temporary nursing station, that the supplies are well organized, and that you are becoming skilled at many of your new duties. It will please you to know that we value your experience and wish your move on to open another nursing station closer to James Bay. Please send a list of supplies that you will need to take with you to open a new station. We will send these with your replacement in Fairlight. Thank you for your wonderful service.
God bless you…

II

Kate learned to ride a horse well. She loved the animals, but riding one had never entered her mind until she realized the distances she would need to go to see very ill patients. She often had to borrow a horse from the neighbouring farm, and she never knew what its personality might be. At times, her nursing bag would be flopping up and down rather violently, and bottles of medicine would be well shaken by the time she arrived at her patient's lodging.

III

Kate opened a letter from her brother in December of 1918. She was shocked at the news about the war. There were some families who had sent sons to war, but mostly they were needed on the farms, so she didn't know anyone who had lost someone.

"What are you reading that's made you so sad?" asked her present landlady.

"Oh, sad news from my brother. His wife's nephew, just twenty-two years old, was killed on the 6th of November, last month. Robert Oscar Andrews had only signed up in April, and now he's dead."

"Did they say where he died?" Mrs. Wheaton asked.

"In battle in France, they believe. The 1st Central Ontario Regiment was with the 75th Battalion when they heard last. Oh, they must be sad to lose such a young man. He hadn't married yet…" Kate's voice dropped off as she remembered that her landlady had been left a widow less than a year ago, and she had been left in this northern climate on a farm with three small children to raise. Despite the challenges, she did an admirable job of coping.

Mrs. Wheaton carried on. "There are so many that have been killed, but I understand the Spanish flu is getting many, both ours and the Germans. Thank goodness we won't be getting in contact with that, like they are in some of the cities."

Kate did not reply that it would only take one wounded soldier returning to the area to carry and spread the disease. She hoped that was one thing she would not have to cope with. Pregnancies, births, gunshot wounds, general childhood disease, outbreaks of small pox, and injuries from falls and axes and other farm equipment were all she thought she could cope with. She stitched cuts, set broken bones, and even pulled a few teeth that were causing abscesses. No need to add to the list.

The group of homes at a crossroads several miles away was proving a challenge for Kate.

"Mrs. R., how are you today?"

Kate's inquiry was met with a stoic, expressionless look on the woman's face. Her well-worn dress hung limply from her sunken shoulders, and her baby lethargically looked straight ahead.

"Have you eaten today, Mrs. R?" Kate asked, making motions of eating, not being sure she was understood. The woman shook her head slowly side to side. "Has your husband left you any animal bones?" Kate asked. The woman pointed to the shed. Kate wondered if the flies had yet devoured it or if it might still be good. She went out to the shed, and once her eyes adjusted to the darkness, she could see the remains of the carcass and two knucklebones. They still felt moist and fairly fresh. Perhaps the husband had slaughtered the last pig just within the last few hours. No doubt, the missus and two children would see none of the benefits of it. Mr. R. would have consumed payment in spirits before he returned home in the next week. She would have to help the mother and two children with making food and cleaning up somewhat so that there would be less chance of infection.

"Do you have a pot, Mrs. R?" asked Kate, holding up the nearly nude pieces of bone. She would boil them until all the goodness from the marrow could be brought out into the broth. Perhaps there was an onion or potato they could use. What the family needed was nutritious food. They were nearly starving, and the husband was not working regularly. He probably could only get a few days here and there because his employers would find out about his drinking habits.

Once the pot was boiling, Kate brought the woman outside to where some greens grew in the wild. "Pick these, Mrs. R.," Kate instructed her. "Chop them up for the soup."

Mrs. R. pointed to what had been the start of a garden. Kate could see a few plants among the grass. She looked at what might be potato plants, and as she brushed aside the grass, she saw a small bunch of potatoes, but they were very green. Mrs. R. hoisted the baby onto her hip and pulled them up.

"No!" Kate said firmly. "Bad for you," and she made a vomiting motion.

Mrs. R tried to pull the plant away from Kate but was too late. Kate had swung the plant out into the field as far as she could. Mrs. R. looked about to break into tears, but Kate knew the green part of a potato would make them sick. She showed Mrs. R. other leafy plants that could go in the soup and then brought them inside. The stock smelled good, and once the bone was out and cooled, she let the baby gnaw on it. She could work her gums and help with the teething process and also get any morsel of meat off the bone. Kate set a bar of soap by the washbasin and left, with Mrs. R. thanking her in some foreign language.

IV

Bancroft, Ontario, 1918

Bancroft was the next place for Kate to go and organize a medical clinic. There was a doctor available and another nurse to assist with the town and surrounding farms in this rugged part of Northern Ontario.

Only one road went south, and Kate thought more and more about heading down it, back to civilization. She thought of the contents of her trunk, which she had left with her brother. There were some good dishes, linens, the silk baby quilt, and at least two fine dresses that she didn't think she would need. Kate thought fondly of the teas she had attended with the mission nurses, of their camaraderie, of the sounds of life in the city. By the time she got notice of her brother's illness, she was ready to leave. The west had cured her pleurisy but made her long for closer humanity.

fifty-two

Stratford, Ontario, 1919

Ada realized her husband was very ill. She said nothing to the children, even fourteen-year-old Sadie. She wrote to her sisters-in-law, Kate and Clemmie, that they should prepare themselves, as he had tuberculosis of the bowel. John made several trips to General Hospital in Stratford and spent a few days each time.

Early morning on the 4th of May, Ada sat up in bed and looked at John. His dark eyes pleaded forgiveness and a knowing sadness.

"I'll get the children up and get help. Just try to rest easy." Ada turned to hide her tears from John, and then she started Sadie and Florence on making breakfast. Ada went to get the neighbour to help transport John to the General as soon as possible. He was in so much pain.

Shirley, Willard, and John Junior stood together while Ada, Florence, and the neighbour helped half-lift, half-carry John out to the neighbour's car. There were no telephones in the house. That was a luxury they could not afford.

Sarah, the oldest Summers girl, was fondly known as Sadie. She fixed the oatmeal for breakfast and made sure the others drank their milk. They got bread and butter for lunch to take to school, and she herded them off.

Willard wondered why no one had said anything about their being late for school. The teachers just nodded them into the room, and they took their places. They would usually get in trouble, but maybe her mother had sent a message. It had been a rather mixed-up morning with their father having to go to the hospital. She wished she could go and visit him like Sadie and Florence did, but she guessed she was just too young to go.

Sadie hurried in the direction of the hospital. She knew her father was dying, just as Mr. Meeks in the next bed was dying. Maybe it was more quickly, though, because John Meeks, the son, never seemed as anxious as she was now.

The head nurse intercepted her as she headed to the green double doors leading to the ward. "I'm sorry, Miss Sadie, but your mother is in with your father, and I believe they would like a little privacy, just for a few minutes. I will let your mother know you are here when she's ready," and the nurse left

Sadie standing at the door peering at the closed curtain. She wished she had asked Florence to come with her, but Florence would need to finish her school year. Sadie knew that she would likely have to go out to work immediately if her father died.

"There you are, Sadie. Your father is resting now. They gave him something for the pain, and I think we should come back."

"Oh, Mother, can't I just see him, even for an instant?" pleaded Sadie.

Ada looked at her daughter, so full of life and energy. She was close to her father, and two hours might be too late. "Yes, dear. Go in, but try not to disturb him."

Ada waited until Sadie came back out the ward door, tearfully searching for her mother's eyes. Ada took her arm, gently leading her to the outside door.

"We have to be strong, Sadie. Now, no tears. Did the children get off to school all right?"

Sadie nodded and turned, resisting her mother's directing her to leave.

"Sadie, there is nothing more to be done for your father."

II

The funeral procession was large, but only Kate was present out of all John's siblings. Walter and Charlotte were too ill, and there had been no contact with either Florence in Montreal or Philip. It was a beautiful sunny day, but the trees in the cemetery gave shade to the new mound of earth near the river, which had been piled with wreaths and bouquets of flowers. Kate had borrowed a camera and took snaps of the grave itself, but the bent head of her sister-in-law was just too sad to photograph. Kate wondered how Ada could carry on with such strength, but she was just as determined to remain strong so she could comfort the children and be of use. Young John was only six, but he remained quiet and somber throughout the burial.

John Meeks stood discreetly behind the family, but Sadie was well aware of his presence. She had such mixed emotions. Emotion welled up inside her at the sight of him, but the overlying sadness of her father's death tempered any joy she might have felt at this time. She was young, and she knew it, but there was a distinct possibility she and John would become more than friends. She wondered if John had any idea what she was struggling with at the moment.

fifty-three

Toronto, Ontario, May 1919

The discussion had been brief.

"Arthur, there is no need for you to sign up. The war is over. You are too young anyway."

Charlotte agreed with her husband. "Your father is right, Arthur. You should stick with the job for the city."

"Mom, they treat me like a second-class citizen. I get angry when they always give me the hardest and dirtiest jobs. Someday I'm going to say something that will get me fired anyway. I need to try to get into the military. There are still all kinds of cleanup jobs to do in Europe. I might get to see more of the world."

"And you might contract the Spanish flu and die needlessly. Please be reasonable, Arthur," pleaded Frederick.

II

Two days later Arthur went to the recruiting office and signed the attestation papers for the Canadian Overseas Expeditionary Force. He had put down his birthdate of January 8, but to be sure they would take him, he said 1901, making him eighteen, which he looked, not the sixteen years old that he was.

At home, Charlotte was lying down, unwell again. She was trying to rest so the pains would ease, then she would prepare dinner.

"Mother? Where are you?" Arthur gently opened the door to his parents' room to see if his mother was awake. She quickly wiped tears away and asked him in. "What's wrong, Mother? I thought you were going to Uncle John's funeral?"

"I just am not feeling well enough. I'm sure that your Aunt Ada is hurt, thinking I am avoiding the family, but with so many of you children busy looking for work, I just didn't feel up to making the trip."

Charlotte's tears continued to fall as she took Arthur's hand and gave it a squeeze. She had tried so hard over the years to keep the family in contact with one another, updating the office at the Barnardo's School in London, England, but the others were not letter writers, and Florence and Philip had not responded. For some years, she had tried to find out from Barnardo's where they were, but she had no luck with that line of questioning.

"What have you got in your hand?" asked Charlotte, and too late Arthur realized he still had his attestation papers with him. His mother would not like the fact they had signed him up immediately. She would be pleased that he would be stationed at the Brant Hospital in Burlington, helping wounded soldiers improve their mobility. At least it was a start to some training.

III

At times, some of the children went with Frederick to Napanee to visit his mother and stepfather. Emma, his mother, was still young, having been only fifteen when she met George Washington Leonard. After Frederick and William were born, she thought George had gone back to the United States. He had said he was going to look for work on the Erie or Welland Canal, but she never heard from him again. Maybe he had died, or maybe he just went back to the rest of his family.

When Samuel James Howard, a twenty-three-year-old bachelor from the Loyalist town of Bath across from Amherst Island, had proposed to Emma, she joyfully accepted. Emma was still young and beautiful, and Samuel was content to accept Frederick and his brother William as his own. He was the caretaker of the Harvey Warner Park and looked after numerous gardens and lawns.

After Frederick left for Toronto and married, Frederick and Charlotte's oldest son, Earl Charles, stayed with Grandma Emma and Samuel when his sister Edith was born in 1899. A son, Frederick, and then Ruby and Arthur, twins, were born in the next three years, followed by Evelyn four years later. Charlotte tried her best to look after the children, but things were difficult, and her health didn't improve very quickly after the last birth.

After reading her sister-in-law Ada's letter again, Charlotte felt a great sadness overcome her. She had hardly had time to correspond with her brother and his family, really didn't know them, and had no idea how they might respond to her darker skin complexion, nor the fact she had fallen in love with and married a black man. Besides all that, she just could not afford the fare all the way to Stratford.

IV

Toronto, Ontario, October 29, 1919

"Mother! I'm home," called Arthur as he opened the side door to 1171 Dufferin Street.

"In the kitchen, son," answered Charlotte. She turned and exclaimed, "Oh, Arthur! I thought it was Earl Charles coming by from the AB Ormsby shop. How are you? Let me look at you." Charlotte gave him a big hug, then drew him back so she could look at him fully.

Arthur smiled widely, and purposefully.

"Oh, Arthur! You have a gold crown. When did you have that done?"

"Just last week, Mom. I had a bad filling giving me grief, and they filled it with gold. How do I look?"

"Older. You look older, son."

"I wasn't on the front, as you know, but I saw the results of those who were. Truthfully, I have seen as much of the war at the Brant Hospital for Veterans as I want to see. Here are my discharge papers. Let's keep them safe. I might need them to get a job soon."

fifty-four

Toronto, Ontario, 1920–1921

Kate Summers – Victorian Order of Nurses

Kate had taken a position at the Toronto hospital after deciding she would like to experience again the city life. She had been examined and entered The Victorian Order of Nurses for Canada on the eleventh day of April 1918.

"Miss Summers, would you please check on Mr. Smith with the iron lung in room 304. Then the men's wardroom has a new patient, a diabetic, so you need to get his charts brought up to date. You can continue your rounds in there, and I'll get Miss Amberly to cover the women's ward room."

Off went Kate as directed, checking her hat's position. She deliberately felt the black strip at the corners of her stiffly starched cap, a sign of the registered nurse. She was newly thrilled each time she thought of having reached this goal, and she meant to do her very best. She flattened the wide starched bib over her abdomen and then checked for her watch, blood pressure pump, and thermometer.

"Mr. Smith, how are you today?" Kate asked with a smile. She never let on she knew his days were numbered. She did her best to make him comfortable within the restrictions of the huge machine surrounding him. He offered a very weak smile, happy to have a change of scene.

Kate came to the ward doors of the men's unit, being sure her shoes were snuggly tied, her apron was straight, her watch was in place, and a look that meant business was on her face. Once the men had found out she was unmarried, she had had all kinds of offers, mainly from young men. They enjoyed teasing her because she couldn't help herself from smiling at their joking ways. Those who were quiet or asleep were too ill to care what their nurse did until she came to each of them, fluffing pillows, checking their pulse, patting their arms.

Mr. Martin, the new patient, looked on the jaundiced side. Kate wondered how his liver was functioning.

"So, how are we feeling now?" she asked, taking his arm from under the covers to feel his pulse. It was racing. "Have you had any water to drink?" Kate looked at the full glass beside his bed and took it to try making him sip some.

"Will you be looking after me?" Mr. Martin asked.

"I expect so, along with all the others," she answered, shaking her thermometer.

"Then I shall be content to keep on living." He smiled.

His answer surprised Kate, and she made the mistake of looking directly into his admiring eyes. She broke the spell with a businesslike clearing of her throat.

"Please open your mouth, sir, so I may take your temperature."

"And where are you taking it? Will you be taking it with you?" He flirtatiously winked but did open his mouth, relieved it was not a rectal thermometer.

II

Kate worked her daily rounds of twelve-hour shifts. As it was, she attended the men's ward with particularly good humour. It could not have had anything to do with Mr. Martin, because, after all, she would be turning forty in January this coming year, and that was too late to be thinking of changing her marital status, wasn't it?

"Ah, Miss Summers! There you are. Mr. Martin has been pestering me with questions today, and I feel I cannot answer them. You can if you wish; just don't let Matron catch you cavorting with the inmates!"

"Really, Miss Knight, have I ever been known to be anything but professional with the patients?" and Kate smartly strode off towards the ward doors with a smile she was trying to tone down before greeting her patients.

PART EIGHT

Martin FAMILY

fifty-five

Cornwall, England, 1818

The wild Atlantic January seas badgered the rugged coast of Cornwall. The ancient Celts called this Belerim, literally Land's End. The Cornish language and many ancient ways had all but disappeared by the time Henry Martin was born. His parents earned a meagre living by raising stock on the open moors. The smallholdings were divided by several Cornish hedgerows, each solidly built of two rows of dry-stone walls, with earth between. Thick shrubs grew on the top of the walls, providing a sturdy windbreak from the relentless westerlies for the small pastures and the sparse population of western England.

The barren moors had been stripped of any trees by earlier generations, and outcroppings of rock determined the face of the landscape: a wild, thinly covered county of moors, small villages, and centuries-old tin mines.

Henry was not a miner, had no interest in fishing, and years later decided that there wouldn't be much of a life for him farming in Cornwall. He wanted to find a better life for himself, and he decided to take to the new industries in London. This way he could earn enough for future passage to North America.

Though not strictly a Cornish man, Henry did love the country, as it was all he knew. Old Dionysus Penryn had reminded him of the verse "By Tre, Pol, and Pen/ You shall know the Cornish men." This meant, of course, that Martin was not a Cornish name, and his ancestors had come from the Emerald Isle, or elsewhere.

London, England, 1848

Requests to members of Parliament were being made frequently by many merchants, labourers, and starving poor who had moved to England from Ireland even before the death-dealing potato famine. Some wrote on behalf of others; some wrote on behalf of themselves. They had their priests write letters to Parliament. Rumours spread quickly that there was free land available in Canada and Australia, and many had hopes of finding help to emigrate there.

They wrote to their members of Parliament, where their requests for assistance were duly circulated for opinion and submitted to the department for answering.

To the Right Honourable Earl De Grey
My Lord,
In sending the following lines, I express the sentiments of a number of persons who along with myself are most anxiously attempting to devise some means to better our conditions. We are small manufacturers excepting two or three farmers who have small families dependant on average about three children to each family. We have long and ardently looked for a time when without external aid we should be enabled to get an honourable livelihood but have been doomed to utter disappointment and the future seems more dreadful than the past. You are perfectly aware that trade has been in such a state that those who most likely seemed to stand have been born down by the pressure of the times. What then must have been the state of those who were only just capable of keeping afloat in the best of times? Why they have dropped off like rotten branches from the sturdy oak that has been uprooted by the tempest… [Can they not expect some] happiness and plenty… [by supplementing transportation and small parcels of land in Canada]…
Should our expectations prove correct and your Lordship deem it prudent to favour our project we should feel greatly obliged by your advising us on the same and transmitting the conditions as soon as possibly you can.
I am, my Lord,
Your Lordship's most humble servant
Joseph Ineson

Responses

W. Elliot: This is one of, I am afraid, many similar representations of distress which could be made from parts of England—but how to afford relief except by the application of some very expensive measure I have really not the means of stating.
A. B.: The writers describe themselves as chiefly small manufacturers and what they ask is a Grant of Land in Canada. They seem to be under the impression that grants are still made there and also that people were sent out last year by the Government…

In answering letters such as these, a reply from the principal secretary of state was written and sent in return:

> *Downing Street*
> *12 June 1848*
> *Sir,*
> *I am directed by Earl Grey to acknowledge the receipt of your letter of the 27th describing the distress to which you and your neighbours have been reduced by the depression of Trade, and expressing a wish to emigrate to Canada provided the Government will assist you to pay your passage... explain to you that you are mistaken is supposing that at any time this was being offered...unfair to the tax-payers of this country.*
> *The expense of a passage to Australia is about L14 and the expense of outfit bedding at about L6 more making in all L20. The expense for children under 14 years of age is about half...the funds are obtained by the sale of the Crown Lands which are applied to paying the passages of Immigrants for whose labour there is in a very great demand.*
>
> *The Right Honourable Earl Grey*
> *Principal Secretary of State*
> *For the Colonial Department*
> *1 March 1848*[5]

In a letter dated April 13, 1848, William McFertes and Clark Matheson suggested a plan for military families of good character to be sent to Canada, where they would receive less land than the huge tracts given members of Parliament and in return would be ready to be called out for military duty. In this way, they "could have prevented the blood and cost of the Rebellion of 1837."[6]

fifty-six

London, England, 1849

Henry Martin held his two-year-old son tightly as he stared down at the fresh grave. He bid his wife a final goodbye and headed out the gate of the church cemetery. Henry and his son, Edwin William, would board the ship for North America the next day, and in two months or less, if the weather was good, they would arrive in Montreal, Canada. It was a long way from Lands End, Cornwall, where Henry had been born. He had left all that and come to London, married, and had a son.

Before his wife became ill, they had saved almost the amount needed for three passages to Canada, where they could start a new life. Now there was plenty for their fare with just the two of them. He could use any extra to start business or buy land, but there were those who were begging to go with him. The Irish were starving, and many English families were destitute.

II

"Here, sir. Let me help with that bag."

Henry was startled when a fellow his own age jumped the queue onto the ramp ascending to the opening of the ship's hull. The man began to help Henry pull his large, heavy pack along the gangplank, shouldering his own bag.

"Thanks," answered Henry. He had no choice but to allow the assistance of the stranger through passageways to the berths. Crowds were pushing and struggling to get trunks and crates into storage areas while children tugged at parents' hands or struggled with their own burdensome packages.

"Edwin, don't cry. It's just—there are so many people," Henry comforted his son as they were jostled along the deck and down narrow steps into the dark hold where hammocks were hung end to end.

"Name's Robert Morrison of the fine city of Liverpool. Care to get above on deck for some fresh air and a last look at our homeland?"

They climbed a solid wooden ladder to the starboard deck and emerged to cooler air and heavy grey skies. Henry was glad to have someone to talk with.

He had felt empty and lonely since his wife died, and he was somewhat anxious about taking his young son on such a long voyage by himself.

Robert conversed easily and appeared genuinely interested in Edwin and Henry. He, too, was probably lonely.

"What trade do you plan on engaging in when we reach Canada?" Henry asked as they began to enjoy the regular swells of the open sea.

"Well, they say it's a land of many opportunities, and eeeh, I want to try something where I can own a bit of me own land and not be cheated by a rent collector and fat landlord. I can do some carpentry, and even tried my hand at blacksmithery," answered Robert.

"Ah, yes! The land. That's what I wish for too. Since the time I was a small boy in Cornwall, surrounded by the sea, I wanted to own a piece of my own land and grow great crops. My family thought I was getting above myself, but my wife shared my dream, and we worked in London to save for the passage." Henry averted his eyes to the rough planks of the deck to prevent any unwanted tears from appearing. He hugged Edwin, who had barely left his hip.

"Your wife died then?"

Henry nodded. Robert was silent for a moment. "My intended got herself in the family way with another bloke, and then I decided to make a new start. Some women are hard to figure out, but I'm sorry about your wife."

The two men met on deck daily and became fast friends. Time passed more quickly, the yearning for good food lessened, and the fresh air was always better than belowdecks. Gradually little Edwin became accustomed to Robert, allowing him to entertain with ropes and songs. Henry and Robert discovered they were within a year of each other in age and had a common desire to start fresh in the new world.

fifty-seven

Montreal, Canada, 1849

After parting with a handshake and promise to meet up, Robert and Henry joined the crowd surging in toward the railings and gangplank. Henry gripped his son in his left arm while hauling the canvas bag that an old sailor friend had donated to him for their Atlantic crossing. The air was thick with fishy smells, the same as the wharves in London, but the hollering and excitement here was overwhelming. Fishmongers, trades people, and orphan boys dominated the crowd around the arriving ships. Everywhere there was movement as Henry tried to establish his bearings from above, using his uncle's description. Wagons and carriages awkwardly wove their way through the crowds.

Once the gangplank was lowered and ropes as large as Henry's arm harnessed the ship in place, the disembarking passengers surged to the barrier holding them back and shouted to some of those waiting on shore. These greetings were mostly in French, as were the responses, but English could still heard above the din. After he showed his papers to the first mate, Henry gripped Edwin even closer. Edwin, wide-eyed and frightened because of all the cacophony, clung to his father as strongly as a two-year-old possibly could. They moved slowly down the gangplank, everyone stepping carefully over the crosspieces to avoid catapulting forward.

"Henri! Henri! Assai!" bellowed a Frenchman, but Henry was disappointed that the speaker was directing his gaze elsewhere. He could be sure that his Uncle Martin was too busy to meet them at the dock. If he had, he would be puzzled by Sarah's absence, for Henry would be arriving before any notice of his wife's death had reached Canada.

II

Forcing his way through crowded streets just blocks from the dock, Henry stepped into a small grocer's shop that had English signs plastered in the windows. Some light entered through the remaining square panes of dingy glass. The shop was surrounded with shelves and bins of the usual food staples, but there were some root vegetables with which Henry was not familiar.

"Good afternoon, sir. May I be of assistance?" asked an apron-clad young woman from behind a counter at the back of the store.

"Good day, ma'am." Henry hesitantly. Could he ask after his uncle's grocery without offending the young woman?

"I'm looking for the store of my uncle, Henry Martin. Do you know of him?

"Henri Martin? Oui, of course. Are you his nephew from England?"

"Yes, I am, and this is my son Edwin. Can you tell me how to get there, please?"

"Certainly. Is your wife waiting for you somewhere? I can get a cart for your luggage if necessary."

"No, my wife died just before we left England. This is our luggage," Henry explained, lifting the sack, where their entire belongings were in an unsavoury tangle after the weeks at sea with limited facilities.

III

Within days of settling down to help his uncle in the mercantile, Henry met a delightful bright-eyed woman and a sturdy gentleman who entered the store. Henry smiled in greeting, wondering if they would be speaking Upper Canadian French or English. He was relieved to hear them speak English, and his uncle hurried over to introduce them.

"Henry, I wish to introduce you to my good friends, Louisa and her brother Felix Hooper. They are the children of John Hooper, a fellow countryman from Devonport." Henry shook their hands. Just then, little Edwin came waddling over and stood staring at Louisa. His gaze covered every inch of her taffeta dress, short cape, and large bow securing a large-brimmed hat. Then he thrust his arms high to be picked up. Louisa was surprised but delighted and put her parcel down so she could reach for him.

"Oh, I am sorry, ma'am. There is no need for you to pick him up. He is usually quite shy. Perhaps he was thinking of his mother," a blushing Henry managed to blurt out.

"What a sweet little boy. What is your name, young man?" Edwin stared into her gentle eyes but said nothing.

Weeks passed, with frequent visits from Henry and Edwin to the Hoopers' home. There were many lively talks about Lower Canada and the opportunities of owning land and opening business there, instead of the crowded French quarters of old Montreal.

"Edmund and Augustus are doing well for themselves. Augustus has established a mill downstream on the Napanee River from Clark's Mills. He and his wife and son Edmund are building a large stone house in the village of Clark's Mills. Samuel Clark, who built the earlier mills, is the postmaster. At present, our second oldest son, John Douglas, and his wife, Lydia, live in a well-established little hamlet to the west called Newburg. There are rivers available in every town, they say, so mills can be run. The area is tops in farm production in the county, and every description of animal and crop is grown there. They insist we think about joining them," John declared.

"Is there a need for more mercantile stores?" asked Henry.

"Oh, my, yes. I don't know if there is a full mercantile in the village or not, but I believe we could establish one when we got there. Augustus is in the lumber business, and our son Edmund has successfully been running a mill. Douglas and his family are not far away, and there are others who would need the supplies."

PART NINE

Hooper, Martin
FAMILIES

fifty-eight

Canada West, Addington County, 1851–1856

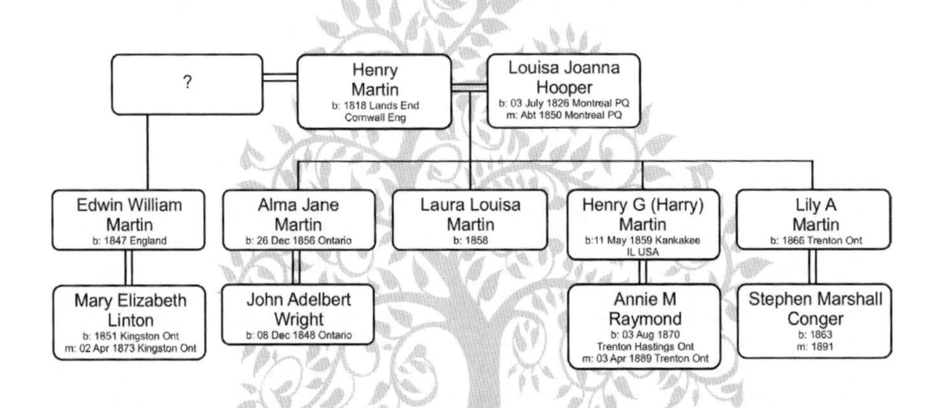

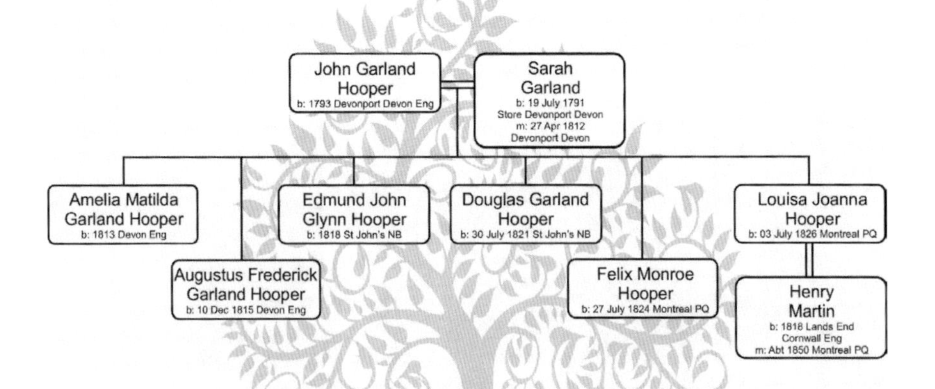

When Henry spoke to John Garland Hooper and his wife, Sarah, about the possibility of marrying Louisa, he was surprised by the ease with which they agreed. The two had watched from a not-so-far distance and had seen Louisa and Henry take to each other from the start. Louisa was a strong-minded young woman, and her parents wanted to see their youngest daughter happily settled.

Although John Hooper had the position of lumber inspector, as well as owning and operating a corner grocery store in Montreal, he was as anxious for new adventure as his sons. Felix, Louisa's brother, had operated the store with John's help, but they quickly sold it for a substantial profit just before they packed up for Lower Canada.

Louisa had grown up with the mixture of French and English, but Henry found it disconcerting, and he happily agreed that he, Edwin, and Louisa would follow her parents and younger brothers to join the older Hooper boys. There was also Aunt Amelia and Henry's friend Robert Morrison, who had shown up on the street one day near Henry Martin's doorstep. They joined the group who were headed to the newly established townships north of Napanee and Trenton.

Henry had wanted to farm, and because he was able to get land near Clark's Mills, Louisa had been doubly pleased to marry him. She left the city of her birth to become a farmer's wife.

II

Louisa was still nervous being left alone so far out in the Camden East township house.

"Edwin! Stay close to the house. I don't want you to be lost." Louisa looked up the grassy lane, hoping to spot Henry returning from town with supplies. They had oats and eggs to sell this time, and she had made quite a list of necessities.

"Edwin, come here to me, please," said Louisa, extending her arms. Edwin was a bit shy with Louisa at times but accepted her as a substitute mother. The move west to Camden Township had been difficult for him. Perhaps time would heal his unsettled early years and the losses he endured.

"Edwin, would you like a piece of bread with your water?" She felt badly, but there was little food in the larder of the one-and-a-half-storey frame house. They indeed needed Henry to return with supplies. The land was fertile but untamed. Each season new weeds appeared and strangled the crops. Henry kept at them. He enjoyed the fresh air and outdoor work, as well as keeping the store in stock, and did not miss the crowded streets of London or the noisy bustle of Montreal.

Henry stopped at the lean-to to tether the horse. Edwin, already in bed by this time, was the first to be aware of Henry's return. "Papa," Edwin shouted as he leapt out of the cot. "He's home, Louisa. I heard him." With that announcement he opened the door to allow Henry inside so he might scramble up his papa's shoulders. Henry managed to greet Louisa with a hug and quick kiss before swinging his son around, holding him tightly by the chest and arm. Edwin loved the feel of his father twirling him around and giggled as they stumbled to the floor in a dizzy heap.

"All right now, Edwin. Off back to bed, and you can talk to your father first thing in the morning."

Edwin obeyed Louisa, and Henry brought in packages from the Kingston Market and then settled down for a late supper. He had already delivered the mercantile supplies to the general stores that he and Edmund managed.

Louisa exclaimed with delight and happily organized the dry goods on the pantry shelves and the perishables in the cellar's cold room.

"Well, Louisa, it looks as though Toronto and Montreal are the two cities in the race to be capital of Upper and Lower Canada. Kingston is now relegated to being a midway trading post. There's been quite some discussion about it. There's also the fact that within months we can expect the Grand Trunk Railroad to connect Kingston with Toronto and Montreal." Henry began eating the poached eggs and toast Louisa had prepared for him. His mouth was already open when Louisa made her announcement.

"We can expect someone else within months as well. I'm in the family way, Henry," and she smiled at his pleased surprise.

"Well, good news," and he stood, awkwardly hugging her, not wanting to squeeze her too tightly but excited at the prospect. There had been no sign of children in the first few years of marriage, and he had wondered whether they would ever have children.

"Your sister-in-law Lydia is not well again. I spoke with Douglas at the general store on my return," said Henry.

"Lydia just hasn't been well since their darling Garland died. If she would eat more, she might gain her strength back," commented Louisa.

fifty-nine

On the highest point of the hill in the northeast corner of town, above the mills and nearly in the centre of the churchyard, John G. Hooper had dug up the sod and placed something on the ground. Louisa had seen a mysterious box being carted to her parents' home, and now curiosity got the better of her. Her father finished planting a tiny yew tree and was leaning on the shovel, head bowed.

"Papa, what are you doing?" Louisa gently called.

"Come and see, Louisa. I hope to put this part of my life to rest at last. Your mother agrees it's time. You see, Louisa, before I was married to your mother, I was married to another young woman. We were fishing off the shore near Plymouth when she nearly drowned. I've always blamed myself, although I don't know exactly what possessed her to stand up so suddenly. A wave came and knocked her overboard. I found her and managed to get her to shore, but she never woke from that coma."

"Oh, Papa. I never knew. How you must have loved her." Louisa gently put her arm around her father's waist as the two stood silently studying the white marble stone: "Isabel Richmond—wife of John G. Hooper—departed this life Sept. 12, 1817—aged 27 yrs. 2 mo."

"Your mother and I will be buried here, and any of the family that wishes. Your Uncle Richard and I have purchased a large plot from St. Luke's here for the entire family." They stood at the top of the hill, studying the village that had become home. John hugged his daughter, and they returned to the house where Sarah quietly waited for them.

II

In the early winter of 1855, Felix Hooper and Henry Martin were brushing a light layer of snow from the front stoop of the mercantile when they saw a blackened, dishevelled figure slowly shuffling along the road from the direction of Fifth Depot Lake.

"Edmund!" exclaimed Felix as the figure got closer. "What happened?"

"A fire." His shoulders drooped in exhaustion.

"Not the saw mill?" asked Henry.

Edmund nodded.

"Had the big order from Napanee been sent on yet, or was it still in…" Felix's question trailed off as Edmund's head bent lower and he shook his head slowly. A great stockpile of lumber, then, had been lost as well as the mill.

"It just went up with a boom. The blades made a spark that hit the dust, and whoosh! It's all gone," Edmund despaired.

"Were any lives lost, Edmund?" asked Henry.

"No, but there could have been. Philip Richards had the sense to jump out the second storey window and only twisted his ankle in the snow."

Mills, especially sawmills, tended to burn down regularly. There was no insurance for them, and this was indeed a catastrophic loss. Henry and Felix put their hands on Edmund's shoulders, sharing his grief.

III

Alma Jane was born the day after Christmas in 1856. There were no midwives in the area, but her mother and aunt came from town, so Louisa had some female support. Her neighbour with three children had been delivered of them by her husband. Henry figured it couldn't be too different from delivering a calf, but he was not prepared for the groans, the cries, and the dripping perspiration. Edwin had been delegated to bringing in the wood. He was fascinated with his tiny new sister. When baby Louisa was born two years later, Edwin was well-prepared to help both inside and outside the house.

Since 1851 Henry and Louisa had owned land and helped her brother Felix run the general store. There were a number of mills along the river; hence it was called Clark's Mills. However, most of them had burned and been rebuilt. Augustus G. Hooper, Louisa's oldest brother, remained settled a few miles to the east at Newburg. He was now post office master for both Newburg and Clark's Mills, ran the mill and lumber businesses, and looked to a career in politics.

By 1857, Augustus Hooper had ownership of the saw mill in Clark's Mills. Edward Hooper and Henry Martin both ran the general store. Douglas Hooper was a company agent for Equitable Firearms and was the International Life Assurance Company agent in Newburg. Felix Hooper, his wife, Mary, and children, John and Eva, made the move to Kingston so that Felix could become the agent there for North British Fire Insurance Company. They enjoyed a charming home on Rideau Street and the town life of a larger centre. Insurance agencies vied for businesses' insurance dollars, particularly when so many buildings in close quarters were made from wood and were at high risk for fire.

IV

"Henry, your tea is ready."

Henry smiled. Tea was a hot drink in Canada, available at great cost. The dried black leaves were compressed into tight wads and used sparingly. Here, Louisa served tea long after a meal so she could get the last dishes tidied up and the babies to bed. Then she could sit on one of the hard wooden chairs and relax for a few minutes. Tonight they had a fire going, and Henry stoked it while adding a few more branches to chase the chill away.

"Louisa, have you read this article here? It's describing Chicago as the largest hub city in the west. Rail lines from Illinois and Michigan run there, and the canal has been serving it since 1848. Besides all that, the city has a busy port. Apparently the land south of there is being sold up quite cheaply so they can get more settlers on the rail lines. What do you think?" Henry made a pretense of asking Louisa, but she knew he had made up his mind.

"When are you thinking of moving? Are you planning to sell this land, or could we rent it out until we see how things are across the border? You would hate to move there and have to take up arms against Canada and our neighbours, wouldn't you?"

"Oh, I think they have other problems now between the north and south with the slavery issue. They won't be turning against Canada at this point in time. It may well be that Canadians will be called to help out the north, but I wouldn't worry. Now is the time to get a hold of land before the price rises. If we pack up in February, we can be settled before the spring planting. What do you think?"

Louisa smiled at Henry's ambition. The house was getting cramped, and Edwin was nearly ten, but Alma was not yet three, and baby Louisa was only a year old. There would be plenty of work in the move, but it would be exciting too.

sixty

Kankakee, Illinois, USA, 1859

Henry had been most impressed with how efficiently the barges carried the carts, horses, and passengers smoothly across the river at Detroit. The Windsor area had many well-established farms owned by the French. These ran from the river separating Detroit and Windsor, out about half a mile, and each of these farms had water from the river, flat land and fertile soil. As Henry and his family drove the cart along an Indian path called Tecumseh, he saw how well organized the place was. It was mainly French Catholic, though, and he was happy to press on through Fort Detroit and across Michigan.

After the busyness of the city of Chicago, the rest of the trip south was quiet, breezy, and open-spaced. They headed to Kankakee, which had been founded as a town only six years before. The Kankakee River was surrounded by an outwash plain from the glacial retreat, leaving sandy soil, easy for tilling. Henry and Louisa came into the town, saw an empty store for sale, and looked at each other. Henry turned the cart towards the post, where he tied the horses.

"I'll just take a look, Louisa." Baby Louisa was whimpering, so Louisa fed her and then changed her nappy. Edwin was talking the whole time to Alma, pointing out signs and reading them to her. He told her about the different types of stores, the horses, and the people.

Before they had time to get restless, Henry was out with a piece of paper in his hand. The owner had been inside tidying up and was happy to have Henry offer to take over immediately. He couldn't believe his luck. They would make a trip to the Wells Fargo Bank next and meet with the owner in an hour.

"Well, this gives us a place to stay, anyway. We can live upstairs, can't we?" asked Louisa.

"We sure can. Edwin, you help me get the boxes inside, and Louisa, you take the girls in to look around and decide where you want the household things. We'll probably need to buy some furniture and a few other items before we set up a store. After I finish at the bank I'm going to take a quick survey to see if a grocery would be a better idea than general merchandise."

II

By the time the 1860 census was taken on June 8th, Henry and his family were settled in and doing well. Henry was an astute businessman, and Louisa often had valuable ideas from a female point of view, gained from the experience of working for her father in his store. Now Henry Junior was one month old, the building was worth much more than when they had purchased it, and Mary Abrout was their eighteen-year-old domestic help from France. Edwin and Alma were attending school. All in all, the family was quite happy and healthy.

They had learned that Kankakee had been home to the Mormons under Joseph Smith, but after he was murdered in the nearby Carthage jail, they had migrated much further west to a valley surrounded by desert and badlands. They also learned that some of their neighbours were Canadians, like Joseph Leamory and Joseph Mitchell and their families. Most of the people in Kankakee were immigrants from other eastern states.

There was a general setback in the area when an epidemic of the fatal glanders disease killed many of the horses. It was a very difficult infection to control, and only the winter weather brought relief. The railroad was selling parcels of 80 to 200 acres of land cheaply to families in the hopes of getting the area settled.

Some groups of people who were sympathetic to the southern states' cause of keeping slavery began to rile up others in the Midwest. Some less liberal Democrats were a part of this group, which became known as the Copperheads.

III

Henry returned to the store one evening looking tired and deflated. "Louisa, I'm afraid we will have to return to Canada."

"But Henry, we're doing so well here! Why would we move? What's happened?"

"There's been a call to civil war. There are thousands just in Illinois who've signed up. They've already formed more than 100 infantry troops, 10 cavalry, and even light artillery. I'm afraid for Edwin. They might have a draft law in effect soon, and he would be just old enough to join."

"But Henry, he's only fifteen!"

"Yes, but that is just the age when he might think of war as an adventure, without considering the consequences. What is to stop him from telling them he's sixteen?"

"Do you think it will reach this far? Won't we be safe?"

"The Southerners are well-trained militia. They'll be sure to try to force their way north, and besides, there are sympathizers in this state. They would make it easy for troops to make their way here. I'm going to see about selling the store in the morning, and you can hire another cart and driver. It won't be too cold yet that we can't sleep outdoors. What do you think?" pleaded Henry.

Louisa paused to think for a moment. She had heard talk, of course, in the store, but she had not heeded the warning signs. Henry had, and for that she was grateful. She understood his concern for Edwin and could just picture her stepson in uniform telling them he had signed up as he headed out the door. She nodded her head and drew close to Henry. They were a long time getting to sleep that night, thinking of all that needed doing before their return to Canada.

Hooper-Cresser-Martin plot – Camden East

sixty-one

Kingston Township, Frontenac County, Ontario, 1866

The Hooper family gave Henry, Louisa, and the children a warm welcome. One or two families at a time would drop in to hear about the American adventure. Douglas and his wife Caroline brought Samuel, Alice, Flora, Douglas, and Ann with them. Business in Newburg was doing as well as Clark's Mills. The townspeople still called it Clark's Mills, but after Samuel Clark died, it had been renamed Camden East. It was a hub for the county and township meetings. John G. Hooper, Augustus, and Edmund owned lots on the 26th and 23rd concessions, where Henry Martin and Louisa had also owned land before renting it out while living in the United States. They now took back the responsibility of farming the land, and after the house became available, they improved it and widened the lane before moving in.

II

"It's Augustus, Louisa. I never thought I'd have to bury any of my children, but it's happened. His wife needs some help, so your mother and I are going over, but I wanted to let you know. Can you have Henry let the neighbours know? I think the Hinch family, Beeman, Charters, and Galbraiths are the main ones. I'm going to get the Reverend Thomas Stanton and bring him down. Take heart, Louisa. Your brother Augustus had a good life. Maybe not long enough, but he gave much to his family and community." With that, John put on his warm hat, for the wet November winds were blowing fiercely.

A few days after the funeral, Louisa read the obituary in the Napanee Standard of December 6, 1866. She read of Augustus's partnership with their brother Douglas in the mercantile business, his building and operating a saw mill, and his milling grain that gave Camden East a boost in the grain trade. What surprised her was his involvement in politics: warden of Lennox and Addington, and also reeve of the township. Then there were his Masonic brothers who came from far and wide for the funeral. Louisa had been most impressed with their procession and realized that Augustus had been a well-liked and influential man. Her sadness was lifted with the pride she felt in the success of her older brother.

III

Kingston, Ontario, 1867

Edwin had been a clerk at the grocers on the corner of Princess and Montreal Streets in Kingston for a year now. Once his father and the rest of the family were settled on a farm near Camden East, Edwin sought employment in town. His father was disappointed that he didn't stay to help him longer but understood Edwin's wanting to be more independent now that he was twenty years old.

His uncle Edmund John Glynn Hooper had set up and worked as a general merchant in Camden East until four years before, when he moved to Napanee to open up a store on Dundas Street, situated between the John and Centre Street intersections.

He had gone to command the Napanee Battery of Garrison Artillery during the Fenian scare. The garrison patrolled the narrows between Kingston and Prescott. Since the attacks ceased, his uncle had gone back to his store. Edwin wondered how he could be in uniform directing military men as a captain one week and back in his store the next. It was a strange world.

"Edwin? Did your father say anything about bringing butter when he brings the eggs this time?" asked the proprietor where Edwin worked.

"Yes, yesterday after service, he said he would bring what Louisa had ready. He wasn't sure how much it would be," replied Edwin. The two worked at sorting through the apples and plums, then the garden greens, which were just becoming available. Edwin took care in washing the windows and sweeping the wooden steps and front boardwalk. They were getting ready for the bulk buyers, who would be in before they were opened to the general public. Small stores in the areas outlying the town needed to get certain supplies. That often included his Uncle Edmund in Camden East. Edwin hoped his father would be arriving soon with his produce and meat.

"There you are, Father." Edwin greeted Henry and immediately began putting wooden crates of eggs, vegetables, and the needed butter into the store. Henry left the hog in the wagon to be later taken to the meat cutters for butchering.

"Well, I say people sure are excited about tomorrow's celebration, are they not?" asked Henry.

"There are certainly a great number of people and carts around and about. What do you think, Henry? Should we have stayed with the motherland, or do you think it was time for this new confederation?" asked Henry's cousin, also named Henry Martin.

"It's a good thing. There were too many problems without our own government, and although the Nova Scotians don't like being dictated to, there is safety in numbers. We don't know for sure that the United States won't try to make us another state. We need Britain's protection, and those Acadians should recognize that they might not have been spared from the Americans had it not been for the Brits allowing them to settle in Nova Scotia. They'll have their representation along with New Brunswick and Upper and Lower Canada. So, as I say, there's safety in being united."

"Well, let's hope there are no fiascos like the Orangemen's Arch in 1860!" emphatically exclaimed Edwin's uncle. At Henry and Edwin's puzzled looks, Uncle Henry went on to explain. "When King Edward, the Prince of Wales, was to visit here in Kingston in September of 1860, the Orangemen created a huge arch of branches and flowers that could be seen from the dock. No one thought much of it until they put up a banner: 'Our God, Our Country, and Our Queen, 1690,'" and Uncle Henry waved his arm in a large arch for emphasis. "No wonder Edward refused to land." Henry and Edwin looked at each other in stunned surprise. "There was such an uproar after that, the Orangemen had to lie low. It still has not been forgotten." Cousin Henry leaned heavily on his broom handle, reminiscing.

PART TEN

Linton FAMILY

sixty-two

England to Canada, 1843

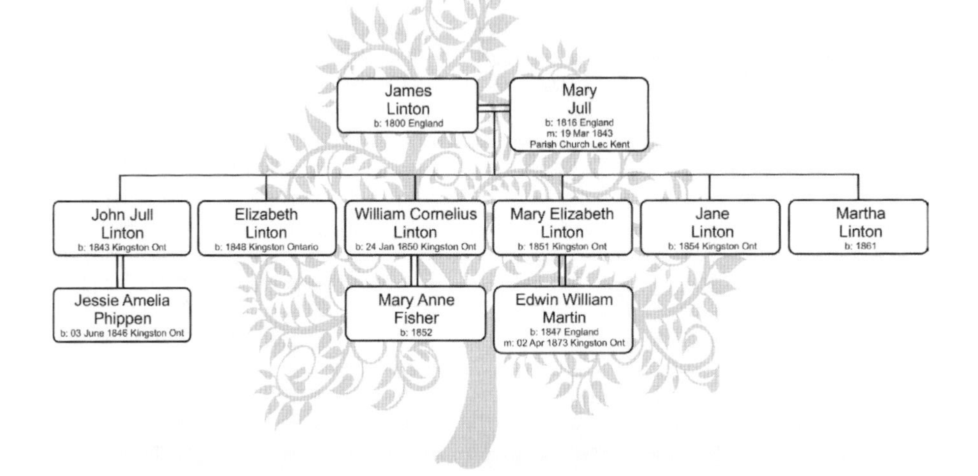

Linton Residence, Kingston, Ontario

James Linton was already a widower when he met and married Mary Jull in March of 1843 in the County of Kent in southeast England. At the time he was a merchant, as had been his father, James.

"There are so many more opportunities, Father," argued Mary when she tried to convince John and Ann Jull, her parents, that it was a good idea she and John emigrate to Canada.

"But dear, we will never see you again," cried Mary's mother.

"Mother, you have the others here, not far away. We need to go there for a better life. I must go with James; you know that."

Mary's heart was heavy while they stood on deck, watching until the land was out of sight. Then her spirit lightened as she hooked her arm through James' and drew her shawl tightly around her. Their little family of two would expand soon to three. She must try to look at this as a great adventure and not feel overwhelmed with fear of the unknown.

John Jull Linton was the oldest of their children, born months after his father and mother's wedding in England. Their second child, Elizabeth, was born in 1848. William Cornelius was a strong boy, born two years later. Mary Elizabeth, born in 1851, was followed by her sisters Jane and Martha.

By 1855 James Linton had established himself as the owner of the family's auction house. He was also a trustee of the Kingston Waterworks and the Permanent Building Society, helping to maintain the city's business area and keeping new residences hooked up with water lines. His father had come to Canada in the mid-thirties and established auction rooms in the market square of Kingston. James continued to keep a profitable business running. William Johnson was a black barber and hairdresser next door, and James gave him something to have his business named in Mr. Johnson's advertisement. His own ads usually announced the dates and goods at upcoming auctions.

James found the advertisement his father had saved among a pile of newspapers.

Wm Johnson Barber and Hair Dresser
Market Square, Kingston
Next door to Mr. Linton's Auction Rooms
Begs to return his sincere thanks to the public
for the liberal support he has received since
his residence in Kingston; and humbly requests a continuance of the same.
Hair cutting to every fashion, performed in the neatest manner.

Razors Honed and Dressed
Kingston, March 1, 1839

There were other ads in the newspaper, including three pages of crown lands for auction. The Napanee Mills were for rent, and there was a wet nurse available. On page four there was a list of unclaimed letters that would be sent to the Dead Letter Office, Quebec, if they were not collected in six more weeks from the post office. A pew was for sale in St. George's Anglican Church that was well-lined and in a central location of the sanctuary. He laughed at this. As a Wesleyan Methodist, he had no idea that church seats could be purchased.

The Chronicle and Gazette and Commercial Advertizer of Kingston, Upper Canada, was situated on the corner of King and Brock Streets. There were already numerous government buildings established near the harbour, impressive structures built of the local limestone. There was hope that someday Kingston would be the capital of both Upper and Lower Canada. For now, it was a heavily fortified city, with many commercial buildings of brick or wood along the earthen streets lined with boardwalks.

James tidied up as much of the clutter as he could in preparation for the next load of furniture from a couple who would be returning to Britain. They disliked the winters and had not been warm since they arrived, they had complained. He added the 1857 City of Kingston Directory to his mounting pile of papers to file. It featured a half-page ad on page 100 for Linter & Linton, Carriage & Sleigh Manufacturers, which James had been involved with for years. Now that his auction business was busier, he only occasionally assisted John Linter and his sons in the business. Soon his oldest son, John, would be helping out.

II

"James? Are you there?" called Mary from the doorway. She held the hand of Mary Elizabeth and carried baby Jane on her hip.

"Oh, is it dinner time already?" inquired James.

"Not right away, but you must be hungry. I just came to warn you that Mr. Robertson was getting anxious about the items he had with you and stopped by the house to see if you could push up the date for the auction."

"Well, I cannot. The dates have been sent to the printers, and if we have it on another date there will be few attending. These things can't be rushed. He doesn't have that many items to be so concerned about. Besides, I have to help John with a few sleighs he's getting ready for customers who've been waiting since early fall."

"Can we buy that, do you think?" Mary asked, pointing to a large piece of fine furniture. "It would fit so well into our dining room now that our family is growing. It's a piece of Gibbard from Napanee, is it not?"

"You have a good eye, dear. Well, it does happen to be Mr. Robertson's. Perhaps it would calm him down some if I asked him about purchasing it for you."

"For us, James. You and the children eat at the table too!" but she smiled at him, with love and appreciation, knowing that he would buy it just for her.

Mary Anne Fisher, wife of WC Linton – Iowa

William and John Jull Linton – Ottumwa, Iowa

Jessie Linton and children – Kingston, Ontario

Sons of William Cornelius Linton and Mary Anne – Iowa

PART ELEVEN

Linton, Martin FAMILIES

sixty-three

Kingston, Ontario, 1872

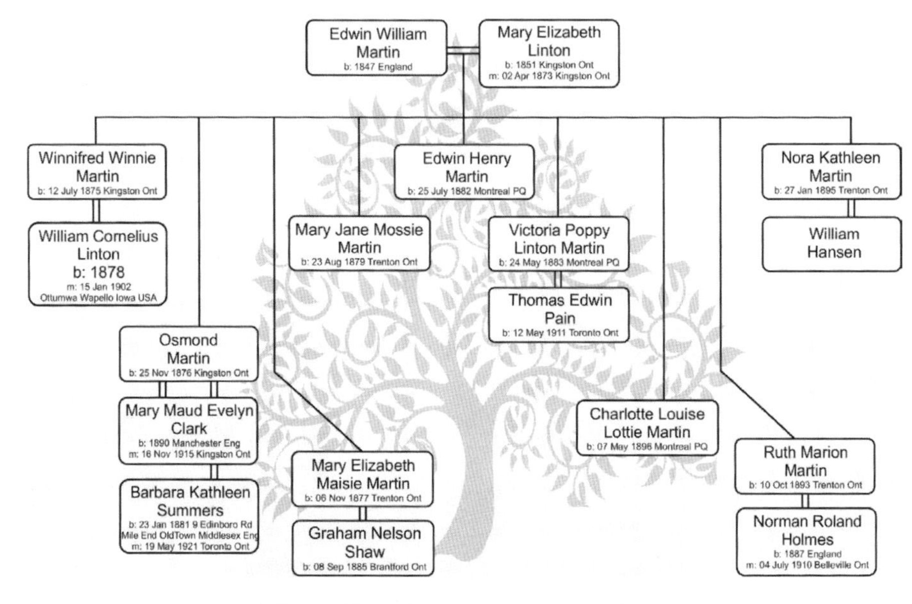

Edwin Martin

Edwin adjusted his tie and collar as he mounted the steps outside of Mary Linton's family home on Gage Street.

"Good evening, ma'am." Edwin was squirming somewhat. "I was hoping to see Mary this evening."

"Well, come right in. I'm Elizabeth McGregor, the housekeeper. You'll be meeting Mary's father, I suspect, when he comes in from the shed. Will you wait here, please, and I'll tell Miss Linton you've arrived?"

Edwin sat up straight on the small parlour chair. He took note of the solid, well-made, though well-used, furnishings lining the walls of the dark room. He repeatedly thumbed the brim of his hat until he heard Mary's voice in the hall. She was speaking to her father as they both entered the room together.

She gave Edwin an encouraging and genuine smile in greeting. "Father, you've heard me speak of Mr. Edwin Martin. Edwin, this is my father, Mr. James Linton."

"How do you do, sir?" Edwin managed to ask as he shook hands with Mary's father.

"Please, call me James, Edwin." Mr. James Linton had the strong voice demanded of an auctioneer but a kind demeanour that put Edwin at ease immediately. "I asked Mrs. McGregor to bring us some tea and biscuits, if that suits you, or would you prefer a glass of sherry?"

"Oh, tea will suit me fine, thank you, sir…ah, James," responded Edwin.

"Ah, true to your Wesleyan Methodist beliefs, I see. Good for you. I like a fellow who sticks to his beliefs. Now, tell me something about yourself, young man. Mary has recounted many of your outings lately, but I'd like to know something about you. Were you born in Canada?"

"No, sir. I was born in London, England, where my mother was raised, but she died while I was still an infant. My father and mother had planned to come to Canada, but it was just my father and I who made the trip to Montreal. We lived there where my father worked in the grocery business. He married my stepmother and worked at Camden East in one of the general stores with his brother-in-law. Our farm helps supply the store with produce."

"I understand from Mary that you lived south of the border for a while."

"Yes, we did. In fact, my brother was born there, in Illinois, but things began to get uncomfortable just before the civil war. My father was concerned about my being drafted, so we returned here to the Kingston area, where all of the family still farm."

"Well, you've had an interesting life by the sounds of it. Did you not want to take up farming with your father?" asked James.

Mary had poured and passed the tea and now spoke up. "Edwin enjoys the retail end of the business, father. He is most impressed with the Kingston market. His father, Henry, helps supply Mr. Martin's grocery distribution business. That Mr. Henry Martin is a cousin of Edwin's father. Edwin hopes to have his own grocery store in the near future." Mary was not timid in speaking out. Being the middle child meant she had learned to make her views known to the family.

"Mary tells me you are wanting to take her to Fort Henry for some military manoeuvres they are performing. That sounds like quite an evening. I don't suppose you would mind taking along Jane and Martha, Mary's younger sisters, would you? Mary is the oldest at home since William left for work in Seattle and John married. It's been a blessing to have these young girls at home to help, though Mrs. McGregor is the head housekeeper." James glanced at Mary fondly, and she smiled back. She wasn't quite ready for marriage yet, but she knew whom she wanted for a husband.

"That would be fine, sir. We can all go in the open trap, as I expect the weather to be co-operating," answered Edwin.

"Fine. Mary's mother, after whom she was named, would have been proud of our girl. We miss her still, and Elizabeth, our oldest daughter. You know, Mary and I married just before we left for Canada. I was a fair bit older than she was, and I always thought she would outlive me, but that was not what God had in mind, I guess.

"This town has been good to our family though. Never been without work, and we all have been healthy, 'cept my wife Mary of course. There was always work in the limestone quarry or at the shipyards. You know, we're the oldest established town in Lower Canada. Our Kingston has grown to have many of the modern conveniences that are not in the rural areas. There has been an advantage to having rail connections to both Toronto and Montreal, as well as steamer transportation. What with that new electric carriage running along the south side of King Street and the new boardwalks with fences and hitching posts, the business section of this town has become quite profitable. The new Royal Military Academy has sure been an important addition—almost as important as Queen's University. It was too bad that we lost the bid for capital, but I guess Ottawa is closer to Upper Canada, and that might appease the French a little.

"Well, I should be getting back to the shed to sort out a consignment. An old gentleman has died and left all kinds of things from his carpentry trade to sell. His family left the area recently and didn't want the furnishings or the tools. It'll make some young families that are starting out very happy to get a hold of these things. Dozens of awls, wooden planes, chisels, and hand saws, not to mention all the wardrobes, desks, and sofas. Well kept, they were." James rose to excuse himself, leaving Edwin and Mary alone.

"Oh, Edwin, Daddy liked you. I think that went well for a first visit. I hope you don't mind my two sisters tagging along with us, but they will so enjoy it. Daddy doesn't take much time off working to socialize. He still misses Mother so much."

Edwin nodded in agreement. He had been too young to really know his birth mother before she died, but he remembered how much happier he was after his father and Louisa married. "Maybe sometime he could come with us to watch the hockey played on the bay. Those military boys sure know how to skate."

sixty-four

Kingston, Ontario, 1873

Edwin and Mary were thrilled walking to their little cottage off the main street for the first time as man and wife.

"It couldn't be a lovelier day than it is today," Mary said with a satisfied sigh.

"And what day is that, Mrs. Martin?" teased Edwin.

"Oh, you! Stop teasing. Don't tell me you don't remember signing the register back there with the former Miss Mary Elizabeth Linton? Perhaps we should go back and look at it again." With a playful tug, Mary pulled on his arm.

"I have no doubt that I will remember April the 2nd of this year 1873 without any difficulty, and by this evening, I have no doubt you and I both will be so overcome with joy, we won't know what to do with ourselves." Edwin lovingly pulled her close and gave her a lingering kiss. He affectionately caressed her blushing cheek, and they moved on toward their cottage.

Business was doing well in Kingston. Queen's University, established in 1841, was growing, the brewing business was picking up, and there was talk of putting new tin awnings over the boardwalk along the length of King Street, where three-storey brick buildings housed all types of businesses.

Edwin was a fair and astute businessman and managed the grocery business for his cousin very well. However, after the birth of their first child, Winifred, on July 12, 1875, there was an influx of grocery businesses, and Edwin was forced to work long hours. Mary was exhausted with seeing to all the housework, laundry, cooking, baking bread, and feeding a crying infant.

"Edwin, I need some help. Is there anyone you know who we could hire to do some housekeeping?" Mary asked.

Edwin's brow furrowed while he was in thought. "What about Lilly, my youngest sister? I know she's only ten, but she could help until the fall term of school starts, then maybe on Saturdays until you are able. What do you think?"

Mary nodded her head. It was a practical arrangement, and Lilly was a sweet girl. She would do her best to settle down the fussy Winnie.

II

William Osmond Martin was born on November 25, 1876, when Winnie was about eighteen months old. While Winnie had been a colicky, crying baby and difficult toddler, Osmond was a placid, happy baby. There was the usual sibling jealousy, and Winnie would often resort to pouting in a corner. Her baby brother just did not want to do as Winnie wanted.

"Winnie! Leave Osmond alone. You have a doll to play with. We'll be going out to get your photo taken, so don't spoil your dress." Mary continued tidying up so that she might get the children down to the photographer's. Winnie's hair was parted in the middle and her curls tied in a short cluster at the back of her neck. The white lace bow around her head matched the trim on the four layers of gathers at the bottom of her blue straight smock, and her black leather shoes were held tightly with a strap around her ankle. Her mother tried to make her smile, but she did not.

Trenton, Ontario, 1877

"We set everything up with the houses, and Father is looking at buying a business. You'll like it here, Mary. It's beautiful country right by the estuary of the Trent River," Edwin said, hoping to encourage his wife with their move.

"I will be happy to see us settled, the kettle on the stove, and the beds made up." Mary gently massaged her expanding belly and took in a sharp breath as the baby kicked back, apparently protesting the jostling ride in the carriage. The furniture and household items had gone ahead in the cart driven by young Henry, Edwin's half-brother.

With the late fall move and the birth of baby Mary on November 6, 1877, the Martin family didn't have time to register her until December 25th. A Dr. Williams was in attendance at the birth, and all were well and happy. Edwin's father, stepmother and four half-siblings joined them in the New Year. They travelled from the farm they had purchased outside of Trenton, making it a large celebration that year with eleven of them in the small house.

"Edwin, your brother Henry and I have been looking at a building on lot 21. I think it would house a business very well," Henry told his son. "Young Henry needs to build up his own business skills, but what say you join us?"

"I will, Papa, providing that we each have our specific areas and duties. Groceries are my specialty. How is the farming going, anyway?"

"Well, I just am not convinced the land here is any better than Camden East, but we'll give it a try. Louisa wanted to leave the area after her father died. She misses her brother Douglas and their eight children and Augustus's family though. They were all such a happy group, even if they were noisy. We never had a moment's peace around them."

The family had a surprise a few days after Christmas. Mary's brother William C. Linton sent a telegram to let them know he would be stopping to visit on his way to the United States. William wanted to discuss a few aspects about moving there and needed the advice of his sister's father-in-law, Henry Martin.

"So you plan on moving to Ashkum near Iroquois, Illinois." Henry drew out a rough map that showed where they had lived nearby in Kankakee. "This part of the river floods. We found that out in the third year. This part is a huge grassy plain, and if you had intentions of farming, it would be excellent. Now that things have settled down after the civil war, business should be good."

"William, is it really necessary to go there? It seems so far away. You haven't brought much with you either," commented Mary.

"I figure it will be easy for a bachelor to move with very little and not be encumbered at the border."

"How are John and the family? I hear from them so infrequently. Has everyone been well? I thought I would have heard that you and Elizabeth had married by now. Can you tell us what happened?"

"I don't know. I thought I was making progress, but she suddenly started cutting our visits short. Then she refused to see me at all. Next, I hear the banns of her and some fellow from Montreal announced in church. It was a painful shock, I tell you, but never mind, I'm getting excited to be on the move. I'm sure there will be plenty of ducks in the lake south of the border."

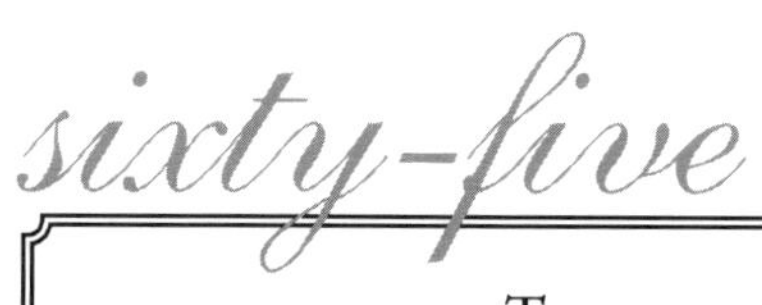

Trenton, Ontario, 1878–1879

Mary's brother had not been gone more than eight months when a letter came from him announcing that he had married a lovely young woman from Missouri. He was doing well with business, he said, and hoped that he would have more news next year. Mary was surprised, but pleased because William sounded so happy finally.

More news came later. William Cornelius Junior was born in June of 1878 and another was expected before the end of the next year.

II

Edwin was rather dumbfounded that his father was suggesting he move again. He and Harry had had their squabbles, but it wasn't enough to dislodge the whole family again after what seemed so short a period of time.

"Edwin, I have two reasons for you to move to Montreal. The confectioner's trade is a very good one for you to learn, and our cousin is willing to teach you and set you up in business if you wish. Montreal is one of the greatest trading cities in Canada. And the second reason is that I've been looking over the books, and there is a downturn in commerce here. It may just be a minor slump, but it wouldn't hurt to go to Henry's in Montreal. He will train you and even find accommodation for all of you."

"I'll have to think about this. I don't know what Mary will say. She'll have to agree to it. Four children are not too easy to transport."

"One advantage of going there is that you should be able to find an au pair to help with the house and children. Think about it." Henry smiled in a somewhat puzzled expression just thinking about Edwin and Mary's relationship. They conferred with each other and made decisions together, and they certainly enjoyed each other's company. Henry had caught Edwin swinging Mary around in a dance in the kitchen on more than one occasion. He shook his head, pondering how they still seemed like young lovers after all this time.

III

The final decision was to make the move to Montreal, but they would rent out the house and let Henry look after the warehouse business.

A few days before the family was to leave, word came from Louisa's older sister, Lavinia, that her husband had died. It was arranged that they would all make a visit to Camden East, using two wagons, and then Henry Junior would take them to the train in Kingston.

"Can I go with Aunt Wis?" asked Winnie. Their Aunt Louisa was affectionately called Aunt Wis, Alma was Aunt Duck, and Lilly was Aunt Lil. The family fondly referred to these pet names, and new family members were often nicknamed according to their comments or behaviour.

"Yes, Winnie, that will be fine. You mind them, you hear," answered her father.

sixty-six

Camden East, Ontario, 1879

Camden East still had the mills by the river, the old stone school on the main street, and St. Luke's Anglican Church on the hill. There was now a Presbyterian church and, of course, a very large stone house, which Augustus Hooper had built in 1850. There were also four inns and hotels, a brewery, a candy and bake shop, a blacksmith shop, a shoemaker, an undertaker, and a veterinarian.

Louisa greeted the family with tears in her eyes but very much in control of her actions. She herded them into the house and allowed them to tidy up before walking up to the church where the funeral was to be held.

Louisa Martin held her cousin Louisa Cresser close as the Reverend Elliot prayed and committed Richard's body to eternity with Christ. The family stood there for a long time after the service ended. The grave diggers stood discreetly near the south wall of the church out of the wind. They would wait for as long as it took.

Henry walked around the family plot, which now had a wrought iron fence and a gate surrounding three tall monuments.

"Young Louisa, these are your ancestors here, and my friends." The Rev. John Hooper led his younger cousin on a tour. He wanted her to feel the same sense of respect and fellowship with her ancestors as he did.

"Do you remember Robert Morrison? He was the first friend in Canada your father had. Henry met him on the ship in Liverpool, and he was a great help to him with little Edwin, who wasn't even two."

Louisa read the flat stone on the earth: "In memory of Robert Morrison, late of Liverpool, England, who died Nov. 6, 1867, aged 48."

They stopped at the new Cresser monument, which would have Richard S. Cresser's death date chiseled on later. There was room for other designations and dates, and Louisa silently wondered whose names would be placed there.

"Here is our grandmother and grandfather's monument. Have you read it before?"

"No, Uncle John. It must have been completed since we came to Grandpa's funeral." Louisa felt the urge to read it aloud, despite the noisy flapping of her skirts.

"Sarah Garland, Beloved wife of John G Hooper, born at Store near Devonport, England. July 1791. Died May 18, 1871. "When life is strong and conscience clear and words of Peace this spirit cheer, And visions of glory doth appear, 'Tis Joy, 'Tis triumph here to die.

That's beautiful, Uncle John. Grandpa must have loved Grandma very much."

John nodded. "And there is the inscription for our grandpa, the man I was named after: 'John G Hooper died June 6, 1873, aged eighty years. Among whom are Ye also the called of Jesus Christ.'

"And here is your great-aunt Amelia Hooper, who died in February 1875, aged sixty-two years. Family has been very important to all of us, as it is to you as well, I think."

Louisa nodded her head. She felt a much greater connection with Camden East than she did Trenton. Maybe she would return someday.

Louisa and her uncle moved closer to the flat stone under the tree. Louisa did not remember this one. "Uncle, who is this? 'Isabel Richmond, wife of John G Hooper departed this life Sept. 12, 1817, aged 27 years, 2 months.'"

"That was your grandfather's first wife. Do you know her story?"

"No. I had no idea that Grandpa was married before Grandma."

"Well, get your father to tell you about it. Lavinia was really his daughter, but after her mother was put in the asylum, John's brother Thomas took Lavinia in. After John Hooper, our grandfather, remarried and had two sons—that was your Uncle Augustus and Uncle Edmund—he and your grandmother Sarah decided to move to Canada. Sarah found out that Lavinia was his daughter and insisted they bring her as well."

Louisa stared in awe at her uncle and his story and wondered how she had never known anything about it. She would certainly think about returning here, or at least try to visit more often. What other mysteries were waiting to unfold?

Henry was anxiously awaiting Edwin and the family to take them to Kingston. He would return to Trenton the following day if he could. In the meantime, his father, mother, and sisters would return right away.

Henry was surprised when Edwin suggested they visit their mother's brother, Uncle Felix, but remembered it had been discussed earlier.

"It's on King Street, Henry. The number is 543, so it will in the next block or two." Edwin was studying the street and seeing new structures, more two and a-half-storey brick buildings, new awnings, new boardwalks and fences. It had certainly changed since he and Mary had been there four years ago.

It was late evening, and so they tried to make as little noise as possible, but Felix, Mary, and the children were awake and greeted them fondly.

"Well, Henry, how are you? And you, Edwin and Mary? Still growing a happy family I see."

Winnie was in her commanding mode, trying to make her brother Ozzie stand up straight and holding Martha's wee hand perhaps a little more tightly than necessary. Edwin was carrying a sleeping Mary, and they were all glad to get in out of the wind and sit in comfort.

"Your father sent a telegram saying you'd be stopping by on your way to Montreal. We have enough space for everyone to have at least a mat. The children can bunk in together. Won't you have some buns and meat? We have fresh milk and some egg tarts if you wish. Come into the dining room while I get things ready."

Mary followed Felix's Mary into the kitchen to help. "How are you, Mary? You have a lovely home here in Kingston." A little envy crept into her voice, even though she didn't feel strongly that way. "I guess you have so many selections in the stores here. We seem to have very few decorative choices in Trenton, although I must say it's not as windy as Kingston is. Your gas lamps are lovely and you have water running from taps right here in the kitchen."

"I am very fortunate indeed, though I expect that you will have plenty of options in the shopping district in Montreal. All the new fashions seem to arrive there first. Ah, what varieties and colours of fabric you will have to choose from, and furnishings. I would so enjoy a shopping trip there."

"Well, you must come, Mary. Does Felix manage on his own very well?"

"Not at all. I could have someone come in if I take the children with me, but shopping is more difficult with small children in tow."

Mary Martin nodded her head and followed behind Mary Hooper with a tray of cheese and meats. They were very generously fed, and after the children were settled in their makeshift beds, Edwin, Henry, and Felix sat smoking pipes and cigars in the parlour.

"Well, gentlemen, this is a pleasure. I had wanted to see the family soon but was unable to go up to poor Richard's funeral. I think the air in Canada must have been very different than what he was used to in France." Felix looked relaxed, entirely enjoying his visitors.

"Tell us, Felix, what is the brewing business like? Are there any profits to be made?"

"I tell you, Henry and Edwin, it's the best business to be in. I don't mean because a person gets to sample the products, but there is always a need for beer and ale. It's for the regular bloke who likes a flavourful beverage after a meal or after work. We've had very good sales."

In the morning, Mary went to visit her brother's widow, Jessie Amelia, and their children, Mary Elizabeth and William Noon. It was a special visit as it had been several years since they had left Kingston. Mary wanted to be sure to see everyone and study them face to face so that she could later recall how they looked and how much they had changed.

"Do you hear anything from your brother William?" Amelia asked.

"Not too often, but certainly when there is news. They have three boys now, all doing well. Do you ever hear from them?" Mary inquired.

Amelia hesitated. "Not since John died. I believe they were as shocked as I was when I got the letter saying that he had died of a gunshot wound."

"I'm sure it has been terribly difficult for you." Mary thought there were some unanswered questions around John's death, but she didn't want to ask anything that might upset Amelia, so she changed the subject. "Do your mother and father help you at all?"

"Oh, yes! They've been wonderful. I help in their dry goods store when I can. The children are wonderful, too. They try to do their bit to help. I'm so glad to see you, Mary, and you with four children already! They seem quite delightful."

Mary was contemplative. She couldn't help think about John and his trip to visit William—a journey from which he had never returned. There were puzzling things about John's death, but Mary was sure that Amelia and her family believed the news and mourned his loss.

Edwin went to his sister-in-law's house to bring his family back to Felix and Mary's house for the evening meal. At the Hooper's home, while enjoying another delicious feast, they recalled so many happy times together in their youth. Winnie, Ozzie, Mayzie, and Mossie joined their boisterous cousins under the scrutiny of Edwin and Mary.

sixty-seven

Picton, Prince Edward County, 1881

Alma was very excited. She was thrilled with her marriage to thirty-two-year-old John Wright, an established lawyer in Picton. When he came home for dinner she would approach him about having her family come to visit. She wanted to show off their lovely two-storey home and the gardens she was cultivating. She also wanted to share the news with them that she would be having a child within the next few months.

"John—here. Let me take your coat and hat. Was it a very gruelling day?"

"No more than the usual property and wills to deal with. I'm looking forward to a dinner with my lovely wife and then putting my feet up. How does that sound?"

"Wonderful. Nellie has things ready, I'm sure. I'll head to the kitchen to let her know you're ready to be served in the dining room as soon as you wash up—sorry, freshen up." Alma left him with a smile but still annoyed with herself for using a term he thought coarse. Oh, well. She was learning.

After their dinner was cleared away and they were enjoying a hot drink, Alma broached the subject of a visit. "Do you think we could invite my family to come for a short visit, John? They wouldn't stay too long, I'm sure. I wanted to share our news with them, as this will be the first grandchild for my parents."

"Well, I'm sure they're welcome for a short visit. You wouldn't expect Edwin and all his brood, now would you?"

"Oh, no! Montreal is too far to come with all those young children. In fact, Louisa will also most likely want to stay at home as well."

"Why don't we wait to invite them a little closer to the baby's birth; then perhaps Lilly could stay and help you with the baby for a few weeks."

Alma was a little disappointed in not having them visit sooner but quite liked the idea of Lilly staying with them to assist. The first baby was usually somewhat difficult, she knew, and she was more than a little nervous. She was also a little lonely, having no close friends to share the time with. Many of John's associates' wives were already busy with two or three children, so she settled to writing a letter to her parents in Trenton.

Dear Papa and Mama,

John and I have been talking about having you for a visit. It would be wonderful to see you both, and Louisa, Harry, and Lilly if they will come. We are hoping to have Lilly stay until after the baby is born. Yes, John and I are expecting a new member of the family by November. What do you think about coming around the middle of October, when the leaves will be very colourful?

The ferry will get you to the island, and then carriages come to town every day so you have no need of staying at an inn. You will notice the roadways are a dark grey shale and very firm, but sharp underfoot. Where you first land on the north side of the island, you will think the land very hilly, but after a few miles you ascend a steep ridge, and then the land is quite flat all the way to Picton.

Although a small town yet, Picton is quite delightful. The water at its lakefront is clear and blue. There are no reeds or mud flats to dirty the waters around the sound as in Trenton. It helps that the shore is rocky. The town is the most interesting you will ever see. Every building has its own design and trimmings. Another barrister-at-law, Mr. Merrill, has a wonderfully large Victorian-style home with steep roofs and so many gingerbread gables it looks like a house out of a fairy tale. John and I enjoy touring around somewhat on our way to and from services on Sundays. Of course there are many more that are simple two-storey houses such as ours. Many kinds of stone and brick are used, as well as the trees, which are harvested at an alarming rate. There seems like a good supply of timber, yet there are places where the logging has left scars and no one has cultivated the fields. In some places they quarry the stone for export and local use.

There are many park areas and beautiful gardens. We are very happy in our new home and wish to have you come mid-October. Thank you again for the letter of the tenth, and I do hope that Edwin and the family are doing well in Montreal. I have not heard from Harry for some time, but perhaps you can let me know how his family is doing in Hamilton when next you write.

Please give regards to all of the family.

Your loving and devoted daughter and son-in-law,

Alma and John

II

"Oh, Alma! You have a lovely boy. John thinks you should call him Charles. Do you need anything?" Lilly was beside herself with excitement and wanted to chatter. Alma was exhausted and just wanted to hold her new son. Once Charles started crying loudly in a piercingly high-pitched wail, Lilly got the hint and handed him gently over to his mother, who began trying to nurse him. John watched the infant for a few minutes while Lilly cleaned him up, and then he gave Alma a firm kiss on her perspiring brow.

"Well done, love. Now you just rest up, and we'll see you a little later if you feel like getting up." Alma gave John a weak smile, thinking she might get up tomorrow if she had to.

John opened the new family Bible he had purchased. After recording the birth dates of Alma and himself, he wrote, "Charles Adelbert Henry Wright, 21 of Nov. 1881."

sixty-eight

Montreal, Quebec, Canada, 1881

Edwin took the tram to 541 St. Denis St. in Montreal, where he and a cousin had their confectioner's store. He was pleased that his wife had Louisa Folkes, a local fourteen-year-old, to help with the children. Winnie, as the eldest child, tried to help but more often ended up making the others cry because of her bossy ways. It was easier to let little Mary and Martha play with each other; then Osmond would pleasantly ignore Winnie if he didn't want to do what she wished. Winnie was anxious to be active and enjoyed helping with housework.

Oh, they were a busy family, but Edwin couldn't be happier. He had wondered if he would remember anything about Montreal from his first time there years ago, but he recalled nothing. Perhaps he had been too young back then.

II

"Edwin, I need to get down to the mercantile to find some flannel for new nappies. Tomorrow Louisa is prepared to stay with the children while I go shopping. Will you direct me to the correct tram I should take? Winnie will be in school, so if you want to come home for dinner at noon, you may have to heat it yourself."

"Shall I come along with you for the morning? I'm sure William can manage the store by himself. We could look at some furnishings if you like. I know how you admired Mary and Felix's home in Kingston. I do love to see you happy," he said, tucking his arm around Mary's expanding waist.

Mary feigned surprise at his offer. "Are you sure that you want to look at furnishings with me? I didn't think that would interest you."

The neighbourhood furniture store smelled slightly stale. The heavy drapery of the sample window dressing was darker than either Mary or Edwin cared for. They browsed up and down the aisles looking at tapestries and beautifully embroidered fabric on ornate furniture. Chairs and matching fainting couches were clearly popular. Mary stifled a yawn.

"You must be exhausted, dear. Shall we have bit to eat?"

"Oh, that would be a good idea, Edwin. I am feeling a little peaked."

Edwin led Mary up the steps to a cafe where they could stop for a cup of tea and some scones. Mary was thankful indeed, as her feet were swelling despite the cool summer air. Mary thought she must look like a balloon with her bulging stomach in front and her bustle in a poof behind her.

The hostess sat them and brought their cups of tea.

"I'm so happy to hear that your sister Alma had a healthy boy. Charles is a fine name, though not a family name."

"Yes, I think they wanted something different. I don't believe that John's family has anyone with that name. They will spoil that child, I think. Alma is a very loving person, and John will try to provide the very best. Being a solicitor, he will expect his son to be educated. I think education can take a person only so far; then experience becomes more important."

Mary suddenly clenched her teeth and clutched her stomach. Her face paled.

"Mary! What's wrong? What should I do? Do you need a cab to go to the hospital?"

"Edwin, sit down. It will pass in a moment. I don't think I need the hospital, but perhaps I will see the doctor later."

Edwin stood immediately and went to the desk to pay the bill. He was not convinced that Mary was all right. "Do you have a telephone here?"

"No, I'm sorry, sir; we have no telephone. Do you need a taxi?"

Edwin nodded.

"I will find one for you, sir. Please wait at the front door."

Edwin helped Mary to the door and assisted her down the steps. Within moments, a horse-drawn taxi pulled to the front steps and waited while Edwin helped Mary up into the carriage. Edwin silently thanked God he had chosen to go along with her today. She was still weeks away from delivery.

After a short visit to the doctor, Mary was required to rest in bed for most of the following weeks.

Despite their precautions, Edwin Henry was born too early. July 25 was a hot day, and the premature baby was small and somewhat underweight. Edwin paced at night while Mary tried to get the baby to nurse. His weak cry pierced Edwin's heart. He blamed himself for bringing Mary to Montreal during the early stages of her pregnancy. It had been too much, but only the good Lord could help now.

A few nights later, Edwin had just finished kissing the children goodnight before Louisa, the au pair, took them to bed when he heard Mary crying. He hurried to her side, and it was as he had feared. Edwin Henry lay limp and lifeless in Mary's arms. Edwin clutched Mary's shoulders and wept. Despite the usual male reserve of the day, Edwin's love for Mary allowed them to share the intimacy of their sorrows, as well as their joys.

sixty-nine

Montreal, Quebec, 1883–1890

Life carried on. The Martin family worked, played, and attended church. They were especially full of joy when Victoria Linton Martin was born on May 24, 1883. They had both agreed that the baby born on Queen Victoria's birthday must take on the British monarch's name. However, at a young age she blurted out "Poppy," and that became her name.

The next month they celebrated the birth of Poppy's cousin, Nina Wright, born in Picton, a sister for Charles and a daughter for Alma and John.

In Trenton, Henry Martin and Louisa purchased lot 21, west of Queen Street, from Thomas Sketch. They had been renting it but now thought that purchasing it would be less expensive in the long run. The lot was on the corner of Queen and Joseph Streets. Joseph Street ran in front of the residential section of the building and then curved south to head up a steep hill. The warehouse and office stood behind the home and faced Queen Street.

II

In late July of 1884, Mary received a letter from Eldon, Iowa, telling her of the death of her youngest niece.

"Edwin, I've just heard from Anna and William in Iowa that their daughter Louisa Mary has died. Oh, how sad to lose their only daughter! The boys will be heartbroken to have lost their little Lulu, only a year old," sympathized Mary.

"They lost their first boy too, didn't they?" asked Edwin. "Well, they have four strong boys." He could empathize with his brother-in-law. Losing a child was so tragic, yet society didn't allow people to grieve for any length of time. A person just had to get on with it.

Late that night, Edwin could hear the thunder rolling in. There was no rain as of yet but just loud claps of thunder. "Mary, there's a thunderstorm coming. Time to get up and get the children."

Mary wearily sat up, sliding her feet into slippers, and quickly put her dressing gown on. She went into the youngest girls' room first and helped them into their slippers and pulled blankets off the bed to help keep them warm while they cuddled together on the sofa. Edwin always did this. He wanted to know they were together and safe.

"Ohhh! That was a big one! I'm afraid," cried Mayzie. Poppy was already in tears. Sometimes Mary thought the children would be better off in their own rooms, but they were all afraid of thunder and lightning storms.

There was another very loud clap, much closer this time, and the rain started. It pelted against the windows as drafts flicked the flame of the oil lamp Edwin had lit, causing eerie shadows to move on the walls.

"Now girls. You'll be fine. We're all here together, and if lightning strikes, we will all leave together." Mary wasn't sure if he meant they would all leave the house together or this earth. They knew of families who had had their houses burned down because of lightning strikes and some who had lost family members as well.

"It's important to be alert when there's a storm should we ever have to leave the house in a hurry. Ozzie, stay over here with your sisters." Edwin was somewhat pale and startled with every thunderous boom.

They started back to bed when the lightning's flash and the thunder's boom slowed and faded into the distance.

III

On Sept. 12, 1884, Henry Martin Junior was charged with cruelty to animals. He was required to pay a dollar fine. It was an embarrassing situation for Douglas and some of the other Hooper relatives in Camden East, but most didn't let on they knew about it. Henry Senior was livid with his son, so he sent a letter of apology to his brother-in-law with the dollar owing.

IV

Charlotte Louise was born to Edwin and Mary in Montreal May 7, 1886. Her young sisters had difficulty pronouncing Charlotte, so it became Lottie.

Ozzie and his five sisters grew rapidly. Their lives in Montreal centred around the English school and Anglican church. Mary became her trim, youthful self again months after Lottie's birth, being busy with six young children. Just keeping them fed, clean, and dressed took most of her time, but she valued her life as a mother and wife.

The weather added challenges. Winter made travel difficult, and even walking to church or school caused everyone to bundle up, or the harsh wind and extreme cold forced people to stay indoors.

seventy

Trenton, Ontario, 1890

Edwin and Mary came to the conclusion that they should return to Trenton. They had missed Edwin's half-brother Henry Martin Jr.'s marriage to Annie Raymond on April 30, 1889, in Trenton and were anxious to meet her. Perhaps she could settle him down.

When they told the children about their move, Winnie had her own ideas.

"Mother, I would like to become a nurse, and I believe I can attend the Montreal Homoeopathic Hospital for their two-year course."

"I must say I'm surprised, Winnie, but I think you would make a good nurse. You have always been efficient and organized. Have you thought about how you would pay for this course?"

"Do you think if you spoke to Cousin Henry that I might stay there? I can continue to work in the store and maybe be a nanny to the neighbour's children. Please, Mother? I would be ever so thankful if you could talk Father into letting me stay."

Mary and Edwin discussed it, but it was decided that Winnie was too young to be left so far away just yet.

Winnie saved her money with great diligence and determination. She worked for other employers besides her father, feeling she would actually receive fair wages elsewhere. Working for the family seemed to have little monetary gain.

Two years later, at age eighteen, she asked again but was put off by her father for another "year or two."

Winnie found a confidante in her Aunt Wis, who still lived with her parents and seemed quite happy to do so. She often stopped to visit her Grandfather Martin and Wis, who lived just down the street.

"Didn't you ever want to become trained in something, Aunt Wis? How have you survived being at home all the time looking after your parents? Grandfather needs more care these days since Grandmother has become sick."

"I do have quite enough to keep me busy. Have you not thought that much of what I do is like nursing?"

Winnie paused in thought for a minute. She had never looked at her Aunt Wis as a nurse, but it was true. She was doing at home what Winnie wanted to do in hospital.

"Did you know I have even made and sold twenty-one hats this season?" asked Louisa.

"Have you really? You must be doing very well. You could have your own place."

"There's no need. Someone has to look after my parents, and we all have to eat; you see, it's not such a burden as you think." Louisa smiled at Winnie. Wilful Winnie. She was sure that someday Winnie would get her wish and attend nursing school.

II

Henry was concerned with business declining. A few years before, an enormous dam had been built upriver from Trenton, and this had given the town and industry limitless electric power according to the town fathers. It might help perk up business as well.

Lilly was to marry Edward Marshall Conger from Picton that summer, but Henry was concerned with the health of his wife, Louisa. Henry and Louisa would arrive in time for the wedding and would help out the family as much as they could under the circumstances.

Edwin and Mary were returning to live in Trenton, perfectly timed for the upcoming wedding. The family took the wagon along the river road in order to inspect the new power dam, and then crossed over the Trent River through the old covered bridge, still used more than fifty years after it had been built.

"Oh, Edwin," exclaimed Lilly at their arrival. "I'm so happy you and Mary and the children have returned to Trenton in time for the wedding. Your daughters are so sweet, and Ozzie is so brave to have so many sisters," she said as she ruffled his hair fondly. "Edward and I will be very happy. You know that it was John and Alma who introduced us. I was worried that I would be an old maid before Edward proposed. Mr. and Mrs. Conger will be pleased to meet the rest of the family. I only wish we could have been married in Trenton. It will be a hard trip on Mother. She hasn't been that strong, and our poor sister Louisa has had the burden of housekeeping for Mother and Father, although I think she is determined to remain a spinster."

"Well, I'll be around now to help, so perhaps that will free Louisa up." Thinking of little Edwin Henry, Edwin said, "We should have stayed here."

"There is no point in regrets, Edwin," and Mary put her arm through his.

"Well, I've got the grocery store to set up. I know Father was disappointed that I didn't want the warehouse, but it's too large for what I want to do. The store on West Front Street will be ideal. I know he was disappointed, too, that Henry and his wife are moving away. He and Mother should retire. Louisa is doing well with her millinery. Perhaps she should set up shop."

III

After much discussion, Henry and Louisa held the mortgage for James Henry Stewart in the amount of $850 for the fifth of an acre that comprised lot 21, west of Queen Street. By the end of 1892, James Henry Stewart purchased the remaining mortgage of $425 from Henry and his wife.

On October 10, 1893, Ruth Marion Martin was born to Edwin and Mary. The family was just getting adjusted to its newest member when Louisa, Edwin's stepmother, took ill.

"Edwin, what will I do without your mother—well, your stepmother? She was the one who nurtured you from the time you were two. I just can't believe that she's dying. The doctor says there's nothing he can do. I wonder if I took her to other doctors in Kingston whether they—"

"Father, I'm so sorry, but I think you know as well as I that there is little we can do but make her comfortable. You've given her such gentle care since she was ill. You know that she appreciates that, don't you? We will all miss her." Edwin put his hand on his father's shoulder. Henry wasn't taking Louisa's decline well.

IV

The Trenton Courier and Advocate printed the announcement that Louisa Martin died on July 8 and was buried on July 12, 1894. Henry was beside himself with grief. Louisa had followed him wherever he had chosen to go. She had been his faithful soulmate, and now she was gone, far sooner than Henry had ever imagined.

"Your mother will be buried in the family plot up at Camden East, Louisa. I'm thinking maybe it's time to return there. We had such fond memories of our early days. I know you feel that you are past the marrying age, but I don't want to saddle you with looking after me for the rest of your life if you choose to go with me."

"Father, I never plan on marrying. In fact, I have never met anyone whom I felt would make a suitable husband. I would love to go back to Clark's Mi—I mean, Camden East. Actually, I have been working up the idea of having my own millinery business, and that would give us a fresh start. Do you think we could rent a storefront?" Louisa made plans to go with Henry to stay permanently in Camden East.

seventy-one

Montreal, Quebec, 1894

Winnie was so pleased and excited that she had found a place to live and work in Montreal, right in the neighbourhood where they had been before. There was something sturdy about the charming houses with winding stairs to the main floor and steps to the apartments belowground. She thrived on the independence she felt going to and from work in the busy crowds and thriftily saving for schooling. Her sister Mayzie had written that their mother was in the family way again, but Winnie was determined to stay in Montreal.

Trenton, Ontario, 1894, 1895

Edwin was concerned about the upcoming delivery of the child. It was twenty years since Winnie had been born, and after eight children, here they were having another.

"Mary, you must rest. Let the girls finish the cleaning up. Here, sit in this chair while I get you a cup of tea," said Edwin as he led a reluctant Mary to a chair.

"Oh, Edwin. Don't make such a fuss. This isn't our first child," replied Mary. She made no resistance to sitting down though. This baby would be due in a few weeks, sometime about the middle of February if her calculations were correct.

"What dress are you wearing to the Christmas concert?" Mayzie asked Lottie.

"I don't know yet, but I wanted to wear something festive, not too dark. Why, were you wanting to borrow my grey skirt?" asked Lottie.

Mayzie smiled. "That would be very generous of you, Lottie. May I?" The waist size and height of the sisters were very similar. They were all growing and often shared clothing to save money. In fact, they would have been expected to share or hand clothes down whether or not they fit well. All of their friends did the same thing in their families. Only Ozzie needed his own clothing, but even then, Mary would often rework one of Edwin's suits to fit Ozzie, and at some point they could share clothing, until Ozzie grew broader than Edwin.

The quiet of early evening was broken by a cry from Ruth Marion, their two-year-old. Mary prepared to get up from the table where she and Edwin were sharing a pot of tea.

"No, let Winnie go and look after her, Mary. You need to stay put. Are you too warm? You look flushed." Edwin kept his hand over hers.

"I'm fine. Just weary. I think I will lie down for a while," Mary said. "Don't be concerned, Edwin. It's just that I'm not getting any younger, but I will be fine. I'll be forty-five next birthday, you know."

Edwin was concerned, so he got up and helped his wife to their room, where he gently took off her shoes and massaged her swollen feet. In minutes she was asleep, and after covering her with a quilt, Edwin left the room, closing the door as he prayed for God's protection for Mary and the unborn baby.

II

A quiet Christmas season passed that year, and January came with a vengeance. Edwin and Ozzie would walk along Front Street, mufflers wrapped around their throats twice, hat flaps down, and long coats buttoned knees-to-neck.

"There won't be much activity down at the docks today," Edwin hollered to Ozzie.

"There should be good skating if the wind dies down," Ozzie shouted back, always the optimist. He looked forward to putting on a pair of blades so he could play a little hockey with his friends. He didn't have much spare time for recreation, but he took it whenever he could. By no means was Ozzie a serious athlete, but he loved winter for its sports.

"Looks like a standstill in the harbour," Edwin noted. Icicles hung from yardarms and ropes all the way to the mast tops decorating the stationary fishing boats, frozen along the wharfs of the Trent River. Water ran under the frozen canopy of the dam. Trees, silhouetted in snow and ice, gave the scene an ethereal beauty.

On the 27th of January, Poppy came running into the store, calling for her father. He was pulling on his coat and galoshes while giving Ozzie instructions.

"Your mother may need the doctor. This is a little early, so be prepared to stay to closing time, Ozzie. The girls will bring word if there is any news. You could go over those invoices and the lower shelves of tinned goods stocked from the back room. I doubt you will be very busy today with the weather." And Edwin was out the door, still buttoning his coat while ducking his head to face the wind. Poppy's tracks were already being covered as Edwin followed, only a yard away.

"Father, you need to send for the doctor. Mother is struggling to keep from shouting. She must be in great pain," and Mayzie turned her father around at their door.

Mary was biting the bedsheet when the doctor arrived. Perspiration covered her forehead. The doctor got to work immediately.

"Ah, this little baby wants to enter the world backwards. Breathe deeply, Mrs. Martin; I'm going to turn this little fellow around." With an expert hand, the doctor got the head down, and things began moving quickly. Mary groaned a few times, and another tiny but healthy baby appeared.

"Oh, thank you, Doctor. Thank you. Please tell the girls and Edwin," and she breathed a sigh of relief as she cuddled her newborn.

The family trooped in, the girls all trying to make their mother comfortable; Edwin just held on to the baby's hand, thankful that both Mary and this little one were healthy.

"Mossie and Mayzie, why don't both of you go down to the store and help Ozzie. You can tell him the good news." The girls left somewhat reluctantly, but there was plenty of help, so they bundled up for the cold and headed out.

"What?" Ozzie lamented. "Another sister! Seven sisters! Father'll be a poor man by the time he gets all you girls married off." Although teasing, Ozzie felt somewhat lonesome within the family. His only brother had died as an infant, and here were seven busy sisters now, and their mother. He wished he and his father Edwin were closer, but Ozzie felt that his ideas and dreams were often being downplayed.

III

Harry Martin and Annie Raymond, his wife, made the move back to Camden East to be with Henry and Louisa. It wasn't long before Harry was getting itchy feet. His father couldn't blame him, having moved his own family so many times and such long distances on occasion.

"Father, Annie and I have decided to leave. I have an opportunity to set up business in Hamilton. You remember John? He and I used to chum around together when we were here in Camden East," said Harry.

"Henry—I mean Harry—I can't get used to calling you that. Harry, why all the way to Hamilton? Why not Kingston, or Napanee, or Trenton? You aren't leaving because of some dispute with Edwin, are you?" Henry Senior slumped in his chair.

"Well, not really. I just want something different, and Annie and I have talked about moving to a larger city for a while. I know you miss Mother, but we think you are getting along well now, with Louisa's help, of course."

"Your sister has been a godsend to me, Harry. If she didn't seem so happy, I would think she should have married and raised her own family. It seems she really is content to look after an old man like me and work on her hats," said Henry.

"She is doing a good little business. Besides, she's involved in St. Luke's ladies group, she has many friends, and she's a wonderful sister. I shall miss her, and Annie will too."

Harry and Annie left soon after to set up business in Hamilton. They found friends and a good Presbyterian church to attend. Their daughter Marjorie was born in February 1896, and the family seemed to be happily settled.

Montreal, Quebec, 1900

In the fall of 1898, Winifred Martin enrolled in the two-year theoretical and practical instruction program at the Montreal Homoeopathic Hospital. It seemed to her that she had completed the course and was about to be graduated in no time at all.

"Father, I'm so glad you could come," Winnie said. "How are Mother and baby Nora?"

"They are well, Winnie. Your mother was disappointed that she couldn't come, but Nora is still a bit fragile. She certainly has become stronger and is beginning to look like a healthier four-year-old, but she came down with a cold, and your mother didn't wish her to travel on the train with all those people."

Winnie studied her diploma. The hospital was sketched on the top half. The red wax seal held the black and green ribbon firmly to the page at the bottom. On the seventh day of June in the year 1900 she had walked proudly up to the president of the hospital board and had shaken his hand before receiving the certificate from the secretary. Her father had looked as pleased as she felt.

seventy-two

Trenton, Ontario, 1900

"Well, if you aren't going to be in the photo, Father, neither will I. Let the girls and Mother dress up and fuss with the photographer. I think the boys are meeting down at the Union Hotel. I hear them calling me."

"Calling for your turn to foot the bill likely. Don't be too late this afternoon. We have stock to distribute."

Edwin was kept busy in his store warehouse. On the same fifth of lot 21 that his father had owned sat a barn for the horses, a house of eight rooms where the nine of them lived, and a building lot. By November of 1901, the town of Trenton had taken possession of lot 21 for taxes, and Henry never collected all his mortgage money.

Edwin found it difficult to get ahead of the expenses, but he appreciated having so many wonderful children. They remained in the house and paid rent to the town. Times were challenging, and many were in the same position. The town took what they could get in small rents, rather than remove people to the streets.

Mayzie was particularly interested in the green grocery business. Edwin just wished his son showed more of an aptitude for commerce. He had great ideas for spending but was far too carefree with his money. All too often he would be down at the local watering hole or Armstrong's Restaurant on Front Street with his friends, having a few rounds. He was a well-liked and friendly chap, funny when in a lighthearted mood but too easily led by his friends to spend more time than he should in the pub. Then he would come home and sweet-talk his mother, making light of the fact he hadn't been in the shop to help his father all afternoon. Well, someday he would have to look after his own business. Edwin wouldn't be running it himself forever.

II

Mary gathered her girls around her. They all had lace collars or bows of light coloured material, except for Poppy, who wore a light cream blouse with a black bow, pleated like a fan, from her neck.

"It will look like a funeral picture if we all wear black," Poppy insisted.

Mary smoothed out Nora's ringlets and placed a bow at the side of her head. She turned to her eldest daughter.

"Winnie, try to keep from frowning. It spoils your face, and you do hope to marry someday, I hope."

Winnie did frown, wondering how her mother could think she would be marrying someday when she had so little chance to meet any suitable young men. Helping to look after the house with seven younger siblings was no easy task, and she made sure that they knew it. Besides, she had her father's height, which was too tall for a woman, and she tried to stoop her shoulders somewhat so that it wasn't quite so evident.

Ruth and Nora gazed at the black cloth surrounding the photographer's camera with youthful curiosity. The girls were a formidable fortress of females surrounding their mother in protectiveness. They didn't question the decision that their father and brother were not to be among the group.

III

Winnie overheard her mother telling her father about her cousin W. C. Linton coming to visit. She wondered if he had married. They didn't hear too often from her mother's brother William Cornelius Linton Sr. He had gone to the United States before Winnie was born, married Mary Ann Fisher, and had four sons, who were born in Illinois. They had settled in Ottumwa, Iowa, where W. C. Sr. was an insurance agent. The oldest boy was married, Walter was left to look after business, and William and Lester were accompanying their father to visit.

"Grandfather James Linton would have been one hundred years old now if he had lived. Some of the family said he was from Ireland, but we never knew for sure. He was a widower already when Grandma Mary married him. Your Uncle John got her maiden name, Jull, as his second name. They didn't talk much about their family though," concluded Mary.

"Did I hear that your brother is coming to Kingston to visit? When is that?" interrupted Winnie, her interest piqued.

"Winnie, they are already here, and I wanted to surprise you all. We're going to visit Uncle William's family at our sister-in-law Jessie's home in Kingston after your father closes the store Saturday afternoon. Can you help pack some overnight clothes for Poppy, Lottie, Ruth, and Nora? We'll need a brush, comb, and some clean underclothes. Mayzie, can you help Mossie get your things ready, and we'll put everything in the carpetbags."

Everyone was excited to be going on a very rare trip to Kingston. They didn't travel as a family often, so even Winnie was looking forward to the change. Mary had not seen her older brother's family for some time, and this was too good an opportunity to miss. Edwin and Ozzie would only come for the first two days and then return the next week to pick them up. The train and the steamer were available, but with so many needing to pay full or half fare, it was decided that their own carriage was a much less expensive way to travel.

IV

They pulled up in front of the Linton house on Gore Street. Mary was first off, the most anxious to see her brothers' families. She nearly hopped up the veranda steps in her excitement.

"Shall we bring in the baggage, Mother?" called Ozzie from the rear of the carriage.

"We can do that later after we get these travelling clothes off. Everyone is anxious to meet the family." Mary held Nora's hand as she moved to where the screen door was being held open by a man older than she expected. He couldn't possibly be her brother, could he?

"Mary! How are you? This must be Ruth, is it?"

"Will? Oh, it is so good to see you. This is Nora. She's our youngest, the eighth. Will, you remember my husband, Edwin. And this must be your second oldest, young William Cornelius."

A small-boned serious lad stepped forward and shook hands. He politely took time to greet each of his newly met cousins, taking only slightly longer over Winnie's handshake. He appeared somewhat nervous around all these young girls, having only brothers himself.

Jessie Amelia, John Jull Linton's widow, herded all of them into the dining room to where chairs, stools, and benches had been brought in as an attempt to seat most of the guests. Fruit breads, generously buttered, scones with jam, slices of meat, cheese, and pickles were arranged on the sideboard. Jessie had brought out her best silver and china dinnerware, and she insisted that the youngest fill their plates first. Her daughter-in-law, Mary Urquhart Linton, and her daughter Mary put out the plates and served. With Mary Martin also helping, there was much laughter over the confusion of names.

Edwin talked enthusiastically with Will, while the Linton and Martin male cousins made their acquaintances in the vestibule. When the din in the dining room had quieted down, they joined the females in satisfying their hunger.

On the eve of the family's expected return to Kingston, Edwin requested that Ozzie take care of the store and warehouse while he left early in the morning to pick up the rest of the family.

"What should we do with these oranges, Father? Some are looking a little soft."

"Your mother and sisters can make marmalade when we return if you haven't sold them by tomorrow night."

Edwin was met by a tired but happy team of young girls, and he greeted his wife with a fond hug and stolen kiss. He noticed that Winnie actually had some colour to her cheeks, and her seemingly permanent frown was not as pronounced as it was before they had come. He wondered at the change until he noticed young cousin William standing close to her and offering a hand as she stepped into the carriage. He looked at Mary and raised his eyebrows, silently questioning the situation. Mary just held her head straight and restrained a smile as best she could. They would talk later.

seventy-three

Trenton, Ontario, 1899

Young William came by the Queen Street house in Trenton, as promised. He had taken the train on his own, ahead of the rest of the family, and would join them later.

It was obvious to all that he had intentions with Winnie. The glow of her cheeks alone would have been enough to show the spark between the two, but the fact William promised to write when he went home was the clincher for Edwin and Mary.

"Well, thank God for huge kindnesses. I never thought Winnie would ever interest any man, but I am concerned they are first cousins."

"I don't think that will be much of a concern. They aren't like royalty who marry cousins every other generation. It will take some doing on William's part if he's to thaw that young woman enough to produce children."

"Edwin!" Mary giggled despite her reprimand. Edwin drew her close and rubbed her back through the layer of her flannel nightgown. They snuggled under the layers of quilts that the cool fall air demanded.

"Oh, you are a naughty one, Mrs. Martin. Have a good sleep. In the morning, I'll have to see that Ozzie has put in the advertisements for this week's produce and has organized the shop."

Winnie never let on that she was corresponding with William Linton, but as soon as the mail came in, she would go through the letters quickly, and if a letter with an American stamp came in, she would grasp it and have it in her pocket before any of her younger siblings could announce with a shout that she had received mail, which was what they were bound to do. So it was somewhat of a surprise, and to Mary a relief, when the oldest daughter in the family made a clipped announcement the day after Christmas.

"I'm leaving for Iowa in the new year. William has asked me to marry him, and I'm going to. Uncle William has asked me to stay with them for a few months until then. You can't stop me."

"You are nearly twenty-six years old, Winifred. We have no intention of stopping you," responded her father, a twitch at the corners of his mouth.

Winifred was slightly deflated, having expected at least some argument.

"You girls are all growing so quickly. We'll soon have an empty nest, do you think, Mother?" asked Edwin, winking at Nora, who at this time was only eight.

"Oh, Papa. I'm not going to get married! I'm always going to live with you and Mama."

Nine-year-old Ruth snorted. "No, you're not. We girls are all going to grow up and get married some day. You have to get married, to have children, you know."

"And that will be enough, thank you, Ruth. Nora will grow up soon enough. There's no rush for any of you to go off getting married," and that was the end of that conversation at the dinner table.

Edwin insisted that Ozzie accompany Winifred, as it was not safe in what he considered the Wild West. Having lived in Illinois as a young lad, he remembered some of the wilder behaviour of horsemen on the streets. There had seemed a proliferation of rifles and guns.

"Father, I'm a grown woman. I don't need an escort!" Winnie tried arguing.

"You are going six hundred miles and have several changes of trains to make. Indians are restless at the moment, and you are not going unaccompanied. Osmund will go with you, and that is that."

Every spare minute was spent knitting, sewing, and quilting for Winnie's trousseau. Ozzie came into the parlour one evening to find six of his seven sisters busy. Nora had gone to bed, but even Ruth was helping to hem a new nightgown. Mossie was embroidering, Poppy was helping her mother quilt the pieced bed covering, and Mayzie was pumping the treadle of the sewing machine while Winnie held up the fabric, guiding it along as Mayzie pushed it gently under the foot and needle.

"Well, what are you knitting there, Lottie?" Ozzie asked.

"A woolen jumper for William to match the shawl I made for Winnie. I understand it's very cold in the winter in Iowa."

"Well, that's good of you to think of William, but don't you think Winnie will keep him warm?"

"Osmond! Enough of that," scolded his mother, and with a smile to see such industry at such a late hour, he quickly ducked out down the hall to find his father, who was probably sitting by the stove in the kitchen reading a newspaper.

Winnie and William were married in mid-winter, January 15th, 1902, in Ottumwa, Wapello, Iowa.

To her father's delight a birth announcement arrived stating Harold Martin Linton was born on the thirteenth of October 1903, and all appeared to be well with the family.

II

"Edwin, are you worried? asked Mary.

"No. Thomas Sketch is an honest man. He knows that Father lost a great deal on the mortgage, and the town has allowed Sketch to pay the back taxes of $100. He told me confidentially that our family could have it for that cost at any time. I'm sure that we will have no trouble with renting from him. The town is probably happy to have the account cleared after three years. At least we have our own home here now, free and clear. We can hope for better times, and better management from Ozzie.

"I hope he will take over at some point, but it won't be soon. He really does not have a good head for business. He pays for things without thought about getting any profit. He could spend less time with his friends at their local. I don't expect the temperance movement to make much headway just yet, so we just need to be a little firmer with him. He's old enough to settle down any time now."

"Oh, Edwin. Sometimes I think you are a little hard on Ozzie. He is our only son, you know, but he can't be perfect. He does have a kind heart and would do anything to help others."

Edwin nodded but refrained from further comment. He hoped to interest Ozzie in expanding the ice-making business. There was a need for ice all year round, and the capital outlay was minimal. It would give Ozzie a chance for physical work and a profitable sideline.

Trenton, Ontario, Christmas 1904

The Martin family was busy helping others to prepare for Christmas. It was the height of the baking season. Housewives had already made their Christmas cake, some with brandy, some without. Mincemeat tarts would be next.

Ozzie checked over the advertisement at the counter of the Trenton Courier.

"E. & O. Martin—for our rendered Lard; 10 barrels of candies, 10 crates of oranges, 5 tubs oysters, 10 boxes of Haddies, 100 lbs. Mincemeat. Must be sold in next 10 days."

His other endeavour was the sale of new typewriters. He had gotten a deal on them and thought they were reasonably priced. He wasn't aware of their being available anywhere else in town, at least with the wide selection he had.

"Twenty-five different kinds of type-writers for sale, price in reach of everyone. Call and inspect at O. W. Martin & Co."

"This will go into the December 15th paper, will it, Harry?"

"You bet, Mr. Martin. How are those sisters of yours doing, eh?" laughed Harry.

"Well, since you are married yourself, Harry, what interest would that be to you? If there were a few more appropriate suitors, I wouldn't have to help keep them, now would I, Harry?" Ozzie was joking in a friendly manner, but underlying was a concern that money just never went as far as he hoped.

II

The twenty-fourth of December was very busy for Mary and the girls at home. Edwin would bring in what produce had not been sold, and the girls would get busy and bake or cook. If there were excess oranges, they made marmalade. If it was mincemeat, tarts and pies were prepared. There was often fruit and some of the dry crusts for bread puddings. Mary always made sure she had lard available, usually rendering it down on the back of the wood stove for days. Not a thing went to waste. Greens left over from the store would be used as vegetable dishes or, if too wilted, chopped up to add to the soup.

Edwin opened the front door of the house to look outside. New snow had already covered the veranda, the steps, and the walk. He would have to get the corn broom out again and sweep so his aging father and the rest of the family could get in without slipping. It was crisp, cold air that tickled the nose hairs but felt refreshing to the lungs. The snowbanks were piled quite high this year, but there was still room for carriages or the odd automobile to be parked on the street.

III

"Harry is bringing Father in," Edwin warned his wife. They would make a comfortable place of honour for him in the parlour where he could see the kitchen, dining room, and front entrance.

"There you are, Father. Let Mossie here hang up your coat in the hall. How are you doing? Is Louisa taking good care of you?" Edwin spoke loudly and directly to his father's face so he could read Edwin's lips. His hearing had declined in the past few years, as had his stature. Edwin was saddened to see the stoop in Henry's upper body but pleased he managed to move around so well with the aid of a cane.

"What's that you said, Edwin? Is there moss on the wall? How did you take care of it? I never heard of a problem like that."

Edwin glanced over at Harry and Mossie, bending his head to hide his laughter, but Mossie came to the rescue.

"Everything is fine, Grandfather. How are you?" She carefully and slowly enunciated every word.

"I'm not too bad for an old man of eighty-four. Oh, I wish your mother were here to see how all you young folks have grown up. Look at you, Nora. What lovely hair! And little Ruth. What are you now, fourteen?"

"Oh, Grandfather! You know I'm only eleven, but I wish I were fourteen. Then I wouldn't be a child any longer and people might actually speak to me. Why do so many grownups ignore us children, Grandfather?" and Ruth gave the old gentleman a big hug. She was finding it difficult to grow up with so many older sisters, except Nora, who seemed content to be the youngest and happy to be a child. Ruth pulled up a stool to her grandfather's knee and held his strong, gnarled hand. He would listen to her.

Edwin stood at the head of the table surrounding the large, happy family. His two married sisters, their husbands, and their children had joined them this year. Louisa, his only unmarried sister, was helping Mary and the girls with the food. Harry and his family were with his in-laws, so they were missing. Winnie and her family were in Iowa, which was too far to come for the holiday, but it was nearly everyone, and the tables filled the length of the dining room and parlour.

Mary had read the passage of the Christ child's birth from the Gospel of Matthew, and Edwin had prayed a prayer of thanksgiving for all their blessings. Now he was standing poised to cut and serve the goose. Ozzie, who had filled a few glasses with small amounts of sherry, stood up, raising his glass.

"I'd like to propose a toast to the most wonderful mother a son could have, even if he has to share her with seven sisters. May you live many more years and be happy to often organize a feast like this for all of us who appreciate it. To Mary Martin, and may God bless you." Ozzie's flushed cheeks indicated that he had already tasted the sherry, but his mother chose to ignore that and smiled on her son, then her father-in-law and brothers-in-law, before resting her gaze on her husband. The men raised their glasses and toasted Mary with love and fondness.

seventy-five

Trenton and Camden East, 1907

Edwin had been thinking of his father, Henry, more often lately. He had made it a habit to visit once a month because he could see that his father was failing. Louisa was doing a remarkable job taking care of him. It suited her that she could work on her millinery from home and still assist their father when needed.

Edwin thought that more and more his father was losing interest in living. He had hardly made comment when a second little girl, Doris, was born to Harry last year. Edwin brought Nora, his youngest, a few times, thinking she might distract his father, but he took less and less notice of any visitor.

It was no surprise to receive a telegram on the first of November saying his father had died.

"Louisa, you look exhausted. Here, why don't you sit down while the family get their clothing off, and I'll make us each a cup of tea." Edwin helped his teary-eyed sister to a comfortable chair and walked into the back kitchen searching for the kettle. At least the water pump was inside, so he just needed to stoke the fire and look for some pickles and beets to go with the bread, butter, and ham his wife had brought.

"I need to speak to you, Edwin, about Father's finances. You may not know that Father lost a significant amount of money last year when the Farmer's Bank failed. After that, he changed his will and signed the house over to me. I hope that won't upset you and the others."

"You deserve it, Louisa. You have devoted your life to looking after our parents, even turning down suitors to do so. Don't you give it another thought. All of us are married with families and have means of our own. Do you plan on staying here, now that Father is gone?"

"I've settled in well, Edwin, and I like it better here than Trenton for some reason. I've made friends, believe it or not, and belong to the women's auxiliary of St. Luke's. By the way, the cousins are giving money for a memorial communion rail from the Hooper and Cresser families. I don't think we can afford to contribute to that, but I've talked to the Reverend Spencer, and he said a few more Books of Common Prayer would be most useful."

"That sounds fine with me. I know how much Father loved his in-laws, and the Cressers left the church a significant amount of money, never having had children. I'll speak with the Reverend Spencer when I discuss the arrangements of the service. Do you know of a mason who can do the engraving?"

"Yes. It's the same one that did cousin John Hooper's last year. It seems like we've lost so many aunts, uncles, and cousins in the last while." Louisa returned her teacup to its saucer and bent her head down. Within minutes she was asleep sitting up. She had intended to plan out some of the new hats that had been ordered for the Christmas season. The Edwardian style of a large, highly flared straw frame worn on top of hair piled high and tilted over the face was beginning to move to a much flatter and wider brim, though netting, artificial silk flowers, and velvet ribbons to edge the brim were still popular.

There had been so much extra washing to do the past few weeks. Her father's incontinence was the hardest to deal with. "It's only water," he would say. "It'll dry." Well, she would have more time now, and would keep herself busy with hat-making for the next few weeks. Tears for her father came even in her sleep. He was eighty-nine, after all, but she would miss him.

Picton, 1907

"Would you like an apple with your sandwiches, Charles?"

"Yes, Mother. That will be fine." Charles was scowling a little, partly because he felt his mother was fussing and partly because he was a little nervous and excited about making the long train trip all the way to Calgary, where he would be articling at Blaylock and Bergeron Solicitors. He had a room in the Armstrong block at one dollar and fifty cents a day, and the offices were right downtown in the Alberta block. He had been very pleased when his father and mother had presented him with a leather travelling suitcase and a leather briefcase, both with his initials, C. A. W., embossed in gold.

"Are you all ready, son?" John asked. "We still have plenty of time to get the train in Trenton. Did you say goodbye to your sister last night?"

"Oh, yes, Father. Nina was nearly in tears. She must think she will never see me again." The two had been close growing up, and each had promised to write. Nina was to look after her mother and make sure her father didn't work too hard.

Alma hugged her son tightly, handing him his lunch. She used the hem of her apron to dry her tears. She should be so pleased—and she really was—that he was going to follow in his father's footsteps. After all, they had survived the flu epidemic, and Charles had been too young to enlist, so unlike other families who were still getting over losses of the last few years, they were indeed fortunate.

Trenton, Ontario, 1907

"We're going to Toronto!" exclaimed Mayzie. "There was an advertisement in the Courier that Eaton's store in downtown Toronto was hiring clerks, and we've been accepted."

"Who do you mean, we?" asked Edwin, glancing at his wife, who was standing at the stove. She turned around to listen.

"Well, myself, and my friend Laura, and Poppy. We have lodgings near the streetcar for the winter weather, and maybe we can walk in the nice weather."

"How did this come about?" asked her mother.

"Well, Laura and I answered the ad. Then I wrote to Uncle Harry, but I never got a response, so Laura wrote to her cousin and went down to Toronto and has found us a boarding house where we can stay."

"Poppy seems young to be going off to a big city like this. Are you sure she will want to go?" asked Edwin.

"It was her idea to join us. She asked. She'll do fine at a big store like that. I'm sure that it will be very busy, and she will have so many customers that she won't have time to worry or be shy," replied Mayzie.

Toronto, Ontario, 1907

The three girls were thrilled with their positions in the big city. They enjoyed travelling on the streetcars. They went to live theatre or music productions when they could. Lunch was in the cafeteria in the basement, and for very little they could have a hot meal. They would climb onboard the tram along with the crowds at the Shuter-Louise stop and return to the boarding house. This was a stone and brick building of substantial size. The front stone steps led to the heavy wooden door at the front.

In a letter home, Poppy wrote,

We are doing well. Mayzie has taken a different position, which involves more paperwork, and she is enjoying that. We talk and laugh all the way downtown with some of the other girls at the boarding house. Our favourite is to rhyme off the choice of meals: steak, sausage, liver and bacon, cold roast beef, shepherds' pie or stew. We see who can say it the fastest, and end up laughing as our tongues get twisted. Then we have Laura trying to rhyme off our family names: Winnie, Ozzie, Mayzie, Mossie, Poppy, Lottie, Ruth, and Nora. We look forward to our next visit, and hope all are well.
Your loving daughter,
Poppy

Poppy, Mossie and friend in Toronto

seventy-six

Trenton, 1907

Two doors down the street from the Martins' home were Daniel and Annie Jackson. At nineteen, Mossie had offered to help with their newborn daughter, Maggie. She would often show up to help with the baby while Annie prepared supper. Sometimes Mossie would be asked to stay for meals, and the four became close friends. Daniel was also in the grocery business and became a good customer of Ozzie's through wholesales and ice.

Ozzie would saw through thick solid ice in the winter, cut it into blocks, and store it in the icehouse on lot 21, Queen. Bales of straw kept the ice rather well, until by late fall only smaller chunks were available to sell to people for refrigeration.

"There's your order, Daniel," said Ozzie, dropping the last of the ice blocks into the box-like refrigerator and closing the lid.

"What do you hear of Calgary these days?" Daniel asked.

"They seem like a wild bunch of crazy horsemen to me," said Ozzie.

"I've heard they have two soapworks, two candy factories, and even a macaroni factory. Their mills are doing a great business apparently. I hear they will have two electric power plants, another cigar factory, a meat processing plant, and two breweries within the next year. Have you ever thought of moving west, Ozzie?" asked Daniel.

"No. I like it here, and besides, what would my father do without me?"

"They have two breweries there," offered Daniel, knowing of Ozzie's fondness for the beverage.

"I'm working on some unique type of bottling equipment myself. Maybe if you do go, you can let me know what the conditions are. I hear they don't have good roads and that they are deep with mud most of the year."

II

By 1908 plans were made by the Jacksons to move to Calgary and start up a business there. Mossie planned on joining them. She knew the grocery business and would be a help in staffing a new store. Apparently the city was booming. Buildings were being constructed as fast as contractors could build them, and still people, even businesses, were purchasing tents to start with. There were two tent and mattress manufacturers already. Six fire stations and 100 alarm boxes kept the city safe after the devastating downtown fire of 1886.

Toronto, Ontario, 1909

Thomas Pain was trying to make eye contact with the attractive young woman behind the counter at Eaton's. It was difficult to casually be looking at women's gloves and scarves when all his family were in Portsmouth, England.

"May I help you?" the young woman asked.

"Oh…yes. Have you had your lunch break yet?" he asked.

Poppy's face neck blushed rosy red. "No," was all she could manage.

Thomas Pain had been sixteen when he had made his way to Canada in 1894. His family were butchers, which he worked at in Montreal, but he wanted to work with the hides. He loved the feel of soft fur pelts and soon approached a furrier to apprentice him.

"Mr. Fairweather? I was wanting a job and would like to be a furrier."

Mr. Fairweather looked at the earnest young man, thought a moment, and then handed him the broom that he himself had been using.

"This cutting area needs sweeping, then around the cleaning drum. After that you can go into the front sales area and sweep there when the doors are closed for dinner. Get into the corners, mind you, and when Penny returns, she will add you to the payroll."

Fairweather Furriers soon found that Thomas Pain knew about skinning and cleaning furs. He was soon learning about the quality of pelts, the favourite animals for the fashions, and cutting. Montreal was a very cold city in winter, and both men and women needed fur collars and coats to help keep them warm.

"Thomas, I need you to make a delivery of furs to Toronto and pick up orders from the store there. You can stay overnight with Gordon near the station and leave on the afternoon train to return. You've become a very valuable member of our staff." Fairweather dropped his heavy hand on Thomas' shoulder, slapping it with power enough to convey the confidence in which he held Thomas.

This was how Thomas came to be in Toronto and wondering around the Eaton's store. He had seen this attractive young lady the last time he had come to Toronto, and now he had surprised himself by asking her to lunch.

"We could head down to the cafeteria in the basement, if that suits you? When are you free?" he asked.

Poppy blushed, hardly knowing what to say. She had seen him before in the store and thought that Mayzie would be joining them anyway, so it would be quite safe.

"I can go in ten minutes," she said looking at her watch. "Do you have a name?" she asked, looking up at him through her lashes.

"Thomas, Thomas Pain. Just plain Pain. I mean, not that I want to be a pain, but it came with my birth."

A few minutes later, Mayzie, Poppy, and Thomas were in line with trays, chatting and laughing like old friends. Before the lunch date was finished, Thomas had given Poppy his address, hoping against hope she might write to him in Montreal.

"Have you received another letter from Thomas already?" her friend asked.

"Yes, I asked about the fur business and how he liked working with the furs of animals. He was explaining to me about how they can tell the quality of a fur by gently blowing on it, and how they mark out a pattern's cutting lines with chalk. It sounds quite complicated, but he is enthusiastic about his work."

"Do you think we'll be able to get seats on the train next Friday?" interrupted Mayzie. "There will be crowds going home with Christmas on a Saturday. At least we will have two whole days off and can return on Monday."

"Our seats are reserved, so as long as we make it to the station on time, we will be fine. Union Station will be a madhouse, though. I'm glad my parcels are small and we have some clothing already there," responded Poppy.

seventy-seven

Trenton, Ontario, 1909–1910

Suddenly, it seemed the remainder of the Martin girls were all growing up. They were taking positions or moving away. Lottie had been asked by her sister Winnie and brother-in-law William Linton to work at the insurance office in Scott, Iowa. She had been practicing on the typewriter that Ozzie had given her for her birthday. Not all the typewriters had sold at Christmas. She looked at going west as an adventure. She thought Winnie might be lonely, and she liked her brother-in-law and her fine young nephew, Harold, well enough to make up for leaving her parents and younger sisters.

Poppy, rightfully named Victoria Linton Martin, was also away from home, still working at Eaton's in Toronto. She had saved money to purchase lot 21 from Thomas Sketch and his wife for the $100 they had paid the town. Ozzie convinced her he would be making a great business out of it one day, and she could see he had plans.

Equipment began taking shape, and soon a bottling processing plant evolved. Poppy continued to work the mortgage back and forth between James Kinney, Jesse Fernell, and Arthur Edwin Bywater. Ozzie was challenging to deal with, since his idea of handling money did not match the careful dealings of the rest of the family. Edwin had warned his daughter, but the girls all had a soft spot for Ozzie, and they tried their best to keep him afloat.

Edwin and Mary were having their own problems. Edwin was having a difficult time getting over the death of Lilly Conger, his youngest half-sister. She had suffered throat problems for years and lost the fight to the disease in May. As well, Ruth had taken to going to nearby Belleville to the cinema. Moving pictures were all the rage, but her parents were concerned about the late nights she kept. She also performed at the theatre in Trenton, but they really were not sure of her schedule.

"Ruth, you cannot go again this week. You have seen this same moving picture before. What is the attraction?" asked Edwin.

"Oh, the music is wonderful. It's amazing the way Norm—the pianist can play such exciting music for fast moving horses or the train going through the mountains, and he plays such sad music when someone dies and romantic music when the hero kisses the lady he rescues." Ruth was blushing with pleasure of it but failed to mention the looks the pianist sent her way when he played those romantic parts. She may have been only sixteen, but she knew love when she saw it.

Rather than go all the way home from the main street where she worked, Ruth would stop in to leave a message with Ozzie or her father, who would be busy at the grocers. They were never sure they got the full story, but one evening Ozzie was sent to Belleville to view the pictures. When the film ended and Ozzie had not seen Ruth exit, he went around to the back of the building. There, on their way up the steps to rooms above the cinema, were a suave dark-haired young man and a giggling, blushing Ruth.

"Ruth! How about you introduce me your young man?"

"Ozzie! What are you doing here? Have you been sent to spy on me? You can just—"

"Who is this, Ruth?"

"I'm Osmond Martin, Ruth's brother, and you are..."

"Norman Roland Holmes. Pleased to meet you, sir."

Ozzie felt there was a little freshness in his attitude when he emphasized the "sir." "I think, Ruth, it's time for you to come home, and the next time you wish to see my sister, Mr. Holmes, you may call at the house at 24 Queen Street, in Trenton. Goodnight," and with that he took his sister's arm firmly and guided her to the station.

"What were you thinking, Ruth? Or I don't suppose you were thinking about what he might do to you in his rooms. I assume it was his rooms he was taking you to."

"Oh, Ozzie. We were just going to talk. Norman is really a gentleman. You just have no idea what it's like to be in love. I feel so humiliated with you taking me like that," and Ruth stomped on ahead. It was several minutes before she would speak to her brother, and he let her simmer. That was Ruth: spunky, fun-loving, but naive.

"What are you going to tell Mother and Father?" Ruth later asked, somewhat contritely.

"I'm not going to tell them anything except that you should not be allowed to go to the cinema in Belleville on your own and that someday soon they can expect to have a 'gentleman' by the name of Norman Roland Holmes come by the house. If he doesn't propose marriage, then I might suggest he should." Ozzie gave his sister a protective hug around the shoulders. He would have to tell his parents they were right to be concerned. Ruth was still too young to be married, but it might have to happen sooner than expected.

On the afternoon of Monday, July 4, 1910, Ruth took particular care with her dress, patting her new hairstyle gently as she gathered her purse with whatever money she had and made her way to the station for the Belleville train. Her friend Minnie Grant met up with her. Upon arriving in Belleville, they followed the directions Norman had given her to the home of the Reverend Bishop.

"Oh, Norman. You're late. I was worried you…something happened." She rolled her eyes at Minnie, knowing by the smell of them that Norman and his friend George Cook had imbibed a little something before arriving. She had experience with her brother's drinking habits to know all about it, but she was not going to let anything stop them from getting married now. Norman had promised, and she could be having a baby; she wasn't sure.

"I now pronounce you man and wife. You may kiss the bride." Norman knew what was expected and gave her a sweet, gentle kiss on the lips, not with the hungry passion he usually demonstrated.

"Did you bring the envelope for the Reverend?" Norman whispered as they finished the signing of the registry. Ruth nodded and pulled out the five dollars for the minister. She smiled, knowing they were really married. Norman had confessed to leaving a girlfriend in England, and although he had not said outright that he had deserted her at the altar, it was enough for Ruth to have been slightly wary before they were really married.

When Ruth returned to her parents' home that evening, she was not greeted as well as she hoped. She certainly didn't get the excited attention that Winnie had been given.

"You're sure it was a legitimate preacher?" her father asked doubtfully.

"Yes, it was. We signed papers and everything. It was all aboveboard. Minnie was there and Norman's friend George to witness. Aren't you going to put it into the paper?"

"Yes, that is a good idea, Edwin. Can you see to the details? I think Ruth and I need to have a talk," and Mary slowly got up from her armchair to speak privately with her daughter.

seventy-eight

Calgary, 1910

Osmond William Martin

Dear Poppy,
I miss being with the family, but the Jacksons have become my family. Daniel has a store quite a few blocks south of where we live, and it seems to be doing well. The city is growing so fast, one can hardly believe it. The winter is extremely cold, so you must tell Thomas that he should come here and start his fur business. The Blackfoot and Sarcees camp nearby and bring in their pelts. The Hudson's Bay Company doesn't deal with furs as it did in the pioneering days, but there are still furs available. Some days there are auctions where they are sold as well. With the town population growing, particularly females, there is sure to be a need for fur coats and muffs. Thomas could bring some of the modern Montreal styles with him and update the old furriers already here.

I hope Mother and Father are well. How are Nora and Ruth doing? Is Ruth continuing her music lessons? Please write when you have time, and do tell Thomas he should come to Calgary. Perhaps he can bring you too, as his wife of course.
Your loving and affectionate sister,
Mossie

Trenton, 1910

Ozzie wanted a more permanent building to house the ice he took from the lake, and he had been asked to draw up blueprints for his proposal.

"Alf, can you draw up a simple blueprint for me for the icehouse? I've talked to Granger about the use of the shore, and he said I just need to get permission from the town. They want a blueprint and an estimation of how much ice I will be taking."

"Sure, Ozzie. Why don't I come by the house on my way home to get your specs?"

"Great, and thanks, Alf. How much will I owe you?"

"Well, including last week's pints at the pub, about two dollars," Alf answered.

True to his word, Alf came by with his notepad and paper. "Good evening, Miss Martin. I say, you are looking smashing. Do you have a beau?"

Nora blushed but smiled shyly. She knew he was teasing because she was only nine. She took his coat and hung it up on a hook by the door, calling Ozzie from out in the kitchen. The two men spread out papers in the dining room, and Alf drew up rough sketches.

"The icehouse is to be here on the shore of Bay of Quinte. I have three gin poles in there, about forty-three, no, forty-four feet from shore. In fall I put booms out and attach them to the shoreline booms. These first two are twenty-eight by forty-four by eighteen inches thick; the next two are seventeen by forty-four by eighteen; and the last two are nineteen by forty-four and eighteen inches thick. Here are the calculations for the weight."

"Holy mackerel! Do you take that much ice off every year?"

"It's about the same most years, but this is the first I have had to calculate it. The town is likely going to start charging a healthy permit now. Seems as though they need the money."

"As usual. Do you sell all this ice?" Alf inquired.

"There's never any trouble selling the ice. Most people don't have electric refrigerators, and the stores all need it for their perishables in summer. I could sell even more in the summer, if I had better ways of keeping it from thawing. Depends on the season, though."

"I'll have this ready by tomorrow afternoon and will drop it off at the planning offices at city hall, if you like. I'm right in the same building. Well, I had better get home to the wife before supper is cold. When are you getting married, Ozzie?"

"Not soon, if wedding preparations are anything like I think they are," laughed Ozzie.

Trenton, Ontario, 1911–1913

Ruth came home the first of March to wait the birth of her first child. She was somewhat nervous, and tired too. Norman had had to go to Toronto to do a stint there with a cinema. He said it would be more money and they could save to rent part of a house, rather than just have two rooms. That would be heaven, because it was going to be awfully cramped if three of them had to fit into two crowded rooms.

Lionel Martin Holmes was born on a cold morning in March 1911. He was not a strong baby and picked up a cold within days. His little sneezes worried Ruth and her mother, who recalled how her little Edwin Henry sickened and died.

In the meantime, Winnie was home to be at the celebration of Poppy's wedding.

On May 12th that same year, Victoria Linton Martin married Thomas Edwin Pain at her parents' home in Trenton. They were a wonderful match and just so happy with each other. Ruth looked on, teary-eyed. Norman had looked at her like that before they married.

The family was deeply saddened when Lionel died in August. Ozzie sent a telegram to the Toronto address Norman had left with Ruth. To his credit, Norman was in Trenton within a week, having quit his job, and took Ruth to find a few rooms to rent so they could have the privacy of grieving together. Norman had seen his son only twice, but still he understood how Ruth felt, as he was heartbroken himself.

He wasn't aware that what she was feeling was exacerbated by morning sickness. On March 28th of 1912 Phyllis Holmes was born to Ruth and Norman. She was a strong baby, cried loudly when hungry, and seemed to need more attention than Ruth had energy to give her.

"Norman, I'm going home for a few days so Mother and Nora can help me with Phyllis. I just can't seem to get enough sleep."

"Seems to me you're giving that baby too much attention," and Norman watched as Ruth put things into two carrying bags.

"Can you help me get this over to Queen Street?"

"I'll be late for work. Here, let me help you to the store, and your father can bring the bags home with him." Ruth let out an exasperated sigh. She felt Norman would have lots of time to help her if he didn't go to the restaurant and have coffee and cigarettes, which they could ill afford.

Six days later, after rest and help with Phyllis, Ruth was ready to tackle a generally good tidying up of the rooms she and Norman rented. She hadn't expected to find him home, but she hadn't expected to find an almost empty apartment. Her hand continued to hold the key in the door as she stood shock still, viewing the litter of papers, open drawers, and empty cupboards. He had taken the dishes, the silverware, the kettle, and his clothes. There hadn't been much food anyways, but there was a lingering smell of cigarette smoke and decay. He had walked out on her.

Ruth couldn't face cleaning now. She would have to come back. What was she to do with Phyllis? Would her parents let her come back home to stay? There was more room now with Poppy married and gone. Ruth closed the door, turning the key mechanically, and walked home in a dream-like fog.

seventy-nine

When Poppy and her husband made the move west to Calgary, the others were sad to see the happy couple leave.

"Poppy wants to rid herself of lot 21 across the street," Thomas Pain declared on behalf of his wife. "We need to be free and clear of mortgages and holdings in Ontario if we are to move to the west. I need the capital to equip the fur store. "

"Can you find someone interested in taking over the mortgage, Ozzie?" asked Poppy.

"You've been putting a great deal of money into the bottling system over there," commented Edwin, his lips tightening and forehead furrowing.

"Well, yes, I have," Ozzie replied. "Arthur Bywater has an interest in it with Kinney and me. We've talked about forming a corporation. I don't really feel I can bow out at this point. Things are starting to mesh together, and I've invested a lot of time and money in the bottling works."

"Are you ever going to settle and marry, Ozzie?" asked his mother.

"Oh, yes, someday. But I would like to get the business going first. I haven't met anyone to my liking yet, and I blame you girls. You haven't allowed me to meet any of your friends." Ozzie smiled at his sisters, liking to tease the lot of them.

Edwin sat quietly while Ozzie discussed the bottling works. He was fairly certain that beer would be bottled, and he wasn't sure his son could handle having such an easy source of it close by without excessively partaking of the product. Arthur Bywater was a good businessman, having acquired several properties around town. He had sold his jewellery business to Rixon a few years before. Now he could concentrate on his other properties, his position as town councillor, and his captaincy with Company F in Trenton.7 Edwin would have preferred Arthur to run the business.

II

By July 2, 1913, the Berlin Brewery had been registered and hops delivered for brewing. There were other breweries in town, but the bottling system of Ozzie's was unique. Ozzie furnished the rooms above the factory into an apartment. Steam from the works would do well to heat the entire building, and the factory would be quiet at night. He was looking forward to the prospect, for by now he enjoyed a few drinks on a regular basis, and what better way than to run a brewery!

Trenton, Ontario, 1914–1916

Everyone was buzzing with war news. An ammunition plant was to be built in Trenton, and numerous jobs would be available. This was good news for Ozzie. His age and the pains in his legs prevented him from enlisting, so he was free to provide an essential service to the workers of Ontario. Most of the liquor and beer bottled in Trenton was shipped to Quebec, where the province had rejected the Prohibition Act of 1898. There was no preventing the people of Ontario in purchasing it in Quebec and bringing it back to Ontario. Some government officials were complaining, but nothing had been done to stop it.

"Well, Ozzie, you by yourself here again tonight?" asked Frank.

"Yup. Been awfully quiet around here lately since most of the family left for the west."

"I bet you didn't think you would miss all your sisters so much. They sure were a great bunch. How about you come down to the Armstrong Hotel and meet some girls? There are a few who came from the Old Country to work in the ammunitions factory. What say, eh?" and Frank nudged Ozzie's arm, spilling his beverage over the workbench.

"Hey, don't waste my drink. I've got to check quality control, you know. But, yah, I sure miss everyone, so let's go."

There were several girls who were taking their evening meal at the Armstrong. They were staying in temporary quarters while they worked for the war effort. Some had worked in ammunition factories in Britain as soon as the war broke out. One young lady looked Ozzie's way a few times, noting his clean-shaven face, sad brown eyes, and thick straight hair.

"I think there's a girl looking at you, Ozzie. Probably wondering if you're married or not. Should I introduce myself and bring her over to introduce you?" Frank laughed. He knew Ozzie would be horrified, because despite having seven sisters, or maybe because of that fact, he was rather shy of women.

The next evening, and several evenings after that, Ozzie took his dinner at the Front Street Hotel, where he quietly observed the gaggle of girls, and one in particular. She appeared to have an interest in him, but she looked so young. Ozzie didn't feel so old, but he was thirty-seven.

III

On November 16, 1915, there was a blizzard from the lake. The fury of flakes whipped around their ankles as Ozzie and Mary made their way back to lot 21, Berlin Brewery and apartment. Ozzie had never met anyone with so many given names. His young wife was Mary Maud Evelyn Clark, a twenty-five-year-old orphan, lately of Manchester, England. He had learned more about her during the registration of their marriage than he had in the previous six months of courting her. He looked at her dreamily, having wanted to take her in his arms as his wife for weeks now.

"Are you happy, Mary?" he asked.

"Oh, yes. I'm so excited to be moving to our own place. I'll have such fun decorating and cooking meals. Are we really going to get a greenhouse built in the spring? I really hate this cold weather and so look forward to having some green plants around." Mary turned her smile towards him, and his heart melted.

Mary was still shivering when they entered the rooms above the factory.

"Here, Mary. Leave your coat on while I set the stove ablaze. I'll just run downstairs to fill the coal bucket. You can unpack your bags in the bedroom. We may have to get another wardrobe for you, but move my things around as you need. I'll be right back," and he gently pressed a kiss on her rosy cheek.

It took a few minutes for the stove to make any difference to the temperature of the kitchen, and then Ozzie went in the bedroom to bring Mary in where it was warmest. He should have thought of getting the rooms warm ahead of time. He didn't want to waste any coal, as it was expensive, but he should have thought how Mary hated this freezing weather.

Once the brewery bottling works was running on a Monday, it was much warmer in the apartment above than on a Sunday. Still Mary Maud wrapped herself in extra shawls and often wore half-gloves with the fingers open that Ozzie had given her. He was quite happy to be married, never noticing that Mary Maud only smiled when he smiled at her. She tried to go back to the ammunition factory, but they wouldn't take a married woman. There were plenty of older men and single women who needed employment.

"I'm meeting Claire and Susan at the restaurant for a meal tonight," Mary Maud told Ozzie. "There is some pork shoulder and pickle for your supper. You can open a can of mushy peas if you like. They're in the cupboard above the counter. I'll see you later this evening," and she brushed his cheek with a kiss as she made her way to the stairs. There was just the beginning evidence of a pregnancy beginning to show around Mary's waistline.

"Do you want me to meet you later and walk you home?"

"No, I'll be fine." As an afterthought, she turned and said, "Thanks anyway, Ozzie."

Ozzie nodded and set about to cut some bread and pork for his dinner. Oh, he missed his mother's and sisters' cooking and baking! Mary Maud had a very different menu based on English meals. He certainly didn't like mushy peas or lard on his bread. The puddings like spotted dick and bread-caramel were tasty enough, though.

A five foot five inch dark-haired man with piercing grey eyes, at least according to Mary Elizabeth Martin, also known as Mayzie, caught her attention. Graham Nelson Shaw from Brantford courted Mayzie by letter, visiting her as often as possible in Toronto or Trenton. Then the war drew him away from his trade as a drug clerk.

"I have my attestation papers, Mayzie. Will you come to Calgary and marry me?"

Mayzie knew that was what she wanted to do.

"Mother, Graham has asked me to marry him. He's stationed in Calgary, but I hoped that since Father has closed the store you and he will come out to Calgary with me. It would mean so much to me to have you there for the wedding. You have only seen Poppy married out of all your daughters, and then Ozzie of course, but that was a party after the fact. You would see Mossie, Poppy, and baby Maxine. Ruth and Nora are in agreement. They would like to come west but don't want to leave you both on your own."

"Well, it's something your father and I will have to discuss. As you know, he has not been happy with Ruth these past few years, but I hate to leave them behind. Phyllis is only just four. We'll think about it."

Edwin and Mary discussed it for several days. Since the store had closed, Nora was not working outside the house, Ruth worked only part time, and Edwin helped Ozzie with a few sales at the warehouse. Ozzie's wife kept to herself or Ozzie when he was available, but Mary wondered when she was going to announce that she was in the family way. Mary knew she was. She had seen the symptoms and the way she walked. Mary would just have to ask Ozzie if he knew.

Edwin approached his son's bottling works and waited while he finished with the hoses and turned off the water.

"We've decided to make the move, son. Your mother is anxious to see your sisters and of course Maxine. Is there any chance you would come with us? Sell up here, and come out west."

"Father, I think you and Mother and the girls should go. You've worked hard all your life, and maybe you could take it a little easier. Mary Maud and I were going to let you know that you'll be having a grandchild soon, in four or five months." Ozzie smiled, thinking of that coming event. He was most anxious to be a father.

Weeks later the Martin family loaded their baggage and crates on the train. They were bustling about with bags and packages, excited about the prospect of riding all the way across Northern Ontario, the prairies, and then within a week they would arrive in Calgary. They would see the famous Rocky Mountain range!

Ozzie saw them off, a sense of loneliness overcoming him as he helped his mother, three sisters, father, and eldest niece onto the train. He waved, then stood back from the steam as the engine moved forward. When would he see them again, he wondered.

IV

On the Thursday after Christmas Day, Mary Elizabeth Martin had married Sergeant Graham Nelson Shaw of the 89th Battalion. The Reverend S. W. Fallis of Central Methodist Church performed the ceremony. Now Mary and Graham were living in Calgary southwest, waiting until Graham was shipped overseas. Ozzie was worried that his sister would be a widow before the end of the war the way the casualties were adding up so quickly. He couldn't believe the numbers recorded in the Courier.

He sat down at his desk with his food in order to do books, but first he needed to retrieve the letter from Mayzie about her marriage so he could place it in the Trenton Courier by January 20th, 1916.

"I might as well go downstairs and get the bottles ready for sterilizing tomorrow," Ozzie said to himself. It would be a while before Mary Maud was home. Ozzie breathed in the aroma of hops and smiled. He began placing empties on a rack, which would be placed on the drain table where washing and sterilizing took place. Ozzie had hooked up the hose, which had a long spray nozzle on a heavy spring attached to an arm at ceiling height. It was a great timesaver and helped keep up a heavy pressure when hot water was pumped through.

Ozzie thought he would sample the day's work while getting the racks of empty bottles ready. "Mmm, this is delicious, Mr. Martin," he said to himself. He was nearly halfway done when he heard Mary Maud calling.

"In here, Mrs. Martin," he called in return.

Mary Maud stepped tentatively into the warm steamy room, tiptoeing around the puddles. "You've let the fire go out upstairs, Ozzie. It's freezing again." Ozzie's happy smile sagged when he saw the annoyed look on Mary Maud's face. "I'll be right there, love. Just give me two minutes to finish this tray of bottles, and I'll bring up the wood and some coal so we get a nice fire going." Ozzie hurried, as he realized Mary would be cross. The sooner he got the kitchen stove lit, the better.

eighty

Calgary, Alberta, 1916

Edwin's half-sister Alma, her husband, John Wright, and their younger daughter, Nina, were in Calgary, having joined their son Charles.

"Edwin, do you think you will be staying?" Alma asked. "We wondered where Mary and Graham are living." The city was growing very quickly, and it was difficult to find a home.

"Mary is at 825–4th Avenue, Aunt Wis. It's so good to see you and Nina, and you, Uncle John. When did you decide to come out?" Mossie had joined the group in the living room of the Wrights' home on 29th Avenue.

"It was Charles' idea, of course," answered John.

"You know he and Gertrude have a new baby, and they called her Mary," smiled Alma, and she nodded towards her sister-in-law. "I'm sure you were the influence there."

"Oh, nonsense! I'm sure English royalty has more to do with it," but she was grateful for the compliment. "How is the baby doing?"

"Oh, just fine. So pretty. We are pleased. We weren't sure that Charles would even marry, and then when he did find Gertrude, they were both thirty-four, you know; well, I wasn't sure they wanted children. Nina here has decided she will be an old maid because we need so much looking after." Nina frowned at her mother, partly because it was true. She had just never found the right man.

"Where is it that Charles lives?" Edwin asked.

"Just behind us on Glencoe Road West. Number 3002, to be exact. After he articled with Blaylock and Bergeron, who had offices in the Alberta block, he formed a partnership with a Mr. Aitken. He and his father are hoping to form their own partnership. John just can't keep retired. "

John grunted in response.

"I understand," Mary said. "Edwin here doesn't want to stay put either. He is going to be clerking at Jackson's Grocery. They were neighbours from Trenton, you know."

"How are Ruth and Phyllis?" asked Aunt Wis.

Mary glanced warily over at her husband. Edwin had not yet forgiven his daughter for running off and eloping with Norman Holmes, who turned out just as Edwin had warned Ruth he would. "Ruth is a clerk at Snells' dry goods store, and she and Phyllis are with us at the 18th Avenue apartment. It's a long way to work for Edwin, but the trams run on a line close to us."

"Has there been flooding in this part of the river near you?" Edwin asked, changing the subject.

"No. There doesn't seem to be any trouble here with the Elbow River," John Wright answered. "I assume you heard all about the Bow River flooding last year? The old Central Bridge was wiped out. That was the main connection to the north side of Calgary. People were lined up near the shore watching all day as the river rose. One section was washed out; then hours later the rest washed downstream. There was a terrific amount of damage to other bridges and buildings on the north shore. Some large homes were like islands, completely surrounded by water."

"I see they've started construction on a cement bridge to replace the Centre Street one."

"Yes, they have. I think the arches are quite graceful in their construction, and hopefully it will withstand any flooding in the future."

An hour and several scones later, the visit ended, and hugs and handshakes were given all around.

II

Calgary, Alberta, October 11, 1916

Edwin had a firm hold of his wife's arm as they pushed, or were pushed, along the sidewalk of Stephen Street on their way to Thomas Pain's store. Mary's tiny frame was no match for the angry mob of soldiers, who seemed to be increasing in number as the minutes went by.

"In here, Mr. and Mrs. Martin," said Thomas as he gently pulled them in out of the general flow of the crowd on the street.

"What's happening, Thomas?" asked a worried Edwin.

"They seem to be at it again. Back in February there was terrible destruction, with hundreds of soldiers and civilians breaking up furniture, china, and mirrors in the Riverside Hotel. Here, let me close this blind. At least I don't have to worry about large glass windows that could be smashed." Thomas pulled the window blind for the door down and double locked it. He escorted his in-laws to chairs farther away from the noise on the streets. He just hoped the police would get things under control quickly.

"Would you like a cup of coffee, or some tea, perhaps? We can't go out now," said Thomas. Their earlier plans to go out to tea had been thwarted by the uprising in the streets.

"That would be lovely. I think Mary here could use something to perk her up." In truth, they were both pale and still a little frightened by the noises going by. They suddenly felt as though they understood what people in war zones must be going through.

"Why are the soldiers going on a rampage like this?" asked Edwin.

Thomas brought them tea and some stale biscuits, which were all he had on hand. "Last February it was really an anti-German riot. It started at the Riverside because the owner was German. Then Nagels' White Lunch Cafe was destroyed because the owner apparently hired an Austrian immigrant instead of a returning soldier. The problem is that the mobilization camp is so near the city that too many recruits are here while waiting deployment. They gather in large numbers, and soon things get out of control." He looked over at the elderly couple with compassion and decided immediately to distract them with an intense tour of his business. As soon as he saw they were finished their tea, he got up and led them over to the fur-cleaning equipment.

"This is what we call the dry-cleaning drum. This sawdust is used with a solution in the drum where a fur coat is placed. Then we rotate the drum so the cleaning solution and sawdust will clean the fur."

"That sawdust smells like hickory," commented Edwin.

"You're right. It's hickory and oak. We have to get this from the United States, where they have an excellent quality."

Mary was studying the drum. "How do you get the sawdust out from the furs?" she asked.

"Well, see this door? We replace it with this screen," Thomas said, bringing it out to show them. "The sawdust drops to the floor as the drum is again rotated. Then we have to use one of these rug beaters to beat the rest of it out."

"I have one of those," commented Mary. "I would never have guessed that you would use one to clean these beautiful furs."

"Most people wouldn't. Over here, Mrs. Martin, we have the cutting tools, the touch-up crayons, the combs, and here is the machine table with foot pedals and motor. This is new, and we find it works very well."

Suddenly, there was a pounding on the door. Thomas stopped talking and hesitated before going to the door. The pounding continued.

"Please, stay here, and I'll check who that might be." Thomas thought most of the mob had passed earlier. He opened the side of the blind slightly, then hurried to unlock the door. "Marius! Come in."

"Gracias! I was worried about 'dis shop! I thought I saw 'dat "Two Gun" Morris Cohen leading some troublemakers. Da police. Day do no theeng." Marius stopped his excited talk to stare at the couple standing watching him with anxious surprise.

"Mr. and Mrs. Martin, this is Marius Lenzie, who works with me. He purchases the skins from the natives and cleans them. He also raises mink and fox, which we use in the fur business. These are Poppy's parents, who have come to Calgary. After today's excitement, I hope they stay!" exclaimed Thomas.

"Ah, eet ees my pleasure, Mr. and Mrs. Marteen. Do not be alarmed by dees wild boys. Day weel be sheeped out to da war, and den dey will become men."

The group stood talking for some time before it was quiet on the street again. Thomas raised the blind and then opened the door to scout around. "I believe it is safe now, Mr. and Martin. Would you like me to accompany you home?"

"That won't be necessary, Thomas. And it's Edwin and Mary, please. We hope to see much more of you and Poppy and that cute Maxine granddaughter of ours. We will be fine on the way home, and thank you for your tour."

Edwin and Mary headed out, hoping to find the electric streetcar in working order and still making its rounds. The Royal Northwest Mounted Police barracks were several blocks in the opposite direction, but Edwin and Mary felt reassured that things had settled down for the time being.

eighty-one

Trenton, Ontario, 1917

"Mary, you can't leave. You mustn't. There's too much danger on the Atlantic. Goodness, we're in the middle of a war, for heaven's sake!" exclaimed Ozzie.

"I need to know where my brothers are. I haven't heard from them in months. They could have been killed in action." She paused to pin her hat on. "It hasn't worked out very well, has it, Osmond? Admit it. You are in debt, and Bywater is really the owner here. Even changing the name from the Berlin Lion Brewery to the Heuther Brewery will not make a difference when you spend all the profits."

"Please, Mary. I know things haven't been easy, but you can't take our child and just leave." Ozzie knew she could, and she would if he didn't stop her. "You made a vow to me as I made a vow to you, 'until death do us part.'"

Mary tucked the baby under her arm and pulled away from Ozzie's desperate grasp. Picking up her valise, she determinedly marched to the head of the stairs and awkwardly down them. She was not going to let his dark, pleading eyes break down her determination.

Ozzie dropped his head into his hands, and tears began. He knew she meant it. At least she had not snuck off later in the day when he was busy, but how was he going to live without his only child and Mary? There would be no family around at all. Would she return at the end of the war?

After weeks of dragging himself through the routine of daily work, consuming beer rather than food, he began to feel ill—really ill. Art Bywater came by when he didn't appear downstairs at work one day and found him nearly in a coma. He looked for a telephone, but there was none, so he had to hurry downstairs and outside to the loading dock and find a helper or two to bring Ozzie down to his vehicle. He was one of a few with a motorized vehicle these days, and now he used it to take Ozzie to the hospital.

II

"Arthur. I want to thank you. I guess you saved my life, they tell me. I just haven't been the same since Mary left."

"You were in quite a state, I can tell you, Osmond. You cannot consume alcohol in your condition. Do you realize you have diabetes?"

Ozzie's face paled, even under jaundiced flesh. "No, I didn't know," he answered quietly.

"I understand that your wife and child were returning to England," Arthur said gently.

Ozzie looked away from him, embarrassed. "She hadn't heard from her brothers, and she was so worried about their safety, since they had both enlisted."

Arthur pursed his lips, wondering if Ozzie was well enough yet to share the news he had, but he decided now was a better time than when he returned home alone. "There were some ships destroyed last week in the North Atlantic. I'm sorry, Osmond, but your wife and son were on one that went down. All crew and passengers were lost."

Ozzie's chin dropped. He looked directly at Arthur, hoping it wasn't true but knowing these things were happening. It had been a concern when they left. After all, it was wartime.

"No! No," he cried, and he rolled back his head, clenching his fists. Anger and frustration forced tears to bubble up and release the sorrow he could no longer contain.

Arthur patted his shoulder, and taking his walking stick and hat, he left the hospital bedside, knowing there was little he could do. His heart went out to the kind man grieving for his loss, no family to help carry him through the rough days ahead. Ozzie was no businessman, but he had an affable and gentle heart, if only the drink hadn't got him in its grip.

III

In 1918 a new law put a stop to the production and bottling of beer or spirits. The temporary cessation of production was because of pressure from the War Office. Soldiers needed to be protected from the evils of alcohol, even those who had returned injured from the European fronts.

"We have to try bottling other beverages, Osmond. The law is quite clear that booze production is illegal until a year after the war's end. It can't go on long. There are signs that a treaty will be signed any day now," Arthur said.

"Well, we can start with bottling soda pop. The Coca Cola company has been doing well for twenty-some years now. Is there any call for bottling that pop with ginger as a basis?" inquired Ozzie.

"I'll look into it while you clear out the beer. You might look up Charlie Mills, who is still in business with the Americans," Arthur added slyly. Everyone knew that this law was going to inhibit the honest, but there would be those who made huge profits by dealing with spirits illegally.

Ozzie struggled to keep on top of the bills and manage the brewery. The business was beginning to heat up somewhat with all the temperance talk, although Trenton was not a centre for the Temperance Society's greatest activities.

Another personal blow came to him in a telegram.

"O. W. Martin: Father died last night. Funeral Monday. Mary."

"And I can't even be there. Poor Mother. How will she survive this?" Then Ozzie pictured the seven girls around her. Winnie would not make it to the funeral either, but the others were there to comfort their mother. Who would comfort him?

He sat in the front office. He had never felt so alone, but he must not give in to the evil of that beverage he had bottled. The doctors had told him he was fortunate to have survived the last bout in hospital. He must go upstairs and write to his mother and sisters. Perhaps he should have gone out west with the family, but what would he have done out there in the untamed city of Calgary?

Iowa, 1918

Winnie was devastated when her mother-in-law, Anna Fisher Linton, died on the second of February.

"Will, I tried everything I could think of to help your mother recover."

"Winnie, I know you did. We just have to watch Father now and make sure that he takes care of himself. People everywhere are dying from this Spanish flu bug. There doesn't seem to be anything we can do to stop it."

A few weeks later a letter arrived from Calgary. Winnie was always pleased to have contact with her mother and sisters. They seemed settled into the western city and were enjoying the increase in industry and population. She would have to get up soon to see her great nieces.

"Oh, no!" she cried after reading the first few lines. Her father had died. "I must get to the office and tell Lottie. Oh, she will be so upset."

Then, a few weeks later, on July 23, Winnie knew by the look of William's face as he entered the door that something was seriously wrong.

"It's my father, Winnie. He died this morning. Walter was with him."

There was just a sorrowful silence. It seemed to thicken the steam of boiling potatoes sitting heavily in the kitchen. They would have to inform Harold of his grandfather's death, and just when he was about to start his college education. When would God put an end to this devastating flu?

Calgary, November 6, 1918

"Listen to this, Mother. 'If the Dominion Government had acted as promptly and effectively as the Alberta Health Department, there would have been much less "flu" west of Toronto, and hundreds of lives would have been saved.'" Ruth had been reading aloud from the Albertan Non-Partisan. "Just think. Aunt Anna, Father, and Uncle Will. Others have lost as many of their own families as well. No wonder there is such resentment towards the east." Ruth studied her mother's unchanging face, still grief-lined, and decided not to say anything further.

Davenport, Iowa, November 1919

Lottie looked at the telegram that her fiancé's father had handed her across her desk at Will's insurance office. Her hands and eyes seemed to belong to someone else as she read "Russell…killed in action…sorry…" Her tears welled up, blinding her to anything else but those dreaded words.

The man before her had a puzzled look on his face, as if asking, why now? Why now when the war was as good as over? They had all been making plans for Russell's return, and fate had driven a cruel blow into their lives.

Lottie handed the telegram back, hardly daring to look at the stricken man. "I'm so sorry," she said softly. He nodded and left without saying a word.

Will, who had been standing behind his sister-in-law, had understood immediately the implications of the message. He moved over to the door and turned the Open sign to Closed, then shut the blind. There would not do any more business today.

"Oh, Lottie, I am so sorry." He was at a loss for words. Lottie's tall, normally erect frame was bent over and shaking. She had lost her aunt, uncle, father, and now fiancé in a matter of seven months. Will stepped towards Lottie and put both hands sympathetically around her shoulders. He admired her so much for all her skills, her lady-like demeanour, and her pleasant thoughtfulness. Now he would try to show that same kindness.

"Let's go home now, Lottie. You need a rest after this shock." William gently put his arm around her as they walked along the boardwalk. He figured Lottie was in shock by the way she walked tall and stiffly. Will felt such sympathy for her. She was such a smart, attractive young woman, and he couldn't imagine what she must be feeling.

Charlotte (Lottie) Martin

eighty-two

Calgary, Banff, 1920

Thomas Pain ambled over the rough foothills of Kampkilkare, surveying the lot with the cabin he was about to purchase. It seemed like the ideal summer retreat to enjoy with his family.

Later, he arrived home in Calgary. "Poppy! Are you there? We have ourselves a cabin in the mountains," and Thomas hugged his wife happily.

"Oh, the children will love it there. We will have to watch them near the lake, though."

"Well, it's quite a walk to the lake, which is good. No surprising accidents will happen. Would you like to invite your sister Ruth and Phyllis? I bet they would like some time at the lake. And of course we'll bring Grandma Martin."

Poppy smiled and nodded her head, thinking she'd better get baking if they were having company on this trip. She would make several pies to bring. Water needed to be brought, and the wicker picnic baskets and thermoses needed to be packed. There was much to do.

Trenton, Ontario, 1920

By the time the United States passed the Volstead Act in 1920, inhibiting Americans from producing, buying, or consuming alcoholic beverages, it was again legal for Canadians. The federal government, however, could not stop boatloads of spirits going to the United States, since it was up to the U. S. Coast Guard to stop them. Twelve bottles of Corby's Old Whiskey, which sold in Canada for $24, sold on the U. S. black market for $200.8

Ozzie kept looking for a way into the legal production of beer, but it wasn't until later in 1920 that the law changed, a year after the end of the war, as promised. There were too many businessmen in the federal government against the temperance leagues for prohibition to continue permanently. Petitions, speeches, and picketing did nothing to stop the production of alcoholic beverages.

On March 23 Lieutenant Colonel Arthur Bywater became owner of the Huether Brewery Ltd. and all of lot 21 for the cost of one dollar.

Toronto, Ontario, 1920–1921

"Mr. Osmond Martin?" asked the doctor.

"That would be me," answered the jaundiced patient lying under the pristine white sheets of the Toronto Hospital. Besides very swollen ankles, his stomach was distended considerably. Ozzie had been transferred from the Kingston Hospital to Toronto in hopes of dealing with his diabetes. Banting and Best were working on a cure but had yet to develop one that was widely used.

"You are a very fortunate man, Mr. Martin. We've been able to reduce your blood sugar considerably, but tell me, how are the pains in your legs?"

"They hurt. As much as ever. I just feel like having you amputate!"

"No need for that. A few more days, and more normal functions will begin to reduce that pain considerably. You will be on a very strict diet and are not to eat anything, even fruit, that visitors might bring. Do you think you will have many visitors?"

Ozzie shook his head, realizing again how lonely he was. He couldn't return to the life he had before, or he would very likely die.

"Well, try to get some sleep," and the doctor replaced the chart at the end of the bed.

PART TWELVE

Summers, Martin

FAMILIES

eighty-three

Toronto, Ontario, 1920–1921

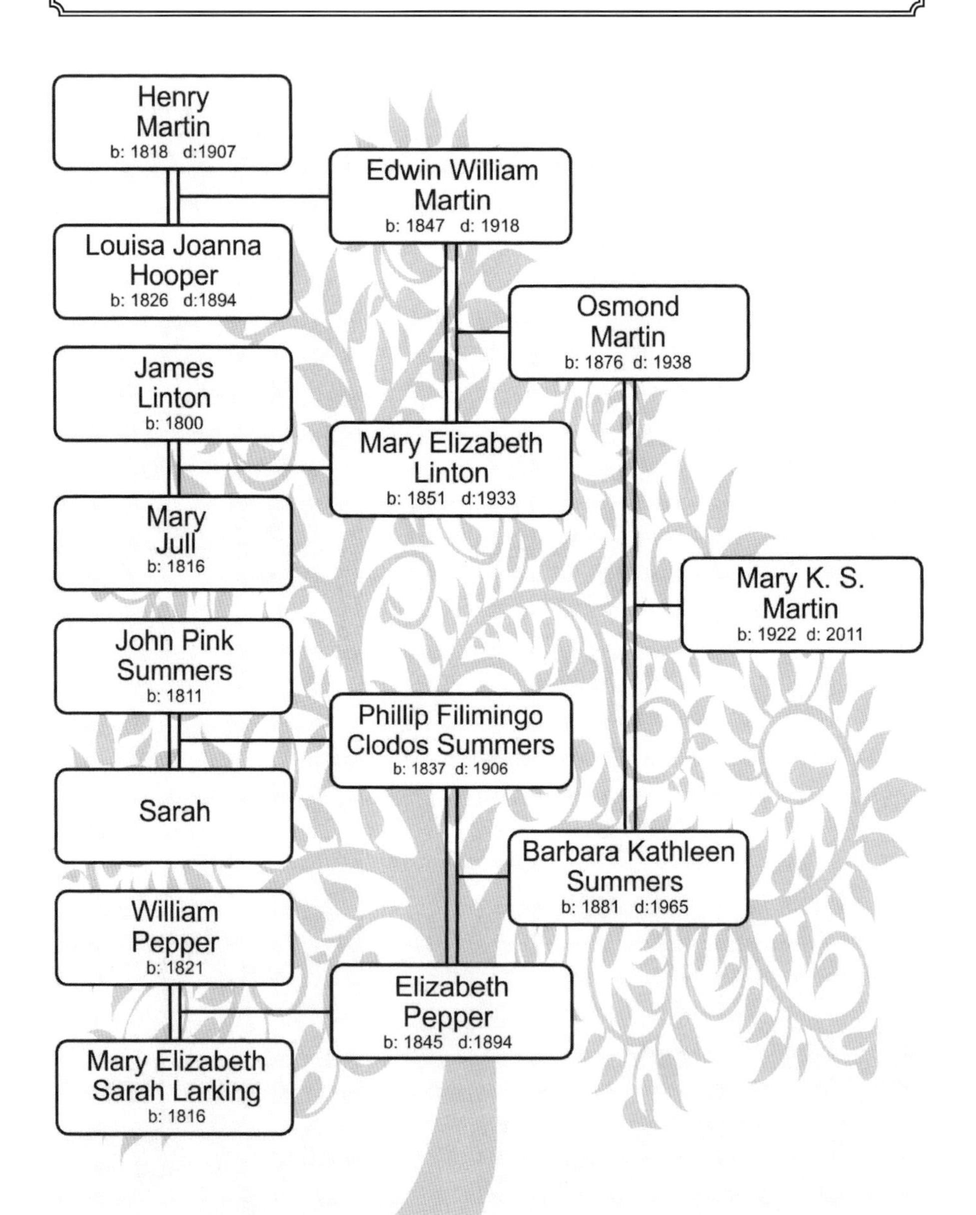

OZZIE WAS FEELING BETTER THAN HE HAD FOR WEEKS, BUT HE WAS A VERY SICK man, and he knew it. His legs still gave him a great deal of pain, but his colour was better. He started to look forward to when the nurses came to see him, or rather when a tiny, businesslike yet cheerful nurse came, checking his temperature, his pulse, his comfort. She had wispy black curls that would not stay tucked into her bun at the back of her cap.

"Ah, the lovely Miss Summers!" said Ozzie, looking at her squarely in the face. "Do I correctly understand from the other chaps that you remain unmarried?"

The heat rose to Kate's face, and she made a point of being busy with the chart. Finally she answered. "Yes, but I can't see how that concerns you. Now open up your mouth and say ahh." Kate felt bad as soon as she realized how sharp her response had sounded. "I'm sorry, Mr. Martin, but I have my duties to perform. Perhaps at the end of my shift I can return and check on you again," and Kate left the bed of a smiling Ozzie.

Kate returned after her shift, tired but still smiling. She asked about his family and realized they had something in common. Both had large families but were basically on their own.

"Please, Miss Summers, call me Ozzie."

"I could when off duty, but it's Mr. Martin while on duty." She tried to give him a stern look, but her determination broke down, and she ended up laughing playfully.

"A few days ago I saw you were wearing a rose. Do you have a beau?"

"Oh, that was on January 25. It was a special rose from Dr. Bartlett on my fortieth birthday. He said I should have something to celebrate it and very kindly brought one to the nurses' ward desk. I don't think Miss Wright approved, but he does this for many of the nurses on special occasions. He's such a thoughtful old gentleman."

Ozzie sighed with relief. He had seen other nurses wearing a rose on occasion, and Dr. Bartlett was elderly, although very alert. More alert than he felt most days. How could he lead this lovely woman on into a relationship with him? He would have to change his ways.

"You must rest now, Mr. Mar—Osmond, and I will see you tomorrow."

II

Ozzie remained in Toronto until he had convinced Kate they should marry, that neither of them were too old, and that he loved her with all his heart. May 19,

1921, was the day they walked to the Beverley Street Baptist Church and entered the chapel.

"Oh, Kate! You look wonderful," exclaimed her friend Mary Ethel Grant. "You know my husband, Alfred. Alfred, this is Osmond, Kate's betrothed." Mary squeezed the arm of a blushing Kate and whispered, "Oh, he is so handsome, Kate. He certainly looks better than when he was in the hospital."

"I should, with the wonderful care I've received," said Ozzie. Having overheard the comment, he was quietly laughing and in a joyful mood.

The four moved forward to the minister, Ernest Forde, for the quiet ceremony. Kate and Ozzie both wished that some members of their families could share this day with them, but all were too far away or too busy.

"Thank you, Alfred, for standing up with me. I appreciate you and Mary coming to witness. I believe Kate has a special tea planned for us. Shall we go?"

A smiling Kate and Ozzie led the way to the street and down to a local café where they would have tea and cakes. The Martins had a train to catch to Trenton that afternoon so they might arrive before dark. Kate's trunk would follow the next week. Her heavily embroidered crepe wedding nightgown was packed in her valise with her toiletries and new dreams of a happy marriage.

Kate and Ozzie on their wedding day

III

"We have only a short walk, Kate, so I would like to carry your bag if I might."

"Oh, no, Osmond. You need more time to fully gain your strength back. I may be short, but I'm sturdy, as you will find out." Kate laughed, just so thrilled to be a missus now rather than a miss. It would take getting used to, but she felt she could take on the world with this tall, handsome man beside her.

"You will see the factory and our apartment as we go around the corner here. I don't know what condition the place will be in, but Arthur was aware we would be coming today. He was so glad when I told him about you. I think he expects you to help keep me on track." Ozzie smiled seriously at Kate, who looked so much younger than he, though there was only five years' difference in their age.

"Oh, there's the greenhouse! It's grand. I shall enjoy working in it. I never had a chance to grow anything before coming to Canada. Oh, I see a few panes need repair, but never mind. It has a good location, facing to the south. I'll have it in shape in no time." Kate surprised herself with how excited she was to have a home that they owned where she could arrange, decorate, and become very domestic. She would not worry about nursing again for some time, she thought.

Ozzie led the way up the steps, thinking he would be brushing the cobwebs away from the stairwell. He couldn't remember what condition the place was in when he left. He didn't remember leaving at all. He might not have been living if Arthur Bywater and his other friends hadn't been keeping a close eye on him.

Ozzie stopped Kate at the top step before the landing, took both bags, and unlocked the door. "Wait here, Kate. I…I just need to see what shape the place is in before I take you over the threshold." Kate waited primly with her gloved hands crossed in front of her, standing her full height in her heeled oxfords. She had spent considerable money on the cream-coloured French-crepe nightgown and dressing gown. Unfortunately, she had to turn the hems up about eight inches so that they wouldn't drag on the floor, but she was still excited to have them and was actually looking forward to showing them to Ozzie.

"Mrs. Martin, you may enter," Ozzie said as he bowed and took her hand. She wasn't sure what to expect because he had explained to her the conditions under which he had left, and that was months ago.

"I believe some friends have been in and taken care of tidying the place up in honour of your arrival," said Ozzie with a swoop of his arm.

"Oh, and they have left some beautiful flowers. The card says Colonel and Mrs. Arthur Bywater. He's your partner, is he not?" asked Kate.

"He is indeed, and he has saved my life on at least one occasion. Would you like to see the kitchen, my dear?" asked Ozzie hopefully.

Kate just smiled and said, "Of course. I'll have a brief look, but I must confess that I cannot make pastry to save my life. A cake I can bake, and other meals with meat, potatoes, and vegetables, but not pastry. I can also make soup, but if you want anything fancy, you must be the chef." Kate was still thinking of the greenhouse and how she would love to spend her time in good weather outside growing both vegetables and flowers.

After discussing the money situation with Ozzie, Kate S. Martin now became the grantee of lot 21, only two weeks after their marriage. She felt secure in knowing they could now make the business run without the profit being drained by rent and taxes.

Kate smiled as she signed, because she was married, she could vote, and she was now allowed to sign her own papers of property and not have to have her husband do that on her behalf.

"There you are, Kate! I wondered where you got to. Am I to make my own noon meal?" Ozzie asked jokingly.

"Oh, no! Is it that time already?" said Kate, looking up to the sky. She had been so preoccupied with planting some zinnia seedlings and geranium cuttings, which a neighbour had offered, that she lost track of all time. "I'll come right now! Can you wait while I boil some potatoes?"

Kate looked back with satisfaction at her work in the garden. She loved the fresh earth and the little hopeful plants that edged the greenhouse and the building. Brushing her gloved hands over her knees, she straightened her back to attend her kitchen duties.

"We're going to bottle for the O'Keefe Company. It will be O'Keefe Agent, Ice and Beverage in the business directory," said Ozzie. "I'm going to see about getting the ice house in order for next winter and see the town about a licence to take ice off the Bay of Quinte again." He had been doing it for several years but didn't know for sure what had happened last winter while he was in hospital.

"That sounds satisfactory," answered Kate. She placed their plates of steaming hot food on the table and bowed her head.

Ozzie, who kept forgetting that she liked to say grace before meals, quickly put down his knife and fork as he also bowed his head. He must try to remember from here on.

"Father, we ask your blessing upon this food, our home, and each other. We thank you for all the good that you have bestowed upon us, and ask that you be with all our family and friends. Amen." Kate and Ozzie looked at each other, the looks of love and mutual admiration plain and unabashed.

After eating heartily, Ozzie informed Kate that he wanted to have a telephone installed.

"Will that be costly?" Kate asked.

"No, I think not. The Bell Company has been putting up new poles and lines everywhere in town; there's just the monthly cost of the line and of the installation. I thought it would be best to have a line up here as well as the office."

"Who would call us here?" asked Kate.

"Well, you could use it to call friends or family," suggested Ozzie.

"My family is too frugal to call that far. Why don't you install one in the office, and if I ever need it, I can go there? I don't think I would like to waken in the night with the thing ringing either. Aren't there several people on a line?" asked Kate.

"Not so many in town. I understand two to four share a party line in the country. We can have a private line if it's a business."

"Well, let's have one in the office, then, and you can use it as an expense against your taxes. I will need some housekeeping money for the groceries and a cupboard installed in the kitchen. Those shelves are just a little tippy."

"Well, yes, of course. I can look into the furniture in the downstairs storage room. My parents and sisters left quite a few things they didn't—or rather couldn't—take out west. You know, I forgot about housekeeping money for groceries. When we had the store, there was always leftover produce, or if Mother needed something, one of the girls would run down and get it." Ozzie's eyes glazed slightly as he remembered his family and their growing up years.

Kate cleared her throat. Ozzie smiled. "I'll look after that this afternoon."

"Thank you, Ozzie. What do you think of the gardens I've dug?"

"They're going to be spectacular, Mrs. Martin. It should be easier next year after the preparation you've done now. I can't wait to see things in bloom. It's been a long time since anyone did gardening around here."

Kate smiled. "I miss the green in England, so I can imagine how my father must have missed the green in Jamaica when he moved to England. Except for the heat, I think that would be a very exotic place to visit."

After clearing away the dishes and preparing a pudding for tea, Kate began emptying one of her trunks. She had purchased a few things before she left England and wanted them out so that she could enjoy them as well as use them. The silver and glass pickle jar was one of the things she wanted to get out. The little gold-rimmed tea plates with violets were another.

eighty-four

Months had passed, and Kate knew she was "in the family way," as Canadians said. After helping to deliver so many babies and look after other mothers' children, she was finally going to have her own. She could hardly believe it. She was forty, soon to be forty-one, but she knew many women who had healthy babies after forty, just maybe not their first one.

"Kate! What are you doing standing on that chair?"

Kate looked down into the alarmed face of Ozzie and smiled. "I'm dusting the top shelf. You know I can't reach as high as you with my stature. It's all right. The chair is steady."

"Oh, Kate, I don't think you should be doing heavy work in your condition."

"Ozzie, it is hardly heavy work, and I still have months to go." Kate tried not to sound annoyed. She was the nurse, and she always rested in the afternoon, just to keep any swelling in her ankles to a minimum. What did he know of having a baby?

"My mother had some trouble having Nora. She had to take it easy the last few weeks."

"Well, yes, Ozzie. But your mother had seven other children before that, and it couldn't have been easy. Are you going to dust this top shelf for me?" Kate asked with a smile at Ozzie's sheepish look. "No, I didn't think so. Perhaps you can hand up some of those larger plates and bowls, so I don't have to get down again," and Kate carried on working.

One evening as Ozzie was taking the trash to the main floor, he started talking about the heat. "If we had a fireplace in here, we could burn much of this and have a bit of added warmth. There are always scraps of wood around at the base of the woods out back. It would save on the coal bill."

Kate looked at Ozzie. He had mentioned the coal bill several times, but she couldn't understand where they were using so much coal.

"Is the bottling works using so much coal? I don't think I'm using too much. I always wear a sweater and sometimes a shawl to keep from burning extra." Kate hesitated to ask too many questions about Ozzie's first wife, so she was left wondering if the girl had burned coal needlessly and if she was one of those English people who were always cold in the Canadian winter.

"Are you warm enough now, dear?" Ozzie asked.

"Yes, I'm fine, but I have extra weight to help keep me warm," and she patted the bulge on her lap. "Are you warm enough, Ozzie? I worry that you are still a little thin after last year's illness." She worried about his controlling the diabetes; so far there didn't seem to be a problem. She tried very hard to stick to the diet the doctors had recommended when they left the hospital. Kate wondered how he would have made out on his own if they hadn't married.

II

Kate struggled up the stairs with the clean sheets. She had hung them outside to dry, and they smelled so fresh. Ozzie complained that she was doing too much and should just hang the sheets inside, but the March day had been so sunny she couldn't resist. He had not offered to carry them down or take them off the line and carry them up, though.

Kate battled to make the bed. Her nurse's training could not be compromised. The ends of the bed had the bottom sheet pulled tightly. Then the leftover was tucked under the side. Finally, the side of the sheet was tucked firmly under to make a very tight and neat corner fold. They made them like this in the military as well, if she was not mistaken.

After making up the bed, Kate brewed herself a cup of tea to revive herself while she rested. She looked at the pile of papers on the desk near the door and decided to tidy that up while she enjoyed a cup of tea. She piled a few invoices up that should be paid. Ozzie didn't seem to realize that he should pay his bills before the extra charges were laid. If he kept the bills paid, he would not fall behind.

Under some of the other papers, she found an envelope that had remained unopened. It looked like a bill from the Hill Coal Company in Toronto. The postal date was weeks past, so why had Ozzie not opened it? She needed to open it and warn him again about paying his debts.

The letter opener was handy, so she slit the top and took out the bill. Her heart seemed to plummet, and she had trouble breathing. The bill was for an unheard of $600 dollars! Unheard of! Kate sat there in shock staring at it.

"Hello. I'm home. Kate?" Ozzie stopped short, his right hand still on the doorknob he had just opened. He just looked at her face to know what she must have found. He waited.

Unshed tears welled up in her eyes, and it took her a moment before she could speak. "Osmond! When were you going to tell me about this debt? I can't believe you didn't tell me about this. How did it come about that you owe them this much?" Kate turned to face him, tears now on her cheeks. Moments ago she had been the happiest she had ever been in her life. Now she felt defeated, betrayed, and stunned.

"How did this happen, Osmond?"

Ozzie opened his mouth to speak. He closed it, then tried again. "Oh, it's not that bad. I have every intention of paying it back. I didn't want to worry you with business things…" and his voice trailed off. He knew he was not going to succeed in putting this off, or his few other small debts, any longer. She was too astute, too good a money manager to let this type of thing slide.

"I promise, Kate, please, I am going to deal with it."

Kate straightened her back as much as her advanced pregnancy allowed her. She squared her shoulders, swallowed her anger, and simply said, "Yes, you will, and before this baby is born."

"Why don't you come over to the sofa and put your feet up…" Ozzie's voice trailed off. How could he explain that things got out of hand when he married Mary Maud, who was always so cold and unhappy?

"I will not move from here until we have discussed how we can pay this off and what you are going to do to change some things. Why don't you pull over another chair, and we will start." The firmness in her voice was more powerful than either his father's or mother's commands had ever been. She meant business. He didn't think she would allow him to put off what should have been done long ago.

"First, tell me how much we can be guaranteed per week in profits from the business. Not the high, but the minimum. Anything extra will be a bonus."

"Well, before the expenses—" Ozzie began, but Kate sharply interrupted.

"I'm talking profit, not what you take in to start with."

"Well, it would be about $450 per month, minus expenses, minus the taxes, the phone, the trucking…about $45 a week."

"I want you to start by paying the expenses, which, by the way, are how much for coal per week?"

"I think roughly $20 a week."

"Plus the $600," and here she visibly swallowed, almost choking, "owed to the Hill Coal Company in Toronto. Do they have an office in town?"

"Yes, down on Albert Street, just a little desk at the hardware store. They ship larger quantities by rail, where I have it delivered directly."

Kate and Ozzie worked on the details: the exact expenses, how much of the profits they would use, how they could save on home expenses, and finally how much they would have to use of her savings.

eighty-five

One evening Ozzie came upstairs before their tea, carrying an armload of what looked like bricks.

"What are those bricks for, Ozzie?" Kate had gone back to calling her husband Ozzie, somewhat softened in her demeanour but still vigilant in keeping track of expenditures.

"These are firebricks, and I got a great deal on them from Fred, who said they were in good enough shape to use again. I'm going to put them under the fireplace I will build. Then we'll be able to save on heating and enjoy the fireplace as well. It should remind you of the houses you worked in back home." He smiled, thinking of his plan and dreaming of cosy evenings by the fire in winter with just the three of them.

"How are you going to stop the fire from burning a hole in the floor?" asked Kate, who knew about some of these things, having as a child watched workmen put in fireplaces in the houses they were building.

"The firebricks will stop the fire going through. There will be a grate above that on which we can place the logs."

"There will be cracks between the bricks. You can't just put the bricks on a wooden floor. Come on, forget about that for now. Your tea is ready, and then I want to show you the wonderful parcel that your mother and sisters sent from the west."

Ozzie brightened up after that, forgetting for now about the fireplace. Kate opened the box and carefully took out each item: baby nightgowns, blankets, flannelette for diapers, special pins, and bonnets with matching booties. Ozzie smiled as he recognized some of the handiwork of his siblings and mother. Kate was thrilled to receive so many wonderful items at once. She had put off making too much or buying anything, hoping that she would feel more like it after the baby was born. Now she felt much more prepared, and the two weeks before she delivered would go faster.

"I think I will see if Sadie, Ada and John's oldest, would mind coming for a few weeks to help me with the baby. I'm sorry that you never met my brother John."

"Bringing Sadie sounds like a fine idea. We can set up a cot in the far bedroom and maybe find a dresser or small wardrobe as well. There are still more pieces of furniture downstairs in storage."

"That sounds fine, but don't go and buy anything. If Sadie can come, she will be here only a matter of weeks. I'm not sure if she's engaged in any position or not."

Mary Kathleen Summers Martin was born on April 20, 1922. Kate was doing exceptionally well, having taken care of herself before and after delivery. The doctor had been amazed at Kate's understanding of the process, but of course she had attended many births. Sadie had arrived two days earlier and was helping at every step. She would burp little Mary, bathe her, and change her without being told.

Despite money worries, Kate didn't even flinch when Ozzie came home with a new perambulator so that the baby could be outdoors while she did the laundry or worked in the garden. She would allow him this one extravagance, because it was a practical one. Kate and Ozzie were thrilled with their new baby and loved her dearly. Mary was a contented child, for which Kate was glad, because she still had concerns with debts and spent time with paper and pencil doing figuring frequently.

II

Ozzie was adamant. "We need a photo to send to the families in Calgary. Wouldn't you like to send some to Ada and the girls and Charlotte and Walter? We'll get a large one for ourselves, and some smaller copies for the family. What do you say?"

"I can hardly argue with you. With all the help I had from Sadie, I guess it would be nice to send a picture of Mary near Christmas. You arrange the sitting then, and I'll have Mary ready."

Mary sat up very smartly for a seven-month-old. She looked so seriously at the camera draped with black cloth. Her blue eyes were wide with curiosity. Kate was reminded of her young brother Walter, who had pale blue eyes, and Mary's hair was dark as well.

"She has your straight hair, Ozzie.

"But she has your dark beauty, Kate." He embraced his wife lovingly.

III

Ozzie had taken to calling his wife "Mother" after Mary's birth. "Here we are with the framed picture, Mother."

"Oh, it's large! Let's set it on the table to unwrap it." Kate and Ozzie carefully tore the gummed brown paper strips where they crossed the seams of the brown paper wrapping. The photo of a rather startled-looking baby peered out from the gold and red frame. The shiny bevelled glass reflected the sunlight, highlighting Mary's chubby cheeks.

"Oh, it's grand, Ozzie! Thank you so much. I won't ask the cost, because I will enjoy it more not knowing. She is a beauty, isn't she?"

"I couldn't agree more, Mrs. Martin."

Arm in arm, they stood in wonder of the little girl they so adored. Each thanked the good Lord.

Winnie, Mayzie, Mossie, Poppy, Lottie, Ruth, and Nora with their mother

epilogue

Mary Martin trained as a teacher. While at Queen's University Summer School, she met Robert Thomas Bailey, son of Gladys and Jack.

Their lives continue in book 3 of the BMD series by Beverley Hopwood.

ENDNOTES

1. Records of the Colonial Office, Commonwealth and Foreign and Commonwealth Office, book CO 137/87, British National Archives at Kew, page 266, Aug. 24, 1788, Jamaica.
2. Records of the Colonial Office, Commonwealth and Foreign and Commonwealth Office, book CO 137/87, British National Archives at Kew, page 203, 1780, Jamaica.
3. Records of the Colonial Office, Commonwealth and Foreign and Commonwealth Office, book CO 141/3, British National Archives at Kew, supplement to the Royal Gazette, 1 January 1813–31 December 1813, Jamaica. Saturday June 26 to Saturday July 3, 1813, page 16.
4. Records of the Board of Trade and Successors, book BT 99/798, British National Archives at Kew, from the Olga, registry number 60222, January 12, 1871, to June 26, 1871, London, England.
5. Records of the War and Colonial Office: Emigration-Original Correspondence, book CO 384/81, British National Archives at Kew, March 1, 1848, image 3356.
6. Records of the War and Colonial Office: Emigration-Original Correspondence, book CO 384/81, British National Archives at Kew, April 13, 1848, page 439.
7. Thomas Jarrett, *The Evolution of Trenton, 100 Years 1813–1913* (Trenton, Ontario, 1913), page 47.
8. C. W. Hunt, Gentleman Charlie, *The Lady Rumrunner* (Bancroft, Ontario: Billa Flint Publishers, 1999), page 14 and throughout.